SOLOMON'S KEY: THE CODIS PROJECT
A CONSPIRACY THRILLER

▲ ⌐ ∩ ∨ ∩ ∪ ∩ ⊏ - ∇ ◁

By
R. Douglas Weber

ERISTA BOOKS

THE PROCESS IS HIDDEN

Code:

Clues made with Sir. Francis Bacon's "Bakish" code can be found in different *typeface* throughout. A more complex version of Bakish code can be found in Chapter 20.

Dear reader: Find the codes highlighted in **bold** type and *italics* somewhere *within* these pages. Hint: look for this ---------- line.

An ancient target: The Vatican. An ancient book that brings truth to all who look upon its pages. A book that holds forbidden knowledge and secrets … Secrets worth dying for.

First published by Novo Seculo Editoria
San Palo, Brazil ISBN:8576790645
Portion adapted from Protocol-17 coypright©2002
ERISTA BOOKS

An imprint of Hutton-Hauser Publishing
23 Hobbs Lane, Middlesex, England
The website address is: www.eristahutton-hauser.com

Library of Congress Cataloging-in-Publication Data

Weber, Richard D.
Solomon's Key: The CODIS Project A Conspiracy Thriller
ISBN 9545857366

BT670.P23 2006
223.97—dc23

10 9 8 7 6 5 4 3 2 1

R. DOUGLAS WEBER

SOLOMON'S KEY

For
Peaches and Cream
Erick,Punky
And Mom
My Stalwarts

ACKNOWLEDGEMENTS

From true-life experiences I would like to thank the dedicated men and women of the NSA, The State Department, Mossad, OSI, and the Department of Homeland Security, specifically Special Agent Robert Kyle of ICE and Ernest Buck of INTERPOL with whom I had the privilege of working.

I would like to thank Lt. Colonel S. Curtis "Chewy" Johnston U.S. Air Force retired for his valuable technical assistance. Last but not least, Professors Otto Nemo and H. D. Carr, without whose knowledge of religious history and vivid imagination this work would have not been possible. Writing a novel is a long journey. But every journey begins with the first step. For me, that first step began in 2002, long before religious thrillers had become a genre. That is when the seed or the premise of this story began to germinate. Over time, it took root and grew. It required a lot of pruning, but took nourishment from fans and fellow writer's group members. It sought its own light source, took its own path, until eventually, it blossomed into this tale.

R. Douglas Weber was formerly a U.S. Foreign Service Officer, Special Agent in Charge of Dignitary Protection with the U.S. Department of State's (DSS) Diplomatic Security Service. The unit responsible for the protection of the late Diana Princess of Wales—and Prince Charles, the Secretary of State, the Prime Minister of Israel, and Saudi Arabia's and Jordan's ambassadors to name but a few. He has traveled extensively and roamed the hallowed halls of Foggy Bottom, various embassies, and the Pentagon. His last position was Deputy Assistant Regional Director with the U.S. Department of Justice. He currently works as a security consultant.

Map of Solomon's Temple

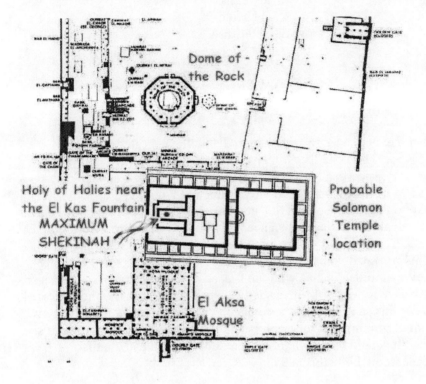

Temple of Absalom, King David's son, located in Jerusalem.

Solomon's Temple in Kashmir.

Left: Isis and Horus.   Right: The Black Madonna of Tindari and Christ.

Dark I am, yet comely, O daughters of Jerusalem, dark like the tents of Kedar, like the tent curtains of Solomon.
Song of Solomon

Isis, represented in the Song of Solomon by the dark maid of Jerusalem, is symbolic of receptive nature, the watery, maternal principle which creates all things out of herself after impregnation has been achieved by the virility of the sun.
Manly P. Hall

For I am the first and the last.
I am the honoured one and the scorned one.
I am the whore and the holy one.
I am the wife and the virgin.
I am the mother and the daughter.
… I am the bride and the bridegroom, and it is my husband who begot me.

The Thunder, Perfect Mind. Nag Hammadi Library

AUTHOR'S NOTE

You will find a variation of the Masonic Royal Arch Code on the title page and after the signature at the end of these notes. The key to decoding it can be found in chapter 36.

Author's reference to locales within the Vatican and Chicago, IL, are factual with a few exceptions: Swift Hall at the University of Chicago does not have thirteen floors, but does house the Divinity School. Contact the author at:

E-mail: solomonskeyweber@yahoo.com

While most events and persons in this novel are made from the whole cloth of my imagination, others are not. *Le Cahier de la Rose Noire* actually exists in the form of *Le Cahier Rose* written by the Abbé Boullan and is, indeed, locked away in the Vatican's Secret Archives. Likewise, *The Key of Solomon, Clavicula Salomonis,* can be found at the British Library, Sloane MS. 3091.References to Occult Secret Societies, their rituals, and their practitioners are historically accurate. The *Steganographia* is an actual historical codex written by the German abbot Johannes Trithemius, the father of cryptography and the *tabula recta,* a geometric pattern used to arrange alphabets, numbers, and symbols to make encryption.

Break this Vigenére cipher and discover the Templar's secret.

VSE OMOJWATD TJWM NSEKC SZKTYE TQ EHZ OTUGE
ESRDAV MFRXTVZL VBP CTFCDNKRTOP

Hint: You'll need a little Internet help …
http://cryptoclub.math.uic.edu/vigenere/vigenerecipher.php
And the key word:

U L K I D
C A E N E
I I Y T C
V S T O O
A T Y B D
L H P O E
C E E X S

References to Kashmir's tombs, Durer's art, archeology, genetics, and the Roman Catholic Church's history are accurate and widely documented.

Protocol-17, however—while being the author's invention—is based upon a historical document: *The Protocols of the Learned Elders of Zion*. While attributed to the Russian Czar's Secret Police, and later adopted by none other than industrialist Henry Ford as anti-Semitic propaganda, some believe it to be in reality, the hidden plan of the Illuminati. Let's hope not! After all, this *is* a work of fiction.

R.D.W. ∴ ∴ X

PART I

SOLOMON'S TEMPLE

We are split off from a relationship with our creative feminine, our rational mind devalues and ignores it as we refuse to listen to our intuition, feelings, the deep knowings of our body. As we have moved more and more into the realm of logos over eros, left brain over right, there has been an increasing sense of alienation from the inarticulate sources of meaning that can be called feminine, the Goddess, the Grail.

Joseph Campbell

CHAPTER 1

Zurich, Switzerland

The woman sat bolt upright as if in school, her slender right wrist manacled to the armrest of a blond-wood, over-sized, high-backed chair secured to the floor, looking incredibly striking—but shocked, remote.

Sat wondering …

Watching …

Waiting, fearing the worst.

Alone.

Mouth soft and trembling, Laylah sat perched in the center of a single-room flat; it was dust-covered with half-eaten plates of food, piles of empty fast-food wrappers and pizza cartons that blanketed the floor. The only movement came from the whispery scuttling of cockroaches, crawling over the cracked and rust-stained porcelain of the kitchen sink. Strobelike flashes from a closed-circuit TV monitor's flickering screen pulsed and played across the woman's face.

Pressing a cigarette to her quivering lips with her free hand, Laylah took a deep drag and exhaled.

Terror-glazed eyes cut to the door. Counted the triple brass deadbolts. Darted to the window. Checked it was locked and covered with security screens.

Looking closely now, she gazed vacantly at the reflection in the windowpane.

Some would say that face with its flawless, sun-bronzed skin and cherubic good looks was perfect. Almost *too* perfect. The jaw set a bit too firm. The lips at times slightly cruel. The neck a bit too long, swanlike. The cold, piercing, powder-blue eyes, like a porcelain doll, held a certain sadness. A flatness. But sometimes they sparked. Became windows that revealed nerves that were like the frayed ends of two charged wires. Separated they held only the potential for violence. An offhand remark, an innocent bump and jostle on the train, might only draw a smile. Or the naked ends might touch, releasing a current of rage. That's when she lost control.

Overhead, a moth trapped in the light fixture fluttered its wings in desperation.

Below, Laylah sat quaking. Her T-shirt drenched in sweat and outlining the mounds of her breasts, teeth clenched firmly and grinding.

Her eyes closed tightly now, she softly mumbled in a druggedlike stupor, "Don't sleep, can't sleep. Can't let them in." The cigarette held weakly between long fingers dropped to the floor.

The wall clock tick-tick-ticking as the dark minutes of the night wound down.

Each breath grew shallower, uneven.

She opened her eyes.

The mirrored face stared back, eyes probing. In her mind's eye she thought it whispered.

I am, therefore I Kill?

Footsteps sounded in the outer hallway ... drew closer—

Her eyelids snapped wide. Breath held tightly and ears straining, Laylah's tear-clouded gaze shot to the door, searching obsessively. *Still locked tight. Safe. Don't let them in!*

—and then paused briefly. A reaching shadow poured from beneath the door, shrunk away. The footfalls moved on and then gradually faded.

Caged breath exploded from her lungs. She breathed a sigh of relief.

The shrill ring of the telephone shattered the air.

It rang again. Stared back from the floor. Rang a third time.

Trembling hands fisted. Finally her free hand reached down and palmed the receiver.

For a moment, the caller breathed heavily, raggedly into the phone but said nothing. Then he spoke in a whispery yet forceful voice:

"Let's play a game—"

Eyes blinking twice in rapid succession, face sculpted by unseen hands, the killer squirmed through flesh and bone to the surface. Took control and said in a wooden tone ...

"I'm listening—"

"You have a new target. Kazim Rahman."

"Rahman," she repeated.

"Yes," the voice rasped. "He's patiently waiting for you at the Club-Q on Bergen Strasse in the Zone. Look at the monitor."

Laylah's eyes flicked to the monitor mounted on the wall. The image of a swarthy, Middle Eastern man with a pencil-thin mustache appeared on the screen.

Face blank, eyes opaque, she sat listening intently.

"Rahman will respond to the recognition code: I favor chess."

"I favor chess."

"He'll be expecting you to make a trade, you won't. Neutralize target and obtain document in his possession."

Click.

The hum of the dial tone.

The steel wristband that cuffed her to the chair rolled back and disappeared flush into the armrest. With three loud clicks the electronic deadbolts unlocked in succession. A slight hissing sound and the outer door slowly swung inward.

Silhouetted in the doorway stood a figure. Cautiously, the figure advanced across the threshold and stopped. The extended arm proffered a suit bag. In a hushed whisper a voice said, "You'll have to change. Do your make-up."

* * *

A pounding Techno-Euro beat raged from the loudspeakers at the Club-Q. Strobe lights pulsed, revealing stuttering glimpses of purple neon, a black lacquered bar, and black faux-leather booths that ringed the jammed dance floor. The air was clotted with smoke, sweat, violence, and pheromones.

Rahman was at the bar, looking for a refill, and sweating profusely. The leather pants and jacket he'd chosen to wear didn't breathe like the sheer robes he was accustomed to wearing in his homeland, Saudi Arabia. His work had taken him to stranger places. His business was exchanging art and antiquities for death. He sold priceless, stolen ancient artifacts on the black market. The money received financed al-Qaeda's suicide squads. His most recent offering was the writings of the eighth-century Arabian sage and alchemist Jabir ibn Hayyan, better known as Geber, which had been part of the booty from the recent looting of the Baghdad Museum.

A woman snaked her way through the crowd toward him. She moved with her shoulders back and her head lifted haughtily. She radiated self-confidence and vitality.

He noticed the reaction she had on every man in the club. Their sullen faces came alive and their eyes tracked her, but looked away as she passed, as if they somehow knew a single cutting glance from this woman could render them into eunuchs.

When the woman edged past a girl with lavender spiked hair and a black PVC outfit, the girl shot her a challenging stare, as if she was trying to decide if she craved her sexually or sadistically or both. Rahman thought that most of the patrons, like him, were seeking something that transcended sex and violence. The difference was that he'd experienced the power of having a woman's life-force, her essence, drain from her as he held her body close, gazing into her lifeless eyes.

The woman sidled up next to him at the bar.

She wasn't having any luck getting the bartender's attention. He hoisted a large euro note, and the bartender shot over and filled her order. A longneck bottle of Heineken. As he studied her face in profile, she turned. Her eyes were the same shade of blue as a flickering gas flame, but icy. Her gaze was direct, coolly sensual, slightly playful. Everything about her exuded a savage vitality. She was physical perfection. Glistening olive skin. High cheekbones. Her lips were full, her mouth generous. Although dressed somewhat modestly, her silk blouse was unbuttoned just enough for him to sneak a peek at her cleavage. She flicked her tousled mane of raven, silken hair and smiled.

As she slid onto a barstool, his gaze lowered, drinking in her narrow waist, the long, supple lines of her legs, the way the straps of her spike-heeled pumps caressed her delicate ankles.

She took the beer and looked at him across the top of the bottle as she slowly brought it to her mouth, her lips parting as she might have welcomed his erection. He flashed a greasy smile and stroked his mustache. "I'll only be in town for just the night."

In a silken voice she said, "You don't like to play games, do you?"

She took another sip. He studied the way her throat muscles worked as she swallowed. Imagined a straight razor slicing across her soft flesh.

"Games?" he asked.

"I favor chess."

The reference to chess didn't go unnoticed. *So this is my contact for the exchange,* he thought. *Rahman, He who is great has sent you a gift.* Absently, his hand patted his chest, assuring himself the manuscript was still nestled safely in the lining of his jacket.

She ran her tongue along her upper lip, slowly for effect, and winked.

He reached out and cupped the firm mound of her buttocks. She moaned, slid off the stool and pressed against him, her eyes fluttering. *She's so smug, so vain, and so full of herself.* He imagined neatly slicing into each eye socket, reversing those arctic orbs so that they looked inward. Condemned for eternity to gaze upon herself.

She leaned in close, her breath hot on his face, her eyes never wavering, effectively blocking their intimacy from curious patrons on either side. Her hand moved upward and she tried to reach inside his jacket. He pushed it away. "Not so fast," he admonished. "We'll make the exchange outside in my car."

"Okay," she said from between pouting lips. "But let me give you a preview."

That's when he felt it. Her hand sliding up his inner thigh. He flinched. She laughed as her hand rose higher, her eyes still locked on his. Her practiced hand undid his zipper, reached inside. His heart pounded in his ribcage.

She whispered into his ear, "Do you like it rough?" and bit his earlobe. He winced.

A bolt of sharp, stabbing pain shot from his groin, traveling down his thigh like molten lava. Her expression changed from smoldering arousal to apathetic disdain in an instant, and she said, "Checkmate!" Then nuzzling his ear with the tip of her nose she explained, "That burning sensation rippling through your body right now… is a deadly neurotoxin." And then she kissed him lightly on the cheek.

Rahman saw her face begin to darken, then the room around him began to spin, slowly at first, then at a sickening speed. He heard snatches of music, muted voices, sounds that slowly faded, became weaker and distant. He rasped for air and slumped forward. With a swift pull, Laylah hiked his zipper, and deftly tucked the syringe she'd palmed earlier back into the clutch purse that hung at her side. She moved with the precision and stealth of a stage magician.

With a flick of her wrist a razor-edged knife filled her hand. She glanced around and simultaneously reached beneath his jacket while continuing to nuzzle his ear. In one silken movement the blade sliced the jacket's lining, and she removed the document. She tucked it beneath her skirt, snuggly between garter and thigh. The music raged on, the crowd so self-absorbed that no one noticed as she slipped into the press of bodies and into the night.

CHAPTER 2

And they (the Jews) said (in boast),
"We killed Christ Jesus the son of Mary,
the Messenger of God":
But they killed him not, nor crucified him,
but it was made to appear to them so,
and those who differ therein are full of doubts
with no (certain) knowledge,
but they follow only conjecture.
For a surety they (Jews) killed him not.

Holy Qur'an 4:157

Dome of the Rock: Al-Quds, Palestine

Overhead, Israeli fighter jets streaked against the afternoon sky.

The tall man stopped to listen to the tour guide addressing a group of American sightseers.

"Construction of the Dome began around 688 C.E. by Caliph Abd al-Malik. The Prophet Muhammad's mystic night journey, atop a winged stallion with the Archangel Gabriel at his side, brought him here, where he prayed with the great prophets: Abraham, Moses, and Jesus. Then he ascended to paradise and to Allah on a golden ladder."

A heavyset woman with a floppy, wide-brimmed hat shook her wattle of double chins and said, "Sure… but tell us about those secret chambers."

"The Mount is actually riddled with tunnels and passages, chambers and caves, deep wells and cisterns," the guide went on. "There are thirty-eight major documented wells and cisterns, eleven minor cisterns and forty-three catalogued conduits and passageways. The most famous of which are Solomon's stables and a couple of other large chambers."

A skinny young man asked, "Isn't that where the Knights Templar searched for lost treasure?"

The guide nodded and smiled.

17

"Ah, I see. You want the magical mystery tour. As you wish. In about 1118, nine warrior monks traveled from France to Jerusalem. Their avowed mission was to protect Christian pilgrims visiting the Holy Land. But legend states that they had a secret agenda: the excavation of the mount in a search for buried treasure and relics."

"Did they find it?" another asked.

"They found something all right," the guide explained. "When they returned to France, they received a hero's welcome. St. Bernard of Clairvaux gave a powerful sermon that resulted in the expansion of their order, a religious order of warriors who only reported to the Pope. The sons of rich European nobles swelled their ranks, pledging their wealth. Eventually their Temple became Europe's first bank, even loaning money to monarchs."

"Isn't that what got them into hot water?" the woman asked knowingly.

"More like hot flames. Yes, the bad luck associated with Friday the thirteenth all started with the arrest of the French Knights by Philip the Fair on Friday the 13th of October, 1307. Many were burned at the stake based on false accusations of sacrilegious acts either involving the Crucifix or on an image of Christ."

"Didn't they worship some sort of mysterious silver head?" the young man said, his eyes probing.

"Who knows?" The guide shrugged. "All their admissions were made under the pain of torture. The Dominicans, the Hounds of the Lord, were the French Inquisition's master torturers. The Templars were spread-eagled and had lead weights stacked on their chest, or had funnels rammed into their mouths and were filled with water until they bloated and suffocated. If that didn't make them confess, their feet were burnt, then they had wedges driven under their fingernails or had their teeth pulled out, the nerve endings deftly probed with sharp instruments."

"You mean like in that movie *Marathon Man*, when Olivier, the Nazi dentist, keeps asking Dustin Hoffman, 'Is it safe?' as he digs into another cavity?" the young man offered.

"Where do you think the writer William Goldman got the idea?" the guide said.

The woman's face blanched. "But why did they attack them?"

"Oldest reason in the world, money. King Philip was into the Templars for a fortune in loans; he even borrowed money for his daughter's dowry from the Templars. They were a lot of other monarchs all across Europe deeply in debt to the holy warrior monks."

"But they were accused of heresy," a man wearing a nametag identifying him as a Baptist minister admonished in a self-satisfied tone, his jaw jutting, eyes squinting in the harsh sunlight.

From the rear of the group came a voice. It was deep and precise and conveyed intelligence. "Perhaps you should look up the meaning of the word." The crowd parted and heads turned as a tall man of aristocratic bearing strode to the front. "Heresy is from a Greek word, *airesis,* signifying a choice, the opinion chosen, and the sect holding the opinion." His cold, dark eyes studied the crowd. "It was a label used to describe early Christian sects. St. Paul was described to the Roman governor Felix as the leader of the heresy of the Nazarenes. The historian Josephus applied the name to the three religious sects prevalent in Judea: the Sadducees, the Pharisees, and the Essenes."

"But Christ was an Essene," the woman managed around a mouthful of candy bar, clutching her over-sized hat.

The tall man smiled thinly and moved on, leaving them staring in awe-shocked silence as he made his way into the Dome.

Another man, dressed in dark western clothing, except a white-and-black checkered *gutra* double-banded with a black *igal* that covered his head, pushed his way through the knot of people. He followed the tall stranger at what appeared to be a calculated distance, his eyes nervously darting around as he moved.

Recovering quickly and trying to save face, the guide said, "I won't be able to show you, but beneath the *as-Shakra*, an ancient sacred stone believed to be part of the original wall of Solomon's Temple, is a cavelike crypt known as *Bir el-Arweh*, the Well of Souls. Here, according to ancient folklore, the voices of the dead may sometimes be heard along with the sounds of the rivers of paradise.

"Rumor has it that archeologists are quietly exploring the elaborate honeycomb of subterranean tunnels, cisterns, and secret passages under the Temple Mount."

NSA Fort Meade, Maryland

Kenny, the scrawny, carrot-top intern, pounded the keyboard, instructing the mainframe to access the "Patsy" cut-out system. It was a software program that disguised the source of various computer searches and data mining conducted by the NSA. If any congressional committee or rival agency like Langley or the FBI ran a back trace, the trail would point to the NSC. And no one inside the beltway wanted to lock horns with the bull-necked chairman of the NSC.

The intern was running a crosscheck on the FBI's Combined DNA Index System or—CODIS for short: a database of DNA markers compiled from convicted felons, runaway kids, victims of UNSUB serial killers, or known and suspected terrorists. Kenny took a hit from a can of Coke and brought a bag of chips to his mouth. Tilting it, he devoured the last few crumbs. He'd been working for Dr. Sanger, a ranking genetics egghead, for six months now, and he'd run this program without fail for the umpteenth time, always with the same result: NO MATCH FOUND. Hell, Dr. Sanger didn't even confide in him the identity or history of the base DNA marker that he'd been trying to match.

Data streamed across the face of the oversized monitor.

He glanced at the wall clock. Midnight. He sighed.

From the corner of his eye, he caught the flash of the amber light.

His gaze cut back to the screen. In bold letters the words—POSITIVE MATCH MADE. NOTIFICATION TO MESSIAH PROJECT DIRECTOR COMPLETED. EYES ONLY—pulsed in red.

Kenny's main talent was computer hacking, and he resented doing this grunt work as he called it. But even more, he resented being kept in the dark. "Screw it," he said as he rubbed his hands together quickly and blew on them before letting his fingers fly over the keys. He'd figured out Dr. Sanger's password months ago. Stupid shit for brains had used his golden lab's name: Old Yeller. *How f'ing original*, Kenny thought. Determined to find out what the hell the professor was up to, Kenny hacked his way in and called up the detailed results.

Ice carved dominos tumbled down his spine as he read the screen:

99% probability match of terrorist subject with base DNA marker from Shroud of Turin sample.

He sat frozen, speechless. Somewhere in the back of his mind, he heard the hiss of the security door as it opened behind him. He heard the fall of footsteps drawing closer.

He sensed someone standing directly behind him. The familiar scent of Dr. Sanger's aftershave wafted around him. He knew that Sanger had no life, usually slept on the old leather couch in his office upstairs.

Without turning he said, "Hey Doc … I've done it. We've gotta match."

Then it hit him. He'd violated security protocols by accessing the results. His hand flew to the keyboard.

Before he could delete the screen, he felt it. An odd sensation, something cold …metallic pressed against his throat. Tighter and tighter it constricted, cutting off his air supply, razoring into tender flesh.

Instinctively, he clawed at the piano wire looped around his neck.

Dark motes swarmed at the corners of his vision.

His fingers became slick with blood.

His legs kicked spasmodically. He writhed and twisted his torso but an overpowering force was yanking him backward out of the chair now. A starburst of light flashed on the screen of his eyelids, dizziness and then … blackness everywhere.

An arthritic-bunched hand reached across Kenny's limp and lifeless body and hit the Cntrl, Alt, and Delete keys simultaneously.

CHAPTER 3

Palestine

DR. FAISAL BIN AL-SALADIN stumbled, cursed under his breath, and turned to the man behind him.

"Be careful, it gets a bit steep here," he said, smiling weakly, holding an outstretched hand toward the tall Italian. He had to swallow his annoyance, his irritation at being here at all. He had urgent work to do back in Riyadh at the university, and not much time to accomplish it. He'd wanted no part of this assignment, but Bin Laden had insisted, saying Faisal was the only man he could trust for this sacred mission.

It is not your place to question the will of Allah, Faisal, Bin Laden had said. *If He commands us to lay with the whores of Rome to achieve a higher purpose, then so be it. Deliver the artifact into their hands.*

"How much farther is it?" the Italian asked.

"Not much farther. We're entering the burial chamber now."

Faisal arced the lamp high, playing the light across the loculi—long, narrow shafts hewn deep into the walls of the chamber to serve as burial niches, some for whole bodies, others for limestone ossuaries that held the brittle bones of an entire family.

"The generator isn't working or we'd have plenty of light."

"All the more melodramatic this way, isn't it? I feel like Carter just as he was about to enter Tutankhamun's tomb. I hope there's no curse," the Italian said, his voice cracking slightly.

"Have no fear, for He who is great shall protect us from harm." As the overwhelming stillness and closeness of the underground crypt blanketed him, Faisal secretly hoped that his words were true.

They were deep beneath the *as-Shakra* now, The Noble Rock, the focus of the interior of the Dome of the Rock, located directly beneath the lofty golden dome and surrounded by the highly ornate inner circular and outer eight arcades. The mosque itself was octagonal in shape, each side having a door and seven windows, with rock crystal carving. The dome was made of gold. Muslims believed that this was the rock upon which the Prophet Muhammad stood, before he was raised to heaven. And in his heart Faisal knew that this work would insure that he, too, would see paradise.

The air was damp and chill. The rock walls that ensconced them wept with moisture.

***

The Italian, known simply as the Cleric, was tall and barrel-chested but moved with an economy of grace like an Olympic athlete. He had a presence that dominated the chamber, filling it, not by his mere bulk but by the simple fact that he was there.

When the Cleric had heard of the discovery of a fragment of the scrolls, he had been simultaneously awed and frightened. *The Book of Q* had been, up until now, only the conjecture of biblical scholars. The similarity of the Gospels of Mathew, Mark, and Luke all pointed to a much older source, a *Quelle* in German, hence the lost book of *Q*. And when he heard of their contents and the bodies, his heart seized. The pangs of guilt he'd initially felt as a high-ranking Roman Catholic cleric, who'd taken a holy vow to maintain the integrity of doctrinal truths at all costs, were soon replaced by the raw intensity of power these artifacts held. He knew they held the power to quake the very foundations of The Holy Church and Christianity everywhere.

"Is this where you found the bones of the man you believe was crucified? The ones you sent us for examination?" the Cleric asked.

Faisal shook his head. "No, we must continue south through this passage to an area beneath the *El Kas* Fountain. The fountain is located approximately midway between the Dome of the Rock and *Al Aqsa* Mosque."

They continued on, their footsteps echoing in the darkness, the Cleric's broad girth forcing him to turn sideways, squeezing through narrower sections.

Finally they stopped. The Cleric found himself standing in the center of the mirror image of the Dome above. The chamber was an octagonal space from which eight loculi radiated.

"Over here," Faisal said, hoisting the hurricane lamp and illuminating a shaft to his left. "The bones were in an ossuary."

The Italian remembered studying the bones. The heels were pierced by a long nail; the shattered insteps, victims of a hammer's heavy blow delivered on the Mount of Golgotha.

Faisal raised the lamp and it flickered. Shadows leaped and danced across the walls.

"Was there a name on the jar?" the Italian asked.

Faisal turned, swallowed audibly. "Yes … in Aramaic. 'J'acov, my brother, who died in my place.'"

A wry smile crept across the Italian's face. He fumbled in his pocket for a small, high-intensity flashlight and flicked it on. Its beam slowly arced across the wall above the crypt. There, etched into stone, were a series of murals. The first depicted a man accepting the burden of a cross. The second showed three figures looking down from a hilltop at the scene of the crucifixion. Beneath the man who bore a halo was the name *Issa al-Nagar*, and beneath the man at his side, the name *St. John* was written in Aramaic, Coptic, and Greek.

Panning the light back toward the third figure, he noticed that the face had soft, feminine features and her left hand held the hand of the haloed figure next to her. The Italian read the name aloud, "Magdalena, *Pistis Sophia.*"

Mouth dry and heart pounding, the Cleric focused on the third panel. Entwined in and around the limbs of a tree that resembled a cross, a serpent peered back. The serpent had the head of a woman, cherubic but definitely feminine. Above it a white dove pointed downward. The naked figures of a man and woman, Adam and Eve, bracketed the tree. The man pointed to the picture of an empty tomb. The woman pointed toward the east, to a cityscape. Letters that floated above it read Nin igi *nagar sir*.

"What does it mean?" the Cleric said, pointing to the inscription. "I don't recognize the language."

Fiasal stroked his chin. "That's because it's ancient Babylonian. Its use doesn't fit with the other inscriptions."

"Well … can you translate it or not?"

"It means 'Great Architect of Heaven.'"

The Cleric scoffed. "These drawings look similar to Gnostic symbolism from the second century. And the Great Architect is a reference to the Masonic God. So far, you've shown me nothing of any consequence. I also suspect this whole mural may be a forgery." He stared evenly, maintaining his poker-faced bluff. But when he panned the light across the top of the third mural, something caught his eye. Obscured by a layer of dust, a faint outline was barely visible.

"Faisal," he said, tapping his shoulder. "See that faint tint of red near the top?"

Squinting and raising his lantern, Faisal grunted. "Yes, beneath the dust."

The Cleric looked more closely. "No, it's almost as if someone has deliberately covered it over with chalk."

After quickly searching the immediate area, Faisal found a crate, placed it beneath the mural, and gingerly climbed on top. The wood looked old and creaked as Faisal shifted his weight.

"It's chalk all right."

While Faisal began dusting the mural with a brush, the Cleric stood watching.

Faisal may already know too much, the Cleric reasoned. The Cleric knew the true meaning of the imagery of the serpent and the temptation in the Garden of Eden.

His mind wound back to lectures he'd heard while studying at Rome University, based upon the work of Joseph Campbell, the American authority on the origins of myth and its relationship to religion.

Professore Lorenzo had shown the class a slide titled *The Tree of Eternal Life*. "This is from a document in the 'Ring of Nestor,' an actual ring of solid gold found by a peasant boy in a huge beehive tomb. It's of Minoan Crete origin dating from about 1550 to 1500 B.C.E." He flicked the controller. "Look at this painting by Michelangelo. Some have criticized it because the serpent bears the head and curvaceous torso of a woman, then tapers into a snake's body. But maybe the old Master was simply hiding the truth in plain sight. In this case, the ceiling of the Vatican's Sistine Chapel."

A student asked, "So you're saying that the story told in Genesis was borrowed from much earlier beliefs?"

"Indeed."

"And that a serpent goddess ruled over mankind?"

"No, just the opposite: liberated mankind," Lorenzo explained. "The Gnostics believe that the true God sent into the world a savior, a redeemer, not only once—but twice. The first time was in the Garden of Eden, where the serpent, previously the symbol of wisdom and self-moving energy, who was later transformed by patriarchal writers into Satan, gave Adam and Eve free will. Eve symbolized the divine Sophia, the female aspect of God, not a lust-filled temptress. Sophia mystically entered the serpent, who became the instructor and taught Adam and Eve about their source, informing them that they were of high and holy origin and not mere slaves of the creator deity—Jehovah."

"Sounds like they turned the story upside-down," another student offered.

Lorenzo shrugged. "We could say the same for the Israelites who demonized the gods of the Canaanites, and then later, the Catholic Church followed suit, erecting churches upon old, so-called pagan temples and adopting their holidays."

"Like Passover and Easter are celebrated on the date of the resurrection of Adonis," a girl said. "And how the death, descent, and resurrection were also attributed to previous gods like Adonis, Mithris, Dionysis, and then finally Christ?"

"Or how the rabbit and egg, symbols of fertility, became the Easter Bunny and the egg hunt," a second student offered.

Lorenzo nodded. "Cultures adopt each other's mythos. Make demons of their gods."

"And their women," someone wisecracked.

"Genesis Chapter One states that God created *adam* in his own image. The word *adam* is correctly translated as humankind, the species, not solely the male. So the Gnostics believe that since Adam and Eve were created together, in His image, then God must have not been only male but androgyne. Beyond gender. Therefore, why shouldn't God be worshiped as both male and female?"

The room was silent. Then from the back a girl shouted, "It's about time someone told the truth."

"So originally we were kind of a freak, half man and half woman?" a boy asked.

Lorenzo shook his head. "The word you're searching for is hermaphrodite, divide it into two parts and you get—"

The same girl broke in. "Hermes and Aphrodite?"

Lorenzo nodded. "As Jung said, meld our two natures and be whole again."

The silence of the classroom was broken by the bell.

***

Finished with his work, Faisal stepped down and faced the Cleric.

"My friend, you seem lost in thought," Faisal said, jolting him out of his reverie.

"I'm sorry …what were you saying?"

Faisal shook his head. "Your suggestion that this is somehow a fake wounds my heart. If nothing else, I take great pains with my research. I think you'll find the results of the carbon dating and chlorine isotope tests most interesting. I took scrapings of the images."

"And?"

"It predates the Gospels, making it—"

"From the actual time that Christ walked the earth, a firsthand account." The Italian drew a sharp breath.

"Exactly. I've managed to remove most of the chalk." Faisal hoisted his lantern.

The Cleric's eyes cut to the image above the dove that perched nestled in the clouds. A red-ochre-faced demon stared down scowling, and its hand pointed directly behind him. He recognized the face. It was *Asmodeus*, the demon Solomon used to build his temple. From nowhere a cold draft bit at the back of his neck.

Instinctively, he spun and probed the darkness with the flashlight's narrow beam, eyes searching, hand shaking.

***

High above them, after flashing a permit issued by the Muslim Supreme Council—W*aqf*—at the guard dressed in the drab, olive-green uniform of the security forces, the man who'd followed the Cleric into the Dome made his way down the steps into the Well of Souls.

Absently, his hand ran over his outer clothing, checking that the explosives hidden beneath were still securely taped around his chest. Holding a maglite in one hand and black-light stick in the other, the intruder entered the mouth of the excavated tunnel. As he made his way through the winding passageway, he aimed the light stick toward the ground. Like a trail of breadcrumbs, the phosphorescent glow of the powder that had been intermittently sprinkled marked the way.

CHAPTER 4

IN THE LOWER CHAMBER, the Cleric stood frozen, gripped by an unreasonable fear.

"Perhaps you have offended the Jinn," Faisal taunted

Ignoring him, the Cleric moved quickly across the room. "What's over here? There seems to be a blank wall that's been left untouched."

"Maybe they had no more relatives to bury."

Running his fingertips along the wall, the Cleric noticed a few indentations, as if someone had worked it with a chisel.

"I need more light."

Faisal scurried to his side, and shone his lamp on the wall.

As the Cleric's fingers wandered up and down the limestone, Faisal looked on. The Cleric paused and pressed his cheek to the wall's surface. He pulled back and nodded vigorously while pulling a Zippo lighter from his coat pocket. Thumbing the wheel, he held the flame to the wall. It flickered as though it were kissed by a light breeze. He knelt and studied the floor, then rose slowly and took a step back.

"There's a seam in the wall here." He reached out and dug his finger along a narrow fissure. Flaking limestone fell to the ground. He turned and looked at Faisal, whose face was half-cloaked in shadow, his eyes invisible.

"This isn't part of the original wall. It's been inserted to conceal an entrance. What are you hiding, Faisal?"

The Arab's brow furrowed in confusion, then smoothed. "Nothing … nothing that money can't buy."

"So it's blackmail then, you want—"

"Three hundred thousand dollars wired into this account by noon tomorrow." He smiled and handed the Italian a slip of paper. "As you say in the west, 'it's nothing personal, just business.'"

"I can't wait until tomorrow!"

Apparently, the Bedouin code "give me a good camel, a skin filled with goat's milk and a place to rest my head" is not to Faisal's liking, the Cleric thought. Having to deal with this man offended his sensibilities. The man's sallow cheeks and close-set beady eyes gave the impression of a weasel.

"We're gentlemen, are we not? Your word will suffice."

"You have it."

A greasy smile creased Faisal's face. "That's a satisfactory down payment. But if what I deliver into your hands pleases you, I'll require an additional seven hundred thousand in U.S. dollars."

"Done, now show me what I'm buying."

Moving closer and hoisting the lamp, Faisal said, "Your observation was only half correct. The reason this section appears different is because it's part of the original wall. See the inscription?"

At the top of the slab were the more recently added Modern Greek letters:

Ï ÍÁÏÓ ÔÏÕ ÂÁÓÉËÅÀÙÓ ÓÏËÅÌÌÌÍÔÏÓ

Squinting as he read the hen-scratching-like Paleo-Hebrew letters beneath the Greek inscription, he grimaced and said, "Beth-zur… means temple, and Shelomoh …" He turned on Faisal, glaring. "I'm not in the mood for any more games. People have searched for The Temple of Solomon for years. It doesn't exist. It's just a bedtime story."

"But they were never allowed to search beneath a sacred Muslim shrine with modern technology." Faisal paused for effect. "We beamed ground-penetrating radar, GPR, through the outer walls of the Mount and ran high-frequency seismic tests as well as magnetic mapping and thermal infra-red imagery. The results of both the radar and seismic tests were interesting, but the infrared imagery was most revealing."

"How does it work?" the Cleric asked.

"Infra-red imagery registers changes in thermal or heat radiation above the surface of bodies of varying thermal capacity, such as boulders or walls buried beneath the surface. During the day the surface of the Temple Mount heats uniformly from the sun, and this heat is conducted into the ground beneath. At night the surface cools; however, heat flowing back up from the sub-surface is non-uniform because of cisterns, voids, bedrock, old foundations, and channels. This variance forms images. Here, see for yourself." With a quick flick of the wrist, Faisal unclipped the hard-drive video player-recorder from his waist that was a little larger than a pack of cigarettes. Next he clicked and scrolled to an image and then held it so that the Cleric could clearly see the two-inch screen. It was an aerial shot of the Dome compound with two darker areas in the shape of an octagon. "These were taken from a helicopter at dusk."

Clicking to the next image, he said, "Now for a closer look."

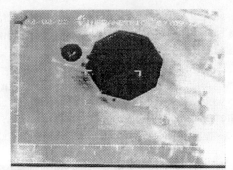

"Notice the larger octagon and then the smaller version. This is where we are now."

The Cleric leaned closer, carefully examining the glowing screen. Here, surrounded by an ancient darkness, it seemed eerily ghostlike.

"Of course, I had a little help from a wise old sage," Faisal went on. "Using the baffling codices compiled by the seventh-century Arabian alchemist Geber, whose enigmatic writing style fostered the word 'gibberish,' I was able to locate the site."

The Cleric's eyes cut to Faisal, probing for deceit, and searching found none. "Wasn't that part of the booty of antiquities stolen from the Baghdad museum?"

"Our operative, Laylah, recently procured it from a dealer in Switzerland."

"Black-market?"

Faisal shrugged. "I wouldn't know of these things."

"Of course not, you're a man of sincere integrity," the Cleric said in a sarcastic tone.

"Believe what you wish, but here's the map. The Hebraic Goddess Shekinah of the mystic Jewish Kabbalah does not play games. She tests us. Take a look at this panel." Faisal moved to the side of the slab and dusted off a golden plate, covered in symbols, that was embedded in a shadowed cubbyhole. A pentagram whose center outline formed a pentagon, nestled on a field of odd letters, stared back enigmatically.

Beneath it was a phrase.

ΙΑΩ ΑΒΡΑΣΑΞ ΑΔΩΝ ΑΤΑ

"Can you translate it?" Faisal asked smugly.

"It's Greek. 'IAO Abrasax, thou art the Lord.' Just more Gnostic mumbo jumbo. A god with the head of a rooster and snakes for legs, who clutched a shield in one arm and a whip in the other. They put his image on amulets to ward off evil."

30

"Yes, but it's missing the divine feminine aspect, which was part of their original trinity: The Father, The Mother, and the Son. Look at the words below it."

AH ELOHIM SABAOTH ADONAI ELOAI

"They're Hebraic names for God. All masculine," the Cleric replied.

"To think a Muslim has to instruct a Christian on the names of his god. Think of your Bible. Think of how God told Abram to take a letter from his wife Sarah's name, signifying the merging of masculine and feminine."

"You mean Ab*raham*? After Sari was changed to Sa*rah*?"

"Yes, now insert the symbol by pushing on its corresponding symbol on the plate."

Stepping aside, Faisal urged him on with a nod.

His hand trembling as if he were about to throw the doomsday switch, the Italian punched the symbol that corresponded to *AH*. It wouldn't budge. He pushed harder. Nothing. Just as he lowered his hand and was about to speak, the symbol sank into the wall. Still the wall remained motionless.

Faisal smiled. "Now insert the more obvious combination of the last letters of their names … ham plus ah."

"Hamah?" the Cleric questioned.

Faisal nodded.

Without hesitation this time, the Cleric pushed the corresponding symbol.

A great rushing sound, like tons of sand pouring through a grate, roared from below the wall. The slab moved a little at first and then several inches at once, and slowly began to sink into the floor. The sound of stone grinding against stone echoed in the emptiness of the chamber. Over the din, Faisal shouted, "It's quite fitting. *Hamah* means roar, a boisterous yearning. Or as your westernized feminists would say, 'I am woman, hear me roar.'"

A foul odor resembling pungent ammonia poured through from the other side.

"Maybe the air is going bad," the Cleric said with a worried look washing over his already haggard face.

Faisal shook his head. It's just the perfume of the cave dwellers …bat guano."

The slab suddenly shuddered and ground to a halt.

"It's a two-part test. Look here." Faisal pointed to an odd-shaped funnel sticking out from the side of the plate. As he moved closer, the Italian shone his flashlight down the funnel's throat. Sparkling crystals danced in the light.

"Are you familiar with words of power?" the Arab asked.

"Don't tell me that I've got to shout 'Open Sesame' like Ali Baba into that thing."

31

By the glow of the lamplight, he could see Faisal's pained expression.

"No, the reverse of the Abrasax amulet holds the key." From beneath his tunic, Faisal pulled out a medallion and turned it over. He held it under the lamp.

The Cleric squinted, straining to read the tiny ancient Greek letters.

‖ ΒΒΒΝΑΘ   ΑΝΑΛΕΛ

"You were almost correct. The word is known to children the world over. If we combine the last two lines in English, they'd read Ablanathanalba, a palindrome in Greek letters, meaning it reads the same forward and backward."

Sounding out the word in his mind, the Cleric smiled wryly. "Abracadabra."

"A crude mispronunciation, but basically correct. Some say that it's a variation of the Hebraic *Ab Ben Ruash a Cadesh*, the Father, Son and Holy Ghost."

The Cleric's eyebrows bunched and he sighed loudly.

"Shall we try it?"

Palms raised in a gesture of capitulation, the Cleric said, "Be my guest."

Faisal pressed the front of the amulet into a circular niche in the wall. With a clicking sound, it slowly revolved counter-clockwise a full turn and stopped. Then he leaned over the mouth of the funnel and intoned the incantation.

At first nothing happened and the Cleric smirked. Then a high-pitched vibration resonated from the mouthpiece of the funnel. His ears rang; the fillings of his teeth pulsed in sync. Suddenly the slab slowly dropped away, sinking into the floor.

"I don't claim to understand exactly how the mechanism works or how it even could work," Faisal offered. "But I'd hazard a guess that it has something to do with the proper pitch of the sound waves and their effect on the crystals within the tube."

"At this point, my friend, I wouldn't be the least surprised if Atlantis itself lay beyond that threshold."

"After you see what's in store for you, you may wish it was *only* a lost city."

Taking the lead, Faisal stepped into the dark heart of the cavity.

Hesitating at first, the Cleric followed, guided by the pendulous glow of Faisal's lamp as they moved through a narrow tunnel. From up ahead, a leathery, rustling noise drifted toward him.

CHAPTER 5

WITH FAISAL STILL leading, they traveled a maze of passageways. Around them, the darkness was a physical presence. As they went deeper the grade became even steeper. Twice the Cleric tripped over an outcropping of jagged rock, skinning his shin.

Without warning, Faisal stopped in his tracks. Taken by surprise, the Cleric plowed into his back, knocking him to the ground. As he fell, the flashlight flew from his hand, tumbling end-over-end and clattering to the ground. It spun like a revolving pointer on a board game, casting luminous spirals over the hard rock wall and floor. As the spinning flashlight slowed to a stop, its beam fell upon a face. From ground level, Faisal stared upward with panic-driven eyes. "Help me," he cried.

Hands fumbling desperately, the Cleric found the flashlight.

On all fours, the Cleric crawled toward him, the rough-hewn floor sending sharp spikes of pain through his arthritic kneecaps.

"Careful," Faisal shouted. "I've fallen into a hole." By the light of the flashlight, the Cleric could see Faisal's fingers clawing for a handhold on the edge of the pit.

He tucked the flashlight under his arm and sat, his legs extended in a V. Then gripping Faisal under the armpits, he heaved and slowly pulled the Arab toward him as he scooted backward. Once clear of the hole, they lay on their backs, sucking deep, ragged breaths from the thin, damp air.

"You saved my life," Faisal managed.

"You would have done the same."

Faisal wheezed and coughed. "Don't be so sure. I'm a selfish coward."

Looking past him, the Cleric saw a faint glow. "Your lamp?"

"I must have dropped it."

They moved to the mouth of the hole.

The Cleric stabbed the flashlight's beam downward into the darkness.

About fifteen feet below, jagged spikes of razor-edged flint lined the bottom of a pit roughly six feet in diameter. In the center, the lamp lay on its side nestled against a skeleton. Slowly, he panned the remains. A large black scorpion crawled out of the skull's eye socket and scuttled across the ribcage and down the arm, finally resting on a black-and-white shield emblazed with a faded red cross.

His voice breaking, crawfish skittering up his spine, the Cleric said, "It's a Templar's shield."

They exchanged bewildered glances.

"So the legend's true," he said. Then the Cleric cautiously rose. He bent and pulled Faisal to his feet. A dark, disturbing thought struck him. "How is it that you didn't know the pit was there?"

In a sheepish voice, Faisal said, "We must have taken a wrong turn."

"We? Can you find the way back?"

"In a word … no."

"Then we'll have to jump."

"But how do we know there isn't some booby trap waiting on the other side?"

"We don't."

Taking a few steps back and measuring the distance, the Cleric stood poised. "I'll go first."

"May Allah be with you."

The Cleric sprinted forward, leaped and cleared the pit by inches.

He turned, back stepped to a safe distance, and aimed the flashlight across the pit.

Faisal closed his eyes, mumbled a short prayer and ran, springing at the lip of the pit and landing hard, face down at the Cleric's feet. He brought his hand to his bloodied nose and cried, "It may be broken."

Bending and examining his companion's nose, the Cleric's hand shot out and tweaked it roughly.

Faisal winced and blubbered, "You have a heart of stone, my friend."

"You'll mend," the Cleric said sarcastically and pulled him to his feet.

They pressed on.

As they crept along, eyes straining to see beyond the reach of the flashlight, cautiously checking for more holes, the Cleric would occasionally pause and check to the right and left. At one point, a warren of passageways appeared on his left. He thought of Dante's Inferno. Maybe this was what awaited him on the other side, an endless maze of tunnels, all leading to torment in the seventh circle of Hell. He struggled to hush the whispers of doubt that haunted his thoughts.

Then up ahead he saw it. A steep, winding staircase littered with fallen rock.

Searching his memory, he recalled a description of Solomon's Temple. Two winding staircases that eventually led to the Holy of Holies and the Ark of the Covenant. His mind grappled for a foothold. *This is insanity. I'm walking through some waking nightmare.*

They exchanged furtive glances and mounted the stairs with exhausted legs.

"Does anything look familiar?" the Cleric said, his eyes scanning the vastness of the chamber around them.

"By the grace of Allah we have found it. I can find our way back from here. But first you must see the mysteries with your own eyes. And the artifacts you seek are just—"

They'd reached the top. Looming before them was a massive door made of olive wood and gold plating.

Faisal drew up short and stared as if he'd seen a vision. "There's no turning back once you've entered. Are you sure that you're prepared for the truth?"

"The truth shall set you free," the Cleric said, laughing to relieve the pent-up tension that racked his body. "I've come too far, searched too long for an answer to turn back now. It's time the world woke from the slumber of false doctrine, from the lies of Rome, the lies of the Protestant pulpit."

Gradually, they walked closer.

"The lies that bind, my brother, may be more comfort to your soul than the raw truth."

"Let's get on with it, or don't you want your money?"

"Oh, I want it all right," Faisal answered, drew himself up, took a deep breath, and put his shoulder to the door.

At the far end of the vaulted room stood a large, golden altar. Behind it, two giant statues towered, their stone-carved eyes staring, silent and enigmatic. Affixed to the front of the altar was a bronze figure. Scattered across the altar lay gold goblets. Mouth gaping in awe, heart slamming against his ribcage, the Cleric stood stunned. Along the sides of the wall, small oil lamps flickered, sending shadowy fingers crawling up and down the wall.

"The alchemic lamps of eternal flame," the Cleric said with reverence. "It's impossible. I've read about them but…" He moved to the wall and noticed a long stone trough that connected the lamps and ran the length of the wall. Standing on tiptoe, he dipped his hand into the trough. The inside felt sticky, thick with oil. Then he gingerly pulled down a lamp and examined it. "Just as I thought. It has an asbestos wick and a perpetual supply of lamp oil, amazing."

"We wouldn't want the world to learn the properties of that oil, my friend. Or the Kingdom might go bankrupt," Faisal said, and turned back toward the huge statues. "Magnificent aren't they? The great Goddess of the Canaanites in her twin aspects: Ashtoreth and Adam's first wife, Lilith."

"I don't understand?" the Cleric stammered. "The Bible, the Torah, and the Talmud. The Israelites, the Jews worshiped JAHWEH. They were patriarchal societies."

Faisal laughed so hard that tears came to his eyes. "Chauvinists yes, but not originally patriarchal. Did you know that Lilith's great sin, for which she was banished from the Garden of Eden, was that she'd become a westernized woman? Didn't care for the missionary position and always wanted to be on top. As an Arab male, I can relate to Adam's anger. Have you ever wondered why so many Arab men turn to fundamentalism or hashish or other men for company? It's because the law dictates that we circumcise our young women, remove or split the clitoris. They feel no sexual gratification and we can, therefore, never please them."

"I don't see the humor in this. Nor do I care about your legends of Lilith, Adam's first wife, or how you mutilate young girls!"

"You asked a question. So again, I'll quote your Good Book. 'The King defiled the high places overlooking Jerusalem … with graven idols, which had been built by Solomon King of Israel, to Ashtoreth or Asherah, goddess of the Sidonites, and to Lilith, hag of the desert, consort of the jackals, and to Moleck, god of the Ammonites.'"

"But—"

"Look around you." Faisal indicated with a broad sweep of his arm. "The Edenic or sexual references to procreation. Take the lozenge-shaped porticoes, signifying the womb for example. Solomon was an initiate of the Mystery schools and the temple that he built was actually a house of initiation . . .containing countless pagan philosophic and phallic emblems. In Hebrew the goddess's name Asherah also means pole and living tree. The pomegranates representing the seed, the palm-headed columns, the colossal, erect pillars before the door, the Babylonian cherubim, and the arrangement of the chambers and even the goat hair draperies which once hung here, all indicate the temple to have been patterned after the sanctuaries of Egypt and Atlantis. Are you going to tell me they look that much different from the great Gothic cathedrals of Europe?"

"No, I can't deny it. We, too, encoded messages into the architecture of our places of worship and our Masonic temples, concealing our worship of the divine feminine. But seeing the reality of it all, the antiquity of the secret knowledge from its ancient source, in the flesh, is a bit unnerving."

"Then prepare to be totally shocked." Faisal made for the altar. "Come along with that flashlight. I want you to have a good look at this."

* * *

In the Dome above, a young schoolgirl turned from the railing overlooking the sacred stone below and almost tripped as her foot hit something. Stooping, she snatched a knapsack from the floor at her feet. She glanced around to make sure her teacher wasn't looking and peeked inside. A box of candy lay at the bottom of the sack. Hunching her shoulders and turning her back, she reached in and hefted the box. Awfully heavy for chocolates, she thought. Quickly, she closed the flap, slung the bag onto her shoulder and rejoined her tour group.

CHAPTER 6

BEHIND THE ALTAR, in the floor, lay a huge block of marble with a ring in its center. Perched above it were the legs of large tripod fitted with a pulley and winch mechanism that appeared to be made of steel. A cable ran from the winch, upward through the pulley, and then back down to a hook that had been inserted into the ring.

"Look familiar?" Faisal asked. "I had this tripod especially made. Had a devil of a time getting it down here." He pointed to a pile of chains and something that may have once been timbers. "Of course, there wasn't just one temple on this site. There was the original temple, the new temple, and Herod's temple, which I believe some of the remains of this original device came from. The Knights Templar probably used a horse and ropes to raise the slab."

Immediately, the Cleric recognized it as the same device captured as a scale model and found in all Masonic Lodges. His heart thudded in his chest, his palms slick with sweat. He blotted them on his trousers.

Together, they grasped the winch's handle and cranked, faces taut, arms aching from the muscle strain. With a scraping sound, the marble block slowly ascended. When it reached nearly the apex of the tripod, Faisal said, "That's good." Then he threw a locking lever on the winch. He rose, hand pressed to the small of his back and groaning.

Beneath the hovering block was a dark, square-shaped hole about six feet by six feet.

They moved to the rim, and the Cleric speared the dark cavity with the narrow beam of his flashlight. Stretching down into the blackness was a rock-carved stairway.

"The entrance to the underground vault that the Templars discovered?" the Cleric asked.

Faisal nodded. "Age before beauty," he said, grinning widely and motioning for the Cleric to go first.

The air was stale and thin, the hungry darkness that surrounded them complete. As they made their way deeper and deeper down the narrow steps, the only sound was their searching footsteps and the Arab's incessant wheezing. Between gasping breaths, Faisal said, "My curse since childhood, asthma."

"Can you make it?" the Cleric asked, his free hand hugging the side wall to steady himself as he moved.

Faisal coughed. "It's not much farther and the air gets better, cooler."

From below came a faint fog of light and soon they reached the bottom of the staircase.

They found themselves in another smaller chamber.

In the center, suspended from the ceiling, a large gold mobile twisted in the air as they stood before it in the antechamber and below it, Hebrew letters decorated the floor. The walls and floor were limned with the faint orange glow of the eternal flame lamps that ringed the room.

"Study how the segments move, my friend," Faisal said, nodding toward the mobile.

The Cleric watched patiently, trying to detect a pattern. Then he saw it. From this angle the dancing segments merged, forming a winged serpent eating its own tail. "It's an *Ouroboros*, the sign of regeneration, the 'mystical marriage' of the micro and macrocosms. The Inner and Outer Worlds," he whispered as he stood staring, his mouth gaping.

Although the symbol was commonplace today, even used in the form of a coiled circle of light by Lucent Technologies, the Cleric knew that it held a far deeper meaning. Because of the Inquisition, the scientists or alchemists as they were called, had to conceal the secrets in the form of allegory and symbols. Only if you had the key, could you decipher the hidden knowledge. The "dragon with wings" symbolized our Interior guide, or Holy Guardian Angel as the Gnostics called it, and the dragon "without wings" our ego, or "little King," who blocked the way.

"Focus on the center," Faisal ordered. "The inscription beneath it reads: 'Let your eye lead you beyond the whirling energy of the *esoptron*.'"

Now staring back from the center, the image of the Star of David formed. As the Cleric studied the center of the star, he thought of its meaning. The triangle pointing downward symbolized the feminine principal, but conjoined with the triangle pointing skyward, it symbolized, like the Ouroboros, a mystical marriage. *Let your eye lead ...*

That was the clue. Looking through and past the center of the star, he saw something in the far corner of the room: a pale flicker of light reflected from the eternal lamps. Fishing into his pocket, he pulled out a laser pointer, thumbed it to life, and aimed its beam through the center of the hexagram at a crystal that dangled and twisted there. The laser's red beam was bisected and bounced back, snaking through the darkness and finding the mouth of Ouroboros. It sprang back as though it had been reflected by some unseen, mirrorlike surface. And within the mouth, floating in the darkness, was a 3-D, holographic image. A whirling golden door. He bolted across the room with Faisal following.

...beyond the esoptron or mirror in Greek, he thought.

Stretching the expanse of the far side was a wall of polished bronze, the only type of mirror yet invented in Solomon's time. From a distance the surface worked like a magician's trick mirror, reflecting the darkness that surrounded it and giving the impression that nothing but emptiness lay in this direction.

"Now how do we get through it?" the Cleric asked, turning to his companion. "You're not much help, you know."

"Your words wound my heart," Faisal said, shaking his finger and feigning a hurt puppy look. "I'm now acting only in the capacity of a guide who has brought you to the threshold. Solving the riddles of the temple and seizing the bounty must be accomplished by the seeker. So it is written."

"Have you ever considered becoming an actor? 'So it is said, let it be written.' You sound like a bad impersonation of Moses in *The Ten Commandments*."

"I'm not sure that I like your tone. Don't spin my words."

The Cleric was about to answer but paused. "Say that again."

"What? … not sure I like your tone?"

"NO! That last part."

"Don't spin my words?"

Making for the edge of the wall, the Cleric shouted back over his shoulder, "You said the inscription read the energy of the … '*whirling* esoptron', correct?"

"Yes … but—"

Placing his palms against the cool metal and bracing his feet, the Cleric said, "Don't just stand there, push."

Shoving with all their strength, the wall finally began to move, rotating on its center axis like a revolving door. The scraping sound of metal against stone reverberated in the darkness.

In moments, they were standing on the other side.

There, lying in shadow, were three sarcophagi. Hesitating, the intruders moved closer. The first was white and delicately carved, but appeared to be very solid, as though it weren't hollow but a single oblong slab sculpted magically from living stone. Faisal stood looking as the Cleric ran his fingertips lightly along the lid. A raised seal and characters fought for meaning in the dim, wavering lamplight.

Probing with the beam of his flashlight, the Cleric struggled to read the inscription, written in Aramaic, in a faltering voice. "Here lies the body of MAR-ee-yaam, Mariamene e Mara, Tribe of Benjamin, daughter of the house of Herod and Chusa, sister of Lazarus and Sarah, Tower of Jerusalem, high priestess and Master of the Essene healers, wife of ee-SHOW-ah, Jehoshua."

For a long time they stood not speaking, the Muslim and the Christian separated by years of misunderstanding and bloodshed.

Finally, the Cleric broke the deafening silence. "Mary Magdalene, wife of Jesus." As he sighed deeply, his eyes lowered to the side of the sarcophagus. Then his eyes darted to the other two coffins and back. "What's this?" He dropped to one knee. "There's a ring of rosettes sculpted here interspaced with Templar crosses. Besides, they buried only the bones in a small limestone ossuary … never the whole body … this is a fake!"

"I assure you it is not a forgery," Faisal countered. "Everyone assumes that the Templars only took something of value from Solomon's Temple. It now appears obvious that in fact, not only did they take the Ark of the Covenant, but they also *returned* something or someone to their rightful resting place. After Mary Magdalene's exile to southern France, she was probably temporarily buried somewhere in the Languedoc region of the Cathars, where the Pope waged the first European Crusade for forty years and massacred over a hundred thousand of them during the Albigensian Crusade. But the Templars, fearing that Rome had learned of Magdalene's resting place, returned her to Jerusalem. This secret of her marriage to the prophet Jesus and the location of her tomb were the true secrets that Pope Clement V and Philip the Fair tried to force the Templars to divulge."

Shaking his head and staring coldly into his companion's eyes, the Cleric said, "You're a con artist. Show me proof!"

"Help me slide back the lid, then. And you'll see with your own eyes." The tone of his voice sounded more like an urgent prayer than a statement of fact.

Together they struggled, backs straining, temples pulsing and necks cording, to move the heavy lid. Inch by inch stone grated against stone. The sweet odor of spices and something that resembled the scent of crushed rose petals perfumed the air. "That's sufficient," Faisal said, breathing heavily. He reached into the sarcophagus and removed a vellum scroll that lay atop the chest of the mummified body, whose head was adorned in a jeweled crown.

With trembling hands, the Cleric took the scroll and gently laid the goatskin parchment on the lid. Next he carefully unraveled a tiny section and by the beam of the flashlight, he read the text.

As he read, he felt the blood drain from his face. It was the Book of *Q*, and more importantly, the little he could make out showed it to be closer in content to the Gnostic Gospels than the orthodox P text, or the King James version's account of the life and times of Jesus. His throat parched, his muscles cramping with tension, he pondered the consequences. In his trembling hands he held the one true Gospel, written in Jesus's own hand.

He read on and came to a passage that was a letter addressed to Caiaphas, High Priest of the Sanhedrin. Referring to himself as Yahoshua Teacher of the Righteous, Jesus outlined a plot that included Judas Iscariot's betrayal and the subsequent staging of a crucifixion.

The Cleric's blood ran cold; his fingers became numb.

It told of a plan to substitute Barabbas, who Jesus referred to as his brother J'acov the Just, on the cross. The Cleric knew that Barabbas meant literally "Son of the Father." He'd kept silent about the mural, but the fresco that Faisal had shown him earlier, when combined with this document, was explosive proof that the so-called heretical texts were in fact true. Then he remembered the other two sarcophagi.

He straightened and moved on rubbery legs to the second tomb. Its cover lay against one side. When he searched its interior with the bright beam of the flashlight, nothing but emptiness leered back. His eyes cut to the lid. Scanning it with the light and translating the Aramaic, he read aloud, "Yahoshua, son of Miryam and Rabboni Joseph. Issa al-Nagar, who suffered not, but having shown the way journeyed far and rests in the city of the great serpent."

"Are you satisfied with the authenticity?"

Bracing himself against the cold stone, the Cleric nodded slowly. He turned and met Faisal's eyes. "It's everything you promised and more. But did you know Yahoshua's sarcophagus was empty? And how did you know that the Book of *Q* was inside Magdalene's?"

"What I have shown you and told you was discovered by my father. But he died suddenly before sharing all the secrets of the temple with me. And some things are beyond my control. It would appear that the legend of Issa al-Nagar is true, also."

So he knows of the meaning of nagar and understands the message portrayed in the fresco, the Cleric thought. The Cleric knew that in the original Aramaic texts, Jesus was referred to as *Bar Nagara*. The underlying Hebraic and Aramaic word is *nagar,* which meant wise serpent or the expression "good with his hands," an allusion to a Magi. A similar Sumerian word—*nanger*—which meant carpenter, accounted for the mistranslation that labeled him a carpenter and son of a carpenter. Even Joseph's importance was confused. In the Greek, both he and Jesus were referred to as *ho tekton*—which means "scholar or teacher," or more specifically "master of the craft." And the craft-working was knowledge—not woodworking. The term was carried over into present-day Masonry: Master of the Craft.

His resolve stiffened. *This man knows too much*, he reasoned. *One minute he plays the fool and the next, the educated scholar. He's an unacceptable risk.*

"Tell me, Faisal. This city of the great serpent …do you know where it is?"

Smiling knowingly and rubbing his palms, Faisal said, "But of course, my friend. And for a small additional fee … I could be persuaded to tell you."

***

Having maneuvered the winding tunnels, the intruder mounted the last step of the colossal staircase and entered the temple, eyes searching, his handgun held out before him. He heard distant voices and followed the sound, flowing silently through amber lamplight and shadow like smoke.

CHAPTER 7

THE CLERIC SHRUGGED. "We'll talk more of Christ's tomb later. But let's take a quick peek at the third sarcophagus as long as we're here."

Faisal nodded and they moved to the next stone coffin.

The lid was cracked in two. Playing the flashlight across it, the Cleric stopped on a gold seal.

From behind him, came a strangled gasp. The Cleric spun at the sound.

In the beam of the flashlight, his companion stood shuddering and praying fervently to Allah.

"What is it?" the Cleric asked.

Shaking his head vigorously, perspiration streaking down his cheeks, Faisal answered, "We must leave this place now. Gather what you came for, but do not—"

"Get a grip and help me lift the lid."

"Never. That is the seal from *Clavicula Salomonis, The Key of Solomon the King*. Its purpose is to bind evil. Break the seal and—"

"Okay, how much money do you want this time?"

His eyes pleaded. "Forget the money … it's not worth my life, my soul."

Sighing deeply, the Cleric grasped the lid and shoved. It moved slightly. When he put his back into it, spurred by adrenaline, the top half tumbled to the floor with a loud thud.

Something brushed against the Cleric's arm, through his hair. From nowhere the thunder of flapping wings thrummed the air. Shrieking and mewling, the frenzied, winged vermin swooped and dived from the ceiling, revealing the glint of tiny fangs as they plunged closer. But at the last moment they congealed into a black mass that swarmed over the two intruders and disappeared as quickly as they came.

He clawed frantically at his hair, brushed his clothing and pulled back a palm coated with bat guano. Looking down, he saw Faisal on his knees cowering on the floor, head tucked beneath his tented arms.

"They're gone. Just stay where you are," the Cleric admonished.

Turning back to the coffin, he peered inside. The body was desiccated but with a different appearance than the remains of a mummy you'd find in a museum. Instead of looking like petrified wood, dark brown with shades of black running through it, the body was moist-looking and ashen gray, mottled with yellow bands. The face was all sharp angles and hard plains, high cheekbones and deep-set eye sockets. The chin was pointy, the forehead high and flat. The

43

lips razor thin. Looking closer, he saw that the chest was emaciated; each rib clearly defined against the stretched skin. But more disconcerting were the huge, black eyes. It was as if obsidian replicas had been placed into its eye sockets by some Egyptian priest. They radiated an age-old intelligence, and a curious mixture of intensity and fury.

And instead of lying on its back, the body was tucked in a fetal position. The hands and feet were bound in chains. He couldn't make out what they were made of, but they looked like some strange alloy. He moved to the other side. That's when he saw them.

From its back where one would expect to find the scapulas, something sprouted. Bending closer, he froze. Vestigial winglike appendages curled outward and down the middle of its back.

Understanding slowly dawned. His eyes cut back to the creature's chest. Around its neck hung a golden plaque. The Hebrew letters of the Tetragrammaton, the ineffable name of God, were stamped into the soft metal. And below it the name—*Asmodeus.* Something glinted in the beam of his flashlight. A small silver amulet lay near the creature's neck on the bottom of the tomb. The silver scroll, he thought. Without thinking, his hand shot out, snatched the tiny piece of metal, and tucked it into his pocket. His gaze traveled down the creature's arm to its gnarled hand. A golden ring winked back in the flashlight's bright light. He swallowed hard, reached out, and pulled the ring from the skeletal finger. After sliding it onto his ring finger, he rolled it back and forth between the thumb and forefinger of his free hand. The Cleric remembered the texts that told of how King Solomon had bound the demon Asmodeus with his magic ring. After doing Solomon's bidding and building the temple, Asmodeus tricked Solomon into letting him try wearing the magic ring. In an instant, Solomon was flung into the heavens and Asmodeus took the King's seat on the throne. Could the legend be true?

Then something else caught his eye. A tiny vial made of some crystal-like substance lay next to the creature. He snatched it from the coffin and held the flashlight up to it. Written in Hebrew on the side was *Shamir*. Within the amber-colored crystal was a tiny worm. He knew that legend had it that the worm possessed magical powers. When Solomon placed it atop the marble, the stone was cleaved in two. Pocketing the vial, he shouted to Faisal, "I'm done here. Bring me the scroll and we'll leave."

The sound of Faisal's scrambling feet echoed, faded away and returned.

Standing with his back to Faisal and fingering the pectoral cross beneath his shirt, he said, "You've done well, my friend. I think you deserve to be rewarded with an advance payment." His voice was soft, almost fatherly, but when he turned, his dark eyes narrowed to slits. With blinding speed, his arm arced high and he thumbed the release button on the head of the cross, causing a razor-edged blade to spring from its base. Cold steel flashed through the air. The tip of the blade dug deep into Faisal's throat; rose again and flickered, punching into his chest; rose again and flickered, plunging deep into his left eye. Blood spilled down his cheeks, down his throat. His knees buckled and he toppled to the cold floor, the remaining eye staring sightlessly.

The Cleric bent and took the scroll from his hands.

As he began to turn, it hit him. Faisal had shown him digital pictures of the Dome. Dropping to his knees, he searched Faisal's clothing. When he ripped the video recorder from Faisal's waist, he noticed the wire that snaked upward to a miniature buttonhole video camera concealed in the center of the Arab's tunic. *Bastard recorded everything*, he thought.

He spun on his heels and wrenched the gold plaque from the creature's, Asmodeus's, chest. His arm pistoned out and drove the hand that held the ring into its emaciated chest. "I, King Solomon, call you to do my bidding."

Nothing happened. He shrugged, dropped the plaque, and pulled the Zippo lighter from his pocket. As he walked away, he thumbed it to flame and casually tossed it over his shoulder into the sarcophagus. The mummified creature burst into flames. Cracking embers spit high into the darkness. And glancing back over his shoulder, he thought he saw a fiery hand rise, briefly paw the air and then, slowly drop.

The Cleric paused over Mary Magdalene's coffin. He gently caressed her cheek and then abruptly reached down and broke off the petrified tip of her finger. Next he snatched a lock of hair and completed his desecration by yanking out a tooth. "My deepest apologies. But we'll need the DNA evidence quite badly." He tucked the samples into a plastic bag and started for the doorway.

A loud, distant boom echoed. Shockwaves rumbled and shook the walls around him. A second blast, only closer. The ground quaked beneath his feet. A fine mist of dust rained down from the ceiling. He bolted across the chamber and to the staircase. Stumbling, his lungs flaming, he scrambled up the steps. The flashlight in his outstretched hand blinked once, twice, and finally winked out. He froze in the sudden rushing blackness. He fumbled for his Zippo, then remembered he'd pitched into the demon's tomb earlier. Tucking the scroll into his shirt, he crawled hand over hand, his fingers siphoning the air like a blind man.

Above him in the distance, he saw the bright lens of a flashlight.

"Follow my light," came an excited voice. It was the intruder, his accomplice.

Adrenaline-charged limbs carried him up and through the opening into the main chamber.

"This way, over here. We have to hurry," the intruder barked and turned, running.

The Cleric's panic-driven eyes scanned the room. Spider webs of cracks, as if demons wielding ball-peen hammers were pounding at them, ran across the walls. He dodged falling blocks of marble as he ran helter-skelter, eyes searching the dust-clotted air for the beacon ahead. When he rounded the altar, a jagged fissure tore across the floor, knocking him off balance and to the ground. A loud rumble churned toward him and suddenly the towering statue of Lilith toppled to the floor, narrowly missing him, and splintered into huge slabs, sending billowing clouds of dust high into the air.

Rough hands brought him to his feet and pulled him toward the exit door. "There's one more charge, we have to hurry," the intruder said as he dragged the Cleric through the doorway and down the stairs. By now the Cleric was coughing violently, unsteady on his feet.

The staircase began to sway violently as giant veins marbled the surrounding walls and columns. Once at the bottom and clear of the stairs, the intruder laid the Cleric on the floor and ducked into a nearby tunnel. Suddenly a large piece of marble crashed down, pinning the Cleric beneath its weight.

"Come back!" the Cleric pleaded, his gaze sliding down his leg to the deep gash on his calf. "Don't leave me here!" His hand flew to his scalp; it was damp with blood. He struggled to move the slab. It wouldn't budge. Then he remembered the vial. Fishing in his pocket, he found it, and cracked it hard against the side of the marble. Slowly the worm within came to life and inched its way across the hard surface, arched, and then began burrowing its way into the solid marble. The fleeting image of its wiggling tail was the last thing the Cleric saw before the slab cracked in two, freeing him.

From the mouth of the tunnel came a different roar. Squinting and blinking the blood and sweat from his eyes, he saw a huge yellow eye making straight for him. The roar was louder, the eye charging closer. He buried his head in his hands and shouted, "By the ineffable name of God, I command you demon, by your name, Asmodeus, be gone from here!"

The four-wheeler rocketed to his side and shuddered to a stop, its engine percolating loudly. Composing himself, the Cleric struggled to his feet and climbed on. "Did you say something?" the intruder shouted over the din.

"Yes, what took you so Goddamn long?"

The engine revved wildly, and they sprang forward and into a tunnel.

***

High above on the steps of the Dome, tourists fled in panic as smoke and fire bellowed from the mouth of the holy mosque. A young Jewish boy stood glassy-eyed and pulsing with the energy of a zealot. At his feet lay what bloodied parts remained of a young girl. In his hand he clutched a knapsack.

"I have another bomb," he taunted, hefting the bag higher. "What do you care if I burn the *chazar* temple! We must destroy it, level it to the ground in order to rebuild the temple of Jerusalem in its place as Rabbi Mier Khane has prophesied."

A cordon of young, boyish-faced Israeli security forces officers leveled their Galil AR 5.56 mm. assault rifles on the boy. Their eyes were wide and filled with anger and confusion, their fingers heavy on the trigger, their hearts pounding through the roofs of their mouths.

"*A sof! A sof!* Let's end it, End it!" the boy shouted and ran toward the officers.

A blaze of muzzle fire erupted and the boy was cut down in his tracks.

***

Across the giant security wall that divided Palestine from Jerusalem another young man entered a different shrine: the new Holocaust Memorial. His features were delicate, his eyes blue. At first glance, no one would have guessed he was a Muslim. He approached the inner security checkpoint. His eyes were vacant, his face slack and expressionless. When the guard motioned him forward toward the magnetometer, his smile was forced, waxen, but his dimples flashed as though he were boarding the bus for school.

He paused and when his blue eyes sparked, he whispered, "*Allahu Akbar,* Allah is great. Death to the Infidels…" Then punched his cell phone, sparking the detonator. The area exploded in a blast of heat and flame.

CHAPTER 8

Roma, City of Infernal Love

Alitalia Flight #284 was on final approach. As it descended through the cloud cover, the female passenger in seat 4C slept soundly, her head snuggled in a pillow, facing the first-class cabin window. Daybreak's first light bathed her face in a serenity of expression, the subtle play of light and shadow, *chiaroscuro*, as in one of Raphael's Madonnas. She dreamed of earlier times. Visions flooded her mind in waves: images of private school and life in Italy, of Nico—not only her first lover but the only man she'd truly loved, the man by which all others would be compared and found wanting—images of her father, *Tateh*, his back stooped with age and huddled over a table strewn with old books and manuscripts. She pictured *Muta*, her mother's warm Italian features—her beauty.

Her mother's dulcet voice floated through her dreams, singing an old Yiddish lullaby, *"Shlof, Mayan Tokhter"*:

"Sleep my good daughter
Sleep in your cradle
I will sit by your side and sing you a song
I will rock you in your cradle and sing you to sleep.
Lulinke, mayan kind . . . Hushaby baby . . ."

Nico's face appeared again, older now but even more handsome than in youth. Would she have the nerve to see him once more, to leave him once again?

Suddenly, violent flashbacks bombarded her peaceful dream world: muzzle blasts flashing in deep, dark, narrow alleyways; the din of explosions; screams in the night, the screams of children, of mothers and daughters, of fathers and sons—visions of war.

She was a member of Mossad, *Ha Mossad le Modiyn ve le Tafkidim Mayuhadim*, the Institute for Intelligence and Special Operations.

She'd bounced between the States and Tel Aviv throughout her youth, attending private schools in New York and joining the Gadna, youth brigades, in Israel.

Her father was the world-renowned professor of theology, Dr. Max Schulman, of the Hebrew University in Jerusalem. He'd held positions at Rome University,

Princeton University, and now, held a visiting professorship at the University of Chicago's Divinity School.

But more importantly, he served as an advisor to the Israeli government, and a *Sayan*, a volunteer Jewish helper outside the boundaries of Israel.

Her mother, Muta Ennoia, was an Italian-born Jew, but she practiced her father's religion— Catholicism—although her mother's Jewish tradition was scolded and combed and prayed into her very pores. She was a budding Italian rose, an aspiring opera diva, who gave up her career for Max Schulman and their daughter, Josephine. Then when Josephine was only fourteen years old, her mother gave up her life in a terrorist bombing in Rome. Her father never remarried, never gave up his heart to another woman. Instead, he buried himself in his work and shortly after Josephine's sixteenth birthday, he took a position at Princeton, N.J.

Trying to fit in with the other teenage girls at school, she shortened her name to Josie. Even though Josie took to American pop culture, she never completely fit in. "You're too stubborn, Josie," her father would rebuke her. "Why are you such a loner?" She'd shrug her shoulders and march off, alone again, preferring solitude to the company of others. She was too old to adjust to the loss of her mother; like most adolescents who incurred the loss of a parent, she blamed herself. She vowed to right the wrong.

When she finished high school, Josie left the nest and flew to Brooklyn, her father's birthplace. From a small apartment there, she commuted to NYU, where she completed her undergraduate and masters degrees. Upon graduation she returned to Israel, and was soon recruited by one of Tateh's colleagues at the Hebrew University. She trained at Mossad's academy, the *Midrasha*, located just north of Tel Aviv, known simply as Building 28. Her goal set firmly on avenging her mother's death.

She began her career as a courier, then junior intelligence officer, and finally a *Kasta*—foreign case officer—with postings in various third world countries. Lastly she served in Belgium where she drowned in waffles and was busied by keeping tabs on NATO.

She'd been burnt and soiled by the politics of compromise—the eighth deadly sin. She was a lightning bolt that needed to be constantly grounded. A manic-charge. Ground her quickly or she would eventually dissipate, instantly burning out in the atmosphere. But not before setting flame to the world around her. As a result of this flame-out, her career had been grounded, but only temporarily. Her rabbi in the Agency, her guardian, had saved her. She was transferred to *Metsada*, a compartment within Mossad that dealt strictly in Covert Ops. Josie was made a combatant in the *Kidon,* the Bayonet, which only dealt in wet operations: murder and kidnappings. Here, her voltage could be amplified and tuned to its maximum effectiveness.

Josie began to awaken, slowly taking in the world around her, but still slightly groggy from the 2-mg. tablet of Xanax she'd popped to overcome her chronic claustrophobia, her mild panic attacks.

A lithe but buxom flight attendant sashayed down the aisle. Stooping, she hung her derriere directly in the face of the Little Man, a passenger seated across the aisle from Josie. Still not moving her fanny from his face, she just adjusted it in a teasing wiggle. Josie took in the Little Man's ogling session through a purple haze. The flight attendant gently shook Josie's forearm. She bolted with a start, instinctively grabbed for the flight attendant's arm, only checking herself at the last moment.

With a raise of the eyebrow, the attendant explained, "*Scussi, Signorina*, we are about to land. Please bring your seatback upright."

Josie was relieved and pleased she could control her reflex response when needed. A slight smile came to her as she pictured herself grabbing the haughty attendant's wrist and making her knee-walk down the aisle, begging each passenger's forgiveness as she went. These prima donnas were such rude taskmasters, Josie thought. Give them a designer uniform and a little set of wings and look out.

She shook the fantasy off, returning to the moment, and gave a curt but polite, "Thank you."

The Little Man across the aisle, face now flushed by the taunting young attendant's body language and the momentary flash of tension in the cabin's air—a catfight—was apparently overwhelmed. He popped what was likely a blood pressure pill and loosened his collar.

Josie pulled out her compact to freshen her makeup and studied her reflection. Her star-fire, topaz eyes still had their brightness. Her face retained its smooth texture, the glow of youth and a healthy, mocha-hued tan; her mahogany hair glistened like Muta's. *Not so hard on the eyes, a looker, Tateh* would say, she thought and winked. *You bet your sweet* toches, *babe.*

But when she looked deeper into the reflection, the truth glared back. She was exhausted, played out, *osygeshpilt,* and sick of the game. Sick of the lies, the endless stream of airports and bland, expressionless, new faces. Sick of the hotel rooms and hotel lobby bars. She'd slept under many different flags and under many assumed names. Under many different men. Her haunts ranged from the seediest of backwater dives to five-star luxury palaces of opulence. In the end they were all the same. They were not home. She had no *home*. And most of all, she was sick of being alone; she was sick of the whole damned thing.

The flight attendant returned and instructed her to put away her laptop. Josie puffed her cheeks and blew a muffled *"bitch"* from between pursed lips. The Little Man, the voyeur, looked on. Josie imagined that his manhood was throbbing almost as fast as his heart.

The bark of rubber against the tarmac. The thunderous whine of jet engines. The shudder and push of G-forces against her body. These collectively seemed to steel her thoughts. They reminded her of the adrenaline rush that her career had always provided. The fix.

This was a simple assignment. In and out fast. A late evening dinner with Monsignor Scarlotti, *Zio* Lotti, her mother's brother from the Catholic side of the family, pick up the book and on to Chicago for a long-awaited reunion with Tateh. The plane coasted to a stop at the gate.

The Little Man from across the aisle, feeling suddenly very Italian and overcome with sexual fantasy, rubbed up against the flight attendant and pinched her ass as he deplaned. She wheeled round and slapped him hard on the cheek. The Carabinieri were called; he would likely spend the night soothing his pride and protecting his manhood in the Leonardo da Vinci Airport lock up. So much for *La Dolce Vita*.

Later, Josie queued in the shortest line at passport control, plunked down her Mossad-issued Canadian passport, made of authentic paper stock, complete with bonafide cover story and verifiable references, and hopped a cab to the Excelsior Hotel just up the street from the American Embassy. She took a long, leisurely bath. She had the rest of the day to kill. So, she did what any self-respecting women of international intrigue would do; she went shopping in Roma. If the time came or the occasion presented itself, she wanted to look good for Nico.

CHAPTER 9

Roma

THE LITTLE MAN got the one obligatory phone call. It was to RSO Bill Cotter, Regional Security Officer at the American Embassy.

"Cotter—"

"The bird has landed," said the doughy-faced Little Man with a slight lisp.

"Don't say anymore, this is an open line, you fool," Cotter whispered.

"Oh, I will say more. Get me the hell out of here!"

Click.

A grinning, toothless, giant of man sat leering at the Little Man from across the cell. His rancid breath and body odor were in Olympic competition. As the guard pulled the phone back through the pass door of the cell, the lumbering giant rose and moved toward the Little Man. The effeminate Little Man stared intently at the approaching beast. Pearly beads of perspiration dotted his brow but he kept glaring at the beast. The towering beast's tongue protruded between curled lips, salivating like a starving wolf eying a tethered goat. He moved ever closer. The Little Man's hand slid into his pocket and took out an electronic device no larger than a cell phone.

Then the giant began clawing frantically at his ears, as though something was ringing louder and louder, droning in the brute's ears, pulsing in sync with his pounding heartbeat. He screamed in agony.

He froze, clutched his chest and toppled in a heap to the floor.

The Little Man, thoroughly devoid of emotion, strode directly to the collapsed giant and stood over him, studying him for a moment. He drew back his tiny foot, kicked him sharply in the temple. He sat on the lifeless hulk and sighed. "*Oh, tale melodrama!*"

The guard returned. Unseen by the guard, the Little Man thumbed a switch, and pocketed the small device.

"*Scussi, Signoré Dottore. La Madre Benedetta!*" *What happened here?*

"Poor diet, I would guess," the Little Man said. "Am I free to go?"

"*Si, Dottore. Si, mi perdoni . . . Il mio Dio, mi perdoni.*"

CHAPTER 10

Vatican City: Unspeakable Words

IT WAS LATE evening as Monsignor Scarlotti's footsteps echoed off the cold marble floor of the Apostolic Place. He hurried down long, empty corridors. Most of the other priests, cardinals, and secretaries were attending a late mass in the Sistine Chapel with His Holiness, the Pope. The colorful frescos and marble sculptures stood mute, crippled by paint and plaster and the thick dust of time.

As he walked he thought. His old colleague, Professor Schulman, an eccentric, had sent a telegram instead of an E-mail in which he had concealed an encrypted message, asking him to obtain an item hidden in the message.

***

ALL GOING WELL HERE. PLEASE SEND   ITEM DISCUSSED PREVIOUSLY.

STOP. IT'S ENOUGH TO MADDEN ANYONE TRYING TO FIND IT. STOP. AVAILABLE AT ONE BOOKSTORE LOCATED AT **14-23-24** VILLA FLORA. STOP. MERRY XMAS

***

This day Scarlotti, First Assistant Secretary to the Curatore General of the *Bibliotica Apostolica Vaticana*, the Vatican Library, would break his vows of obedience. But lives were at stake. Perhaps even his own.

Monsignor Scarlotti crossed the Borgia Courtyard, crested the hill from the Gate of Santa Anna, through the Via della Fondamenta, and entered a building off limits to the public. He was now headed downward, down an endless series of winding stairwells, deeper and deeper into the very bowels of the library—*Archivio Segreto Vaticano* . . . The Secret Archives of the Vatican.

The musty, damp air filled his nostrils and conjured images of things ancient and arcane: yellowed, vellum manuscripts. Forbidden things. Illicit and denied things.

Over five million bound volumes and eighty thousand manuscripts were sequestered within these walls. Since 1447 learned men, scholars, noblemen, clergymen and magicians—students of the alchemical arts—studied and translated these ancient tomes and treatises from the Greek, the French, the Latin, and even the ancient papyri of Sumer, Babylon, and Egypt.

Monsignor Scarlotti pulled a key from the pocket of his black cassock, inserted it into a tarnished bronze lock and twisted. He put his shoulder to the heavy brass door, forcing it to swing slowly open.

He entered the room. The premonition of some horrific curse that lay in wait leached into the marrow of his bones, forming icy shards where warm blood once flowed. His hand reached out gingerly, fumbled in the darkness, found the light switch.

A large brass plaque stretched across the topmost arch of the ceiling before him. Like a caveat of doom, its bold letters read:

INDEX REGISTRUM LIBRORUM PROHIBITORUM

He was in the Library Registry of the Prohibited. He felt a slow trickle of perspiration crawl down his spine. His mouth was chalky, powder-dry. He willed his legs to move. They reluctantly obeyed, shuffling one foot before the other as he inched forward.

A curtain hung just ahead in the weak light. Scarlotti reached out, yanked back the curtain. There before him stood a glass case, and emblazoned on a wafer-thin oval plate, he saw it. Exhibit *102-24*.

The Seal of Giovanni Caligari—Sigillo II.

Around the edge was a Latin inscription: *Arcanum Arcanorum-Artes Perditae.* Silently, he mouthed the translation: Secret of Secrets-Lost Arts-Forbidden.

In the center were two entwined serpents, crowned by the seals of the Pope: the scepter, the miter and the crossed Keys of Peter—the Keys of Blood.

This was one of the "private cases" of the previous Curatore General of the library. To enter and break the seal was almost a mortal sin and would surely end his career. But he realized that a secret battle was being waged. You either took a stand or would be, as Christ said, vomited from Our Savior's mouth for your indifference. He'd also known and trusted Professor Max Schulman for years. Friendship had its own solemn oaths.

He broke the seal. A gust of frigid air slapped his cheeks and sent distant, icy fingers running up and down his spine. He lifted the glass lid and there, within the case, lay a register and a single book covered in vermilion-rose velvet.

The cover was inscribed in French:

Le Cahier de la Rose Noire
Abbé Boullan

CHAPTER 11

"There is always an unknown factor. That is the ombra."
Benito Mussolini after sketching a figure throwing a cone of shadow.

ROME:

COLONEL NICK ROSSI loved surveillance work because he was good at it,
damn good. Because of Rossi's ability to blend into his surroundings, Romano
his mentor at OSI the Air Force's Office of Special Investigations had nicknamed
him the Shadow. Since they were both third generation Italian Americans who
were fluent in the language of their grandfathers, Romano used the Italian
translation—*ombra.*

When tasked to come up with an acronym for a new counterterrorism unit,
Rossi choose SHADO: Special Hostage Action Directorate Ops.

The collar of his leather jacket turned up against the damp night air, Rossi
made his way down Via Monterone. It was late. Pedestrian and street traffic
were light. The shops and restaurants closed. He held back a safe distance
behind his target, knowing that his squad had the man bottled in. One agent
ahead, another moving in tandem across the street, and a team in place in the
fifth-story office of the building up ahead near the target's destination: The
Pantheon. Two alternate teams were parked in unmarked cars at strategic
locations.

Since 9/11 and Italy's involvement in the Iraq war, the Italian government had
tightened up domestic security. Although the Carabinieri antiterrorism unit
technically held most of the responsibility for what happened within Italy's
borders, a new counterintelligence unit was needed. As with the U.S. and
European nations, al-Qaeda had forced old jealousies and infighting to be put
aside, and a new rulebook set in play that sanctioned more aggressive tactics and
less concern for "civil liberties." This led to a marriage of convenience between
OSI and the SISDe: The *Servizio per le Informazioni e la Securezza
Democratica*, Italy's Intelligence and Democratic Security Service. Secret joint
Presidential findings were made and the *OMBRA UNIT* was born. American
agents under the cover of the SISDe worked hand in hand with their Italian
counterparts on foreign soil.

The fact that Rossi's grandfather had been a high-ranking general in the Italian Air Force Intelligence community, combined with Rossi's service record, propelled him into a posting in Rome as head of the Unit.

Rossi remembered the day the call came through. During a routine traffic stop, a motorcycle carabinieri had encountered two Arab students. The officer's report stated that something about the students' demeanor had caused those greasy fingers to start clawing at his stomach. Call it sixth sense or whatever you wish, but Rossi had come to trust that intuitive warning and more than once it had saved his life.

The driver was too glib, overly cooperative, while the thin young man in the passenger seat quaked with fear as his eyes kept darting to the glove compartment. When the passenger reached for the glove box, the officer instinctively pulled his Beretta. The driver's-side door pistoned out, but the officer was properly positioned far enough to the rear to avoid the blow. A shot rang out, the rear side window exploded, the round narrowly missing the carabinieri. Without hesitation, the officer pumped two rounds into the passenger who held the revolver. The first slug tore into the man's throat, the second into his temple. His face and shirt sprayed with blood, the driver sat frozen, eyes glazed with fear. Pleading to Allah for forgiveness, begging for his life.

When they impounded the students' rental car and did a custodial search, they found a cache of IDs, a large sum of money, and a laptop in the trunk. Two of the false passport identities were on the terrorist watch list as suspected al-Qaeda members. Rossi remembered thinking only amateurs would be stupid enough to carry more than one ID at a time. He remembered thinking that sometimes amateurs, because of their unpredictable nature, their impulsiveness, were even more dangerous than pros. The carabinieri had been lucky.

The boys in SISDe's tech unit found a wealth of information on the hard drive. Files listed contacts, cell members, and locations. Together with the antiterrorism squad, they'd made five unpublicized raids. But Rossi couldn't help but feel that some part of the puzzle box was missing. The results of the interrogations did nothing to dispel that nagging suspicion. The head of the snake had somehow managed to slither away. He was sure of it.

Late one night, his stomach sour from too much coffee, his neck cramped and eyes burning from staring at the computer's LCD monitor, he clicked open a file, and the answer stared back from the screen.

It was an Egyptian hieroglyph. It was … the needle in the haystack, his every instinct shouted. Rossi was born in Italy, but since his parents were posted to the American Embassy in Rome at the time, he held dual nationality. He'd flip-flopped back and forth between Rome and the States, attending most of grade and secondary school in Italy as the son of a diplomat. Later, he returned to the States and graduated from the Air Force Academy with honors, following in his grandfather's footsteps, the Italian Air Force general. He was immediately recruited by OSI. But in his heart, he still felt a close kinship with everything Italian. Especially with his uncle Giovanni who'd assumed the role of father figure when his dad passed.

Focus … he admonished himself.

The cipher used throughout the files had been child's play for the crypto squad. A simple substitution cipher. But what about file names? His eyes ticked to the file name: OLUTSOP/SUNELP/ANUL. Jpg. He fed the name into the decoding program. Nothing spit out that made sense.

He checked his wristwatch: almost midnight. A smile came to his lips as he thought of his wife, Isabella. Thought how she'd hidden the watch in his sock drawer, knowing that he would find it the morning of their anniversary as he hurriedly dressed for work. The smiled faded quickly. Wrapped up in his work as usual, he'd totally forgotten the date, had to duck out at lunch and buy her a cheap card and some roses. Only Isabella never saw them. Never saw the taxi that rainy afternoon as it careened around the corner and took her life and the unborn child she was carrying. He sighed and reached for the phone.

In a sleep-clouded voice, *Professore* Giovanni Battista Alberti answered on the fourth ring.

"*Pronto*"

"*Buon giorno*," Rossi said.

"*Chi*—?"

"Your favorite nephew."

"*Nico?*"

His uncle always called him by his childhood nickname.

"*Zio*, I need a favor."

"Now, at this late hour … oh, I suppose it's official, then?"

"I wouldn't impose if it weren't."

"Yes, you would. But go ahead. Once I'm up, I can never get back to sleep."

"I'm sending you an E-mail on the secure encrypted server."

A deep sigh. "Now, where did I put that password?" The sound of movement, bed springs creaking, feet shuffling across the floor, drifted through the receiver.

Rossi could picture his uncle fumbling for his glasses, shrugging into a worn robe, and plodding down the hall to his study, his cordless phone in hand.

"Let me think ..." Rossi heard his uncle say as he began humming the opening to *The Barber of Seville*.

His uncle, despite his age, was sharp as a stiletto. He preferred that everyone address him as simply Giovanni. He was a professor of Egyptian Studies who now worked at the Vatican's Egyptian Museo. Tucked away on the dusty shelves of his memory were countless volumes of information. When Rossi was a boy, Uncle Giovanni had tutored him and had taught him a memory association trick. He matched categories of data with music, a lyrical Rolodex that floated through his brain.

"*L'OH mio! Come interessando*," Giovanni said. "But for some reason the symbols in the cartouche have been depicted backward."

"Thought you'd like it," Rossi answered.

"Old Kingdom ... let's see, the loaf represents the sound 'T' ... the vase is pronounced *bas*. Put them together and we have *bas* plus *T* plus *T* or BASTET."

"Basset?"

"No not the hound, but rather a long A sound ...Ba then Aset, which means literally the soul of Aset or Isis in its native Egyptian form. Those *maledetti* Greeks changed the spelling and pronunciations all around."

"I still don't—"

"An alternate pronunciation would be Pahst, which is where we derive the English slang term 'puss' or 'pussy' from. And the sacred amulet that she clutched in her paw was the *Uchat*, the unblinking eye of Horus. Now that's where we get ..."

"Are you trying to tell me the hieroglyph means *gatto*?"

"Yes, cat, but more precisely ... The Cat Goddess *Bast*."

Rossi sighed deeply. "I need more, Zio. I'm trying to come up with a name and possibly a contact place or time. Tell me about the Goddess."

"She is usually depicted as an ebony cat, sitting serenely, holding a sacred rattle in one paw or the *Uchat*, more commonly known as the eye of Horus amulet. She was worshiped from the Old and through Middle Kingdom in Lower Egypt, originally with the head of a lioness that morphed much later into a desert cat. Therefore, some mistakenly think of her as the pacified version of Sekhmet, the lioness, the destroyer ... who was an Upper Egyptian Goddess. Hence the saying, 'She of the North, and She of the South.' But trust me, this Goddess is no playful kitty. An avenger would be more like it, who was seen as the fierce flame of the sun who burned the deceased should they fail one of the many tests in the underworld, although her worshipers were, according to the Greek historian Herodotus, quite fun loving. Thousands would cruise the Nile, drinking and singing, but when they came near a riverside town, they would move closer to the bank, where the women would abruptly lift their skirts and shout dirty jokes and insults at the town's females as they passed—"

Rossi broke in. "Did you say ebony ... a black cat?"

"Yes ... but—"

"Hold on," Rossi said, and began rifling through a stack of papers found in the drawer of a desk in one of the raids. Stuck to a laundry receipt was a napkin imprinted with the words:

Le Café du Chat Noir.

Rossi translated the French aloud, "The Black Cat Café."

"What's that?"

"I think I found my needle in the haystack as the Americans say."

"Needle ... why how did you know that?"

Rossi's attention drifted back to the phone. "Know what?"

"That a needle, an obelisk, with that particular hieroglyph displayed prominently, is right here in Roma, in the Piazza della Rotonda."

"In front of the Pantheon? You're sure?"

"You call me, wake me from a sound sleep and then, ask me if I am sure?" Giovanni said gruffly. "I took my assistants on a field trip there just last week."

Slats on the puzzle box slid back and forth in Rossi's mind. "One more question." His eyes shot to the file name again. OLUTSOP.SUNELP.ANUL. Jpg. He highlighted the name, right clicked, and pasted it into an E-mail.

"Here's another message. Can you make any sense of this?"

From the other end of the line came his uncle's voice, humming Mozart's *Magic Flute*. The seconds ticked by slowly.

"Yes, it's written in mirror hand, in reverse just like the cartouche. How's your Latin?" Giovanni said finally.

"Rusty."

"Open your reply E-mail, then."

He did. The words leered back.

POSTULO PLENUS LUNA   NEEDLE FULL MOON.

"If you have an almanac, I believe you now have a location and a time, nephew. Now if you don't mind. I'm going to make some warm milk and rest these tired old eyes."

Click.

Now as Rossi walked along the narrow, disserted street, clinging to the shadows, his heart hammered with apprehension. The bigger question still remained. Who was the target, code-named *Bast*, meeting that night at the foot of the Egyptian obelisk? And why?

CHAPTER 12

The Code

AT FIRST Scarlotti had puzzled over the coded text of the telegram. Then his eyes focused on the address. The sequence of numbers was the key. By picking the 14th, the 23rd, and 24th word he came up with—

MADDEN

ONE BOOKSTORE …

—which still made no sense. Then his gaze drifted to the signature: a merry XMAS; the last word was an obvious anagram of his old friend's name MAX S. This was the second key, signaling that the three other words were also anagrams. It had been so simple, so clear that the words leaped off the page.

Damned

Rose Notebook!

Scarlotti knew something of its history.

As he stood staring, his mind traveled back in time to the seminary. He was now seated in a lecture hall, listening to Cardinal Belini's talk. "Forbidden books, forbidden knowledge is today's topic, gentlemen. And the ultimate price men pay for dabbling in, for eating from, the Tree of Knowledge. The price is madness, death, and damnation. The Black Rose Notebook, the book of *mots indescriptibles*, unspeakable words, was written by a defrocked priest, the inheritor of the diabolical Church of Carmel, associated with the renegade, sacrilegious church of St. Sulpice in Paris. A church that was a breeding ground for the black arts.

"*Le Cahier de la Rose Noire* or The Black Rose Notebook by the Abbé Joseph Boullan is one of the most horrible examples of the insanity that seizes the unwary mind. It was discovered by the French novelist, J.K. Huysmans, author of *Là-Bas,* Down There. In its time, *Là-Bas* was a bestseller that told of a devil cult in Paris headed by the evil Dr. Johannes. Yes, Boullan, both in fiction and reality, was a Black Magician—a practitioner of the Path of the Left Hand, a Satanist, and alleged pedophile. He endorsed bestiality. Remaining true to his twisted nature, he married a young nun, Sister Adéle Chevalier, of the Convent of La Salette. Legend had it that he sacrificed the child of this unholy union during the celebration of the ultimate of blasphemes—The Black Mass.

"Now we must remember the times. This was the age of the continued rebirth of occultism in Europe, an age where The Holy Office—The Inquisition still held power. It was an age of secret societies and their infamous necromancers:

Péladan, Papus, and the Paris Salon Set: Oscar Wilde, W.B. Yeats and Debussy. Paris was a forum and melting pot for an exchange in the so-called heretic belief systems of alchemy and mysticism. Blasphemous beliefs which held sex as a sacrament, worshiped the 'divine feminine,' the Black Madonna, rather than the Blessed Virgin and our Lord Jesus Christ."

Whispering voices rippled across the hall.

"This infernal legacy was passed down through the ages by the mystery cults. Absorbed from the Sufi mystics by the Knights Templar during the Crusades and passed on to the secret brotherhoods when the Templars fled to Scotland. We can lay equal blame at the feet of the British and the French of course. Doctor John Dee, the Welsh necromancer, and Éliphas Lévi, also of St. Sulpice, with his book *The Dogma and Ritual of High Magic* wherein he was first to draw the image of his lord—a goat-headed devil."

Noticing that a frown now creased Scarlotti's face, Belini asked, "Something not clear, Scarlotti?"

Scarlotti had been holding back, but now he took his opportunity to pounce.

"Well, sir, it's just that—"

"Just what?"

"Isn't it true that we Italians also have a long history of involvement? The Medici court of Florence spent a fortune searching for, obtaining, and having scholars like Pico translate the so-called hermetic magical texts, works that influenced even our own Leonardo da Vinci."

Now Belini scowled. "Where are you going with this? Pico, the charlatan, was censured by Pope Innocent VIII!"

Scarlotti smiled thinly. *He's taking the bait*, he thought. "Isn't it true that while on the one hand the church condemned these writings, placed them in the Papal Index, burnt their authors and many women who were guilty of nothing more than asserting their right to speak, act as midwives, and think freely… that various Popes such as Alexander VI and Sylvester II collected and studied these same books and held them under lock and key in the Vatican Archives? Alexander's private apartment was decorated with murals of Egyptian symbols, including the more ancient form of the Black Madonna—the Goddess Isis— while Pope Sylvester II consulted a talking head in the image of the Goddess Meridiana, thought to possibly be some form of early mechanical, calculating machine like those found in Leonardo da Vinci's notes."

Belini's cheeks flamed. "Careful where you tread, young man."

Another student added, "Wasn't Pope Alexander VI accused of having his own son murdered and wasn't Lucrezia Borgia, the infamous poisoner, his daughter?"

SOLOMON'S KEY

Before Belini could answer, Scarlotti cut in, "Yes, Lucrezia's mother was the Pope's mistress. She also bore him two illegitimate sons. Cesare, who was the real-life basis for Machiavelli's *The Prince,* who once ordained as a cardinal, had his brother, Juan, killed out of sheer jealousy."

"Nice family," someone blurted out.

"Oh, it gets even better," Scarlotti went on. "Lucrezia and her father, the Pope, were said to have been engaged in an incestuous relationship."

Scarlotti noticed that Belini was smoldering now, his face knotting with anger.

"Maybe that's why her husband had such bad luck," another said.

"The Goddess Venus ruled under the Borgias," Scarlotti went on, twisting the dagger deeper. "During a so-called orgy on October 30, 1501, known as the *Banquet or Ballet of Chestnuts* choreographed by the Pope, fifty prostitutes, his 'unlawful herd' who were regular guests every weekend and with whom he had dined that night, were forced to crawl naked between narrowly placed candlesticks that held lighted tapers and lined the floor of an apartment in the Apostolic Palace. Their bodies glistening with sweat, the *herd* scuttled in a frenzy to snatch chestnuts off the floor, while Cesare and Donna Lucrezia and the Pope's guests cheered them on. The Pope gave prizes to those servants who could couple the greatest number of times, and those who could 'keep time with the music' the longest without ejaculating, and to those who could 'spend a prostitute, leaving her limp.' Finally, the Pope joined in the orgy that continued late into the next morning: All Saints Day."

"Bet he didn't say mass that day," someone offered.

Mouth set in a grim line, eyes stony, Belini regarded Scarlotti as he might have reacted to a leathery demon squatting placidly while picking at the bones of Christian martyrs for scraps of fleshy tissue.

"Enough!" Belini barked, his fist pounding the lectern. "I'll not have such blasphemy discussed in my class." Then he wheeled on the young seminarian. "Scarlotti, see me afterward and remain silent."

Scarlotti nodded and suppressed the urge to smile.

Belini's fiery gaze tracked across the room, seeking further challengers, and finding none, he squared his shoulders and continued.

"Now, where were we?" Belini went on. "Boullan was accused and marked for death. Accused of revealing secrets to the profane, those outside the Brotherhood. Actual magical and real-life duels were fought. Curses were inflicted by passing a spell-cast parchment that would ensure death to whomever received it.

"But many historians had suspected a hidden agenda. Abbé Boullan was defrocked and imprisoned by the Inquisition. Later, The Holy Office found him not guilty and released him. Some lay scholars saw the despicable trail of conspiracy within the Church itself… " Belini waved his hand dismissively. "Utter nonsense! The Church has reasons not always apparent, not always revealed."

"Maybe he was working undercover to infiltrate the secret society?" another offered.

Belini ignored the question. "Legend also stated that anyone reading *Le Cahier de la Rose Noire,* who was not in a deep state of holy grace, would be driven mad by the twisted letters, glyphs, and formulas that darkened its pages."

Belini looked up from his notes. "Now my pupils, wise before your years, I have arranged a treat for you." A rose-colored book suddenly appeared in his hand. "Here it is! Who will be the first to dare to look upon its pages?" Like an accusing finger, he pointed the notebook around the room, finally stopping at Scarlotti. "Well, young man, care to have a peek?"

Scarlotti shook his head.

"I thought not," Belini said with a smirk.

After class was dismissed, Scarlotti reported to Belini's office. Another young seminarian was introduced. Marsciocco was lean and sharp-eyed. They soon struck up a close friendship. Eventually Marsciocco played his hand and recruited Scarlotti into the secret brotherhood whose name had beforehand been only a hushed rumor within the walls of the Vatican. ***Protocollo Diciassette***, Protocol-17. And it was Cardinal Belini who had cast the net. Like Boullan, Scarlotti was now acting on secret orders. Orders from the Polish cardinal, who'd instructed him to act as an agent provocateur. He'd been instructed to dangle the lure, a mock hatred for the church. And his mentor had been correct. *They bit!*

***

Now as Scarlotti stood before the case, he pondered. What secret had Boullan used to blackmail the Holy See that insured his protection? The very name of the notebook itself was a clue: **Rose** was an anagram for **Eros**—Greek carnal lust— as opposed to Agapé, the Christian unselfish act of love. Was the whole tale surrounding the notebook an anagram for something else?

Monsignor Scarlotti pursed his lips, made the sign of the cross, and said a silent prayer. *Cose diaboliche. La Madre Benedetta lo protegge.*

CHAPTER 13

THE TELEPHONE ON Colonnello Pico's desk chimed. Pico was the head of the Vigilanza, the Vatican's police force and intelligence branch and was working late, waiting for a call.

"*Prontó?*"

"Take immediate precautions with the package!"

The phone went dead but Pico recognized the voice of the American, RSO Cotter, and understood the message. Reaching for the Beretta 9 mm. on his desktop, he tucked it into his waistband and ran for the door. Pico's code name in the Brotherhood was Janus, fitting since serving two masters required the powers of a two-faced god.

***

Monsignor Scarlotti also knew he was living on borrowed time and every minute, every second, counted. But he needed spiritual strength so he knelt in prayer. He envisioned the immaculate heart of Jesus, concentrating on its radiant light, bathing in its sanctified glory. Then from behind him came the clamor of racing footfalls, pounding on the ironwork of the stairwell.

Instinctively, he leapt to his feet, killed the lights, and took refuge in the cloak of shadows that filled the corners of the room. A figure pounced into the room, panting and short of breath. It raced to the "Private Case" and withdrew the notebook and registry. Turning now, a spray of light fell across the face of the figure—Colonnello Pico's face. Pico held a flashlight under his armpit and began to bundle the books in butcher-paper wrapping. Then he produced a candle, lit it, and poured red sealing wax over the twined knot of the package. Next, he took a gold seal and pressed it sharply into the wax—the seal of the Holy Church, *The Keys of Blood.*

Monsignor Scarlotti knew what had to be done. He silently reached high into the towering bookcase at his side. Standing on tiptoe, fighting to hold his shallow breath, fumbling, he finally found purchase. He grasped a heavy bronze bookend perched on the shelf. He struck panther-quick and brought the blunt object down in an arc, crashing into the skull of Colonnello Pico.

"Jesus, forgive me," Scarlotti whispered, sighing.

He bent over the limp body of Colonnello Pico, tore the books from the Colonnello's gnarled death grip.

As he ran he thought—*let God claim his own and be my judge.*

CHAPTER 14

AS ROSSI PURSUED his quarry, he recalled how he'd met the mysterious woman who'd changed his life forever. The *Ombra* Unit had staked out the *Le Café du Chat Noir* for a week. It was one of those New Age, touchy-feely type Internet cafés that were becoming the vogue. Only this one served *Qahwah* along with the espresso. That made things difficult. Middle-Eastern students dotted the tables, sipping their *shy,* Arabic tea, and rattling on in their native tongue, suspiciously eyeing any stranger who entered, their gaze sliding away whenever they happened to look back. Rossi's men stuck out like streetwalkers in war paint and stiletto heels trying to infiltrate a mosque during Ramadan. Rossi tried a different approach. After taking hundreds of surveillance shots of the patrons from across the street and running them through sophisticated facial-recognition programs that crosschecked against databases of known terrorists, SISDe was still stymied. Even highly sophisticated keystroke invasion software only revealed that the patron's laptops were typing out school papers, surfing the Internet for news and the usual … porn.

Next Rossi's analysts produced a list of the café's employees from the revenue service's computer files and again crosschecked against intel files and did criminal record checks. The owner was a French expatriate, with a minor drug record but no known political affiliation. He'd owned the place for six years, lived upstairs. The other employees were mostly Italian-born students who attended Rome University and worked at the café part time. Again nothing of interest.

Rossi decided to give it one last try. It was midmorning as he stood at the door thinking, *maybe I've gotta go back to the basics?* He entered. The café was empty. An attractive young girl came to the counter, wiping her hands on her apron.

"*Posso aiutarlo?*" she said, smiling.

"Cappuccino and a cornetto, *per favore,*" Rossi answered, returning her smile.

When she turned and walked toward the coffee maker, Rossi couldn't help noticing the way her short skirt hugged the contours of her hips. He busied himself by fumbling for his wallet.

"Here we are," she said, sliding the tray toward him.

Rossi flinched slightly, surprised by her sudden switch to English. Apparently she'd picked up on the phony American DL he'd purposely flashed when he opened his wallet.

Eyes, pale blue and feline, held him with the intensity of her gaze. He swallowed visibly and glanced around. "I'm visiting my uncle at the university and thought I'd catch a little pick-me-up first."

She nodded, still staring quizzically. "Trying to pick me up, you said?"

He laughed. "No, I need a jolt of caffeine."

"Long night?"

He smiled sheepishly, as though she could read his thoughts, but it was probably his bloodshot eyes. "As a matter of fact, yes. Out a little late with the guys."

"What's he teach?"

"Who?"

"Your uncle at the university." She studied him curiously as she absently undid her hair, letting in fall in silken folds onto her shoulders. Her eyes slowly rose to his.

"Linguistics, very intelligent man," Rossi managed.

She leaned across the counter, looked around furtively as if she were about to share a secret, and motioned him closer with her finger. "I think you're a liar," she whispered.

Rossi stared blankly.

"I think you had a long night, because you were up late reading that American crime thriller of yours."

Her gaze tracked to the paperback novel in his hand.

"You've got me. But it's actually a conspiracy thriller."

She laughed. "You believe in them?"

"Conspiracies?"

"In secret cabals plotting to take over the world?"

He studied the floor, then looked up, his green eyes softening. "No, just in young, beautiful coeds who have the power to turn a middle-aged man's head with their eyes."

"You're only as young as you feel. What you have to ask yourself is ... how young do I feel?"

Her eyes spoke with sincerity, loneliness.

Rossi invited her to join him for coffee. She accepted. He learned that her name was Gina. He told her his was Tony. Over coffee and cigarettes she told him of her dreams to go to America one day to write for the films. She told him about her parents in Naples, her father's law practice, about the foolish young men in her life who were only concerned with their looks, their studies, or their next allowance check from their parents.

Being good at your work had its advantages. And right now Rossi was taking advantage of his ability to make women feel special. A woman had once told him that he had the singular talent of making a woman feel as if he hung on her every word, as if she alone was the most important woman, maybe the only woman in the world. He sat listening intently, using body language to empathize and seduce, leaning in at the proper moment or beaming his Richard Gere boyish smile and shrugging his shoulders in feigned embarrassment at attention. He kept in shape. Kept versed in the latest subjects, including pop culture and its music. Secretly, he hated most new music, loved old jazz tunes, film noir, and American thrillers.

A few customers trickled in, breaking the mood.

Maybe I'm enjoying this a little too much, he thought as Gina rose from the table, and he studied the way her firm calves bunched and rippled as she walked back toward the counter. He made excuses, saying, "Look at the time. I'll be late for my meeting with my uncle."

"Just don't be late tonight, then too," she said, shrugging her shoulders.

"Tonight?"

"I get off at six. Hope that's not past your bedtime?"

"Dinner and a movie?"

"No, first sex and then dinner." She whirled and slinked away into the back room, leaving him standing with his mouth gaping slightly. From the corner of his eye, he caught a young Arabic-looking man sizing him up with scorn-filled eyes.

Outside on the sidewalk, he looked around. The day seemed fresher, more alive. And he was filled with a sense of satisfaction. The bait was taken.

CHAPTER 15

THE BELLS OF the Church of Trinitá dei Monti chimed.

The vibrations rang down across the canopy of flowered gardens at its feet, down the precipitous Spanish Steps, weaving through ascending columns of pious nuns in flowing, sterile-white habits that appeared luminous in the moonlight, weaving through dreamy-eyed lovers climbing slowly, arm in arm, rapt in each other's very existence, and finally across the Piazza of Spain to Josie Schulman.

Josie was seated at a courtyard table in the Café Dellini', savoring an *espresso ristretto* and the pure ambiance of the moment. The weather was unusually warm for a late October night. She dressed for her role, encased in glove-soft, red leather Versace pants and matching jacket that looked as if they had been spray-painted on. Underneath she wore a black leather bustier that hugged the soft curves of her svelte body. She wore little makeup, just a hint of lip-gloss and eyeliner, subtly applied, that magnified her understated elegance and natural beauty. With those bee-stung, pouting lips, she was stunning, poised—but as tough as nails. Her persona was simultaneously winsome and ferocious.

A dark-kind-of-handsome Italian man dressed in a custom-tailored suit (done with the flare and subtle eloquence that only Italians could achieve) sat at an adjacent table.

He raised his wineglass in a toasting gesture toward her and smiled long—too long. His smile had a strong undercurrent of lechery. He took a sip of wine, maintaining eye contact, undressing her with his eyes, breathing in her scent with his flared nostrils. A white heat seemed to wash over her as she pretended not to notice him. Animal heat. But he caught her reaction. Josie gave the subconscious signal, the body language of the mating ritual: the careless flick of her hair with one hand, and a barely noticeable shudder of sexual excitement between her shoulder blades which crept slowly up to the nape of her neck. The gentleman smiled knowingly to himself.

Catching glimpses of Josie over the top of his menu, the Italian thought, *she's a rare ambrosia. Such a pity that I'll have to kill her without the chance to savor the taste of her.*

The romantic sounds of a strolling violinist playing "Mona Lisa" danced in the evening air, floating between layers of sounds: the *vroom* of passing Vespa motor scooters; the tinkle of a bicycle's bell as it streamed past. The Italian gentleman sipped his wine and dabbed the corner of his mouth with a linen napkin. He frowned. *Americans and Israelis*, his mind spit out the words in disgust.

***

She stared at the menu, then ordered *proscuitto crudo* and *bresaola*, with a bottle of their finest *Recoaro*. After all, this was a celebration. She hadn't seen her Uncle Lotti for years.

Josie saw the towering image of Monsignor Scarlotti as he approached. In the jaundiced lamplight his form bobbed and wavered, levitating phantomlike over the back of an old man stooped to drink from the cool, refreshing water of the Piazza's fountain. Tall and gaunt, shoulders back, dressed in his black cassock with scarlet piping and buttons, he strode with purpose and station.

She rose to embrace him like a schoolgirl, teary-eyed and giggling.

"Ciao, principessina mia. Come stai?"

"Sono bene, I'm fine. *Ed il mio zio preferito?"*

"Cosi, Cosi." The priest, her favorite uncle sighed. "And your father the *professore?"*

"He's fine. Stubborn as ever, I suspect. It will be so good to see him again. It's been five years now."

"Too long. Much too long, but you have your work and he has his. Are you still with the diplomatic corps?"

"You know I am, *Zio Lotti.*"

"Yes, I suppose I do . . . and I imagine that's what brought you here. But indulge an old man a little longer, my sweet *principessina.* You know, I can't help staring at you. Especially here, now, as we are together in Roma. You have your mother's eyes and her beautiful, infectious laughter."

"Always the troubadour. I haven't heard myself laugh much lately."

"We should always take the time to laugh. I am sure God laughs daily. We are such amusing creations. No?"

Smiling now, her dimples showing and face flushed pink, Josie signaled for the waiter to bring the food. Josie remembered Monsignor Scarlotti as a handsome man, with debonair, silver-gray hair brushed back from his forehead, and skin elastic and smooth, almost without wrinkles.

But now as she peered through the flickering candlelight, he looked like a withered, sin-stained replica, the portrait of *Dorian Gray.* His hands were gray and liver-spotted, his flesh pale and translucent as curdled milk; his cheeks magnified all that his eyes betrayed.

Yes, the eyes told the truth, and the truth was brutal as truth frequently is. *Death* glared back at her. The cold, callous fiend that she'd seen before in the marbled eyes of her enemies just before her bullet struck home. The same merciless beast that stared back from the eyes of comrades, of children who had died in her arms. The thousands of pleading eyes that haunted her nightmares and threatened to burst into the cold light of day and someday drive her mad. These were the eyes that now peered back at her. She shuddered. Her blood ran cold. Cold as Uncle Lotti's fallow eyes.

Scarlotti gently folded his hands on the white tablecloth. They trembled. He took a long, hard sip of the wine and pushed his plate away. Fumbling for a pack of Players, struggling to pull the cigarette out of the box and to his lips, his hands were so unsteady now that he couldn't strike the match. Josie lit his cigarette. He took a deep drag, French-inhaled and continued.

"Josie, why does your father want this book?"

"Did you bring it, Zio Lotti?"

He shook his head in anger. His lips glistening with saliva, he said, "Why does he want this damnable thing?" His fist crashed on the tabletop. "Does he realize the danger to you? The perdition and torment its heresy breathes into the world? The menace brought to all who even possess it—merely touch it? The suffering it has already brought into my life? Does he?"

"He doesn't even want it, Zio. *They do.*"

Scarlotti glared harshly with exactness into her eyes as though he'd just been told the earth really is flat and pigs really can fly. "Don't speak in riddles. Don't ridicule what you don't understand. And don't—" He paused as her last words gripped his mind. He stared upward, eyes glistening. He understood.

Nodding his head, swallowing hard, he bit his lower lip and said, "*They* want it. *It* and *you* are the *bait*."

"Yes, damn it! Now you understand, don't you, *Zio* Lotti?

"All too well, my child. All too well."

CHAPTER 16

AS ROSSI MOVED down the street, gliding through pooling shadows, he continued to remember. They'd had dinner at *Osteria dell' Angelo* on the *Via Giovanni*, a small restaurant near the Vatican. They'd sat at a corner table beneath a photo of Muhammad Ali. The owner, Angelo, was a boxing aficionado. Over wine and meatballs with nutmeg and *sultanas*, Rossi had found himself losing control. This young girl, who laughed with her eyes one moment and then seemed to cry the next, grew silent and brooding and quickly changed the subject, as if somehow feeling guilty for enjoying herself too much. This young girl was getting to him. Maybe they shared a hidden trauma, a disappointment. He wasn't sure what it was that she was hiding, but he knew whatever it was, it was a deep, mortal wound that would probably, like his own, never completely mend no matter how much another person cared. No matter how hard they tried.

They finished their dessert, a glass of sweet white wine and aniseed biscuits, and then walked in the rain. He held her close.

Suddenly she stopped, turned, and kissed him hard.

"Let's go to a hotel," she said, her eyes almost pleading.

They did.

They made warm passionate love the first time. He'd forgotten how tender he could be if he tried. They made drinks from the minibar, vodka on ice, and talked.

"This is just about sex, you know," Gina said matter-of-factly.

"It is?" he said, smiling.

"I'm serious." She stood abruptly and moved to the window, staring out as if a million miles away now. "We weren't meant for anything more, Tony. We have too much baggage."

He rose and came up behind her. Below, the cityscape glowed against the night. Wrapping his arms around her, he said, "We'll just take it slow. One day at a time."

She turned, eyes wet and glistening.

He lifted her into his arms and carried her to the bed.

The sheets felt cool to the skin. The soapy sent of her hair was more exotic than the most expensive perfume.

The second time, though, was different. Gina's eyes suddenly flashed, she rolled on top, took control. Lust-filled eyes, wanton eyes, leered down at him, and she took him deep within her. And for a moment, it seemed as though when her lips met his that she was sucking out his last breath, his soul. She seemed insatiable. When they finished, he was exhausted, drained. He climbed out of bed and made for the bathroom on rubbery legs. At the sink he splashed his face with cold water and stared into the mirror. *She's dangerous,* he thought. *This is dangerous.* He stiffened and shook it off.

She lay stretched across the Egyptian cotton. From the window, a sliver of moonlight spilled across her flesh. When it met her body it became golden, and her creamy, olive-toned skin seemed faintly luminous, as though she pulsed with an inner fire. Her nude body glistened with the sheen of perspiration.

He lit her a cigarette. She took a deep drag and let the smoke drift upward, hanging in the ambient light. *Time to get down to business,* he thought. Slowly and methodically he segued into talk about the café, about the clientele, about the young man with the scorn-filled eyes.

Nothing of relevance about the café's patrons but the boy.

Gina rolled over and put out the cigarette in a bedside ashtray and turned back, propping her head on one elbow. The sloping curve of her breast and the dark pigment of her areola peeked out from beneath her forearm, taunting him as she spoke.

"His name's Saud. We dated a few times. But it's over."

"Meet him at school?"

"No the café. He became a regular soon after he arrived."

"As in not long in your country, you mean?"

"Yes, he moved here from the Kingdom. Rich parents, strict. He wanted to get as far away as possible."

"Saudi oil?"

"What else?"

"Why not the States?"

She shrugged. "Maybe it was too far. Don't think he cares for Americans much."

He backed off, changed the subject, then gradually drifted back.

"I have a confession to make," he said, sighing.

"Here we go. A wife and—"

"No, I'm a reporter. I need your help with a story."

"Just using me."

He kissed her lightly on the forehead. "Never. But can you help me?"

"What kind of story?"

"Murder."

She frowned. "Okay, now you've got my attention. Ask away, newspaper man."

He rose and fished something from his coat pocket. "Have you ever seen anyone around the café with this symbol?"

The Egyptian hieroglyph stared back from his hand.

She took the paper, studied it, and cast her eyes to the ceiling. "Well, come to think of it..."—lowering her head, she met his gaze—"... there was this strange guy ... walked with a limp. Really old geezer. Didn't smell too good, either. Kind of a prune face, if you know what I mean."

Rossi leaned closer, breath trapped in his lungs.

"He have a name?"

"Sure, let me see ... oh, yes... it was Imhotep."

Rossi's face slackened. "Imhotep the mummy. Cute."

She threw back her head and laughed. "I really had you there for a moment, didn't I?"

He shook it off. "Gina, this was found at a murder scene. I'm dead serious," he lied. Then he reached over and took something from his coat, hanging on the back of a chair, and handed her a photocopy of the Black Cat Café napkin. She glanced at it and then quickly looked away.

She studied her nails for a moment then sheepishly met his eyes. "Hand me my purse, please," she said, her voice cracking. Puzzled, Rossi fetched her purse.

She was visibly shaken. Hand trembling, she reached into her bag and pulled out a long, gold chain. In her palm lay a gold amulet: the symbol of *Bast,* the Cat Goddess.

Gingerly, Rossi took the amulet and studied it under the bedside lamp.

"Where did you get this?" he asked.

She puffed out her cheeks, blew a long sigh. "From Saud. He told me to always wear it for ... good luck." Tears welled in her eyes, and she broke down sobbing in his arms.

She told him he could keep the amulet. Then she dressed hurriedly and insisted upon taking a cab home. He said he understood.

After she'd gone, he lay on his back in bed, brooding. His hunch, his long shot, had paid off. He had a suspect, a name and a face to go with it. His eyes cut to the door. *But will I ever see her again? Do I just use people and toss them aside? Hell, I'll call her tomorrow.* But he wouldn't.

His eyes had been drawn back toward the window. A three quarter moon had floated in the night sky.

"Three days, old man, and you'll be full," he'd said, talking to the moon. "Then you'll give up your secrets."

* * *

When he rounded the corner, he looked up. Tonight's full moon hung suspended and drew him back to the present. Back to the chase.

CHAPTER 17

THAT NIGHT IN a tiny flat in the university district of San Lorenzo, Basha lay naked and warm beneath the sheets. Her long, black, silken hair fanned across the pillow. Dreamscapes floated through her mind. She thought of Cairo, her classes at the American University, her home. Basha, the daughter of an Egyptian doctor and a beautiful Polish-American woman, had been born at Cairo's Coptic Hospital. Like many children raised in a home of mixed culture and religion, at times Basha felt almost schizophrenic. On the one hand her father expected her to maintain the traditions of his native land, her Muslim faith. But on the other hand, her mother, Sonia, had demanded that she speak English fluently, embrace Catholicism, and adopt American customs, especially the growing feminist movement.

With her light olive complexion, delicate facial features, and pale blue, catlike eyes, she was stunning, but she possessed the temperament of a panther. Her deep, breathy voice conjured visions of amber-colored whiskey and smoke that clouded men's minds like some wispy, seductive phantom. But cross her, disappoint her, lie to her, and she'd snarl, those eyes would flash raw hatred. The hellcat would emerge and pounce without mercy.

Basha murmured peevishly and stirred, pawing the rumpled sheet with her slender, sun-bronzed foot, all fathom-deep and dreaming. The face of her little brother, Hamal, and her twin sister, Laylah, floated in her mind's eye. Then it happened. Like clouds scudding across the moon, dark visions invaded her sleep. A dark shadow poured across little Hamal's face.

Jack was tall, distinguished, good-looking. Basha's mother had met him at church. He was the kind of man who made a woman feel comfortable, a good listener. But wasn't that part of their job, nodding reassuringly, consoling the anguished heart? Wasn't that what a priest was supposed to do? The woman deep within Basha understood. Her father, like many Arab men, respected her mother, probably even loved her deeply, but he never showed it with outward affection, never with words. And Basha later came to realize that her mother, like many western women caught in the patriarchal society of the Middle East, was simply lonely.

When her mother began coming home late in the evening, always busying herself with church activities, Basha felt the cold fingers of doubt seize her heart. She could have forgiven her mother's infidelity, her betrayal, if only she hadn't involved Hamal.

It was a Saturday afternoon, her mother and Father Jack and Hamal were boarding a downtown tour bus filled with an American church group, after shopping in the marketplace. By happenstance Basha was there when it happened. Basha had taken a break from her studies and was picking up something for a surprise birthday dinner for her father. Seeing her brother, she raised her hand to wave and started to shout, but then she saw her mother walking hand-in-hand with Father Jack, sans collar, dressed in street clothes. Holding hands in public was taboo, but in the hustle and bustle of the crowded plaza few noticed or their eyes slid away as they passed. Basha quickly lowered her hand.

Seized by some uncanny premonition of danger, she pushed her way through the crowd, desperately trying to reach them. A dark, hollow feeling filled her chest as the press of bodies swarmed around her. By the time she reached the bus, they were already onboard. Hamal's face pressed to the rear window, his big brown eyes, his tiny hand waving wildly at her as the bus pulled away, would be forever etched into her memory.

All around her the rabble of the street, the sounds of cars, faded into silence. Heavy. Stained. And tense. Silence shattered by the explosion as the bus burst into an oily ball of flame. The marketplace filled with panic and blood as a second explosion rocked the ground beneath her. She would have run, if she could have run, if there was anywhere worth running to.

But unlike Basha her sister, Laylah, did run. Tired of seeing her father drink himself to death, tired of missing her mother and brother, Laylah just never came home from school one day. Vanished off the face of the earth. Basha heard rumors. Nasty, ugly rumors that told of Laylah's downward spiral into prostitution, but Basha dismissed them as the jealous talk of old women. Besides, she had her own problems.

A year later, after her father's suicide, she did run—straight into the arms of Islamic fundamentalism. The Jihad, the holy war against the infidels. Her lover, Abdul Aziz Alghamdi, introduced her to the world of hate via *Gamma Islamiya*, an Egyptian terrorist cell that was responsible for former President Anwar Sadat's assassination, revitalized by returning freedom fighters, mujahideen, from Afghanistan. The irony was that the freedom fighters had been funded, trained, and equipped by U.S. intelligence agencies, then bankrolled with Saudi oil dollars, only to later bite the hand that fed them by declaring a holy jihad against their masters. Like a bunch of grapes, al-Qaeda was made up of individual cells. When one member of the group was plucked off by intelligence services, the other cells remain unaffected, still receiving nourishment from the vine, al-Qaeda.

After showing promise, Basha was sent to bin Laden's training camp in the Sudan. Al-Qaeda's doctrine of hate fed her rage, blanketed her anguish with the prospect of revenge. Despite that it was actually *Gamma Islamiya* who'd planted the bomb that sent the Christian tourists and her mother to the flames of hell, Basha directed her scorn toward the western world. Toward the Church of Rome that had, in her eyes, seduced her mother, killed her brother, destroyed her sister, and driven her father into despair.

In the terrorist camp, she'd studied hard. There, she'd excelled in the fine arts of terror, blackmail, and murder. After completing numerous minor assignments with ease, she finally overcame al-Qaeda's latent chauvinism toward women. If it was Allah's will to let the hands of a woman do his work, so be it, Osama bin Laden had said. Dr. Ayman al-Zawahari, Osama's right hand man, had taken a special interest in her. The technocrat was a pragmatic man and immediately saw her potential.

Besides, with her mixed blood, she could be a very useful tool. Basha could easily pass for an Italian-American, a Canadian or even a fiery Spaniard. She was provided with false identities under many nationalities and aliases. The intelligence and law enforcement agencies around the world were already profiling males of Arabic decent.

Bin Laden had a strategy that worked well: do the unthinkable. A suicide bomber driving a car disguised with police emblems and loaded with explosives into a Saudi compound in Riyadh, a compound filled with the families of westerners and Muslims alike, was previously unthinkable. Hijacking an airliner filled with American infidels was nothing new, but targeting the Twin Towers, a building filled with people of all races, religions and nationalities, was so brazen and so evil it caught the world by total surprise. So using a young woman to carry out a master plan against the greatest symbol of Christianity, the Vicar of Christ, would also, in what had been the previous paradigm of Islamic terrorism, be an unthinkable act.

Basha woke. Her gaze drifted around the room, then to the window. Her eyes were focused on the full moon, but she was seeing something else. Not a tiny room in Rome, but the bloodied marketplace in Cairo; not the moon, but her brother's gentle face.

The shrill ring of the telephone startled her from her reverie. Rising naked, she padded across the room, her breasts swaying slightly, and palmed the receiver.

"Midnight," a gruff voice said, and hung up.

She cradled the phone. As she began dressing she thought, *if I have to sup with the devil himself, I'll do it for you, Hamal. I'll lay with the Freemasons, the*

SOLOMON'S KEY

Zionist bankers, the Jinn of hell itself. I don't give a damn. Dressed in dark slacks and boots and bra she moved to the bed and pulled a knife from under the mattress. Soft moonlight bathed the blade and her creamy skin in its glow. With a practiced hand, she fitted a stiletto-thin blade into a spring-loaded mechanism on her wrist and locked it in place. Pulling her black sweater over her head and then shrugging into her jacket, she made for the door. As she grasped the doorknob, she hesitated and turned to the window. To the moon, she said aloud, *"Allahu, a'lam,* God knows best, my little brother."

CHAPTER 18

FROM ACROSS THE Piazza, seated in a black Fiat sedan, Josie's backup team watched intently. High above on a rooftop, the sniper peered through the eyepiece of the precision 2.5 10x 40 Zeiss night-vision scope fitted atop the Czech CZ 700 7.62 mm. NATO sniper rifle, complete with lengthy sound suppressor and folding bipod. Loaded with large-caliber, subsonic frangible rounds that disintegrated upon entry, avoiding unnecessary collateral damage, it was silent but lethal. With its detachable stock, relatively short length and minimal weight, it was easily transported. He tucked the butt of the rifle snugly against his cheek and pressed it hard into his shoulder. His finger curled around the trigger. He adjusted the focus of the scope, and the lime-tinted image of the handsome Italian gentleman, watching Josie's every move raptly, appeared within its crosshairs and stadia marks.

He focused on the man's hand, following it as it reached downward to raise his inner pant leg. The man's hand slowly pulled a stiletto from his boot. The sniper blinked as beads of perspiration slowly rolled down the nape of his neck and forehead.

"Uri! Target One has a knife. Tell her," shouted the sniper into his mic.

The strolling musician played faster and faster, raking his bow across the cat gut.

"Is he moving?" whispered the driver into his radio mic.

"No. Just watching."

"Then check the other target. Damn it!"

The sniper panned to another target seated at a table to Josie's rear; and spoke into his lapel microphone.

"Josie, Target One to your right. Knife."

***

As the words streamed into her molded, wireless earpiece, she stole a quick glance at the Italian gentleman to her immediate right, calculated the distance, and continued her conversation. No flinch. No reaction at all. *Never let them see you sweat.*

"But Zio Lotti, what's wrong? What's happened? You can't lie to me. You never could," Josie pleaded.

"No, I never could fool you, *principessina*. Don't worry about me now. I am but God's servant. He will chart the course."

With that, Scarlotti reached into his attaché case and slid a butcher-wrapped package with the Vatican Seal across the table to her. He glanced around warily and removed a scroll, passing it to her beneath the table.

The shrill, dissonant squeal of the violin punctured the air.

***

The eerie, green-hued image of Target Number Two formed in the scope. The man withdrew a Beretta semi-auto from under his jacket and slid his gun hand under the edge of the table. Then he withdrew a sound suppressor, and deftly applied the silencer to the end of its barrel.

The sniper warned, "Josie, Target Two, behind you. Gun. Stand down, we have him." As he took a deep breath, the intense whisper of the wheelman sounded in his earpiece: "Neutralize Target Two, then One. Fire at will, Uri."

Always take the bigger threat—the gun—first, Uri thought.

CHAPTER 19

AS JOSIE LISTENED to the words in her earpiece, she took it all in without as much as the flick of an eyelash. She glanced into her lap and unrolled the scroll just enough to read the title:

PROTOCOLLO DICIASSETTE

"*Protocol 17*," she whispered under her breath. "But I thought this was just some damn legend; some paranoid American talk radio conspiracy theory of a plan for world domination. Has this got something to do with *Le Cahier de la Rose Noire?*"

Scarlotti sighed. "Make no mistake. These people are powerful. They could roll over in their sleep and crush you."

She reached for the package on the table. Monsignor Scarlotti grabbed her wrist hard. "You must be in a state of grace, Josie! I will hear your confession now. Don't argue with an old man. Just look into my eyes and trust me."

Stammering, she shook her head violently.

"I can't. No! I can't."

Gripping her wrist with all his strength, fighting her, he rasped, "You must or you will die. Or even worse—be driven mad."

Josie's eyes met his and then slid away.

"Do it for Mama then." Smiling gently, he repeated, "Do it for Mama."

Though not a Roman Catholic convert like her deceased mother, not even a practicing Jew, Josie held the utmost respect for her mother's faith and beliefs. And so, she did confess, and in that moment, for the first time since childhood, she opened her mind and her heart. Josephine Schulman, the woman, cried out to the heavens and released the anguish, the guilt, and the black resin that had lacquered her soul. Uncle Scarlotti, the priest, the confessor, absolved her and blessed her.

The jagged edges of her sixth sense ripped her attention into a crisp focus. She was a consummate professional who never, under any circumstances, totally diverted her attention from the world around her.

From the corner of her eye, she saw the handsome stranger rise to his feet and cover the few short steps to her side in an instant. But an instant was too slow. Her reflexes were keener, her mind and body remained on the West Bank, the war zone, yet bathed in blood and adrenaline. His movements, as if he waded through mud, were in slow motion in her mind's eye.

Josie pivoted with a blur of seamless motion, raised the bottom of her Dunhill cigarette lighter and mashed the top flange with her thumb. A burst of light from the high-intensity strobe flash embedded in the underside of the lighter's case caught the charging attacker's eyes. He instinctively raised his hands to his eyes, leaving a minute window of opportunity.

Closing the distance in a nanosecond, Josie grabbed the attacker's wrist, twisted violently and drove the razor-edged blade of the stiletto downward sharply. The blade's tip cut across his inner thigh and into the femoral artery. The attacker's eyes swam in terror as blood gushed from his wound.

***

The sniper's finger curled tightly around the trigger. Target Number Two began to rise, his gun hand almost clearing the tabletop. The finger squeezed; a faint puffing sounded from the muzzle. The round found its mark, entering the eye socket and exploding in tiny fragments within the brain. His head whiplashed backward.

Josie turned to the Piazza. Headlights blazed to life. A black Fiat sedan screeched to a halt in front of the café. A Mossad agent leapt from the rear of the sedan, grabbing Target Number One and shouldering him, he hobble-carried him to the car.

Blood ran in torrents down the inside of the attacker's leg, filling his shoe, and squishing with each faltering step. The agent muttered to the patrons something about the man having a heart attack and dragged him into the back seat of the Fiat. Josie spun and seized the scroll and the notebook from the table.

She bent to kiss Uncle Lotti gently on the forehead. Visibly shaken, he nodded and kissed her hand.

"Go now, *principessina mia*. Get out of Italy quickly. And do not open the package. Go!"

Her heart still hammering, she raced for the Fiat, gasping for breath. The car tore away from the curb with a shriek of smoldering rubber. As its tires spun against the cobblestone street, then took hold, it sped off almost as quickly as it had appeared.

Now silence.

Frozen and crystal clear.

The waiter approached Monsignor Scarlotti, pausing briefly, his eyes darting, checking for the watchful gaze of a patron. But everyone was still looking toward the street. With a practiced hand, the waiter stabbed a syringe into Scarlotti's exposed neck. A slight gasp and, instinctively, Scarlotti's hand clutched the crucifix that hung from his neck in fragile, soft, colorless fingers. His lips curled in a faint, angelic smile, his eyes cast upward toward the sky. He slumped backward out cold. As the waiter ever so gently closed the priest's eyes, a second waiter appeared; together, they hoisted him out of the chair and carried him to the curb, where they discreetly poured him into a waiting ambulance whose strobes pulsed in the darkness.

The Brotherhood had claimed its own.

***

A living wall of gray and white exploded into the air.

Pigeons.

First just a rustling, a flutter of wings. Then a shockwave of pulsating thunder, silhouetted against the moon.

***

Above, high on the rooftop, the sniper methodically broke down his weapon and stored it in a guitar case, its lid emblazoned with the name *Lucille* in gold script. Dressed as a student, when he made his way down the elevator and to the street, he would have no difficulty blending into the throng of tourists and calf-eyed lovers who still crowded the street, until he reached a second, nondescript black sedan, whose driver sat patiently waiting for his return.

SOLOMON'S KEY

CHAPTER 20

THE SOUND OF a car caught Rossi's attention. Glancing over his shoulder, he saw the headlights streaming toward him. He was just rounding the corner into the *Piazza della Rotonda* now. The Egyptian needle perched atop the fountain adorned with the papal crest stabbed the night sky. He spoke into his lapel mic: "Command Post, from *Ombra* leader, target's in your grid."

"Confirm, target in sight."

Rossi ducked into the shadows and donned a pair of state-of-the-art, slightly oversized eyeglasses. They used the same technology that was fitted into the visors of Apache attack helicopter pilots. It projected target imaging and data right before their eyes. Each member of the *Ombra*, the shadow surveillance team, was outfitted with the same specs. They'd been an appeasement gift bestowed by a large Japanese electronics firm who had wanted the SISDe to turn a blind eye to shady contracts it was negotiating with the Italian government. The special "shades" were also outfitted with a miniature camera that transmitted what the agent saw back to the CP. The agent at the control board in the CP acted as director, switching between feeds and monitoring transmissions.

Now as the night-vision camera in the CP zoomed in on its target, the green-hued image of the subject, and the Egyptian totem towering in the background, floated in front of Rossi's eyes.

"Car approaching," another *Ombra* agent warned, his voice streaming into Rossi's earpiece.

"Hold your positions. *Ombra* post four, can you get a plate?" Rossi whispered into his mic.

"Post four, by. Yes… they're passing beneath me now."

The image of the target silhouetted against the lights of the fountain that surrounded the obelisk dissolved into a high-angle tracking shot of a black Mercedes.

It flickered briefly and zoomed into a close-up of the car's license plate.

A chill ran up Rossi's spine as he read the letters:

SVC 0002

Immediately, Rossi recognized the distinctive Vatican plates

***

The target stood in front of the needle, all eyes watching his every move. The green oval shape of his head filled the latest RAPTOR night-vision sight that had extreme long-range accuracy, enough to shoot the eye out of an eagle when mounted on a .50 cal sniper rifle and in skilled hands. The sniper's orders, like those of the rest of the *Ombra* Unit, were to take *Bast* alive, but if he ran ... to terminate him.

CHAPTER 21

AS SHE STOOD shivering in the cold beneath the columns of the Pantheon behind the needle, cloaked in shadow and dressed head to toe in black, Basha's sixth sense kicked in. Tugging at her black knit ski cap, she cocked her head and listened. The hairs along the nape of her swanlike neck bristled to attention. It wasn't the sound of the approaching car; it wasn't just a case of nerves. It was something else. Something was wrong, terribly wrong. Nervously, her eyes darted around the *Piazza,* probing the shadows, panning over the looming façade of the needle and beyond. She scanned the buildings that surrounded the square. Heart pounding up through her throat as though it would drive through the roof of her mouth, she stood dead still.

Watching.

Waiting.

Listening.

Nostrils flared, sniffing the air like a hunted animal.

Then she saw it. In her peripheral vision, she caught the stencil of a shadow move to her right. She took a faltering step back, crouched lower, her eyes peering into the darkness and darting upward to the building directly in front of her. Absently, her hand flew to her forearm and fingered the outline of the deadly bracelet concealed beneath her clothing, stroking it lovingly as if for reassurance. She brought a pair of small high-powered binoculars to her eyes and studied the building floor by floor.

As she looked she thought of her failsafe plan. She'd asked Saud, that poor lovesick fool, to close up for her tonight. To meet her at the needle, where she had a delicious surprise for him. Taking no chances, she decided to use him as a decoy target for the meet. Planting the seed of suspicion in that arrogant Italian agent's mind had been child's play for her, posing as Gina the harmless little coed. She'd made Rossi the moment he'd stepped into the café. Tonight she'd arrived hours earlier, hidden in plain sight beneath the titan columns of the Goddess of the Earth, Gaia, for whom its distant cousin the Greek Parthenon was originally built. In case things went south, Saud would be a diversion. And right now she sensed that things had gone far, far south. All the way to Hell.

On the fifth floor, in the third window from the right, something moved, a subtle shift in the pattern of the shadows. She was sure of it.

As the beam of approaching headlights washed across the *Piazza*, reaching for the false target—*Saud*—she ducked back into the darkness and scampered away, her movements sleek and sinewy as a cat.

Floodlights suddenly blazed and filled the square with blinding light and traced helter-skelter patterns across the square. Basha didn't look back. Instead, she poured on the speed, loping in long strides, making for an alleyway just ahead.

From behind, came the sound of excited voices shouting, the screech of car tires braking to a sudden halt, an engine gunning, accelerating, then drifting away into the distance.

Then an agonized cry. Saud's cry. When he turned to run, the sniper's .50 cal cartridge blew open his chest.

Gulping air, eyes locked on the alley ahead, *Bast* ran.

Ten feet.

More sounds.

The ear-piercing wail of Klaxon.

Footsteps pounded the pavement behind her, gaining on her.

Someone shouted in a breathless voice, *"Alto!"*

As she spun around the corner into the alleyway, she felt the spray of pulverized brick against her cheek from a round that had missed its target, her back, and pockmarked the wall. The cough of another silenced round and then it whizzed over her scalp.

Head ducked low she bolted ahead, grabbing crates and refuse as she went, hurtling them behind her into her pursuer's path. She cursed herself as she ran. Somehow she'd missed spotting a member of the surveillance team who was too close, and that mistake had almost pumped a slug into her back. Up ahead she saw it, a fire escape. In one bounding leap she sprang. Her hands found the lowest rung of the ladder and she pulled herself up. With the agility of a child playing on monkey bars, she curled her knees to her chest, kicked upward, and snaked her ankles around the vertical bars of the ladder. Then she released her handgrip and spooled down. She hung upside-down, in the darkness, directly in the path of her pursuer, waiting to pounce.

Backlit by the intermittent glow of the halogen searchlights sweeping across the mouth of the alley from the *Piazza*, *Bast* saw the attacker drawing nearer in a strobelike, stuttering image.

Stutter ... a face ... a hand ...

Stutter ... a semi-auto clutched tightly, stabbing outward, seemingly held by a disembodied hand.

Then directly beneath her... an exposed neck.

Her arm snaked out, the thin blade sprang from its nest on her wrist, swiping cleanly across the attacker's throat.

The handgun clattered to the ground. The attacker crumpled, his hand flailing at his throat. She pulled herself up from the waist, grasped the rung, and lowered her legs, dropping to the pavement in one fluid movement.

She pocketed the Beretta and turned toward the man who'd tried to shoot her in the back. Only it wasn't the face of a man she saw. The youthful face of a woman, twenty-something, stared back. She stiffened and sucked a deep breath. Her eyes cut to the strange looking eyeglasses on the dead woman's face. She snatched the special-optics "shades" from the dead woman's face and put them on. In her right eye, *Bast* saw the herky-jerky image of the backs of dark figures swarming across the *Piazza* toward Saud's body. Then a sudden tilt, a blurred pan, as if whoever was holding a camera had suddenly looked back over their shoulder, and she was watching the image of taillights receding down the street. It was her contact, *Prospero*, named after Shakespeare's sorcerer, running away like a frightened child. Then it occurred to her that she now had a bird's eye view of everything her pursuers were doing. Steeling herself, she searched the fallen attacker, located the radio, and tore it from her belt. *Bast* paused. *If I can see what they're seeing, these things must be equipped with a micro camera.* She leaned forward and looked directly into the eyes of the attacker, knowing the image of the agent's innocent face, her vacant eyes, would be transmitted back to the woman's companions.

Rising slowly, she turned, ripped the camera from the corner frame of the eyeglasses, and crushed it under her heel. Retracing her steps and finding an unlocked door, knowing their every move, eavesdropping on their every command, like a panther, she disappeared into the dark recesses of the building and into the night.

Cloaked in shadow on an adjacent rooftop, the young Arab man stood with a practiced stillness and composure, watching *Bast's* every move. When she disappeared from view, he silently slipped into the cocoon of darkness.

CHAPTER 22

BILL COTTER STOOD silently, watching from his vantage point within the American Express Office located across the street from the Café Dellini. From the corner of his eye, he caught a glimpse of his reflection in the window glass. *You look like shit,* he thought. *Eyes all puffy; lost their spark. Grey, telltale hair peeking out from the temples and sideburns of that cheap blond dye job. Crow's feet starting to etch the corners of your dull, filmy eyes.* He shook his head, his gaze cutting back to the scene at the café. The tableau of chaos that unfolded before his eyes left him visibly shaken. His breath thickened in his chest; his hands shook. Drawing hard on his cigarette, he cursed under his breath and pitched the butt onto the floor, mashing it violently in a twisting motion with his foot. Cotter took a deep breath to steady himself then bolted out the door into the cool night air.

Cotter strode briskly down the sidewalk, looking nervously like a ferret in each direction. Then he ducked around the corner and up the hill to his parked car. He jerked open the car door and climbed inside. There, on the passenger side, sat Dr. Felix Ahriman, the Little Man from the plane.

The sticky-sweet scent of lavender overpowered Cotter's nostrils. Ahriman was the personification of Truman Capote's evil twin. His doughy face, slightly rouged cheeks and effeminate air somehow magnified the cruelty of his persona.

He sat, hands steepled to his lips, cherublike with a thin smile.

"Hi, Billy. Surprised to see me?" Ahriman asked.

"How the hell?"

"Oh now, Billy… shame, shame everyone knows your name!"

"NO . . . I just meant that I didn't expect you to be here."

Slapping his thighs with both hands, Ahriman said, "Of course, that's exactly what you meant." Nodding toward the café at the bottom of the steep incline before them, he lisped, "Such an ugly word . . . *'failure'* . . . don't you think?"

Cotter caught the implication as a fish swallows the vicious hook; it ripped at his intestine. Beads of sweat trickled down the sides of his torso, down his back, matted his shirt to his spine.

A fatherly, reassuring look of concern washed over the doctor's face. He patted Cotter's thigh.

"Let's forget this peccadillo for a moment, shall we?"

"Whatever you say," Cotter said.

"That's better. *Let's play a game.*"
Cotter froze in a fugue state. His eyelids flickered.
"To Know," Cotter responded woodenly.
"To Dare," the doctor said.
"To Will."
"To Keep Silent . . ."
Totally immersed in an altered state of consciousness now, Level Alpha, Cotter was the puppet and Ahriman the puppet master. In fact it was his code name, "*Il Burattinaio,*" within the Brotherhood.

"Failure is a terrible thing, Billy. It brings shame and ruin. It makes one disappointed. Life no longer has meaning. Your life has no purpose, Billy. No meaning. Do you understand?"

"I understand. My life has no purpose." Cotter's cheek quivered, just a slight tic, as a tiny droplet of shame rolled down his cheek. He plunged deeper still, into the Omega Level.

"You're an abject failure, Billy Cotter. An unnecessary loose end. Such a bad boy. Listen and obey," Ahriman said.

"I will listen and obey."

***

The passenger door closed softly and Ahriman's tiny feet walked across the cobblestone roadway, moving in and out of cones of streetlight that marked his path down the steep sidewalk toward the *Piazza di Spagna*. He marched triumphantly, swaggering down the walk to the very bottom, where he purchased a carnation from a beautiful young girl. He pinned the flower to his coat and whistled "Zip-A-Dee-Doo-Dah." As he sauntered away, he stole a last peek up the hill toward Cotter's car. As its headlights winked on, he smiled.

***

Cotter's hand turned the ignition; the engine sparked. He slowly moved the gearshift into drive.

In the distance the "EE-AW . . . EE-AW" of the carabinieri's Klaxon rose and fell. Cotter's two-and-a-half ton sedan began to roll down the steep incline of the street.

The shrill pitch of the Klaxon grew closer now.
Louder. Clearer.
Cotter's sedan began to build speed. Faster and faster.
The Klaxon's wail was much louder now, much closer.
EE-AWW . . . EE-AWWWW.
The sedan now hurtling downward. Faster still.

The sound of screeching tires braking too late, the sound of tortured metal and broken bodies, clawed the air. As Cotter's car bolted into the path of the onrushing police car, his vehicle was catapulted into midair by the force of the collision.

SWUSHHHHH . . .

As if in slow motion, Cotter's sedan flew through still space, turning and twisting, spiraling like a touchdown pass, until it crash-landed, nose first, into the fountain. A single blaring car horn sounded taps for those who fail the Brotherhood.

CHAPTER 23

NSA HQ Fort Meade, MD.

FROM HIS SEAT at a conference table, Senior Agent Manwich studied the meek little man who stood in the front of the room; behind the man a huge plasma screen flickered and displayed a long shot of a cell. In the harsh glare of the cell's naked light bulb, a man's body swayed, casting pendulous shadows across the walls. The camera zoomed in on the man's face. A bed sheet was knotted tightly around his neck. His face contorted, eyes still bulging.

The camera slowly panned down the body to the floor directly beneath him. In a tight close-up, the image of an open book filled the screen.

The agent's eyes cut to the little man at the podium. The field agents called him "the Answer Man."

He was an analyst, a professor-type who headed an agency think tank. If you came across some obscure bit of info, you sent it to the Answer Man who fed it to the geek squad.

The Answer Man keyed the remote. The video dissolved into a riot of pixels that merged into a crisp, digital blowup of the page.

"Gentlemen, what we have here is nothing short of a dying man's finger pointing to his killer."

Puzzled looks washed over the briefing room.

"But it was a suicide," someone protested. "Just another CI who cracked under pressure."

"Was it? Although confidential informants frequently suffer depression, don't be so sure." The Answer Man waved his hand dismissively. "Let me explain. This page we're viewing is Bacon's *Tempest* Act 1 Scene 2."

The Chief of Directorate Bill Loveday cut in. "You mean Shakespeare's."

Frowning, the Answer Man said, "No, William Shakespeare was what you'd call a cutout, a false front. Detailed studies have shown that the level of writing and education required in composing these works point to one scholar, Sir Francis Bacon. Our crypto section has discovered what we refer to as the Bakish cipher. Allow me to demonstrate." A new image flashed.

```
English:    abcdefghijklmnopqrstuvwxyz0123456789
21-letter:  ABCDEFGHIIKLMNOPQRSTVVV-Y--ABCDEFGHI
Bakish:     efghiklmnnopqrstvyabccc-d—efghiklmn
```

"Many times the name Bacon appears in 'Shakespeare's' plays ... but in cipher and backward. Here's a line in English with Bakish below:

When now h*is fat*her's death had freed his will
```
Cmir rsc mna kebmiy'a hiebm meh kyiih mna cnpp
```

"Look only at the italicized letters. The letters 'isfat,' when we look at the bottom row, translate into 'nakeb,' which is backward for 'bekan,' which counts as 'bacon.'"

"Only if you can't spell," someone said.

The Answer Man shook his head. "In those early days of the English language the same word could be spelled many different ways. Phonetically."

"Hooked-on-Phonics," another voice wisecracked.

"Yes, the same way children are taught to read even to this day. And disguising a missive, a secret message, within plain text by the use of different fonts is called?" the Answer Man asked, slowly scanning their blank faces.

"Steganography," the chief answered impatiently. "Al-Qaeda used another variant called Semagram to conceal messages in their E-mails and … rumor had it that they'd hidden instructions in photos by playing with the pixels." The chief's eyes narrowed. "Now, can we get on with this?"

The professor's eyebrows lifted. "That last bit, fortunately, was just an Internet 'urban legend.' But let's get back to identifying the killer. Here's a closer view of the passage from *the Tempest* we found in the cell."

> Begun to tell me what I am but stopt,
> And left me to a bootleese Inquistion,
> Concluding, stay: not yet.

"Notice anything odd, gentlemen?"

CHAPTER 24

Roma

JOSIE'S BLACK FIAT screamed across the tarmac and up to the Grumman Gulf Stream V that sat fueled, engines whining, ready for immediate departure. The plane was registered to an Israeli-owned electronics firm that did regular business in Rome. No one found it suspicious that it filed for an expedited departure. As she entered the cabin, the Rome station's Kasta, case officer, sat at a workstation studying a file. He was a short, barrel-chested man with coarse, wiry hair and pale blue eyes. His features resembled a rock quarry: all jagged and sharp edges, pitted not smooth. As unrefined as his true nature.

"Ms. Shulman, kindly be so good as not to return to Rome for oh, say, the remainder of the millennium!" said the Kasta, looking up and peering through the half-lens of his reading glasses.

"You *momze. Kush meer in tochis.*" Josie took pleasure in knowing how to tell a bastard to kiss her ass in eight languages, especially Yiddish. "It was to be a simple exchange. Why didn't you know a hit was waiting for me? Or maybe you're still looking through the book, trying to figure out how you could have been such a total fuck-up in Cairo?" Josie's face flamed with anger.

"Okay, I guess I deserved that," the Kasta said. His eyes slid away for a moment, then ticked back, quick and furtive. "Did the bastard talk on the way here?"

"He was busy bleeding to death," Josie said. "He just muttered something about being better off to die quickly than to face the death of a thousand cuts. He's barely alive. I assume he was a freelance hired gun . . ."

The Kasta shrugged.

"You can do your own dirty work. I leave him in your . . . capable hands." She mocked him with her eyes, mocked him with the inflection in her voice.

Josie and the Kasta had a history, an ugly history of betrayal. He'd left a good friend of hers with his ass hanging out high and dry in Cairo some years back. She had to inform the mother that her twenty-seven-year-old son died and that the body was not recovered, which was the truth: you couldn't count the poor kid's severed finger, mailed to the U.S. Embassy, as a body could you? To her way of thinking the Kasta was an anal retentive fool, an idiot who did everything by the book because otherwise . . . he was clueless.

Josie hated the very smell of him, the stench of him. She had no delusions about her work, but had always held the belief that people in her line of work should be more of the poet or mad artisan, not a chauvinistic, incompetent *chazar,* a pig. She took her marching orders from the head of *Metsada*, Abraham, and no one else. She was a field agent, not a bureaucrat, and certainly no one's flunky.

"Very well," he said. "Here are some files that the institute sent by express pouch for you. Strange business. They're sealed. Care to fill me in, Ms. Shulman?"

"No. It's strictly on a need to know basis. And you don't need to know. Oh hell, just fuck off!"

"I bring out the best in you, obviously." The Kasta's eyes narrowed into slits. "You *Metsada* people are all the same. I'm warning you, Ms. Schulman. Don't push me too—"

She stepped over his words. "Take this book and document; send it express to my father in Chicago by diplomatic pouch. And do not . . . open it! Understood?"

"Since you're headed straight to Chicago, why don't you take it yourself?"

Josie regarded him coldly. "You'd like that, wouldn't you? Since I'm entering the States covertly, I wont have the benefit of diplomatic status. U.S. Customs could inspect the package."

The Kasta averted his gaze. Looking up, he decided to try a different tactic: destroy her with feigned sympathy.

He softened his voice, referred to her in the familiar. "Josie, you better have a seat. Please? I just received a damage report . . . Monsignor Scarlotti suffered a heart attack at the scene and was rushed to a hospital. I'm terribly sorry; I know he's your uncle."

Josie slumped into the seat and bit her lower lip to stop the tears, but they continued to well up. *I'm not going to let this bastard see me cry*, she thought. Making one last effort to blink them back and failing, Josie gave in as the tears finally erupted. "He's all right, then?"

"As far as we know at this time. I'll keep you posted."

Switching gears again, the Kasta said, "Ms. Schulman, The American RSO…Bill Cotter's body and embassy car were also found at the café. Care to offer any conjecture?"

Josie regained composure almost as swiftly as the Kasta had switched gears.

"I told you once, *Gai tren zich*! I'm sure you know more than I do."

The Kasta's face flamed red then faded into a smug grin. "Screwing myself is a physical impossibility."

"You're a jealous little man. Everyone knows we've been at odds with our cousins over liaison intelligence with the Vatican since the 1960's. I developed and nurtured Monsignor Scarlotti from a distance and you have always resented it. I intend to ask the Institute what the hell is going on here. You're still an incompetent moron!"

Glancing over the top of his half-glasses, the Kasta nodded his capitulation. "If there is nothing else, I suggest you depart immediately."

"No there isn't. Just have the package expressed, don't open it. And have the AL agent contact me at the other end in Chicago with fresh ID and tools." She knew that with the fuck-up at the café, she'd need a deep-cover case officer in the US to set her up with new papers—and weapons.

"Shalom, Ms. Schulman."

"Shalom."

It wasn't until they departed Italian air space that Josie had the strength to go about the business of trying to put the pieces together. An Israeli student with clearance, doubling as a flight attendant, brought her a double scotch. As she fumbled for a cigarette, he began to admonish her about smoking on the aircraft. But one look into her marble-cold eyes was enough. He decided to keep his mouth shut, live long enough to graduate school and—someday—lose his virginity. He took his seat at the rear.

CHAPTER 25

NSA HQ:

THE ANSWER MAN frowned. "Really, gentlemen. This is basic cipher breaking 101. The text has been altered. Take note of the original text. Look at the highlighted letters, and then… compare it to the handwritten version scribbled in the margin."
Another image appeared on the screen with both sections enlarged.

Begun to tell me what I am but stopt,
And left me to a bootleese Inquistion,
Concluding, stay: not yet.

Did begun to tell me what I am but stopt,
Rent my bitter soul,
And left me to a bootleese Inquistion,
Gallows light the dark,
On concluding, stay: not yet.

"The first letters of lines one and two, combined with the first three letters of the third line spell… *BACON*!"
In a flash of recognition, the first letters of the handwritten text leaped out at the agent:
D R A   G … O

The agent said, "Okay, I get it. It's Volante's first name. But that still doesn't make it a homicide.
Another image flashed.
Strange letters, markings, sprawled on a thin piece of parchment:

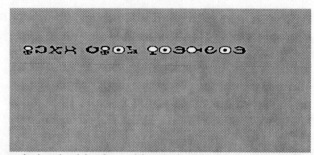

"This was found clutched in the subject's hand. It's a cipher that was found tucked away in the yellowed pages of a book nestled on a dusty shelf in the back of a Masonic library. Does anyone recognize it?"

Agent Childress, who was on loan from MI6, started to speak, hesitated, then looked around sheepishly and said, "It's the Golden Dawn's cipher. A secret society founded in London in the late 1880's." Face reddening with embarrassment, he went on. "Bit of a dark page from England's history. Sex scandals in the tabloids and all."

"Dark?" the chief of directorate said sarcastically. "Which page wasn't …dark?"

Childress stiffened at the barb but went on. "Bunch of daft intellectuals, like the poet W.B. Yeats and that wannabe poet and charlatan, Aleister Crowley. Paraded around in secret. Dressed up in Egyptian costumes, smoked hashish. Played around with hocus-pocus rituals and the like, sir."

"Buncha effete intellectual Queens, you mean… Oh, excuse me; I'm being politically incorrect," the chief chided and turned toward Childress. "I believe you call 'em poufs back in Mother England." He gave a snort of self-satisfaction, leaned back in his chair, and folded his fat fingers on his protruding doughnut gut. "Wasn't Oscar Wilde one of the 'boys in the band'?"

"No, but his wife was a member," Childress corrected smugly, straightening the Windsor knot of his silk tie.

The Answer Man cut in. "They were intelligent, yes. Crowley could play simultaneous games of chess, seated in another room, using his vivid recall to remember each piece's position on the board as he called out moves. Somewhat eccentric, indeed. Crowley would march through Piccadilly Circus, his lantern-yaw jutting, his eyes glaring and wrapped in a velvet cape emblazed with symbols. Thought the cape made him invisible. He almost killed a waiter at the Café Royal for having the audacity to ask him if he'd like a table by the window when he entered, cloaked in his magic cape of invisibility."

"Coulda used a cape like in the field last month," an agent said, snickering.

"Hey, maybe bin Laden's usin' it," another said.

R. DOUGLAS WEBER

"Laugh all you wish, gentlemen, but documented accounts of Crowley's ability to cloud people's thoughts, drive them to suicide or the asylum, exist. Ernest Hemingway recounted how he saw Crowley sidle up behind an unwary passerby, pacing the man in sync down the sidewalk. When Crowley stooped into a duck walk, so did the man. When the magician threw himself to the ground, the man collapsed in a heap."

Manwich hummed the theme from *The Twilight Zone* and stared at he ceiling, rolling his eyes.

The chief of directorate cleared his throat. "Lovely little history lesson, Professor …but what's your point and what's the damn message say?"

Click. "Here's the key. Translate the message for yourselves, gentlemen. And you'll see that the subject was just …following orders."

100

CHAPTER 26

IN THE OFFICE of the *Ombra* Unit Rossi paced back and forth. The clock on the wall read 6:00 AM. His team sat in silence, their muscles aching from the previous night's adrenaline rush, bloodshot eyes studying the floor, trying to avoid Rossi's gaze. Past situations had taught them to wait patiently for their leader to collect his thoughts. Better to keep silent, offer no excuses, and just take what comes.

Rossi stopped. He stood hands tucked in his pockets, solemn and dead serious.

Enrico, the unit's sniper, cleared his throat.

"You say something?" Rossi pressed.

Enrico swallowed audibly, shook his head.

"I believe that what happened last night was what the U.S. Marines call a 'cluster fuck.'" Eyes panning the room, Rossi went on. "No one, including myself, acted professionally. We lost one of our own, Carmela." He stiffened. "When we're finished here, Dante will drive me to her parents home. And I have to try to explain to her mother why someone in my command died needlessly. I've only had to make that long trip once before, and I don't intended to ever make it again. Is that understood?"

Someone coughed. Heads nodded.

"Enough said, now tell me what we've got."

Lorenzo spoke first. "The prints on the decoy target come back to a Saudi national. Age twenty-six, birthplace Mecca. Wealthy family with lots of Halliburton construction contracts throughout the Middle East. We're asking the Foreign Ministry to verify with the Saudi Embassy."

Rossi nodded. "Make it discreet. Did you search his apartment?"

"Yes, sir. Anything of remote interest has been bagged and tagged. Forensics is going over his things now."

"Phone records and computer hard drive turn up anything?"

"Not yet, but they're crosschecking everything."

Rossi scratched his chin. "Tell them to make it priority one."

Hesitantly, Dante raised his hand and finger-combed his thick, black hair Rossi acknowledged with a curt, "Go ahead."

"The black Mercedes, sir. So far I've got—"

Cutting him off with a raised hand, Rossi said, "Leave that to me. Give me what you've got, classify it Ultra ... and discuss it with no one." His steely gaze punctuated the last words. "Gentlemen, that intel is not to be spoken of outside this room."

The ring of the telephone shattered the silence.

Lorenzo answered, spoke briefly, and cradled the receiver. "Sir, they've got something they want you see in Tech Services."

"Dante, Enrico … come with me. The rest of you go over everything again." They headed for the tech lab.

Tech Services was gizmo land to Rossi's way of thinking. They had all the latest software and crypto technology. Compared to what the Brits at GCHQ, signals intel, and the boys at NSA and Langley had, it looked like a kid's chemistry set. Racks jammed with hardware and draped in tendrils of cable surrounded them. They stood in front of a bank of LCD monitors. The pimple-faced tech, Claudio, shoved his thick-lensed glasses up the bridge of his nose, then his fingers flew across the keyboard. "I'm cueing it up now," he said to Rossi.

"Maybe Carmela won't have died in vain," Rossi said glumly.

Multiple images appeared on three monitors.

"What you're seeing is the feed we recorded from the headset cams. When I played back Carmela's, I found something interesting."

The larger middle screen filled with the jerky image of a dark figure running ahead, back turned. The figure ran in long strides.

"That's our man," Dante said.

"He runs like a *dannato* cheetah," Enrico added.

"Can you stabilize the camera movement and enhance the audio?" Rossi asked.

"How's this?" the tech said.

The jitter effect smoothed out. "If we do this,"—the tech tapped a key and a data grid appeared and whirled in the right corner of the screen—"we have a program that can approximate the subject's height and weight based on length of stride, shadow, and comparison to surrounding objects."

"Not very tall," Dante said, staring at the result.

On the screen, the outline of a Beretta equipped with a sound-suppressor bobbed in Carmela's outstretched hand. The handgun spit twice.

The screen darkened as she followed the target into the alley. Carmela's tortured, ragged breaths boomed from the audio.

A few moments of the hollow echo of pounding feet, then a blurred flash of steel.

Rossi cringed in sympathy, hands fisting at his sides.

"Look closely now," the tech said. "I've slowed and digitally enhanced this section." A hand—a small hand, Rossi noticed—fingers extended, reached into the frame. The tech punched the keyboard and an image, a face, magically appeared behind the hand.

"They say the eyes of the dead capture the last instant of life," Rossi said, staring.

At first a straight fall of midnight hair obscured the face. Then with a head toss, bright eyes, pulsing white like some zombie in the distorted emerald hue of the night-vision optics, flashed. Full lips. Delicate features. The image stared downward obliquely.

His breath caught in his throat, Rossi remembered Gina looking down at him as she straddled him in the hotel room, eyes wild and frenzied. He remembered the sweat-dampened mane of silken hair that covered her face as she moved and shuddered with passion. A cold, ice-carved blade stabbed his chest.

"*Figlio di puttana*!" Dante gasped.

"Not a son of a bitch, una *fica*! It's a woman," Enrico corrected.

Rossi's fist slammed the table, knocking over the tech's coffee cup.

Biting his lower lip so hard he almost drew blood, he straightened and said, "Make blow ups and—"

"Disseminate them to the Carabinieri and the Customs?" Dante cut in.

Rossi's cold gaze locked on Dante's. "NO! Just the *Ombra* Unit. I think I know where to find this bitch. And her ass is mine."

Without another word, Rossi spun on his heels and charged out of the room, letting the door slam hard in his wake.

CHAPTER 27

Fort Meade, MD.

The Answer Man resumed his briefing.

"So now that you've broken the code, you have to ask yourselves … how could a simple message induce a man to commit suicide?"

"Maybe the guy was so screwed up it just pushed him over the edge?" Manwich said.

"The informant was a highly intelligent and stable individual. Psychological evaluations revealed no underlying mental defect." The Answer Man clicked the remote. An image of a pasty-faced man with thinning gray hair filled the screen. "Gentlemen, I give you Dr. Felix Ahriman, eminent neuro-psychiatric researcher and …"

"Complete nutcase," Manwich interjected.

The director shot Manwich a harsh glance. As he sat regarding the plump, moon-faced agent, dressed in a crumpled, cheap polyester suit, the director had to suppress a laugh. He considered Manwich a conundrum. The man came off like an unkempt slob, brazen and obnoxious. But behind that rough exterior lurked a devious mind. The word "Ethics" couldn't be found in Manwich's vocabulary, which when combined with his cunning, made him a dangerous operative. The director tolerated the agent's attitude and uncouth manner because Manwich followed orders, never questioning, and never looking back.

Manwich shrugged. "I vetted him when he applied for a position with us." The agent studied the ceiling as if trying to remember. "He was a freelance contractor working for Langley … part of those wackjobs assigned to MK-ULTRA."

Director Loveday said, "That black ops program using LSD and hypnosis for mind control?"

"Yep," Manwich agreed. "Good old Dr. Ahriman was accused of experimenting on his colleagues. He'd dope them up unbeknownst to them, put them through hypnotic programming sessions designed to plant all kinds of crazy, paranoid delusions and then—"

The Answer Man broke in. "His best friend and associate jumped out a hotel room window. Fell thirty floors, landing on the roof of a cab parked on Lexington Avenue."

"That's one way to find a taxi in New York," another agent offered.

"The NYPD called it suicide, but there were a lot of unanswered questions," Manwich added. "Like why he was stark naked?" He paused. "I read the report of an interview taken from Ahriman's secretary at the Agency. She accused him of inappropriate sexual advances, getting physical with her."

"Groping?" Loveday asked

"No," Manwich corrected. "She said that sometimes he'd talk to her about the weirdest stuff over coffee. At first she felt turned off. But after more and more occasions, she found herself compelled to listen. Even found herself attracted to him, although she'd always loathed him. Started having nightmares, missing a lot of work. Said she'd walk into a room and suddenly not recall how she got there. Thought people were out to get her, reading her thoughts, tapping her phone. The kicker was that one morning she woke scared shitless. Lying sprawled across a bed in a cheap hotel, not remembering ever going there, her body a mass of bruises and welts, and painfully sore from sexual violation."

"Probably slipped her a mickey. What did they do to Ahriman?" Director Loveday asked.

"She wasn't doped. They did nothing. They investigated and found that Ahriman had used his plastic to rent the room. Found his prints and pecker tracks all over the place, but … it was the hotel night clerk's statement that put the kibosh on the whole thing. The clerk said that when the woman checked in with Ahriman, she was all hot and bothered …even asked the guy if wanted to join 'em in a threesome."

"Ahriman probably bribed him."

"Nope, they gave the guy a polygraph and he passed with flying colors," Manwich explained.

"What happened to the woman?"

Manwich's eyebrows beetled. Then his eyes opened wide, he swallowed hard. "Suicide… Hung herself."

"And she left no note, did she, Mr. Manwich?" the Answer Man said. "But a slip of paper was found her hand."

The agent's eyes saucered. "That's right, I'd forgotten."

The screen flickered and a photo of a crumpled note written in strange glyphs appeared.

ℵ⦿ℰ⅏Ⴇ ℵ⦿ⴝℵ ⵔⴱ⦿ⴝ ⅭⴱⴲⴱⅭ

And below it the translation read:

SIMON SAYS PLAY DEAD …
The director leaned forward. "You're saying there's a connection with our CI's suicide. Same MO?"

Manwich chimed in. "Don't forget that intern Kenny who we found in the computer room strung up by the neck with piano wire."

The Answer Man shrugged. "I'll let you judge for yourself. Once decoded from the old magical symbols the note reads, 'Simon says, play dead.'"

"Where's this Ahriman now?" the director asked.

"Got blackballed with the G that's for sure," Manwich said, "I bounced his application and put the word out."

"Nevertheless, he has found a patron," the Answer Man explained. "He works as a consultant for the E Institute." The image of a tall building familiar to anyone who's been to Los Angeles flashed onto the screen. "One of the largest 'New Age' churches in the world. This is their headquarters. Its founder and leader is none other than Drago Volante."

"Give me some background." The director leaned back.

"Although you wont find it in Volante's slick bio, he has a rather sordid past. The FBI has a thick file on him going back years. It was part of a security investigation involving a rocket scientist who practically founded the Jet Propulsion Lab in Pasadena.

"Jack Whiteside Parsons. Even had a crater on the moon named after him."

"The Bureau think he was a commie?" the director asked.

"No. It stemmed from his eccentric behavior and a police report. Seems the neighbors complained about some wild goings on at Parsons's Pasadena mansion. It was a hangout for the Bohemian set in those days, writers and artists. Mainly Sci-Fi writers like Harlan Ellison, Robert A. Heinlein, and even Ray Bradbury were rumored to have stopped by."

"Hey, doesn't Volante write Sci-Fi novels?" an agent asked.

Manwich jumped in. "Yeah, Vinny Valentino starred in a film adaptation a few years back. Sucker bombed at the box-office."

"Yes, that was the beginning of Volante's association with Parsons. Volante was a budding writer who wanted to rub elbows with the giants. He took up residence at the mansion. But that's just the half of it. The police received a complaint that a pregnant, naked woman was jumping over a bonfire in the backyard. Some sort of ceremony with lots of people causing a ruckus. Running around in black robes and the like."

"Witches?" someone asked.

"No. A strange occult group known as the Agape Lodge, the American branch of the Ordo Templi Orientis or OTO for short."

"Ordo Templi ..."Manwich managed. "Something to do with the Templars?"

"You're partially correct," the Answer Man said. "It's Order of the Eastern Templar. But their only connection with the actual Templars is that they are an offshoot, quasi-Masonic Lodge. Which means members have to pass through various grades of initiation and similar rituals. Remember our old friend from the Golden Dawn society, Aleister Crowley? Well he was the Outer Head of the OTO. In fact, Crowley, upon hearing of his understudy Parson's association with Volante, wrote Parsons, admonishing him for his connection with a 'con man.'"

"Hold on," Manwich said. The agent prided himself on his encyclopedic knowledge of film. "Wasn't Parson's wife that wannabe actress that stared in some artsy-fartsy film?"

The Answer Man nodded. "That would be Candy Carson, his third wife. Haunting green eyes and flaming red hair. Red hair having some sort of occult significance. Anyway, Parsons called Volante his scribe and magical partner. Long story short, Volante recorded some sex magick ritual called the Babylon Working. Some sexual hocus-pocus Parsons conducted with his then nineteen-year-old wife and ex-sister-in-law, while Volante looked on taking notes.

"Living up to his reputation, Volante swindled Parsons by convincing him to open a joint bank account and then ran off with a small fortune and Parsons's wife. Using the structure and secret rituals of the OTO, Volante created a new form of pop, New Age psychology and outlined it in a book, *CYBOTRONICS*. It became a bestseller. Volante created his own church to go along with it.

"Incorporating the bare-your-soul techniques of the OTO, and other secret societies, they had new members confess all their darkest secrets—drug use, infidelity, crimes and weaknesses, while hooked up to a thinly disguised galvanic response measurement device, a lie detector. By charging higher and higher fees for each 'purging session' on the box, based upon the person's net worth, and not hesitating to blackmail anyone they could, the money poured in. Eschatology temples sprung up overnight across the world."

It occurred to Manwich that this was similar to the technique used by all the intelligence services that routinely strapped their employees to the box. Of course, only an idiot would blather out his darkest sins.

"The *E* Institute brought some ex-intelligence agents into the fold and created a world-wide intelligence division called the Office of Internal Affairs," the Answer Man went on. "They conducted surveillance ops and black bag burglaries against potential opponents and suspected members. In an '80s DOJ indictment they were charged with harboring fugitives, obstruction of justice, and lying before a grand jury. With a database filled with the sensitive information shared by 'purged' members, they weren't above using intimidation and blackmail to advance their causes."

A new image pixilated on the screen. "Gentlemen, I give you Drago Volante," the Answer Man said. Agent Manwich studied Volante's candid, slightly grainy photo.

"Let's try out our new 3D imagining projection system," the Answer Man said as his fingers flew over a keyboard. "This surveillance tape was taken at a speech Volante gave at his *E* Institute in LA."

The lights dimmed and a lifelike image of Volante hovered in midair. Manwich pulled back in his seat. Absently, his hand patted his coat pocket, checking for the outline of the Snickers bar he always kept at the ready, comfort food. Volante's ghostlike face projected peace and warmth; but Manwich nevertheless sensed it was a mask like those worn by lepers to conceal the tortured flesh beneath. His paper-slit mouth and waxy complexion were framed in flaming red hair tightly braided in a socially acceptable ponytail.

The agent looked closer.

The eyes told the truth.

Volante's expressionless, holographic eyes scanned the audience. For a moment they seemed to fall directly on Manwich. And for a moment the agent felt as though Volante's eyes stared through him—and as he looked closer he thought that deep inside, coiling like a thread of smoke, something moved.

Director Loveday took the podium. "Okay, so we're dealing with some powerful, lunatic fringe group. We've learned that our CI was visited by this Dr. Ahriman who may have somehow orchestrated the CI's suicide. Then there's also the mysterious suicide of Kenny the intern." The director panned the room. "So you're asking yourself, 'So what, another kooky PSY OPS deal?' It goes deeper, gentlemen." A computer chip appeared on the screen. "Commerce's Export Security Division has traced the unauthorized overseas shipment of highly classified encryption chips to a foreign company owned by this *E* Institute. A company that is also on the terrorist watch list. A company who we have learned receives donations from the same false-front charity group that funnels funds to al-Qaeda."

Sullen faces stared back at the director now. "Anything to do with classified encryption is our baby, gentlemen. On the desk before each of you is a packet containing your individual assignments. If you'd open them now, please."

Manwich broke the hologram seal and opened the file. There were two tickets to Rome; on the coversheet the photo of a young man grinning broadly and labeled Agent Kyle leered back. The next page was in Italian, written on expensive linen paper. Even with Manwich's limited knowledge of Italian, he could make out dates and locations. And at the very top of the sheet was the Vatican Seal.

After the others had left the room, the director turned to the Answer Man. "You think he'll see through our charade?"

"You mean the cover story about the chip?"

The director nodded.

"Not Manwich. He'll follow orders without questioning. If anyone can locate the al-Qaeda operative, *Bast*, it will be our crude friend."

CHAPTER 28

JOSIE TOOK A long swig of the scotch and let it burn, let it seep its way into her soul. She hoped that it would somehow cut the pain that festered there. It didn't. She lit another cigarette and tore open the security seals on the files. What she read stretched credulity to new heights.

> FLASH REPORT/TEED
> TO: SCHULMAN
> FROM: ABRAHAM/ TEL AVIV COM CENTER
> TOC/009/089 EYES ONLY:
> THROUGH OFFICIAL CHANNELS
> COSMIC
>
> *LOHAMAH PSICHLOGIT* (PSYCHOLOGICAL WARFARE)
> BACKGROUND U.S. INTEL PROJECTS:
>
> **PROJECT ARTICHOKE 1955 AND MK-ULTRA** CIA/ASSASSIN/MANCHURIAN CANDIDATE-STYLE MIND CONTROL PROJECT WAS HISTORICAL BASIS FOR CURRENT ADVANCEMENT IN HYPNOGENIC/PSYCHOTROPIC DRUGS BEHAVIOR MODIFICATION PROJECT. ORIGINALLY RESEARCH UNDER AUSPICES OF PSY. OPS AND NONLETHAL WEAPONS SYSTEMS THAT GRADUATED TO TERRORIST-LINKED ASSASSINATION PROGRAM INFILTRATION AND ASSIMILATION OF TERRORIST ORGS TO ACT AS CONTROL GROUPS AND FUNCTIONING MODELS.
>
> **PROJECT PANDORA/EDOM** ELECTRONIC DISSOLUTION OF MEMORY. PSYCHIC DRIVING/HYPNO INDUCED CONDITIONING/ELF EXTREME LOW FREQUENCY EFFECTS ON EMOTIONS AND BEHAVIOR/EM BURSTS 25 TO 130 CYCLES/SEC. CORNELL UNIVERSITY STUDY ON AUDITORY

SYSTEMS RESPONSES/**SYNCHRONIZATION OF PULSED MICRO WAVES TO MYOCARDIAL RHYTHMS RESULTING IN HEART FAILURE EMITTED FROM HAND-HELD DEVICE.**
DEUS PROJECT/CURRENT BLACK OPS PROJECT/GOALS UNKNOWN AND TO BE ASCERTAINED BY INVESTIGATION OF PROBABLE FRONT ORG SPECIFICALLY THE *E* INSTITUTE/POSSIBLE MIDDLE EAST CONNECTION IN THAT TECHNIQUES ARE UTILIZED TO HEIGHTEN RADICAL ISLAMIC FUNDAMENTALISM/DORMANT AND ACTIVE TERRORIST CELLS IN US/NO FURTHER DATA

The nervous young flight attendant brought dinner. It sat uneaten, but Josie ordered another round of scotch and two packs of cigarettes. A rather handsome young copilot ventured back to her seat. He tried to introduce himself, make small talk as he ogled her body openly.

He was greeted with a terse, "Aren't you supposed to be flying this thing, or would you rather we fall out of the clouds? I'm busy! Why don't you take your cock back to the cockpit where it belongs and leave me alone." She flicked open a butterfly knife with lightning speed and stabbed a cheese blintz on the table for effect.

In a self-protective reflex action, the copilot covered his privates with his cap. It was similar to an infantryman who covers his little head with his helmet instead of his big head. He stayed in the cockpit for the remainder of the flight, his hat still covering the family jewels.

CHAPTER 29

JOSIE CONTINUED TO read, committing most to memory since she could not take notes.

Al-QAEDA THREAT INTERCEPT:

TARGETS VATICAN AND CROWN: ABU ABDEL-RAHMAN AL-IRAQI RECENTLY ACKNOWLEDGED DEPUTY OF TERRORIST ABU MUSAB AL-ZARQAWI THE JORDANIAN-BORN MUSLIM EXTREMIST STATED IN INTERCEPTED SIGNALS TRAFFIC OF DECLARATION TO BE DISSEMINATED BY AL-QAEDA CELLS AT LATER DATE/QUOTE: ISLAM DOES NOT CONCEDE OR MAKE A TRUCE WITH UNBELIEVERS, IT TURNS A DEAF EAR AND EXACTS ALLAH'S CURSE AND REVENGE THROUGH JIHAD, THROUGH THE DIALOGUE OF BULLETS, THE IDEALS OF ASSASSINATION AND BOMBING, THE DIPLOMACY OF THE RAZOR-EDGED SCIMITAR OF HIS WRATH. WE ARE AFTER YOU AS LONG AS YOU ARE ALIVE. WE HAVE TAKEN OUR DECISION, DEPENDING UPON GOD ALONE, TO FIGHT THE INFIDELS, THE HYPOCRITES AND THE VILLAINS/STATEMENT WENT ON TO CITE SPECIFIC TARGETS/EVEN IF YOU GREAT (AL-ZARQAWI) **TAKE US TO THE WHITE HOUSE AND THE BASTION OF THE VATICAN, WE WILL STICK CLOSE AND ACHIEVE OUR AIM: THE DESTRUCTION OF THE INFIDEL'S CHRISTIAN INSTITUTIONS AND THEIR SYMBOLS.**

HISTORICAL BACKGROUND: FURTHER DETAILED DATA TO FOLLOW/TECHNIQUES BEING USED CURRENTLY BY PROTOCOL-17 ORG

FINANCIAL HISTORY: INTERNATIONAL CARTEL/CABAL OF INFLUENTIAL AND INTERCONNECTED BUSINESS LEADERS AND BANKERS FORMED **PROTOCOL 17** SHORTLY AFTER WWII/**STOP**

IDEOLOGY: FASCISTS/RACIST DOGMA

Josie's stomach began to curdle; the acidic taste of bile rose, stinging her throat. She closed the file and pushed it away as though it were contaminated with flesh-eating bacteria. She removed a miniature CD stored in a pocket of the file and placed it into the custom laptop on the table. The disk was TEED, Tactical End-to-End Encryption Device, the latest in spook hardware, and as secure as Monica Lewinski's lips wrapped around a cigar.

She opened the file. As the computer crunched the data, her heart skipped a beat. She somehow sensed that this whole mission would be a trip on the "Good Ship Lollipop," that is, if the ship and she—Shirley Temple—were crossing the river Styx into Hades and eating bonbons all the way.

The screen lit up with her assignment.

OPERATION DANGLE/

OBJECTIVE: USING CONTACT AT "M"/CODE-NAME RUACH ELOHIM/

OBTAIN BOOK/CODE-NAME FLOWER/AND INDUCE US INTEL SPONSORED CHAPTER OF P-17 INTO SURFACING. OBTAIN HARD INFO ON PROJECT DEUS/FROM HUMINT AND ELS COMM INTERCEPT SOURCES. ASCERTAIN IF P-17 INVOLVED IN RECENT RASH OF BOMBINGS IN PALESTINE AND JERUSALEM WHERE SAME MO AND SAME EXPLOSIVE ORDINANCE WERE USED BY BOTH AL-QAEDA AND JEWISH WEST BANK FUNDAMENTALIST GROUPS. POSSIBLE FALSE FLAG TERRORISM ORCHESTRATED BY P-17 IN EFFORT TO FURTHER DESTABILIZE REGION. AUTHORIZATION GRANTED TO UTILIZE OVERT TARGET AS DECOY. ESTABLISH WATCH LIST AND TARGET LIST/NEUTRALIZE TARGET GROUP/SPLASH AUTHORIZED AT YOUR DISCRETION/END.

PRECAUTIONS: NORMAL US INTEL CHANNELS OR SUPPORT TO BE AVOIDED AT ALL COSTS/MOLES ARE IN PLACE AND HAVE COMPROMISED COUSINS/DISSEMINATION OF THREATS TO U.S. INTEL AND ITALIAN CONTACTS NOT AUTHORIZED AT THIS TIME. NONLETHAL WEAPONS AND BIO AGENTS ARE POSSIBLY MAIN THREAT.

CONTACTS: UTILIZE AL AND SAYAN ONLY/END.

Josie stared at the screen for a moment. The words NONLETHAL WEAPONS stood out from the surrounding text like a blemish on Brad Pitt's face. Manchurian Candidate assassins . . . *bopkis, let's see if I am equipped for my style of combat.*

She grabbed the Zero case off the floor, snapped the latches, popped it open, and pried open the case's false bottom. There, snuggled neatly in two socketed compartments, lay her artillery. Two Beretta semi-autos: the first being a Cougar 8045 "F," a 45 ACP that fired both double and single action with custom-tooled action, and a lightened trigger pull, fitted with a Sure-Fire Tactical light, it was a man stopper; the second, her backup piece, was a subcompact, lightweight model 9000S Type "F" also, that handled the large 40 caliber S&W load, with a ten-shot magazine capacity. When she was done, she'd place them in a hidden compartment to avoid detection by Customs upon arrival.

The scent and feel of the gun oil on her hands as she held the weapon restored her spirits. It was like having an old, trusted friend show up unexpectedly. Something a bleeding heart liberal who never learned to handle firearms could never understand, refusing to acknowledge their purpose and necessity. It would be like expecting Gore Vidal and Oprah Winfrey to do the play-by-play coverage of a cockfight in Juarez.

These weapons, however, would be the only amulets of protection Josie needed. That she could fathom and trust.

She loaded the first magazine—never call it a "clip," as her instructor had told her a million times—and then the spares, all but the last magazine.

She thought of Zio Lotti, the Nazi death camps, the stench from the crematoriums, the *oily* smoke wafting through the air, the blank, amorphous face of the unknown evil that assuredly awaited her arrival.

Josie removed ten more rounds from the ammo-box and placed them neatly in a row on the table in front of her. She took one, grabbed a file, and carved an X across the tip of the slug, saying under her breath . . . "This one is for Zio Lotti." She took a second slug and repeating the ritual . . . "This one is for Auntie Frieda—Auschwitz," and then a third slug . . . "This one for Cousin Benjamin . . ."

CHAPTER 30

UNLIKE IN THE movies, Nick Rossi had to answer to superiors who were cut from the transparent fabric of politics rather than the opaque and rough cloth of fieldwork. He was a civil servant who'd displeased his handlers. There would be an official reprimand red-tagged in his file, doubtful looks at staff meetings, and a whisper campaign to the effect that maybe Rossi was not the right man for this position. Suffered from poor judgment, maybe even the recommendation of censure or early retirement. A faction of the Italian intelligence community already had their noses bent out of joint, were just waiting for Rossi to slip up. So the answer was simple. Keep his damn mouth shut. *Son cosi un cornuto, I'm such a cuckold,* he thought. *Who played who like an idioto, Nico? Maybe I am getting too old for the game. Go home to your empty house, feed your cat, and take the bottle of Absolut from the freezer and drink until you're numb.*

But he didn't have that luxury. He had to act quickly. He settled for a couple of shots, a hot shower, and change of clothes. It wasn't hard to find Claude, the owner of the Black Cat Café, since he lived upstairs. Although Rossi figured that Gina or whatever her real name was had disappeared off the face of the earth by now, he still had to run down even the obvious leads.

Claude answered the door in a pink silk robe. After identifying himself as a police inspector conducting a routine missing person's investigation, Rossi made small talk and asked about Gina's whereabouts. Claude offered him a glass of sherry. Rossi declined, casting his gaze around the flat, taking in the multi-colored throw pillows on the pink velvet couch. The lace curtains.

Claude undressed Rossi with his eyes as he took a seat by the window adjusting the hem of his robe to expose a knobby knee and tugged at his black knee socks. "Gina never showed up for work, *la petite putain.* Probably ran off with one of those boys again." He made kissing sounds and a toy French poodle bounded into the room and onto his lap. To the poodle, he said, "Have you been a naughty boy?"

"You have an address and phone number?" Rossi asked coldly, ignoring the comment about Gina being a little whore and the dog who sat glaring and snarling at him.

Raising his long, tapered fingers to his lips, Claude sighed and pushed off the couch. With the poodle tucked under one arm, he moved to an antique desk and pulled out a file card. "*Voilà!*" He turned up his nose as he stared at the card. "Not exactly a better section of Roma, if you know what I mean." Turning, he shrugged and handed the card to Rossi.

"Did … Gina leave any personal effects behind at the café?"

"There's a little cubbyhole in back." Claude moved closer, resting his hand of Rossi's forearm. "We could hop down and check." The poodle growled.

Pulling back, eyebrows creased, Rossi managed, "I think I can find it."

When Rossi turned and went out the door, Claude scampered to the doorway and shouted to his back, "I'm expecting company for lunch. I could always set another place …" Rossi waved dismissively without turning around. "*Mon Dieu*, such a waste," Claude said, shrugging and clucking his tongue.

Downstairs Rossi found the cubbyhole. There was a dirty apron, a blouse, a pair of stockings, and a notebook. With his hands covered in latex gloves, he brought the blouse to his face, her scent filling his nostrils. He squeezed his eyes tightly shut for a moment and then checked the blouse for labels and dry-cleaning marks. Nothing. He checked the pockets. Again nothing.

From the notebook a postcard floated to the floor. He picked it up, studied it. It was a typical tourist shot of St. Peter's Basilica. He flipped it over. On the back a message was scrawled in illegible handwriting. Looked like French but he wasn't sure. He placed the postcard into an evidence envelope and tucked it into his suit coat pocket. Then he bagged the rest of the items, pulled off his gloves and left.

In the car, he punched Gina's phone number into his cell phone. It rang and rang. Finally, a recording stated the line had been disconnected. He clicked off and called Dante, told him Gina's address and the phone number. Instructed him to take five men from the *Ombra* Unit and toss the place if it existed, which he doubted. The phone would probably be a throwaway, pay-as-you-go cell phone listed under an alias.

When he cranked the ignition, his pony car's big block V8 roared to life. It was a dark highland-green '68 Mustang 2+2. Since it was an exact replica of Steve McQueen's, Detective Frank *Bullitt* from the film with the same surname, Rossi christened it Frank. It was one of the small indulgences of his job; idolizing the soft-spoken, tight-lipped actor, the quintessential Gotham detective, Rossi felt empowered by the car's mystique. In some way it eased the pangs of homesickness he'd often felt. He'd purchased the sleek muscle-car for a fraction of its worth from the American Embassy's Diplomatic Security ARSO—Assistant Regional Security Officer—Skip Thomson, who'd hated to part with it, but had been forced to ship out on a disciplinary and wanted to dump it quickly. Rossi and Skip had become drinking buddies after meeting one night at a bar frequented by MSGs (U.S. Marine Security Guards) that served cold American piss-water beer and two fingers of Johnny Walker Black Label neat, Rossi's drink of choice at the time. He liked to rub elbows with his fellow Americans, pick up some loose talk from the soused, lantern-jawed jarheads. Skip had been assigned to guard the ambassador's residence and his twentysomething daughter. Because he was an oil baron from Houston who had a closet filled with over four hundred custom-made cowboy boots, the ambassador was nicknamed "ol' Roy" by his protective detail. Then there were those every-other-weekend barbeques. Ol' Roy had even imported his greasy-haired, yellow-toothed Tex-Mex cook, a grisly faced old coot who reeked of mesquite smoke and chewing tobacco and tequila. After ripping out a seventeenth-century work-of-art fountain in the residence's backyard, ol' Roy, ever the ugly American, constructed a gigantic barbeque in its place, all in the hopes that his idol, the president, would spend a weekend feasting on ribs and ice-cold longnecks of LoneStar beer.

It never happened.

But rumor had it that after returning home from a weekend junket in Venice, the ambassador stormed into the residence unannounced and made straight for his oversized marble tub in the master bathroom, intent on taking a good soak. The tub, however, was ringed with a thick sludge of grime. Red-faced and cursing a blue streak, ol' Roy stormed through the manse, looking for Skip or the maid or anyone to tear a new butt hole. As he neared the end of the hallway, he heard violent screams coming from his daughter's room. Without stopping, thinking she was being violated by terrorists, the ambassador kicked in the bedroom door. There on the floor, buck naked and sprawled on all fours, was his daughter, and behind her, wearing a pair of the ambassador's eel-skin cowboy boots complete with spurs and a ten-gallon Stetson and nothing else—was Skip, bronco busting ol' Roy's little filly. Rossi heard that Skip's next post was Ghana, West Africa, where ambassadors' daughters were scarce and AIDS-infected tree monkeys were plentiful.

Now the low rumble of the dual exhaust changed to a deafening roar as Rossi revved the metallic beast, then exploded as he backed off the gas. He strapped on his shoulder harness, slammed it into gear, popped the clutch, and punched it. The Mustang surged, its radials barking and smoking as he pulled from the curb.

As he slalomed through manic Roma traffic, he tapped the speed dial for Uncle Giovanni at the Vatican Museum.

"*Pronto?*"

"Zio, it's Nico. I'm on the way over," Rossi said.

"More mysteries that need solving, I take it? Wasn't the information on *Bast* correct?"

"Of course it was. But maybe I shouldn't have—"

"Underestimated her powers, eh?"

He clicked off just as he wheeled into the parking garage of the *Ombra* Unit. He took the elevator to the forensics lab, better known as the "Batcave," and gave Claudio the clothing and postcard.

Every inch of the walls were decorated in comic book posters and movie onesheets, Claudio's passion.

"You've got thirty-five minutes to process the card for latent prints and tell me everything about it, *capisce*?"

Claudio shot him a sober look. "Have no fear … Dick Grayson, boy wonder, is on the job, boss."

Rossi rolled his eyes and retreated to his office. He logged onto the computer and into the Bureau's Violent Criminal Apprehension Program and ran Gina as a possible alias. Dozens of hits filled the screen, but nothing in VICAP seemed like even a near match. Then he clicked over to another database compiled by the Carabinieri that listed names and address of aliens who'd entered the country and punched in Gina's data. Sometimes by cross-referencing the identifiers a pattern would emerge. Frequently, arriving passengers used the same addresses and phony names. Then by fishing deeper, an investigator could find corresponding ID, credit cards, purchases, utility bills and a wealth of data. Free enterprise had created colossal private sector clearing houses that tracked health records, even what you eat or read. As the CEO of Sun Microsystems once said, "You have zero privacy anyway." Then he added cynically, "Get over it."

The European Union had adopted a general opt-in rule aimed at damming the flow of information. It was known as the European Data Directive, but the SISDe had standing accounts with American data mining firms. Since 9/11 it had become imperative to prevent further acts of terrorism at all costs. The Saudi hijackers had applied for multiple driver's licenses and purchased airline tickets listing the same Florida residence. Rossi knew that the real problem for the States was the sheer volume of people entering the country each day. By comparison, Italy's total yearly visitors were a drop in the bucket; but the close proximity of northern European countries made travel, once admitted to one of the E.U. member nations, a breeze.

European intelligence agencies were using a system modeled after Homeland Security's "incident data mart," which combs through incident logs for patterns of events. An incident was any event involving law enforcement or a government agency for which a log or record was created, such as a traffic ticket, drug arrest, or illegal possession of firearms. The system looks at crimes in a particular geographic location, particular types of arrest, or any type of unusual activity.

A knock at the door.

"*Avanti*."

"Here's the postcard," Claudio said, laying it on his desk. "I lifted a few clean prints and I'm running them now. The new 'sniffer' picked up something."

Rossi's eyes widened. Similar to the devices used at airports, the sniffer picked up trace elements of chemicals used in IEDs, improvised explosive devices.

Claudio laid the sniffer on the desktop. It was the size of a briefcase.

"How does this thing actually work?" Rossi said, marveling at its small size.

Claudio's eyes brightened as he snapped the latches and opened the case. "It's a chemical preconcentrator unit that is fitted onto the front of a hand-carried, battery-powered ion mobility spectrometer or IMS, of course."

"Give me the short tour, please."

Claudio held up a two-inch-square, metal, felt-covered pad. "You swipe your evidence with this or in this particular case, run a camel-hair brush over the surface to dislodge trace elements. Then I use a hypodermic syringe to punch small disks of paper and ink out of the postcard and place it into this gizmo, the preconcentrator, like so. See, it's about the size of a pocket calculator." He punched a switch. "Then it heats up the swipe and draws the heavy compounds that are vaporized from the felt into the IMS for detection."

"Sensitive as the bigger models?" Rossi said, eyeing the instrument.

"She's capable of detecting less than a nanogram of explosives residue on the swipe."

Rossi's brows scrunched. "And that's how much?"

"For comparison, the fingerprint of a person who'd handled a bomb or a suitcase filled with explosives would likely contain a hundred thousand times as much residue."

The phone chimed and Rossi picked up. "It's for you," he said, passing the phone to Claudio.

Absently fingering his acne-cratered cheeks, Claudio stood nodding.

He cradled the receiver. "That was the CCSIS lab. I copied them with the spectrometer reading just to make sure. They ran it against their database. And I was right."

"Enough with the dramatics."

Claudio pitched a small stack of papers into Rossi's lap. "These are digital images of the traces."

Rossi leafed through the photos.

"The one in your hand is Goma-Two, same explosive used in the hundred-and-twenty-kilogram backpack bombs in Madrid, Spain. They used cell phone detonators, remember?"

Rossi's stomach lurched.

"Goma-Two Eco is a type of high-explosive manufactured for industrial use, chiefly mining, according to Union Española de Explosivos S.A. It is a gelatinous, nitroglycerin-based explosive widely used within Spain and exported abroad.

"It was used by the Basque terrorist group ETA to mount attacks in the early 80's. After security was tightened in Spain, ETA switched to obtaining explosives from the French, stealing large quantities of Titadine and using it in numerous car bombings. MI5 reports that it was also used in the London Underground bombings."

Regarding him with a cold steady gaze, Rossi lit a cigarette.

"And there's more," Claudio continued. "Interpol confirms that Goma-Two was used both at the Dome of the Rock bombing—and at the Holocaust Memorial in Jerusalem."

Rossi dropped his cigarette, bent to pick it up and said, "But that would mean a same-source provider, a connection. But the *Bat Ayin*, the fundamentalist Jewish extremists, whose settlement in Hebron causes so much grief for the Israeli security service, claimed credit for the attack on the Dome."

"They're the ones who detonated the bomb near the Palestinian girls' school and got twenty years for it?"

Rossi nodded, still deep in thought. Then he said, "But I just saw an Interpol bulletin. *Bat Ayin* stole their explosives and arms from the Israeli Army. So how could they use the same explosives as Abbas in Jerusalem and al-Qaeda at King's Cross station in London?"

Claudio shrugged. "You're the crime-fighter, boss. I just report the results."

Rossi nodded. "Anything else?"

"Some sort of organic compound we haven't been able to identify yet and traces of … candle wax and kerosene."

"Good work."

Shaking his head and coughing, Claudio said, "I'll let you know once I …" Then he went weak in the knees and grabbed the desk for support.

Rossi shot to his feet to steady him. "I've been working you too hard. You had any sleep?"

"About forty-eight hours ago."

"Get some rest. I'll check on you later," Rossi told him as he tucked the postcard into his pocket and left.

* * *

Someone rapped softly at the door of *Le Café du Chat Noir's* upstairs apartment. "Coming, my pet," Claude said. He scurried for the door, paused at an antique mirror to finger-comb his thinning, bleached blond locks and examined his reflection in profile, sucking in his stomach. Excitedly, a lecherous smile curling his lips, Claude opened the door.

When Claude saw the young, good-looking Middle Eastern man, he said, "Aren't you a delicious surprise." Then his gaze traveled down the man's torso. That's when he noticed the pistol gripped tightly at the stranger's side. He noticed the wild-eyed look on his sweat-drenched face. He noticed the way tremors shot through the man's hands and body. The man's tremulous gun hand rose slowly.

The thick muzzle of a sound suppressor was now aimed point-black at Claude's face. To Claude's shock and surprise, the young man closed his eyes as if in silent prayer. The weapon coughed once and gouged a third eye into the center of Claude's forehead. The young man stopped quaking and opened his eyes. But when he realized he'd killed the wrong man, realized this wasn't Rossi, he suddenly doubled over and dry heaved in spasms. Which meant Rossi would still hunt *Bast*. Then he spun, slipped down the hallway, and out the window onto the fire escape.

CHAPTER 31

Wheels within wheels

BACK AT HIS office, in a barricaded diplomatic compound tucked safely away at the end of a cul-de-sac known as the Via Michle Mercati, the Kasta was seated at his desk, deep in thought. *The Black Rose Notebook* lay before him, beckoning. Josie's words "Whatever you do, don't open the book." grated like sandpaper. *Such arrogance*, he thought. *Does she think I'm a gullible old fool? Superstitious nonsense. What's she trying to hide?*

He knew that a grimoire called the *Steganographia*, a book of Black Magick, had actually only been the plain text message used by the father of Code Making, Johannes Trithemius, to distract and confuse. His mind wandered back to his lecture on code making at the academy. He could still picture Professor Leiberman standing before the class.

"An interesting work, my students," Leiberman said. "The book was in three volumes, and appears to be about Black Magick— specifically, about using spirits to communicate over long distances."

A wave of tittering voices.

"Yes, your laughing at the implausibility of that concept is just what Trithemius counted on."

You could have heard a pin drop.

"But since the publication of the decryption key to the first two volumes in 1606, they have been known to be actually concerned with cryptography and steganography, the art of concealing a hidden message within plain text."

"I thought stenography was something a secretary did?" a young student said.

Leiberman laughed and shook his head. "Similar root words but spelled differently. Check the spelling in your handout."

Leiberman cleared his throat. "Now if I may continue. Until recently, the third volume was widely still believed to be about magick—but recently the 'magickal' formulae were shown to be covertexts for yet more cryptography content. The work has lent its name to the modern field of steganography."

A student raised his hand.

"Yes," Leiberman said. "Ask your question."

"Then you're saying that by using an accompanying key, the early inventors of secret writing could decipher the hidden message concealed within the spell book, and learn how to write and hide codes—*within* the incantations themselves?"

Leiberman nodded, his eyes twinkling. "Exactly! But there's an even more devious aspect to it all. Trithemius was a Benedictine Monk. One of his prize pupils was the infamous Cornelius Agrippa, whose writing on the occult combined with his strong support of the divine feminine and women's rights..."

"You mean he actually advocated women's liberation?" a female student asked.

"Yes, indeed. He studied the Gnostic and Hermetic texts, which still honored and respected women as active participants in the church. He even advocated that they be ordained."

"Wow, that must have totally ticked off the Holy See," the girl said.

"That, my girl, is an understatement. His writings and the *Steganographia* were banned and locked away in the Vatican's Secret Archives. Which meant of course that only the clergy could read them. And read them, they did!"

***

The Kasta leaned back now and massaged his temples.

Remembering Professor Lieberman's words, the Kasta concluded that this curse mumbo jumbo was nothing but disinformation, a clever ruse to keep away prying eyes. But more importantly, in his world of secrets, knowledge was power. If you allowed someone in Mossad to keep you in the dark, they immediately gained the upper hand. Besides, Rome was his turf. He had a right to digest any intelligence that came into or out of Italy. If this book was the key to some important cipher, he damned well better read it.

The door opened and Holly, his secretary, entered.

Startled, he managed, "Can't you learn to knock first?"

She lowered her head. "Sorry, sir. But you insisted that I notify you when the diplomatic courier arrived."

She was newly posted. Young. He studied her, squinting through the lenses of the reading glasses perched on the end of his hawkish nose. When she rocked back and forth nervously, her large breasts swayed alluringly. The points of her nipples strained against the schoolgirl, button-down white blouse, tucked severely into a short khaki skirt. He figured the stacked heels of her boots were to overcompensate for her short stature, her youthful lack of self-esteem.

He covered his mouth with his hand in an awkward, involuntary motion. "Tell him to wait."

She shrugged and slipped back out the door.

He stiffened and sighed, remembering that Mossad had adopted regulations against sexual harassment. What a pity, he thought. His gaze drifted back to the book.

Reaching for the book, he hesitated, then quickly pulled back his hand. He shook his head, admonishing himself under his breath, and snatched the book from the desktop. Its velvet cover was soft to the touch. Slowly he ran his fingertips across the intricate recesses of its designs, curled his fingertips beneath the edge of the cover and unfastened the ornate silver hasp. When he splayed it open, a sharp pain pricked the pad of his finger. Absently, he sucked the blood from the tiny wound. His fingers felt soiled as though an odd, gelatinous substance had coated them.

The moment he opened it a chill walked through his bones. He glanced at one page, then another. But within moments he began flipping the pages manically, his eyes widening as he scanned the symbols, his heart pounding faster as his mind struggled to translate a bit of French here, a word or two of Latin there.

TOUTE L'OMS A LU CES DERNIERS

MOTS, RENONCEZ AU LEUR

ÂME.

Je crée le prince puissant et efficace de thou du thee O

Lucifurge Rofocale, qui marchent ici et là dans l'Ayre ; avec les ducs thy et d'autres   spiritueux thy d'domestique (d'autre thy)

As he read on, deeply disturbing, dark and strange thoughts flooded his mind. Savage urges pulsed in his blood. Bright bolts of pain flashed behind his eyes, along the length of his spine. His vision blurred, waves of nausea washed over him. He tried to scream, but what he heard was the choked and broken sobs of a child terrified to the brink of insanity.

Someone, please! Help me ...

Dizzy and faint, like a small boy trapped on a whirling merry-go-round, the fun-house darkness began to bleed at the edges of his vision. Then he felt himself sink into the timeless dark.

When he came to, the pain was gone. His thinking crystal clear. He reached for the intercom.

"Holly," he heard himself say.

"Yes, sir."

"Come here, I *need* you."

CHAPTER 32

Zach Talman, diplomatic courier, paced nervously outside the Kasta's office.

Each time Talman passed the secretary's desk, he stole a quick peek. Her enormous, autumnal eyes slid away quickly whenever they happened to meet his. He liked the way her hair was swept back and fastened with barrettes, revealing small, close-set ears. He liked the fact that she wore no makeup, the way she played with her hair each time she caught him looking.

He'd known her mother and father and little brother before they'd been blown to pieces by a suicide bomber as they rode to synagogue on the bus. He knew that she'd been sick and stayed home with her grandmother that day. He knew that since the first time he'd seen her walking to school in his old neighborhood, all others would be found wanting. When the Institute gave her a job, he was delighted. But just as soon as she'd graduated from training last month, they'd packed her off to Rome. He quickly asked for a transfer to the courier section. This was his first trip to Rome and the first time he had seen her in months.

Summing up his nerve, he said, "Next time I pass through, Holly—"

"We'll have dinner, catch up," Holly said, smiling demurely.

Just as he was about to answer, the intercom barked and she stood quickly, smoothed her skirt, took a deep breath, and disappeared into the office.

He sat thinking for a few minutes, planning his response. *When she comes out, I'll…*

Holly's panicked scream severed his thoughts.

Reflexively, he bolted to his feet and made for the door.

The door was locked.

He pounded. "Holly! Open the door."

Another scream.

He shouldered it hard. When the door swung open, he spilled into the room.

There on the floor, her blouse shredded, her neck turned at an unnatural angle, her unblinking eyes staring upward, pleading—lay Holly. And standing over her limp body was the Kasta. His right hand clutched a long knife, its blade wet with blood. Between ragged breaths he kept muttering, "Blood … sacrifice her… sacrifice her … we thirst."

The Kasta's head rose. He sneered, facial muscles twitching, eyes glassy. "We thirst," he whispered. Without warning he lunged. The knife flashed. Talman twisted sharply and threw his left arm out to block the thrust. It worked, but the blade sliced through his shirt and slashed his forearm, leaving a deep gash. He let the Kasta's own weight propel him forward. Then Talman spun with him in his grasp and slammed him hard against the wall. The Kasta lashed out wildly. The long blade sizzled past his face, cutting the air audibly and just missed his head and shoulder. If Talman hadn't pulled back, it would have decapitated him.

A wild, guttural sound bubbled from the Kasta's throat. He charged ... knocking Talman off his feet. The Kasta stood over him, and swung the blade again. It whistled through the air toward Talman's neck. Talman rolled hard to the right, and the blade bit into the floor. While the Kasta fought to free the wedged blade, Talman rolled again and kicked out savagely at his attacker's knee. With the snap of bone, the Kasta fell to the floor near him, howling in pain.

Twisting a kink out of his neck and groaning, the Kasta slowly rose to his feet. He stood with his splintered leg stretched out stiff to one side, staggering only slightly.

"The bitch was asking for it," the Kasta hissed. "We'll send you to her, boy."

Talman stood steely-eyed, gasping for air.

But his hand flew to his ankle and he quickly palmed a butterfly knife. With a sharp twist of the wrist, the blade flickered open.

Talman didn't say a word. The fingers of his upturned hand silently beckoned for the Kasta to make his move.

Wild-eyed, lips skinned back, and screaming like a banshee—the Kasta charged.

Talman sidestepped at the last second and spun. The Kasta plowed headlong into a metal file cabinet. In a second, Talman was on him. Rough hands grabbed the Kasta's hair, wrenched his head backward.

Talman leaned in and whispered into his ear, "This is for Holly!" as he drew the razor-edged knife across the Kasta's exposed throat.

As the Kasta sank to the floor, Talman moved to Holly's side. He kneeled and gently closed her eyes. Clasping her hand in his, he bowed his head in prayer and cried.

***

As if by magic, the pages of *The Black Rose Notebook* were leafed by unseen hands and lay open at the woodcut of ...

... the Pope in miter and vestments, arms folded, his face an ugly caricature, distorted in the rictus of pain, lying in state beneath the wings of a fiery dragon, and on the facing page—the Templar banner.

CHAPTER 33

O'Hare Airport, Chicago, IL

AS THE PLANE taxied to a halt, Josie changed into a pair of faded jeans, a black turtleneck sweater, and an army-surplus field jacket. The grunge look. With a pair of thick socks and Doc Martin boots, her persona was complete. Just another college coed. With one important exception—a Beretta semi-auto was concealed in the fanny-pack holster cinched tightly around her waist.

The plane's door opened as she finished dressing and the El Al agent boarded, greeting her with a warm smile. Actually, he was the local *Al agent*, Benjamin Levine, whose cover was station manager. He was tall and lean with wavy black hair and deep-set, dark brown eyes. They exchanged brief formalities as he handed Josie an envelope containing a clean passport and the key to her hotel room. "Shalom, Ms. Schulman. Or perhaps I should address you by your new name, Anna Spelman?"

Josie smiled and accepted the envelope. "Good to see you again, Benjamin. How's the family?"

"Just fine. The girls are adjusting well and my wife has become a regular suburban soccer mom."

"Good," Josie said. "Any news from Abraham?"

"Yes, he sends his condolences regarding Monsignor Scarlotti's disappearance and wishes you God's speed."

Josie's cheeks flamed. "Disappearance? I was told he suffered a heart attack and was hospitalized."

"Apparently, he never made it to the hospital."

"Any intel on who might have snatched him?"

Benjamin sucked a deep breath inflating his cheeks and breathed out slowly. "So far, no one has taken credit."

Josie bowed her head a moment, looked down at her hands. Benjamin allowed her the moment of reflection and continued. "Down to business, shall we? Your car is waiting on the tarmac. It's a nondescript black Buick with secret plates. The driver's name is Uri. He will be your associate for this assignment. If you need to reach me, use the secure line and the letter drops." Josie nodded her acknowledgment. "Your father is aware of your arrival and will be awaiting you."

A glint of joy shone in Josie's eyes. "Thank you for . . . your kindness and professionalism—"

"One more thing," he added. "Your *friend*, the Kasta, finally cracked. Butchered his secretary. He's dead. Weird thing, though. I never woulda figured him for a drug user."

"How's that?" she said.

"Autopsy showed traces of hallucinogens in his blood and some other psychotropic drugs that they're still tying to identify."

Josie stared in silence for a long beat. Then muttered to herself, "The fool couldn't resist opening the book."

"What's that?"

"Nothing. What about the book?"

He sighed. "Not to worry. It's been delivered by diplomatic courier as planned."

Josie nodded.

"Josie," he said, his eyes dead serious. "I've got a bad feeling about this whole thing."

"Me, too."

"Watch your back," he said, and turned to leave.

Before she could answer the officials entered. Customs, INS, and Agriculture were accustomed to inspecting private aircraft. The perfunctory inspection was completed. The CBP/Homeland Security inspector, pasty-skinned and toothpick-thin with staples hemming his black pants, stamped her passport and I-94. It read: F-1 student visa.

CHAPTER 34

Chicago

SEATED IN THE car, Josie stared out the window as they wound their way through the city, down I-90 east, and onto Lake Shore Drive South. Although it was bitter cold for October and it was beginning to sleet, it was nothing compared to her last journey through the salt-limned streets of the windy city. There had been mounds of dirty slush piled high along the highway, cloaked in a shawl of freshly fallen snow. Five inches and the sheeting snow had continued to pelt the city. Uri's voice startled her, drawing her out of reverie. He briefed her as they drove. He was young, about twenty-six years old, with a jovial disposition. His features were handsome, but sharp. His brown eyes, alert and cautious. As the car curved past the Museum of Science and Industry, Josie again peered out the car window. Her breath fogged the cold glass, trembling against it. Thinking of her father, she sighed and paused for a moment, then drew a heart-shaped figure on the frost-edged glass with her finger.

Their car pulled to the curb and Josie walked east from 58th Street, and into the quads. The University of Chicago's campus was huge, several square blocks. Her father's office was housed in the Divinity School, Swift Hall, a handsome, Gothic, limestone building with huge archways and porticoes, even castlelike turrets. The ice-glazed vines of ivy crawled like skeletal fingers across the old brick and colonnaded limestone.

As she stood in the autumnal silence, again her thoughts drifted back in time. She'd been standing in this very spot, filled with a girlish glee at the winter wonderland scene that had lain before her. A blanket of snow had swaddled the barren shrubbery and dusted the rooftops. Angels could have folded their wings, coming to rest on such rooftops, she told herself. In her mind's eye, the snowfall was heavier now, relentless. It almost concealed the city's grimy face and soiled undergarments in a virgin white wedding gown. In a wedding gown, her thoughts repeated the phrase, taunting her. She was suddenly transported to a vast empty church, wilted lilies decorated the pews; the mocking cacophony of a carnival calliope instead of a solemn, pleasing pipe organ grated the air. Up ahead, standing alone at the altar, stood a bride, stoop-shouldered with long, thin wisps of graying hair visible beneath her veil. The bride turned slowly and when she did, Josie found herself staring into her own craggy, age-weathered face, the eyes red-rimmed, filled with confusion. Then the nightmarish vision dissolved, her imagination snow-blinded in an ever-thickening swirl of ivory haze.

Shaking her head, snapping to, Josie murmured, "Bullshit!"

Pulling the lapels of her coat tightly around her neck, Josie followed a flagstone path across the quad, past freeze-dried flowerbeds, where bare earth lay like a fresh grave.

In Swift Hall now, outside the door of her father's office, Josie's hand reached for the doorknob. She hesitated.

The sound of muffled music and grainy, slightly quivering voices filled her ears. Although she hadn't heard her father's voice for years, nor the song, she recognized both immediately. The song was *"Bei Mir Bist du Schoen,* Means That You're Grand," by the Andrews Sisters: her father's favorite. She entered. Her father stood behind his desk, singing and directing with a ruler as his baton. Outside, the wind, with its invisible baton, conducted a chorus of haunting voices. She swallowed audibly as she took in the sight of him. Max Schulman was a typical professor with a dark bristle of eyebrows and a dark mustache thinning to a gray-speckled beard. Curly, white hair laurelled his balding head. And marble-black eyes peeked out from his dark-framed eyeglasses. His face radiated with the inner glow of the peace that dwelt within. Max paused as if sensing her presence. His smile warmed the room and her heart. She ran to him. They held one another for a minute, which seemed at the same time, far too long and far too fleeting.

Max held Josie at arm's length, studying her. *"Gott,* how you've grown, Josephine!" She blushed and shrugged, soaking in a father's love, a father's attention. Max shook his head. His eyes glistening, he continued: "If only Muta could see you, daughter. She would be so proud." Then a look of confusion washed over his face. "But these clothes . . . don't they pay you a decent wage, girl?"

Josie laughed and explained. "Low profile, Tateh. My cover is a foreign student. Didn't they tell you?"

Max Schulman turned, removed the needle from the record, and motioned for Josie to take a seat. Every inch of each wall was covered in overflowing bookcases. His desk was littered with papers. And on his desk, seated as if on her throne, sat a large, overfed, black Angora cat—Lilith. Purring softly. Somnolent. Indifferent.

"Ah, yes, the clandestine machinations of your profession. It's no matter; you look none the worse for wear on the outside. But tell me, Josephine. Are you happy?" As he said it, Josie's gaze slid away. "Just as I thought. I can see into your heart, *mayan tokhter.*" He moved around the desk, pulled up a chair at her side. He took her hand in his and held it tight. Tears welled up in her eyes and she broke down in deep sobs, finally throwing her arms around him. He held her close and stroked her hair, pressed his cheek to hers.

Her pain, her fear and loneliness, bled into his arms. Regaining her composure, she slowly began to speak: "I'm sorry, Tateh . . . so sorry. I'm too old for this!" She stiffened, the hatred returning. "Those bastards . . . they took Zio Lotti!" She swallowed hard. "I just needed you, needed you so badly that—"

Max interrupted her, and reaching out to grasp her chin, he held her eyes. "Never apologize for being a human being, foolish girl. I know that you think ice water runs in your veins. And maybe, by now, it does. But sometimes you need to let it melt a little, no?"

The cat jumped from the desktop onto the floor. It eeled about her, rubbed against her legs and then curled its tail languidly around her calf.

The blood returned to Josie's cheeks. A faint smile broke through her storm-clouded face. "Of course, you're right. Can we have dinner tonight?"

Max's eyebrows rose like question marks. "Well, yes, if you can fit me into your schedule that is?"

She laughed.

His expression changed and his voice carried a serious inflection. "Josephine, there are matters we need to discuss, personal matters that I have too long put off bringing to your attention. Your mother and I had planned to tell you when you became old enough to understand. But her early passing—"

"It's a little late to explain the birds and the bees, Tateh."

He smiled warmly. "Indeed … no this concerns…"—he paused, turned to the window as if the words he were searching for could be found the dark clouds overhead, and then met her gaze—"concerns something about your past."

Leaning forward, she spoke in a conspiratorial whisper, "You mean how I was an orphan left on your doorstep by wandering gypsies?"

Max regarded her for a long beat. "Let's save this discussion for dinner. It will keep a little longer. I imagine you wish to speak of more pressing issues?"

A tumbler clicked in Josie's brain. Back to business. She rose and paced about the office and halted. Turning to her father, she asked, "Did you receive the book from Benjamin?"

Outside, a gust of wind soughed through the eaves of the building. A singular note played through an ice-carved flute.

"Why, yes. A remarkable book it is. As remarkably vile as it is complex and mysterious. Benjamin told me of Monsignor Lotti's disappearance and of your Kasta's insanity and bloody deeds. "

Josie nodded solemnly.

Speaking as Professor Schulman now, he continued, "I've made the study of man's religions and beliefs my life's work. As the man once said, 'I do not know as much as God, but I know as much as God did at my age.' Some books demonstrate man's finest hour, man's noblest achievement. But others . . . demonstrate his darkest hour, his basest instincts."

"And this book?"

"You already have seen the results of its evil. It can literally kill."

A puzzled looked filled Josie's face.

"The book is booby trapped. Anyone who is not versed in the ancient glyphs that decorate its cover, will open it haphazardly and fall victim to a deadly toxin. The symbols tell the adept how to open the book safely."

"So the Kasta wasn't mad?"

"In the end, yes. But he was driven to madness by the psychoactive toxins emitted by the book."

"But how—"

"The specifics are of no importance for now. What I have discovered is, however, of the gravest consequences. Have you heard of the Atbash cipher?"

"Isn't it some sort of ancient Kabbalistic substitution cipher? I think we studied it at the academy in code breaking."

Her father's eyes sparked. "Precisely, let me show you." He fumbled on his desk for a book and then thumbed to a section. "Look here," he said, pointing.

כ י ט ח ז ו ה ד ג ב א
ל מ נ ס ע פ צ ק ר שׁ ת

"Here we have the Hebrew Atbash cipher." His hand slid down the page. "This is how it would look in English."

A|B|C|D| E| F|G|H|I| J| K|L|M
Z|Y|X|W|V|U|T| S|R|Q|P|O|N

"It was only recently discovered by the Dead Sea Scrolls scholar, Dr. Schonfield. You simply substitute the last letter of the alphabet for the first and so on down the line. Of course in Hebrew we read right to left. By carefully examining certain passages from *Le Cahier de la Rose Noire*, I was able to discover a new version of the Atbash cipher that incorporated Gematria."

"Isn't that like Numerology?"

"Not exactly. First the Jewish mystics assigned a number value to each Hebrew letter. Next they would add the values to get a sum."

"So they converted words and names to numbers?"

"Yes, and then they would look for words that had the same numerical values. For example, if we assign values to English letters A=1,B=2,C=3 and so on … then the value of GOD would be 7 plus 15 plus 4…which equals 26."

Josie took a seat, listening intently.

"It appears that within the mumbo jumbo of incantations and the like, *Le Cahier* holds the key to this modified Atbash cipher. The notebook is written primarily in French and Latin, with a few passages in ole' English, roughly that used in the twelve to thirteen hundreds. The notebook's use of the ancient Hebrew cipher, however, makes perfect sense. I have confirmed that the *Le Cahier* contains the oldest, original translation of the *Clavicula Salomonis, The Greater Key of Solomon the King"*

"Another code book?"

"In a way… you could call it Solomon's Code. It's the spell book written and used by none other than King Solomon himself."

"Must be pretty valuable?"

"Priceless for some collectors. But it gets even more interesting. The notebook refers to passages from Gnostic gospels, even the recently translated Gospel of Judas that was thought to have been lost to eternity." His face slackened and he plunked into his chair. He sat in silence, then looked up weary-eyed.

Josie looked puzzled, tilted her head.

He explained. "The notebook alludes to incontrovertible proof that the Gnostic gospels are the true gospels. It alludes to the Gospel of Jesus written in Christ's own hand: a revelation of staggering proportions to the Christian community."

Josie said softly, "You've been working too hard."

Their eyes locked. "It speaks of proof that Adoni, the God of my Jewish faith, is no more than a lesser god, a fallen angel if you will. The fallen angel who once held En Sof, the Father Almighty's trust and highest admiration."

"But that would be Lucifer—"

For a moment the mere thought strangled their voices into separate silences.

Max broke the silence. "You don't have to believe in or understand thermonuclear energy to be vaporized by a ten-megaton warhead do you? If this missing Gospel of Jesus purports the same heresy and is authenticated, then the world as we know it—"

"But you can't believe—?"

134

"Believe?" Her father stepped on her words, his eyes glaring at her, and then, looking inward, he went on: "Most certainly. Just as I believe in the ancient studies of our faith, *Tokhter*! The *Kabbalah*!" He bowed his head; his fingers ran across a volume of the *Zohar* lying on his desk.

The word flooded her mind with memories. Josie recalled now with crystal clarity occasions in her childhood when she'd been awakened in the middle of the night by cries from her parent's bedroom. Mother would come to reassure her that it was nothing; her father had had another one of his night terrors. Josie would toss and turn and eventually fall off to sleep. But even now she could hear her father's voice, as it had risen in a keening wail of terror, the babbling of a man trapped and tortured by things he could not name. *Dybbuks*. Ghost-Demons of the night.

"Yes, Tateh." Josie saw this was getting nowhere. Her father had perhaps spent too many hours alone with his thoughts, alone with arcane knowledge. "Do you have the book in a safe place, then?"

He patted his jacket pocket and said, "Right here. I've never let it out of my sight. If this notebook should fall into the wrong hands and be used to decipher those gospels…"

"So how do I fight them, Tateh?"

"Their weakness is their pride, their vanity. If you insist upon flushing them out, I suggest that I place a notice in the academic journal announcing a talk on the book as part of our lecture series. You sit back and wait."

"Said the spider to the fly?"

"Yes, but make sure you don't become the fly!"

"Do you have any thoughts as to who is the leader—?"

Then the door opened. A tall man dressed in the traditional garb of the Lubavitcher movement of Hasidic Jews—black clothing, white shirt, dread locks, and a full beard—entered. His face was all hard planes—a prominent jaw line, a large angular nose, and glass-sharp cheekbones. But his eyes were warm, even kind, and his mouth full and generous. She noted the powerful shoulders and arms. Large hands. But when he moved it was with a timid grace, as though he feared he would frighten strangers. His voice had a serious, but mellifluous tone. "O-hh, excuse me, professor, but someone is here to see you."

Lilith hissed and shot back behind the desk.

The professor looked bewildered. "To see me?" he asked, checking his appointment calendar. "Yes, there it is. I'd forgotten. Professor Nemo Bugenhagen of Vienna." He busied himself sorting through pile of documents of his desktop. "Ah, yes here it is." He held up a folder labeled USING GEMATRIA TO DECODE THE ENGRAVINGS OF ALBRECHT DURER.

Josie nodded toward the tall man.

"Oh, yes. Allow me to present Rabbe Jacob Yomach Myers, my associate. Rabbe, my daughter, Josephine." Josie knew that the term of address "Rabbe" denoted that he was a distinguished, deeply respected, and scholarly theologian, not your common garden variety of rabbi. Josie stood and proffered her hand. But she noticed that even though the Rabbi smiled with his lips, his eyes were far away.

Max stood and moved toward the door. "Excuse me, won't you? I shouldn't be long. You could wait in Rabbe Myers's office, downstairs."

She nodded.

To Rabbe Myers, he said, "I found some of this Nemo fellow's notions a bit far-fetched, but his scholarship is impeccable. I could, however, only decode half the messages in Durer's engravings. That's why I asked you to send copies of everything to my old friend *Professore* Giovanni in Rome."

Rabbe Myers said, "They were sent express delivery yesterday."

"This Nemo fellow believes that Durer's three engravings are somehow linked, and that when deciphered, convey an overall message...."

As she made for the door, a diminutive man brushed past her, wearing a thin smile and carrying a walking stick. He was stooped over, had long, disheveled white hair, and dragged his left leg as he moved. He appeared ancient, fragile as tissue paper. In a thick German accent he said, "Excuse me, Fraulein."

For a moment, their eyes locked. His watery eyes twinkled. She paused a beat and left.

CHAPTER 35

The Vatican

BECAUSE OF HIS position, Rossi was able to enter via the *Vle Vaticano* gate closest to the *Musei Vaticani*. The carabinieri and Swiss Guard checked his credentials and waved him through.

Uncle Giovanni had an assistant meet Rossi at the entrance and escort him to his private office. As usual the museum was teeming with tourists, necks craned, making their way up Gluseppe Momo's giant spiral entrance staircase.

Giovanni's deep-set, watery eyes looked on in sympathy as his nephew related the events of the past few days. The seduction, how he'd been played the fool, and *Bast's* mysterious escape from the Pantheon.

Giovanni leaned closer, resting the elbows of his well-worn tweed jacket on the desk blotter. Cupping his pipe in an arthritic and palsied hand, Giovanni brought it to his lips, struck a match and lit it. A cloud of smoke floated between them like a shroud.

Hands folded in his lap as he sat across the desk, Rossi quietly waited for his uncle's response.

"*Cosa fatta capo ha*, what's done is done. Better men than you or I have made far greater errors, Nico. The measure of a man is how he reacts, if he can learn from his mistakes." Giovanni paused a beat and went on. "Your work requires that you deal in duplicity, wearing many masks. But always be true to yourself. Remain centered."

Rossi gave a heavy sigh and nodded.

Professor Giovanni smiled reassuringly. "As you probably know, we've had our own tragedy here within the walls of the Vatican. Colonnello Pico was found viciously murdered in the Secret Archives, and that very afternoon, Monsignore Scarlotti, the biblotica's assistant curator … went missing."

"We heard," Rossi said. "And RSO Cotter from the American Embassy died in freak car crash, taking the lives of two young carabinieri. Any connection?"

"I wish that I wasn't so compelled to think so. Call it the paranoid musings of an old fool, but my instincts tell me the dark tides of a dangerous and diabolical conspiracy lie beneath the surface of this wave of death, drawing the innocent and the guilty without prejudice into its invisible grasp.

"Commander Stato of the Swiss Guard has done little to ease my suspicions. He came to my office just yesterday to inquire about a rare book, *Le Cahier de la Rose Noire*."

"Never heard of it, but why would he show sudden interest in a book and come to you instead of the head curator of the library?"

"You don't understand the 'office politics' of the Vatican. Stato's father was a close friend, and I've known Stato since he was a boy. Perhaps he had his reasons for not consulting anyone within the biblotica itself. And then there's my expertise on the—"

"Your peculiar hobby … your obsession with American superheroes?" Rossi's eyes panned to the piles and piles of collector edition comic books and pulp novels and tapes of old radio programs stacked neatly on shelves in the corner of the office. As a boy he'd spent many happy hours listening to the tales of The Phantom, The Shadow, and Doc Savage in his uncle's study.

Giovanni frowned. "No my other hobby. The occult and secret societies."

"I'm facing a real enemy, not some lunatic-fringe cult of hooded black magicians and mad scientists. An enemy that deals in real-life blood and terror and suffering: al-Qaeda."

Giovanni met his gaze. "And they do it in the name of Allah. Call it a jihad, a holy war, offer blood sacrifices of the innocent with their bombs, even offer their own lives to a religious cause, the purging of the world of infidels and making way for the—"

"New world order?" Rossi cut in, rolling his eyes.

"Scoff all you like. My years in the study of linguistics and Egyptology and its rituals have led me down some strange pathways, indeed. You're too young to remember Mussolini, *Il Duce*, too young to remember the early beginnings of fascism in Germany, how it was nursed and made to bloom in the dark soil of racial bigotry and hate disguised as the science of eugenics by the likes of Lynton and H. P. Blavatsky's Theosophy. And even here within these hallowed walls, the quest for control and power and secret knowledge has turned many good clerics to the dark forces that pulse deep within the human heart and mind."

"Absolute power corrupts absolutely or something like that?" Rossi offered.

"Haven't you had a taste of that in your own life, my nephew? Wasn't the story of your attempting to use this woman just such an example of how easily we can become entrapped? Justify our baser instincts by saying it's all for the greater good?"

Rossi stared blankly for a moment and finally spoke. "Point taken. You never mince words, do you? Even if it draws blood."

"You came here seeking an old man's wisdom. A dangerous thing to do unless you want to hear the truth. Old men neither have time for nor do they enjoy the guilty pleasure of hypocrisy." Giovanni extended his palm. "You said you had something to show me."

Rossi handed him the postcard.

Scowling, his uncle rose, pulled down a slide screen, and moved to an old-fashioned overhead projector. Then he removed the card from the plastic bag and, using a tweezers, placed the postcard facedown in the tray. "The lights, please?"

After killing the lights, Rossi stood at his uncle's side. The whirl of the projector's fan and a blaze of light filled the room. There, projected on the screen, was the blurred image of the card.

Giovanni reached down and twisted a large knob. "Let's bring it into focus. There … much better."

To Rossi it still looked like just so much gibberish.

Humming a Bach concerto, the ambient light dancing off the lenses of his wire-rimmed glasses, Giovanni stared intently.

The minutes ticked by.

Finally, the *professore* raced toward the screen, pulled out a pen and pointed, tracing the symbols and words as he mumbled to himself.

Rossi cleared his throat.

The *professore* spun around, perched his spectacles on his lined forehead, and smiled knowingly. Then his face darkened and he laughed manically, raising a finger. In a deep, resonating voice, he said, "Only the Shadow knows what evil lurks in the hearts of men."

Rossi recognized it as the line from the old radio play. "Zio …?"

"Pardon my exuberance. But it's all beginning to come together. The text of the message is in French but it's just a ruse, a semagram that conceals a message within openly visible writing. In this case, an apparently innocent note scrawled on a postcard from a French-speaking tourist. See this phrase?" He turned and pointed with the pen. "*La Vie en Rose*, a French expression which means 'seeing the world through rose-colored glasses' is our key. Notice anything different about the handwriting here?"

Rossi squinted hard, scanning the text. "The letters tilt to the right as apposed the rest of the text, where the letters are written with a back-handed tilt—"

"Toward the left." Giovanni clapped his wrinkled hands. "Precisely, which sets it off from the rest." Like a boy excitedly following the clues of a treasure map, the *professore* rushed to the projector, donned a latex glove, and snatched the postcard. Next he went to the shelf and pulled out what looked like an old,

139

yellowed, pulp novel. Turning to Rossi, he said, "We'll need a little more sophisticated technology to unravel the rest of the mystery." He made for the door and disappeared into the hall.

As Rossi stood dumbfounded, staring at the doorway, his uncle's voice echoed from the hall. "Come along, Nico. I haven't got all day."

**

Seated before a computer in the museum's artifact lab, Giovanni scanned both sides of the postcard. As Rossi stood at his side, his gaze panned the room. Laymen and clerics alike, dressed in white lab coats, busied themselves unpacking a shipping crate. Others sat hunched over worktables, examining ancient artifacts, handling them with loving care.

Rising and moving to another workstation, Giovanni said, "Now let's use our rose-colored glasses to see the world as it truly is." He placed the postcard beneath the lens of a sophisticated-looking machine and flicked a switch. "It's all a matter of perception you know. In this case the science of light. The world as we perceive it through our five senses is not, modern physics tells us, the real world. When we look at an object it appears right side up, but in reality the lens of our optical nerve, like a telescope, inverts it. It's our brain that uprights the image." From a lunch bag left on the counter, he pulled out an orange and tossed it to Rossi. "What color is it?"

Rossi rolled his eyes. "Orange, of course."

Giovanni shook his head, sucked on his false teeth. "In reality it's blue. The orange light is the spectrum of light bouncing off the fruit. An ancient Zen master once asked his students, 'who is the Master that makes the grass green?' Brimming with self-assurance a young disciple answered, 'God is the Master who colors the world.' The Zen master shook his head vigorously."

"Riddles?" Rossi said, rolling the fruit between his fingers.

"Feels solid to the touch, doesn't it?" the *professore* asked. "But as any schoolboy knows, quantum physics has shown it to be a web of dancing energy. The 'Tree of Knowledge,' our central nervous system with its ganglia of roots emptying into our over-sized mammalian brain, fashions order from chaos, scientific reason from superstition, understanding from mystery. This bio-super computer creates a mystical byproduct we call consciousness. I think, therefore I am. Our neural circuits process the data from our senses into a three-dimensional hologram that we project outside of ourselves and stubbornly label 'reality.'"

A young, mousy, blond-haired tech awkwardly stumbled past, absently powdering her nose as she peered through the thick lenses of her horned-rimmed glasses.

"*Scusi signorina*, may I borrow your compact for a moment?" the *professore* asked. Burying her face in a file, she handed it to him. He held the mirrored lid before Rossi's face.

"You are looking into the face of the god, the face of the Master who makes the grass green."

"Sounds a bit blasphemous, *Zio*. Could've got you strapped to a stake in the Piazza not long ago."

Giovanni laughed, snapped the compact shut, and placed it on the worktable.

"The ramblings of an old man." He winked at the mousy-looking girl whose wide smile was bracketed with dimples, her blue eyes vivid behind the fish-eye lenses. She said, "Not so old, *Professore*. Just a bit eccentric." Then she excused herself and walked off, her high heels clicking on the hard tile floor, her swaying hips belying her plain-Jane appearance.

Pink-cheeked, Giovanni peered over the tops of his glasses at her retreating buttocks and sighed. "These new assistants from the university get younger every day. But let's allow science to … illuminate us, shall we." He whirled around in the swivel chair and tapped the keyboard. "The rose-colored world of infra-red light."

The image of the postcard blazed in a reddish hue on a large projection screen. And between the lines of handwriting a series of letters and shapes emerged.

***

CHAPTER 36

IN THE ARTIFACT room, Rossi stood staring at the screen. "A code embedded between the lines of text. Not exactly the latest thing in 'spook'-ware."

Giovanni laughed. "Effective enough to pass rudimentary inspection and to bring you here, asking for my help, wasn't it?"

Their eyes turned back to the screen.

KNOW WHOS VILE WRATH SULKS IN THE HEART OF MEN

"But can you break the code?"

"No, but *the Shadow* knows." Pulling the pulp thriller from his pocket, Giovanni tossed it into Rossi's lap. From the cover, resembling Count Dracula, a pair of piercing eyes and a hooked nose glared hypnotically from under a black slouch fedora and peeked over a hooked arm draped in a sable cape. Giovanni explained. "The image on the cover is amateur criminologist and millionaire Lamont Cranston: the black-caped vigilante of justice. Each radio program began with the same line. Turn to page fifty-two and read the opening lines."

"The Man from Scotland Yard," Rossi read the title, then the announcer's script. "'Who knows what evil lurks in the hearts of men'?" Rossi's gaze ticked back to the screen. "The phrase on the postcard's a simple word scramble."

"Precisely. It's a reprint from the script of an old radio episode. If you'll recall, the Shadow had certain psychic powers he learned from Tibetan monks that enabled him to read criminals' thoughts and cloud their minds. But occasionally he ran across a cipher that had to be broken. In this case a version of the Masonic Royal Arch Cipher.'"

"*No capisce, Zio.*"

"Well of course not … let me finish. Look at the key in the book, Nico."

He did.

The Masonic Cipher is a simple substitution code once used to keep Alchemist's records hidden from prying eyes. It is borrowed from the aik bekar, a kabbalistic cipher. The code is sometimes referred to as the "pigpen" cipher because the grid shape resembles an animal pen.

In the Masonic cipher, letters are arranged in two grids:

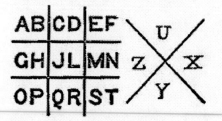

Letters within the grid are replaced by the symbol for their position; the second letter in each grid is indicated with a dot:

Royal Arch

Pointing to the shapes on the screen, Giovanni said, "Can you decode the cipher?"

Rossi frowned. "I forgot my reading glasses. Why don't you go ahead and enlighten me?"

"Thought you'd never ask." Taking a pad and pen and laying out the book in front of him, Giovanni went to work.

An assistant appeared and handed Rossi a cappuccino. As he drank, he studied the screen.

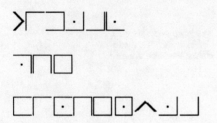

Nervously, Rossi tapped his foot and slurped his coffee.

Pausing and peering scornfully over his lenses at his nephew and then back to his notes, Giovanni said, "Doesn't look good. No not at all."

"Too difficult?" Rossi said, rising and peering over his uncle's shoulder.

"No that's just it. Too simple."

"Easy for you to say."

Turning and huffing, Giovanni looked down, rubbed his chin. Then looked up and said, "Nico, these people have a wicked sense of humor. This message was intended for you!"

Rossi's brow furrowed.

His uncle asked, "What's that silly, melodramatic name that you have christened your intel unit?"

Their eyes locked.

"O … m… b….r…a," Rossi stammered, and slapped his forehead.

Giovanni shook his head. "Yes, a play on words. *Ombra* being SHADOW in English. Which is how I immediately recognized the source of the code."

Rising from the stool and straightening a kink in his back, Giovanni pocketed his notes and the postcard. He noticed the compact lying on the table where he'd inadvertently left it and picked it up. "Now where's that young lady who was so kind as to loan this to me?" He scanned the room and called to his colleague, a thin man with craggy features. "Rosario, did you see that young girl who was here a moment ago?"

"What young girl?"

"That new, bookish-looking assistant."

Rosario frowned and shrugged. "We have no new female assistants, *Professore*."

The hairs on the nape of Rossi's neck prickled.

Exchanging glances of intuitive understanding, Rossi and his uncle nodded in sync.

"Damn. She was right under our noses," Rossi said, his face blotching red.

A sudden commotion came from the corner.

They turned toward the sound.

A knot of workers stood around a packing crate.

After exchanging puzzled glances, they moved to investigate.

To the head assistant, Giovanni said, "What's all the fuss about?"

There, nestled between strands of excelsior, lay a sculpture of a white dragon perched on a post with its head lopped off.

R. DOUGLAS WEBER

"We were going to catalog this, but I can't find any record of requisition.
And it seems to have been damaged in shipment," the head assistant offered.

"Most curious …" Giovanni bent and carefully took out the piece. "Let's take
a closer look." He placed it on a worktable under a magnifier. "I think there is
something etched onto the figure's taloned foot."

Rossi stood behind him, peering over his shoulder.

"Yes, looks like a date in Roman numerals …" He adjusted the magnifier.

The numbers X XIII XIII 0VII floated large under the glass.

Rossi read off the numbers. "Ten …thirteen … thirteen … ooh …seven.
Mean anything to you, *Zio*?"

Ignoring him and turning quickly to the head assistant, Giovanni snapped,
"Find the missing head!"

"What is it?" Rossi asked.

Focusing back on the statue, Giovanni waved dismissively.

"Here it is," someone said.

"Quickly now, place it under the magnifier," the *professore* ordered
anxiously.

After staring for a moment, Giovanni straightened and turned, revealing a
ghostly face.

Rossi's eyes questioned.

"Take a look for yourself," Giovanni said as a pained look washed over his
face.

Rossi moved forward and studied it. Beneath the glass floated a delicately
carved head with the grotesque face of a goat, its eyes pulsing in anger.

Rossi sucked a deep breath.

"October thirteen 1307 was the day that Pope Clement V launched his attack
against the Knights Templar," his uncle explained.

"*Professore*! There's a letter," an excited young assistant shouted as he ran to
their side.

"Let me have that," Rossi barked and snatched it from the man's hand.
"Someone bring me a pair of latex gloves." Holding the letter carefully by one
edge, he held it to the overhead light. *Doesn't look like a letter bomb*. An
assistant handed him a pair of gloves. He placed the letter under the magnifier,
slipped on the gloves, and opened the envelope. Using a forceps and tiny
spatulalike instrument, he removed the letter and spread it out.

It read:
Formal request for apology in the form of the ransom of Eleanor.

We shall witness the 700th anniversary of the persecution of our order on 13th October 2007. It would be just and fitting for the Vatican to acknowledge our grievance in advance of this day of mourning.

Preceptor of the Knights Templar.

With a smug expression, he turned to Giovanni. "Crackpots. And what's this ransom of Eleanor business?"

His uncle's face blanched. "An age-old custom. Send the hostage's body parts in pieces, one at a time until the ransom is paid."

"Call the Swiss Guard," Rossi shouted. "And don't touch anything."

"Someone has sent us a grotesque message," Giovanni said, sighing deeply. Rossi stood brooding, his mind bombarded with dark images of the past.

"Come on, my boy. We've got no time to lose," his uncle added. "They appear to be like phantoms and walk among us unseen." He spun on his heels and limped hurriedly for the door.

Rossi quickly fell in behind him and said to his back, "Where are we going?"

"To see the Holy Father, now hurry!"

CHAPTER 37

JOSIE SAT CHAIN-SMOKING. She crossed one leg over the other, counting away the minutes with each flex of her ankle. After awhile, a feeling of dread leached into her. Fragmented thoughts ran across her mind like fire ants. She bolted from her chair and into the outer hallway. Empty . . . Nobody . . . Zip.

She walked hurriedly, searching, listening; then, she heard it: the ding of the elevator. A muffled cry. She broke into a dead run, screeching to a halt at the elevator door just as it closed.

"Damn it!" Somehow she knew it, knew it in her gut, her father was in danger and in that elevator. Glancing up at the floor indicator, watching the numbers change as it rose steadily upward, she pounded the call button.

First floor.

Second.

▪▪▪

She ran for the *stai*rwell, cra*s*hed through *t*he d*oo*r, and bounded up the stairs. Her Doc Martins, *sla*pping the concre*te* steps, layered echoes, intertwined in a chorus that followed her up the stairwell, barking at her heels.

She climbed two floors and realized this was hopeless—there were ten more floors to her father's office. She rammed the emergency bar of the exit door and tumbled sideways as she rounded the corridor back to the elevator door.

She heard it. Ding.

Standing at the door, lungs burning, she saw the doors begin to slide open. She took a step, hesitated and willed herself to move. Claustrophobia was her Achilles heel. She steeled herself and entered the elevator. Eyes searching everywhere, she strode to the rear and turned sharply.

The elevator became sweltering; the air so thick Josie could hardly breathe. Beads of perspiration dappled her forehead.

Her blouse, equally damp with sweat, matted against the small of her back.

The devil was in the details and in an instant her world became obsessed with details: the sibilant hiss of the closing elevator door, the blinding-harsh overhead lighting, the jolt of the compartment and the creak of cables as it rose.

Third floor. Fourth floor . . . Sixth floor… The soft hum of the ventilation fan.

She wasn't alone after all. There in the corner, next to the control panel, stood a dignified little man. She took him in with a glance. His black overcoat was tailored; his complexion was pasty with a trace of pink like a baby's cheeks—no, more like an elf, with gray wisps of fine hair. His hands rested upon an ebony walking stick with an ornate silver handle. As he rocked on the balls of his tiny feet, he whistled the Disney song "Heigh-Ho."

"Floor please?" he said, turning with an innocuous but naughty smile.

"Twelfth floor, please?" she replied calmly, returning his grin. *Two can play this game.*

The surrounding walls seemed to crush in toward her like the plates of a hydraulic press.

Ninth floor.

Tenth.

Shrugging his diminutive shoulders, he lisped, "These old buildings and old elevators require patience." His watery little eyes stared, studying her, drinking her in. *Are you a patient person, young lady? You appear somewhat distraught. Can you relish this moment, the ecstasy of doubt? The intensity of the unknown? Can you? You little Hmeshe Kurve, hometown whore!*

She heard the words, but couldn't believe her eyes. His lips never moved. No—just that impish little smile. *It must be my nerves*, she thought. Then her eyes zoomed in on the walking stick. Yes, it was the same. Just like the one the old man had carried when he brushed past her in the doorway to Tateh's office. Same man, same stick?

Just as she was about to answer, the elevator shuddered to a stop. The doors opened and in walked a bosomy dowager with her consort tucked beneath her arm—a miniature French poodle—followed by a gaggle of students. The room shrank around Josie now. The thought of sharing this tiny compartment with this press of bodies terrified her.

She peered over the top of the old dame's wide-brimmed hat, stealing a glimpse of the little man. He no longer looked old and fragile, but her instincts told her it was definitely somehow the same man. Had to be. Her hand moved to the fanny pack around her waist; she slid her hand into the Velcro pouch that held her weapon. The cold gunmetal bolstered her courage, bridled her phobia.

Eleventh floor.

She felt something on her wrist, something wet.

Plop . . .

She glanced down. There, against her skin, a tiny blotch of red, and then another. Josie shook as the honed point of a blade ran between her shoulder blades. She looked up. A dark stain was flowering on the ceiling tile of the elevator cab.

Plop . . .

A droplet landed on a young, female student's nose. She raised her hand to wipe it away. The girl looked down and screamed.

149

Twelfth floor.

Like toppling dominos, the first the students, then the dowager, and finally her poodle, fell into panic. A chorus of screams erupted, the poodle threw back its head howling . . . bodies pushing and shoving each other . . . moving in a frenzied wave toward the door.

Ding.

Thirteenth floor.

Josie pushed and scrambled upward. Using the cab's handrail as a foothold, she reached up, and pulled open the overhead trapdoor. There, suspended from the steel cables—a body—her father. His body hung upside down, swaying. His right ankle was lashed to his left knee—forming an inverted numeral four. His throat was cut ear to ear.

The doors parted and the little imp, with the speed and grace of a whirling dervish, was out the door. He held a rose-colored book high above his head. Pointing it toward the bloodstained ceiling of the elevator, his voice changing from a lisp back into a thick German accent, he said, "My regards to, Tateh, Ms. Josie. Oh, and many thanks for retrieving my little book."

The world skipped a beat . . . changing to slow motion.

Josie jumped down. As the semi-auto filled her hand, Josie fired a deafening round into the ceiling to get the mob down.

Everyone half ducked, half tumbled forward; everyone except the dowager, who like a true aristocrat, turned toward the gunshot as if to render her complaint. Her mouth caught the second slug, deflecting the shot so that the little man was bathed in a shower of old blood rather than steel-jacketed hollow-points.

Josie cursed the darkness. And as the elevator doors closed, the little imp bowed as if to make a final curtain call.

Somehow the little man had vanished into thin air. Uri, her partner, also pulled his own variety of magic. He appeared, flashing an FBI badge at campus police, and whisked Josie out of the building and into the car. The witnesses from the elevator were too panicked to protest or notice.

***

As he ran down the alley adjacent to Swift Hall, the little imp, Dr. Ahriman, withdrew a long white wig and make-up stained tissues from his pocket and pitched them into a trashcan. Miraculously, he no longer limped, but sprinted away and into the swirling snow, his coattails flapping like a black, starched witch's skirt.

CHAPTER 38

NUMBED BY LOSS, enraged with anger, Josie sat next to Uri on the sofa. They'd flown to a prearranged safe house. A half-empty bottle of Jack Daniels sat on the cigarette-scarred table. And next to it lay an uneaten sandwich and an ashtray filled to the brim. The minutes and hours since her father's death ticked away with the ceaseless length of centuries. She'd cried until no more tears could flow, as if the burning rage that coursed through her veins had consumed them in their conflagration.

Uri looked deep into her eyes and reached for the whisky-filled glass as she raised it to her mouth. "Josie, that's enough! You've had too much already."

Batting his hand away, she took another long swallow and said, "Enough? NO. Maybe it'll never be enough. Not until I get that little bastard. Not until he pays with his life!"

Uri gulped hard, sensing her pain. "We'll get him, Josie. But you need some rest. The whisky won't dull the pain, it never does. Please, Tateh wouldn't want to see you like this … would he?"

Josie spun around and slapped him hard, leaving a welt on his cheek. Their eyes met and she fell into his arms, sobbing softly again. Her head rolled to the side, and she was out cold. Uri had laced her last drink with a sedative, knowing it was the only way to get it into this stubborn, brave woman.

Violin music . . . the fragrant scent of wild flowers . . . the warmth of the sun on her cheeks. A voice. She looks to see Tateh at her side; leaf-filtered sunlight dapples his face in dancing shadows. Muta is at his side, her long silken hair swept by the breath of a summer breeze. A young man approaches. Longing fills his eyes. It's little Daniel, her childhood sweetheart. He's singing Tumbalayka:

Maiden, maiden tell me true
What can grow, grow without the dew?
What can burn for years and years?
What can cry without shedding tears?
And in a little girl's voice she answers:
Silly boy, I'll tell you true!

Love can burn for years and years; a heart can cry without shedding tears . . .

A tug on her arm and a gentle voice pulled Josie back from dreamland. She woke bleary-eyed with a pounding hangover. Her mouth tasted like the bottom of an ashtray. Another tug at her arm. It was Levine, the local case officer.

"Josie, it's time to move." Levine threw her a bathrobe. "Get showered and dressed quickly now. You're too hot. We need to get you the hell out of Chicago and now."

Josie swung her feet over the edge of the bed and sat up. Her brain seemed to wiggle within her skull like Jell-O in an oversized bowl. Reaching for a cigarette on the bedside table, she hesitated and pulled back her hand.

She glared at Levine. "Out of Chicago? No way in hell! Not until I find that little bastard who killed my father!"

"My sources with Homeland Security say the whole incident was upgraded, taken over by NSA. They invoked national security and buttoned up the whole investigation. But I managed to find out that the shooter left the country."

"Then you know who he is."

Levine nodded.

"Well?"

"Name's Ahriman, on NSA's payroll as a black ops egghead. But his cover is a consultant with the *E* Institute."

"That New Age celebrity name-dropping cult?"

Levine nodded. "The very same."

"Where's he headed?"

Glancing at his hands and then back to Josie, he said, "Rome. But you're under strict orders not to touch him."

Josie studied him long and hard, but decided to hold her tongue.

Levine reached into his coat pocket, pulled out a cipher cable, and tossed it onto her lap. She looked unbelievingly at the cable, reading it twice. Then a different look washed over her face. Anger.

Levine said, somewhat guardedly, "I knew you wouldn't listen to a word I said. Can't say I'd feel any different if it had been my father. But you fucked up. Killed an innocent and not just anyone. No, you had to take out some filthy rich old dame with tons of political connections."

"The crazy old woman just got in the way—"

Pouncing on her now, Levine said, "Does the name Carlyle ring any bells?"

"No, can't say that I've . . . Don't tell me—"

"Yes, you killed Senator Carlyle's great-aunt!"

"But—"

"His rich, deep-pockets-to-the-republican-machine's-war-chest aunt no less. Somebody inside the beltway in D. C. is spreading a nasty rumor that Mossad had something to do with it. Abraham wanted you back in Tel Aviv, but I persuaded him to let you cool your heels shuffling paper at the embassy in Toronto for a while."

"I guess I should've capped a *Democrat* instead."

Uri appeared at the bedroom doorway, shopping bags in hand, shaking his head.

Nodding toward the bags, Levine said, "You'll find some clothing, and a wig inside." He tossed her an envelope. "A ticket to Toronto, a clean Canadian passport, credit cards, and driver's license."

***

Standing at the airline ticket counter, the tall, statuesque blonde said, "Excuse me, but I've had a last minute change in plans." The prim, sour-faced ticket agent strained to smile as she glanced at the woman's passport lying on the counter. "Yes, Mrs. King. How can I help you?"

Josie's topaz eyes peeked over the top of her sunglasses as she said, "When is your next flight to Rome?"

The ticket agent tapped her keyboard. "We have a flight that departs in one hour."

"That'll be just fine."

PART II

> *"Behold our secret. Remember that the end justifies the means . . . and that the wise ought to take all the means to do good which the wicked take to do evil."*
> **Adam Weishaupt, founder of the Illuminati**

CHAPTER 39

Rome

Capt. Enzo Moretti shouldn't have been out past curfew. He shouldn't have had that last glass of wine, and he certainly shouldn't have picked up the cheap call girl. But he was a jet fighter pilot with the Italian Air Force's elite 36 *Stormo groupo* who lived his life on the edge every day.

Besides, there she'd stood outside the bar, stretching those long legs as she lounged seductively against the building, half hidden by shadows, a hint of thigh peeking from the slit of her short skirt. She had moist, pouting lips, giving breasts and buttocks. In fact everything about her seemed somehow moist and giving.

In his arms she exuded a pleasing, musky sent.

Her upper lip and forehead glistened wet.

He should have noticed the uncommon lack of hardness in her pale *b*lue eyes, the w*a*y *s*he kissed him hard on *t*he mouth. And when they were lying wrapped in a sweat-drenched knot of gray sheets in that seedy little room, he should have noticed her hand slipping beneath the pillow as he began to climax violently deep within her. He should have seen the pistol before it filled her hand, before it pressed to the soft flesh of h*is* neck, before *Laylah* pulled the trigger. Laylah, having completed her assignment in Switzerland by obtaining the documents from the Arab in the club, was once again going about her business. Functioning as the perfect killing machine. With no conscience to bar the door, no hesitation—Laylah killed because it was time to kill.

CHAPTER 40

Italy's Lazio region north of Rome

DR. AHRIMAN'S MERCEDES made a sharp turn off the main blacktop of the *Cassia*, tires squealing, and into a private roadway that ribboned over hills mantled in white oak, maple, and ash. Rocketing around a bend, his headlights cut a narrow swath through the darkness. Glancing to his left, the bordering tree line that became denser and thicker with each turn seemed to reach for him. He punched the accelerator; the speedometer shivered to 75 … then 80. Above, the treetops bowed inward, forming a Gothic archway that pressed lower and lower with each mile.

Dissonant chords of Rachmaninoff's *Prelude* blared from the CD player.

A slice of crescent moon glowed unusually bright in the night sky as an armada of black, foreboding clouds sailed by like drifting ghost galleons.

Then, up ahead, he saw it. A huge iron gate sprawled across the roadway.

He slowed to a stop. Caught in the glare of his high beams giant Greco letters formed an archway over the towering gate:

ESCHATOLOGY INSTITUTE

Hinges rasped as the gate slowly opened.

In the distance, perched high atop a monstrous rock formation and bathed in floodlights, stood a dreamlike house of glass.

It was an expression of Volante's eccentric nature, his love of overstatement, his Italian summer palace. Its windows angled out at forty-five degrees, sheer walls of glass and stone, whose overall form was like an inverted pyramid with its capstone hidden below ground level. Tiers of layered rooflines, cakelike, climbed upward, increasing in size as they grew higher.

Ahriman navigated the serpentine drive to the top and parked. Briefly, he stood looking down the steep, studded facing that plummeted sharply to the rock-hewn shoreline below, where the frothing waves of Lago di Bolsena, the largest volcanic lake in Europe, crashed against stone. He knew that the sheer walls of stone on two sides and a dense forest on the third side made the glass fortress almost impenetrable.

He made his way to the elevator door set into the rock wall and placed his eye to the state-of-the-art optical scanner; the door hissed open.

The inside of the elevator cab was paneled in burnished brass. When he hit the up button, the cab rocketed skyward, which made it seem as though he were trapped inside a .30-06 shell fired from a rifle.

The elevator stopped. The doors opened.

A guard posted outside thick, smoked-glass double doors nodded and pressed a wall switch. The doors slid open.

Ahriman entered and scanned the room. At this high elevation wind shears rattled the sloping glass panes. A plush, red velveteen cushion ran the entire length of the window ledge; rock croppings formed interior walls that grew upward, through the floor to the ceiling. Here and there the sandstone walls were dotted with cavelike nooks and crannies. The room was ringed with lights hidden in recesses under the windows and at the bottoms edges of the stone walls. They cast a faint and subtle light that created no window glare.

Dr. Ahriman walked to the far corner of the room, where Drago Volante sat masked in shadow. Thunder, suddenly, pounded the glass walls and rooftop, reverberating like the head of a tympani drum. Moonbeams flooded through a honeycomb of octagon-shaped, beveled windowpanes behind Volante's chair, deflecting and refracting to form a pale yellow corona.

His wife, Honora Celine, lay coquettishly on the cushioned window seat dressed in a flimsy, see-through nightgown. The gloved hands of soft moonlight caressed her lithe and supple body.

The pink bud of her tongue protruded through her pearlescent teeth.

Teasing.

Taunting.

Honora's head arched back, her alabaster shoulders rounding. Long waves of platinum-blond tresses cascaded like molten gold over her back as her palms kneaded her taut thighs.

Ahriman took his seat, crossed his stubby legs, bounced his ankle effeminately and sighed. He drew a white lace handkerchief from his sleeve, dabbed the perspiration from his brow.

Volante reached for the console in his armrest and flicked a rocker switch. A huge, paper-thin LCD screen lowered from the ceiling. The rolling image of a green luminescent Ouija-board tumbled end-over-end into view. His hooded eyes closed in deep concentration. Then suddenly they popped wide open.

"Pleasant trip, I hope?" Volante asked graciously, even affably, but a subtle undercurrent in his voice reinforced their mutual dislike for one another.

Ahriman shrugged.

"What's the condition of our patient," Volante snapped, his true feelings obvious in his tone.

As he spoke, the planchette of the Ouija-board moved in ever widening and rapid circles on the screen.

Dr. Ahriman cleared his throat. "Our flying ace, Capt. Moretti, is at Level Four Delta. The tranquilizer gun had no long-lasting effects. He's in excellent health. He has some residual flashbacks and delusions from the alkaloid compounds we used, but the overall outcome and prognosis are excellent. The false memories of abuse at the hands of a priest have been deeply implanted and his paranoia is at peak levels."

The lightning flashes caused hobgoblin shadows to hopscotch across the cold, curved rock walls. As Honora's pouting lips whispered questions, the planchette on the LCD screen moved in response across the board.

"Go on," Volante said.

"I've prepared a video for our foreign associates and the Eschatology Institute's edification. May I?" Ahriman asked with an upturned palm.

Volante nodded.

Ahriman punched the play button on another console at his side and a second, larger LCD screen crept downward. The symbol of the Eschatology Institute—the *un*blinking Eye of Horus within the Pyramid perched above the letter E entwined within two triangles—tumbled into view on the flat monitor.

Honora Celine sipped her champagne and stared in an erotic stupor at the screen. The planchette moved to "D" . . . then to "A."

An image of Dr. Ahriman dressed in a white lab coat and horn-rimmed glasses appeared. The words **DANOS PROJECT** with the advisory "CLASSIFIED A-2. VOICE CODE RECOGNITION REQUIRED" floated in bold face over the doctor's image.

"Volante, Drago."

A voice from the monitor intoned, "Code Accepted" in a flat, female, computer voice. The image of Ahriman began to speak and, behind him, a picture of two oblong paper-thin or foil-like silver scrolls was projected on a screen.

"The silver scrolls recently recovered by the Cleric have been translated. They are similar in tone and wording with the vellum scroll—The Jesus Gospel—also found by the Cleric in Solomon's Temple. We now know the source of the Templar fragment, which was passed down to our Order through the ages. It's the 'smoking gun' we've been seeking.

"Similar to the silver scrolls found in Jerusalem by Dr. Barkay, our find dates from the late seventh or early sixth century B.C., before the Babylonian captivity. This makes them 400 years older than the Dead Sea Scrolls. Our silver scrolls were amulets, a type of fetish, like the 'prayer object of silver' mentioned in an Egyptian papyrus from 300 B.C. or those of other past cultures or even, the holy medals used by Catholics to this day. The scrolls were worn around the neck as a form of protection to ward off evil. In the Jewish faith, per the instructions of Moses to keep the word of the Lord close to their hearts and minds, even today, Jews wear small cases filled with scriptures on their left arm or brow. They are called phylacteries or *tephillin* in Hebrew."

Another image flashed on the screen, showing a close-up of one section. "When unrolled, we found that the scrolls, which were made of almost pure sheet-silver, contained Paleo-Hebrew inscriptions delicately etched into their surface. We used photographic and computer-imaging techniques to enhance the faint inscriptions. Namely a technique called 'light painting.'

"Unlike the Barkay scrolls with their comforting benediction prayer that is recited at the end of every Catholic mass, ours revealed an unsettling truth for chauvinistic Christians. God was worshiped as both male and female, the female being preferred and embodying the attribute of wisdom. We have discovered the 'Golden Thread' that stretched back to 600 B.C., or earlier, weaving its way through time. Through the time of the Dead Sea Scrolls. Knitted into the very fabric of The Jesus Gospel written in Christ's own hand. And the Golden Thread is that Christ acknowledged in his own words the he was a common man, who like all mankind could, by uniting with the sacred feminine, become the son of God."

CHAPTER 41

The screen filled with the image of a goatskin or vellum scroll.

"The later 'Templar' scrolls were examined using infrared and digital imaging. They confirm that the so-called heretical codices found in Nag Hammadi in 1945 were indeed from this missing Gospel of Q. Securing the key to the variation of the Atbash cipher, *The Black Rose Notebook*, held under lock and key by the Vatican, was instrumental in translating the texts. Years ago, after finding a fragment of the Book of Q hidden in the pillar at Rennes-le-Château, Abbe Saunière, one of our initiates, took it to St. Sulpice in Paris."

"Le-Château … is a church in France decorated with Masonic symbols and abounds with legends of being the resting place of the Templars' buried treasure. Some Indiana Jones nonsense about how when the sunlight hits the guardian demon statue's sapphirelike eyes, the legendary 'blue apples,' the resulting beam of refracted light will point the way."

Ahriman gave a forced laugh. "Nonsense to be sure, but the tourists eat it up. Once at St. Sulpice, Saunière delivered it to Abbe Boullan who used its explosive but factual contradiction of church dogma to blackmail the Pope. Hence the true source of Saunière's sudden, newfound wealth. *Le Cahier de le Rose Noire* contains the encoded text of the Q fragment, hidden in the guise of a grimoire, and the key to a complex variation of the Atbash cipher that, like much of the Dead Sea Scrolls, the text of the Book of Q is written in.

"Atbash was a simple substitution cipher which was used a thousand years after the writing of the Dead Sea Scrolls by the Templars. This could only mean that it was indeed the Templars who had brought the fragment of the Book of Q they had found in Solomon's Temple back to France. Somehow they'd broken the cipher and later, the original document was passed to residents in the Cathar occupied region of southern France for safekeeping, the very same region where lies Rennes-le-Château. But somehow the Templars overlooked the importance of the scroll the Cleric had obtained recently in Palestine. It will lead us directly to The Tomb."

CHAPTER 42

Ahriman's image continued.

"By the way, the legend of the curse that is attached to the grimoire stems from applied alchemy. Hidden within the hasp that binds *The Black Rose Notebook* is a tiny needle that is supplied by a refillable bladder concealed within the book's spine. The needle is laden with an extremely powerful and fast-acting combination of hallucinogens: bufotenine secreted by the sea toad, psilocybin from the mushroom, and finally the alkaloids derived from the seeds of the ancient Syrian rue plant. We combine them with modern MAO inhibitors, which amplify the psychoactive effects of these tryptamines. Like mating toads, once injected, the meddling fools who open the book become psychotic, driven mad by a psychedelically inflamed libido that takes control of their thoughts and actions. In order to insure its lasting effect, a toxin that mimics the brain and central nerves system's debilitating effects caused by general paresis or syphilis, as it is commonly known, is added to the deadly stew. If one is not an adept, if one cannot read the instructions written in symbols on its cover, opening the latch in a haphazard manner is deadly."

A yellowed parchment filled the screen.

"This missing fragment, like the Templar scrolls, proves that the later Gospels were a falsehood, lies created by St. Paul to muddy the truth. Lies perpetuated over time by Rome to insure that St. Peter became the rightful successor, rather than Mary Magdalene. Lies that hid the true teachings of a prophet versed in the ancient knowledge of the Egyptian mystery religions. A prophet, not the son of God, whose true history is about to be revealed to the world."

Volante scowled and punched a button on his armrest console. The video blinked off, and the screen crawled upward.

He turned to Ahriman. "Enough of your reveling in false glory. The truth is that you have bungled everything. You killed Professor Shulman, the one man who could have decoded the real secret of the notebook."

Ahriman steepled his fingers. "Your assessment is not entirely correct. Max Schulman wasn't the only scholar who could decode the supreme secret. I've baited a trap to catch Schulman's colleague."

Volante leaned forward, eyes narrowing to points. "Who?"

A wicked smile curled the doctor's lips. "*Professore* Alberti Giovanni."

"You can wipe that smug look off your face. My sources in the UK have informed me that we're racing against time. Our rivals, the Rosicrucians, may already know about the whereabouts of the tomb!"

Ahriman looked stunned. "But how?"

"Have you forgotten that you let the Palestinian boy slip through your fingers? He was adopted by member of the Rosicrucians who now holds a high position in MI-6."

Tugging at his French cuffs, Ahriman stiffened at the news. "At the time, I had no way of knowing of the boy's importance, nor that of either of his sisters. I won't take blame for not being able to see into the future, for not guessing that something called DNA markers would come into existence. Besides, the boy would know nothing. They must have discovered another secret document that has given them the location."

"Or there's a traitor in our midst," Volante said coldly.

***

On the Ouija-board, the planchette moved to "U"—

—and then to "G"... "H,T,E, R."

After spinning in wild circles for a moment, it traced out ... "OF" and then ..."G...O," finally resting at the letter "D."

When read together, the green flashing letters read ... **DAUGHTER OF GOD.**

Honora rose sluggishly and padded out of the room.

CHAPTER 43

IN A BEDROOM in the complex Honora Cline Volante lay face down sprawled leisurely on red satin sheets. With one long shapely leg raised in midair, she groaned with pleasure as the firm hands of the masseur kneaded her supple flesh. He was twentysomething. A hard-body.

She was blond, stunning, and moved with the feral grace of Uma Thurman.

"Derek, do my thighs," Honora said, moaning.

His broad shoulders and pecs bulged beneath his tight T-shirt as he worked her left thigh.

"Ouch, not so hard!" She squirmed away and rolled over on her back. Her green eyes flashed, then softened. "I'm bored." Her lower lip pouted and she sighed. Hungrily, she eyed him from head to toe.

"Let's play a game," she said, her sensuous voice slinking its way into his brain.

"I'm listening," Derek answered, his six two frame straightening, turning rigid.

Honora slid to the edge of the bed, sat cross-legged, her elbows resting on her knees, and giggled like a schoolgirl. She licked the corner of her mouth; her naturally red and moist lips glistened. "You'd like to screw me wouldn't you?"

"Would I?"

"Yes, long and hard."

He flinched. Started breathing faster, his face flushing red.

"Take off your pants."

His hand moved to his belt, slowly pulling the tongue through the buckle, unfastening his pants, and sliding them over his hips. They pooled on the floor at his ankles and he stepped out of them. He wore white bikini underwear tight as a second skin.

"The shirt, rip it off."

He did, grabbing the V-neck and tearing it down the middle.

"You want me, Derek. Like you've never wanted any woman before. I make you hard."

"I want you."

"Rip off your underwear."

He did and it landed on the bedside lampshade.

Her body rose to him. Turning slowly, she bent slightly at the waist and rubbed her firm cheeks against his erection …her black thong riding higher as she ground her hips. She tossed her long blond hair and arched her back, moaning in ecstasy. Mouth open, gasping for breath, she reached back and cupped hers hands behind his head. Flesh on flesh. She felt the heat pulse through her.

"Touch me, nibble on my neck," she said in breathy voice.

She lowered her arms.

Taking his hand, she slipped it into the cup of her matching push-up bra, guided his fingertips to her erect nipple.

"That's it. Pull on it, squeeze it. Good boy."

Her free hand dug between her smooth thighs.

She shuddered.

The intercom chimed, interrupting her rhythm. Hair matted and damp, bent over the bed, propped on her elbows, her eyes cut to speaker. A metallic voice said, "Mr. Volante wants you back downstairs."

She snarled.

"Fuck," she said, rising and pushing Derek away.

She went to the box and keyed the mic.

"Tell him I'm … indisposed!"

Collecting herself, Honora rang her long fingers through her hair and went to the bedside table. She pulled a pack of cigarettes from her purse, lit one and inhaled deeply, letting the smoke drift out slowly.

Her breasts, her whole body filmed with sweat; she glided like a sinuous shadow across the room to the opposite side, facing Derek. "You feel frightened. Sick to your tummy, but you want to touch me, don't you?" She caressed her breasts, deepening the cleavage.

"Do I?" Derek asked.

"Who's Mama's bad boy?"

His head bowed in shame, he whimpered softly.

"Answer me!"

His voice choking, he managed, "I am."

"Yes, you're racked with guilt, but you can't help yourself."

"Can't help myself."

"Say it."

"I can't help myself."

Derek stood quaking, arms struggling to rise from his side.

"Get on your knees, bad boy. Crawl to me."

Derek dropped to all fours and scuttled toward her, whimpering.

Months before, Honora had enlisted the help of Dr. Ahriman. Ahriman, delighted to have a secret alliance with Honora, trained her in the use of hypnotic drugs and the practical application of the latest mind control techniques. All she had to do was spike Derek's drink and push the right buttons. She knew the domineering, sadistic abuse that Derek had suffered at the hands of his mother in childhood was the key. It unlocked his inner demons, the fear and sexual ambivalence her memory invoked. It was his Achilles' heel. Honora's voice, softly whispering "Who's Mama's bad boy" was the trigger phrase. It turned him into a sniveling, terrified little boy. In fact, it worked so well that Honora had joked with Ahriman about going on Oprah and sharing it with women everywhere.

"Derek, get the hell up. Go sit in the corner," she said with a dismissive wave.

As Derek cowered in the corner of the suite, Honora turned and walked to the far corner. Honora bent and stroked the young girl's cheek lovingly with her fingertips. "Okay, where were we?"

Wearing nothing but a torn T-shirt, sitting with her bare knees pressed tightly together and trembling, knowing somewhere deep within her clouded mind that her turn was coming again, sat Laylah. Her face flushed, eyes vacant—she nodded and rose.

CHAPTER 44

THE GREEN SCRAMBLER phone behind the large ornate desk buzzed, drawing his attention. The Cleric spun in his chair and answered on the prearranged seventh ring.

"*Pronto.*"

"*Buon Cugino,*" Volante whispered.

"*Buon Cugino.* How goes it at your end?" the Cleric asked, reaching under his desk to hit a switch that triggered the electronic bolt mechanism, locking the entrance to his office.

"I look forward to seeing Rome once again."

"Then you're coming soon?"

"Yes, have preparations been made?"

"Everything is in order. They received the letter and the omen today."

"I appreciate your flair for the dramatic. The white headless dragon, symbolizing lopping off the head of the Vicar of Christ, was a nice touch."

"*Grazie*, you're too kind."

"Now down to business. I assume that the virus will be administered with caution, the proper dosage. We wouldn't want to kill him, just yet. And the diversions are in place?"

As he spoke, the Cleric gazed out the window of his office in the Apostolic Palace, overlooking St. Peter's square. "Of course, I tested the virus myself on one of my assistants. He's about the same height and weight and age. All the proper symptoms manifested within an hour. And, how shall I say it, the kindling is stacked and ready for the torch."

"Excellent. And the operative who's snatching the package?"

"*Bast* is as clever as she is stunning," the Cleric said, and fingered the signet ring on his left hand, twisting it nervously around and around the digit. "Her patron, the Bedouin, asked me to thank you for those pamphlets of the Protocols of Zion that you shipped. He's persuaded *ALJAZERRA* to do a three-part special outlining the Zionist conspiracy that will be beamed by satellite all over the Middle East."

"Marvelous, carpetbomb them with hatred. It's a double-edged coup. The Israelis will become incensed and show excerpts from the program, which will in turn be picked up by the major networks in the U.S. and Europe. They constantly fall unwittingly into our scheme. I see that the Israeli Prime Minister toured the Dome shortly after the bombing we arranged. The Palestinians rioted in the square and the Israeli security forces pelted them with rubber bullets, young and old alike."

"Did you approve sending the Bedouins the ninth degree Masonic aprons?"

"Let me check my log notes."

As he waited, the Cleric unlocked his desk drawer and took out a rendering of the design. At the top was a large numeral 9 intertwined with one dagger pointing down and another across, forming a cross—**9...1...1**. Below were two arms, one hand held a decapitated head dripping blood, the other clutched a long, curved scimitar. The Cleric knew that it was the actual ninth degree symbol of the Memphis-Mizraim Lodge, which originated in Milano and then migrated to France and Germany, where it secretly infiltrated Masonic Lodges around the world with the dark Egyptian occult practices. The Cleric's grandfather had been a grand master.

Volante came back on the line. "They went out by courier last week."

"Have we smuggled the gold bullion from the reserves beneath the World Trade Center into our banks?"

"Yes. They found a half-filled truck and convoy in the tunnels beneath the second tower but we left a cold trail. The millions in missing gold have never been leaked to the press. The images of those crumbling twin towers in New York struck a raw nerve. Like the Tower depicted in the tarot card being struck by lightning and bodies leaping to sudden death, the fall of the WTC is an archetypal symbol that instills terror and foreshadows cataclysmic change at the hands of the Muslim fanatics. We are also getting good mileage out of those recent beheading tapes, too. Strikes terror into the hearts of the West, and at the same time, hardens their hearts and fuels more hatred toward Arabs in general."

In a strained voice, the Cleric said, "I worry that our plan is too complicated."

"Your worries are unfounded, *Buon Cugino*. What you fail to fathom is that the Five Stage plan is the natural course of history. We follow in its footsteps, just tweaking it so that we always come out on top. We're just reentering the first stage, Chaos and Discord. And we're dumping a little gas on the fire to accelerate the timeline. By destroying faith in Christianity, and pitting Jew against Muslim, we amp up the second stage: Confusion."

"You're right. And by using this Muslim Fundamentalist group to strike a major blow we'll deliver the coup de grâce. I understand that our program of brainwashing those angst–filled, young Muslim converts is proceeding as planed."

Volante's voice changed in timbre and pitch. "Indeed, we used them for the second London bombing attack, and they are making preparations in Rome as we speak. The intelligence services haven't picked up on the fact that too many of these baby-faced terrorists seem to have manufactured motives that arise out of the blue. When they least expect it, we'll move into phase two of the air terror operation. This time we'll target the heartland of the United States. Since the security provisions for private aircraft are so lax, general aviation will be our next target. Imagine the panic when scores of hijacked Gulfstream IVs and Vs nose-dive into their neighborhood Wal-Mart stores, killing hundreds of local yokels."

"How's the disinformation campaign regarding the Gospel of Jesus proceeding?"

"It's on schedule. Biblical scholars from many faiths are quietly authenticating the Book of *Q* as we speak. We'll leak small fragments to the press, create the usual media hype, but keep the juiciest part for the finale."

"I can't wait to see the old dog's face," the Cleric said eagerly.

"Keep me apprised of how it's going. We'll be in touch."

After hanging up, the Cleric rose and moved to the window. In the square below, he saw a flock of nuns making their way through a rustling blanket of pigeons. Another nun ran to join them, clutching her over-sized white wimple as she merged into the group. *Bast,* having donned a nun's habit, ran with an uncanny *feline* grace.

He nodded and smiled knowingly to himself.

CHAPTER 45

AS THEY MADE their way through the corridors of the Apostolic Palace, they talked.

The flame fading from his cheeks but still breathing hard, Giovanni said, "We'll meet with Commander Stato, but first we must speak with Cardinal Moscato."

"But the security chief needs to—"

Giovanni shook his head. "You don't understand the thick layer of *romanità* which pervades the Vatican. The protocol, the office-politics that must be adhered to. I realize that from your perspective this is a security matter. But Stato reports to Cardinal Moscato. In this case, we must play leapfrog at the Vatican. Unlike in the government, we must respect the chain of command, but start at the top in a matter of such urgency."

"I got the message with the white dragon and the Templars, but they're a lunatic fringe threat at best. I think Stato just needs to be made aware, beef things up a bit."

Giovanni paused and laid his hand on Rossi's shoulder. "You're forgetting the postcard?"

Rossi scowled. "There's a connection?"

They were standing outside of Cardinal Moscato's office now. "Hold that thought," his uncle said and opened the large door.

Monsignore Porcello Bertone greeted them at the door and ushered them into an anteroom where they took a seat on a long settee. After making small talk over coffee, the portly, pig-snout-faced Bertone stood and came to the point. "You must understand. His Eminence has a very full schedule. I'm doing my best to squeeze you in, but it's difficult."

Giovanni lowered his head and then slowly raised it, locking on Bertone's squinty eyes. "It's of the utmost urgency."

Bertone shrugged. "Perhaps if I knew the exact nature of this urgency then—"

"What I have to say is only for his Eminence's ears." Giovanni sat back and crossed his legs, indicating the discussion was over.

"Very well … I'll do my best."

Standing, Giovanni moved to a small desk and scribbled something on a notepad. Then he tore it off and tucked it into an envelope. Thrusting it into Bertone's hand, he said, "Give this to him immediately if you value your life and the widows' sons you serve! Have you no pity? Oh Lord, is there no help?" as he gripped his hand, fingers curled and locking Bertone's in a mirror image, thumbs pressed together.

With an indignant look, Bertone straightened, excused himself, and headed for the inner office door. He rapped gently and disappeared through the door.

Rossi laughed. "You certainly lit a fire under him."

"I just let him know that I was Freemason, too."

"But you're not."

Giovanna winked. "No, but evidently Bertone is. I used a variation of the universal distress plea, the Grand Hailing Sign of the Masons. 'Oh Lord, my God, is there no help for this widow's son'? And the secret Master Mason handgrip."

"But how did you know?"

"His cuff links."

"What?"

"They were thinly disguised Tubal-Cain symbols. Looks like a golf club bracketed by golf balls on both sides of the club's head. Actually, it has a much different connotation in Masonry."

"Do I want to know?"

"Their euphemistic name for it is a clue, Two Ball Cane. It represents a part of the anatomy that's singular to the male gender."

Rossi scratched his head, looked between his legs and smiled.

Pulling a slip of paper from his pocket, Giovanni said, "Here, this is what I made of the cipher on the postcard."

Rossi took the paper and studied it.

Rappini

Il

Pesatore

He read aloud, translating it into English, "Kidnap … The Fisherman …"

He felt the color draining from his cheeks. "If this message was for *Bast*, we have a high-level threat on our hands." He pulled out his cell phone.

"Who are you calling?" Giovanni asked.

"My director, who'll bump it up to the Vatican desk at the Ministry and call this Commander Stato."

His uncle nodded. "We don't seem to be making headway. Go ahead and turn the screws."

Finishing his call, Rossi anxiously paced the room.

"Sit down, Nico. You'll wear out that expensive Persian carpet."

Reluctantly, he plopped down.

Giovanni chewed his lower lip. "This is a bit muddled. I'm trying to figure the possible connection between an al-Qaeda terrorist and a group of old men who call themselves the Templars. We could be wrong. There may be more than one target."

"How do you figure?" Rossi asked.

"Descendants of the high-ranking Curia, who shared equally in the arrest and torture of the Templars with Pope Clement V, are still very much alive, and a few are right here within the walls of the Vatican. And one in particular who has gone missing."

"You mean Monsignore Scarlotti?" Rossi said, staring incredulously.

"His ancestor signed the Venice Papal Bull."

"Then you take that letter seriously?"

"I'm afraid we have to. I'll compile a list of possible targets for Stato, and you concentrate on your Middle East connection."

Before Rossi could answer, the door to Moscato's office burst open. Without acknowledging their presence, Cardinal Moscato stormed past and out the door.

As Bertone passed, Rossi shot to his feet and grabbed his arm.

Looking pained and distraught, Bertone said, "Please gentlemen, The Holy Father has summoned us to his office. An emergency, please excuse me."

Rossi released his grip and Bertone rushed out.

Turning, Rossi met his uncle's stare.

"It's begun," Giovanni said coldly.

Rossi's cell phone rang and he took the call.

CHAPTER 46

Parked on Via degli Scipioni was a white Fiat van. Inside, she sat waiting impatiently, drumming her fingers on the steering wheel and stealing looks across the street. The occasional passerby paid no attention to the nun behind the wheel. Finally, the doors of the Azzurro Scipioni Theater, an independent cinema club that showed art house films and old Hollywood classics in English, opened. A few older couples, a band of students, and a few street sweepers, allowed free admission as a matter of policy, sauntered out beneath the glittering marquee that read: Broadway Melody 1940.

Despite being just north of seventy some years of age, Kystyn Lazarz glided across the busy street with the grace and agility of Fred Astaire. His suit was an impeccably tailored double-breasted pinstripe. His shirt custom-tailored with French cuffs. And like Fred, his tie and socks matched. Robins-egg blue. His hair was thick and combed straight back and he was slightly overweight. But his most outstanding feature was his extraordinary emerald green eyes. Eyes like "homemade" sin one reviewer had said early in his career of song and dance onstage and screen.

He pulled open the van's passenger-side door and jumped in. Winking his dimpled cheeks, he said, "What's up, toots?"

"I've been waiting for half an hour. You're late," the nun said, glaring.

He belched loudly. "Whoa, that giant Coke and extra-buttered popcorn isn't good for Johnny Boy's old pipes. Got any Maalox?"

She shook her head and nodded toward the back of the van. "Your bag is in the back."

Twisting in his seat, he fetched the duffle bag, fumbled inside and found the bottle.

After taking a long pull, he said, "Never leave home without it."

"You're incorrigible," she said.

"Yeah, one time I walked onto the set an hour late for a call, and old Hitch ... he liked to be called Mr. Hitchcock by male actors, but I always called 'im Hitch ... said, "*Good evening*, Mr. Johnny Brett. And welcome to our show." He took another swig, belched again.

"How'd you come up with that stage name?"

"Fred used it in the flick," he said, and nodded toward the marquee.

She fired the engine and pulled away from the curb.

"Huddled in that little movie house in Krakow, I sat watching them float across the silver screen, dressed in glittery white formals against a black mirrored backdrop, just gliding across a pond of shiny black tiles like skaters on ice." He stated humming "Begin the Beguine," staring off into space. "It was sublime, doll. I knew right then and there, I was going to Hollywood."

"Fred and Ginger?"

"No, that one was Eleanor Powell, honeycakes."

She frowned, compressed her lips.

"So what's the gig?" he asked.

Her pale blue eyes flashed from under dark eyebrows. "Why don't you hop in the back and change? We're on a schedule here."

When he rose and squeezed between the seats, he farted. She gunned the accelerator, sending him headfirst to the floor. She smiled to herself and shouted over her shoulder, "And don't call me doll or honeycakes, Johnny Boy!"

Poking his head around her seat and rubbing his forehead, he said, "Understood, sorry about the gas."

She wheeled the van through manic Roma traffic like a veteran cabdriver, blasting the horn and shouting curses as she went. Her hand slid beneath her habit, and she checked that the plastic molded .22 pistol was still strapped snuggly to her inner thigh. A .22 wasn't a manstopper but ammo was cheap. And if you practiced making the kill shot—right in the eye— it would do the trick nicely.

Johnny Boy crawled out from the back and into his seat. He adjusted the Roman collar and tugged at the sleeves of his black cassock. Then he studied his image in a handheld mirror, and ran his fingers through his close-cropped, thin white hair. "Never liked that rug. Makes my head itch something fierce." Donning a pair of thick eyeglasses, he turned and smiled. "Well, boop boop a doop, whataya think, Sister?"

She shrugged. "You'll pass, I guess?"

Fingering his lapels, he said, "Looks like the real thing. Nice fabric and tailoring."

"It should ... it *is* the real thing."

"How'd you ... never mind, I don' t need to know."

"That's correct. Check your coat pocket."

He pulled out a leather credential case and examined it. "You're a girl after my own heart."

"Thought you'd like it."

He straightened and got into character, speaking in a heavy Boston dialect. "Monsignor Charles O'Malley, Boston Arch Diocese, envoy of His Eminence Cardinal Lawless. But please, just call me Chuck."

"Very nice, Chuck."

"And you'll be playing Ingrid Bergman's part, right."

She smiled modestly and lowered her eyes. "Sister Mary Benedict on temporary duty as surgical nurse."

His gaze slid up and down her body. "You know, as a prank on the final scene, Bing asked for another take. Then he grabbed Ingrid in his arms and laid a big wet one on her."

"Save the Viagra for someone your own age."

As the van careened around the corner and into the parking lot of the Gemelli Polyclinic, Johnny Boy began singing "The Bells of St. Mary's" in a deep, Bing Crosby baritone.

CHAPTER 47

Vatican City

THE PONTIFF WAS seated at his desk in the papal study on the third floor of the Apostolic Palace. Towering Palladian windows at his back. On the wall, the sunlight cast dueling shadows from the Pope's pen as he worked feverishly at his daily correspondence.

A sharp rap at the study door drew his attention.

His Holiness's ashen and debilitated face slowly turned to the study door. His face reflected the torment that bridled his soul. He was pale; his eyes, normally a radiant sea-green color, today, were as haunted as old mansions.

"Avanti!" The Pontiff's tremulous hand laid down his pen and he slouched back in his chair with a sigh of exhaustion. It was time for the regular morning briefing. The Cardinal Secretary of State, Luciano Moscato, and the Chief of Papal Security, Commander Gustavo Stato, entered clutching red dossiers. With a nod of his doddering head, His Holiness gestured for them to be seated.

Cardinal Moscato was round of face and round of body, double-chinned, half-bald, and fat-necked. And as if to add insult to injury, a purple-stained birthmark covered half his face. Commander Stato, on the other hand, was his complete antitheses. With his startling combination of Mediterranean features—lush black hair, plum-dark eyes—his good looks, and his fit physique, Stato had the movie star appearance of the quintessential hero: faithful, courageous, and ever-vigilant. He trained with the Swiss Guard. He'd served at the *Ausbildung* in Bern and was posted to the Carabinieri's *Corazzieri* Regiment, their equivalent of the U.S. Secret Service. Following the 1981 assassination attempt on the Pope, he'd been recruited for and assumed the position as Chief of Papal Security.

His eyes bristled with intensity as he spoke:

"As per your request, Your Holiness, I have prepared a detailed account of the circumstances surrounding the death of Colonnello Pico and Monsignore Scarlotti."

"Yes, but if you'd be so kind as to summarize it for us? *Continua, per favore.*"

Stato straightened himself and said, "As you are aware the Vatican has received generous financial support over the years from various western intelligence agencies in the hope that a strong united Church would aid in the combat of communism. Monsignore Scarlotti was recruited through his niece—one Josephine Schulman, a Mossad agent."

Poker-faced, the Pope leaned forward and nodded.

"The Holy See has been the focus of western intelligence exemplified by the Americans' posting of 'special envoy,' Mr. James Wilcox," Stato went on. "Wilcox was a career intelligence officer for the CIA who'd been posted to hot spots and centers of political espionage such as Tehran, Havana, Bangkok, and Tegucigalpa."

Cardinal Secretary Moscato shifted impatiently in his seat, twisting a kink from his neck like a chained mastiff, waiting his turn to speak.

Commander Stato, though aware of the cardinal's growing agitation, refused to acknowledge it. "The suspicious demise of the American Regional Security Officer, William Cotter, at the scene of Monsignore Scarlotti's disappearance demonstrates the American intelligence community's involvement in this affair." Stato paused and drew a breath. "Now to the robbery of the Archive. Colonnello Pico was killed . . . at the hand of Monsignore Scarlotti. Fingerprints on the brass bookend found near Pico's body confirm this."

The Pope lowered his head, sighed, and then returned his gaze to Stato.

Stato continued. "It's my belief that the intelligence community, after years of struggling, has determined that the *Le Cahier de le Rose Noire* is the 'key' to our diplomatic cipher-code. Without that knowledge and without the key, even the colossal Cray 900 computers of the NSA in Fort Meade could not break our code!"

Cardinal Secretary Moscato broke in. "What he means to say, Holiness, is that they could break the code, but without the key it would still be meaningless dribble."

"And now?" the Pontiff asked.

"And now communication between our papal nuncios is an open book," replied Moscato.

The Pontiff regard him coldly, no trace of emotion, as if he were seated across the poker table and did not want to call Moscato's bluff just yet.

Stato steeled himself and went on, "Holy Father, Monsignore Scarlotti was an *agente dippio,* double agent! I recommend that strict protocols of counter-intelligence security be instituted at once." He slid his analysis across the Pontiff's desktop.

Moscato sat in silence, letting the words of the youthful Commander twist in the air like a corpse on the gallows.

The Pope placed a hand on the document without reading it, even glancing at it.

A smirk of apparent satisfaction washed over Cardinal Moscato's face. He turned to Stato, his eyes trying to bore into his. But Stato's eyes were fixated on the Pope's expression, trying desperately to decipher the message hidden behind that pallid face.

"I agree with your assessment fully, Commander." A slight twinkle came to the Pope's eyes as he said it. "I wish to expand your duties, your responsibility. You shall immediately assume command of the *Vigilanza* as well as the Swiss Guard, and all intelligence matters."

Commander Stato swallowed audibly.

The Pope turned to Cardinal Moscato. The cardinal met the steady-eyed, innocent gaze of the Pope as best he could as the Pope asked, "Don't you agree, *Eminenza*?"

"Yes, Holiness. My thoughts exactly!" Moscato nervously fingered his seal ring as he answered.

"*Grazie, Eminenza*." Now, turning his attention to Stato again, the Pope said, "However, first I have a mission for you that must be conducted with aplomb and the utmost discretion. There's much more to this than meets the eye. Even now as we speak, certain forces are at work that have a singular, unwavering purpose."

"I don't follow, Holy Father? I mean—"

"The hounds of the Lord, *Domini Canes*, will brief you."

The Pope hit a recessed button beneath his desk, signaling his secretary to admit the man waiting outside.

"Did you say the hounds of—"

The opening of the study door interrupted Stato's words. Dominican Master-General Damien Spears entered. He could have been a Teutonic Knight, for his German bloodlines had produced a giant. At over six foot five and weighing in at almost two hundred and fifty pounds, he was built like a tank. His nickname in the Vatican, alluding to his compulsory service as a young boy in the Hitler Youth and then later as a young man in Hitler's army, was the *Panzer General*.

But dressed in his cream-colored robes of the Dominican Order, Stato thought that he more resembled a towering, cotton-bedsheet ghost. His pale complexion, silvery hair and dour expression magnified his somewhat haughty German posture. As he rushed to take a seat, rivulets of perspiration poured off his forehead. For a moment, the air lay heavy and thick with silence.

His Holiness folded his hands on the desktop, drew a deep breath and spoke: "What we are about to discuss will never be repeated beyond the confines of this room." His eyes panned to each one in turn. "Is that fully understood?" They signaled their agreement with a simple nod.

The Pope continued: "Commander Stato, your assessment is only half correct." Stato perked his ears at the rebuke. "Yes, Monsignore Scarlotti was a double agent. More correctly an agent *provocateur* who'd been assigned by the Holy Office to infiltrate and report directly to me." Stato's mouth gaped in awe. "And yes, the Church has been infiltrated, but by a far more dangerous enemy than any governmental intelligence service. My dear friend Professor Max Schulman, who persuaded Rabbi Ben Yetzach to invite this Pope for a groundbreaking first visit to a synagogue, has supplied me with documented proof."

Stato's eyes searched the Pope's, and then turned to Spears, whose moss-agate-colored eyes only telegraphed agreement. Returning his gaze to the Pope, he said, "Forgive me, Holy Father . . . but I don't understand?"

"You shall, my son. I speak of *Protocollo Diciassette,* Protocol-17."

"But, Your Holiness, they were disbanded, run to ground by the reform government."

"Are you so sure of this? Is not a snake who sheds his skin still a snake? Does it not lay in wait beneath the rocks, cloaked in shadow, coiled to strike again? The heresy has borne many names: Gnosticism, Humanism, the enlightenment of the Illuminati through pure reason, placing science above God. Their goal is the creation of a New World Order. The Crusades, the Inquisition, may in retrospect seem ruthless, but the *Adversary* is equally ruthless."

Stato met the Pope's eyes and, with a note of apology said, "Of course, one hears rumors. But Holiness, these are only—"

Spears's towering frame rose from his chair. "Your Holiness, if I may?" The Pontiff nodded his approval. Like an enraged spirit, the gargantuan, white-robed Dominican loomed over Stato. "As the Americans say, 'where there's smoke, there's fire.' An all-consuming fire threatens the very walls of this Church, and its tongues of flame lick at the hearts and souls of the clergy and the laity alike." Spears's eyes bristled, punctuating each syllable with a razor-edged glare. "Are you familiar with the term 'THE PROCESS'?"

Stato's flesh crawled. An unreasonable fear slithered in his stomach. He'd read and heard the term in his study of comparative religions and theology at the tutelage of *Professore* Georges Monti. He'd even considered joining the priesthood in his youth.

He recalled Monti's lecture. *Professore* Monti had stood before the class, a somber expression molding his face. "*THE PROCESS* is a Luciferean concept of the plan for the domination of this world by the 'force behind the forces.'" Monti had paused for effect, his watery eyes twinkling. "Or to put it in the vernacular of your popular music, that British group's song, 'Sympathy for the Devil.' None other than: 'Pleased to meet you, hope you guess my name'—Shaitan . . . Lucifer."

Now, Stato stared vacantly into space, digesting the implications.

Spears gave him a moment to reflect before he spoke. "I can see by your reaction that you are indeed familiar with the term."

The Master-General's booming voice jolted him back to the present. "Here," he said as he proffered a parchment to Stato. "See for yourself."

Cardinal Secretary of State Moscato adjusted his skullcap and clutched his pectoral cross. His face was flaming as red as his sash.

With trembling hands, Stato took the parchment. Emblazoned across the top were the words *Protocollo Diciassette (P-17)* flanked by inverted crosses; a white dove soared downward beneath the title. And beneath it, the signatures of numerous high-ranking members of the Holy See and the crest of the Knights of Malta, whose members were frequently top officials in the world's law enforcement and intelligence community. Men like the former director of the CIA who'd stood side by side with the Pope in his hard-fought struggle against communism. Even a former U.S. Attorney General.

Then came a virtual who's who list of the Vatican: the foreign minister, the cardinal vicar of Rome, the head of the Vigilanza, the Vatican's intelligence service.

Stato's eyes burned with indignation as they traveled down the list of names: Archbishop Marsciocco, former head of the Vatican Bank... and at the very bottom, in a wide looping scrawl—Cardinal Moscato.

CHAPTER 48

STATO LOOKED UP into the Pontiff's disconcerted gaze. He'd seen that look before, seen it in the eyes of men filled with the hollow ache of betrayal, with an unappeasable sadness.

Cardinal Moscato's eyes locked on Spears, staring him down like a hungry pit bull. Without warning he leaped across the desk. His arms flailing, he grabbed for the Slavic Pope, his wart-stippled hands clawing at the Pontiff's throat.

He panted like a bitch in heat.

His purple-stained face contorted in madness as he screamed strings of obscenities.   His hand clutched at his pectoral cross and thumbed the hidden release button. With a flash of cold steel, the blade sprang from the bottom of the cross. Arcing it high above him, poised to strike...

Damien Spears's shovel-sized hands seized the mad dog, plucking him off the Pope and hurtling him to floor. Just as the mongrel cardinal rose to launch a second attack, Stato was on him. Beretta in hand, he rammed the pistol's muzzle beneath his chin.

The cardinal's eyes reeked not of terror but undiluted hatred. Stato ripped the crucifix from around Moscato's neck.

Hearing the commotion, two Swiss Guardsmen, replete in their Michelangelo-designed striped jump suits, burst through the door wielding halberds, vicious-looking, long-handled axes made originally for infantrymen to unhorse armored knights. Savage weapons made to cleave armor and flesh, splinter bone, hack limbs. Made to disembowel.

Stato quickly concealed his Beretta, jamming it into the small of Cardinal Moscato's back. "Just give me an excuse, you pig," he whispered into Moscato's ear.

Master-General Damien Spears, bearlike, giant of a man that he was, now stood at the Pope's side behind the desk. A picture of demure demeanor, there was a gentle concern in his manner and expression as he tended to the Holy Father. He dismissed the Swiss Guard with a wave of his large ham of a hand. The Holy Father nodded his acquiescence.

The door closed with the quiet slip of wood on wood.

Stato threw Cardinal Moscato into a high-backed chair and bound his hands to the arms of the chair with plastic field cuffs that he always carried.

A soft light poured through a forest of crossbars on the windowpanes, dappling the Pope's cheeks in a penumbra of tearlike shadows. Stato was struck by the *supernal* effect of the phantom teardrops. In contrast, only a resolute strength, a vitality, seemed to corona the Holy Father's gossamer, white vestments as he sat in profile bathed in light.

The Pope rose slowly on rubbery legs and began to move toward a side door. He turned to Moscato. "Christ is no longer honored in the tabernacle. You have replaced him with debauchery and avarice, but the true body of Christ, the Mystical Body of Christ, lives on. It lives on in the faith of the multitudes who live their meager lives in quiet desperation, sometimes under the boot of tyranny, but they have hope, they have faith. It lives on in the faces of a few valiant men and women who fight the good fight, sometimes against overwhelming odds. Who stand tall in the light of day, sure in their convictions. Who do not cower in the shadows of secrecy, plotting and coveting. They sacrifice, endure ridicule and hardship, but they do not falter, they do not surrender."

Moscato struggled in his chair, fighting against his bonds. "You weak old fool. You haven't the courage, the stomach for it, do you?"

Squaring his shoulders, the Pope said, "I will not allow this papacy to return to its past roots of the tenth century, when it like the old Roman god Janus had two faces, one Christian, one antichristian, one friendly and benevolent, the other hideous and malignant, personified by the antipopes of old. It is painful for me to expose these shocking corruptions; but I pray that God and the Blessed Virgin will guide my hand, give me the strength. With the Blessed Mother's help, I have done my part to silence the snarl of the great bear, Communism. I have done my part to seek the forgiveness of those peoples so wronged by the church. I have flung open the doors to the world's other paths to salvation, and have been accused of being overly liberal, while on the other hand, too much of a hardliner on church doctrine. But in this purge of evil I will not waver, I will not weaken. The truth must be told, with its nourishing lessons of humility tempered by humiliation."

"You don't know anything," Moscato said, sneering and tugging at his bonds.

The Pope's gentle eyes fell upon him. "You have fettered more than your limbs, *Eminenza.* You have bound your soul with the machinations of the Left Hand Path. But it's never too late. Do you wish to renew your baptismal vows, your Holy Ordination, and reject Satan?"

Moscato's face twisted into a sardonic grin as he cursed. "*Basta!* Before this day is done, you and your church will be ruined; the wheels are already in motion. The Nazarene cross continues to crumble. You can't stop us. We move amongst you, visibly and invisibly."

The Pontiff's face became leaden with sorrow. "Stato, learn what you can from him."

"Yes, Holiness. With pleasure," Stato answered. Then pressing his face to Moscato's, he whispered, "You'd be surprised what I have the stomach for."

The Holy Father's brow creased with pain as he said to Stato, "You must cooperate fully with *Professore* Giovanni and his nephew from the SISDe. The Foreign Ministry called moments ago. Giovanni's own life is in grave danger. He is a brave and noble son of the Holy Church. Protect him with your own life if need be, *Commandante*." Stato nodded solemnly. "I have a lingering, grave fear. These turncoat clergymen have something diabolical planned for our Holy Church. We are still trying to decipher the details of their plan. Damien will brief you further as facts come to light. And send an *umo di fiducia*, one of your most trusted officers, to Turin … to *La Cattedrale Di SanGiovanni il Battista*. Secure the Shroud of Turin from its custodian, Cardinal Saldarini, and bring it here immediately."

"As you wish, Your Holiness," Stato said.

Raising his hand in the traditional papal blessing, ring and pinky fingers curved against the inner palm, index and middle fingers extended, thumb hooked inward, the Pope blessed Stato.

A dazzling light streamed through the Palladian windows, washing across the Pope's extended hand and casting a shadow image upon the wall, a hovering, smokelike portent. The diabolical inverse: *Daemon est Deus Inversus*.

The horned head of Satan.

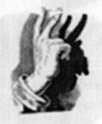

Alone in his study with his trusted secretary, Cardinal Stanislaw, the Pope applied his seal to the last of a stack of envelopes and regarded his secretary. "How many years have we been together, my old fried?" Although the Pope was old enough to be Stanislaw's father and treated him like a son, he liked to make a small joke of it by referring to Stanislaw as an old friend.

"More than I care to remember, Your Holiness."

With a tremulous hand, the Pope slid the envelopes across to his aide. "Have these delivered into the hands of the addressees first thing in the morning."

Stanislaw collected the letters and bowed humbly.

"I have compiled a detailed report and have attached it to the Protocol-17 charter," the Pope said, reaching into his desk drawer and removing a red dossier. As he handed it to Stanislaw, he added, "Place these documents along with my will ..."

Suddenly the Pontiff slumped forward and his hand shot to his forehead, rubbing his temples.

"Are you all right?"

The Pope nodded. "Some water, please. I am feeling a bit weak today."

After handing him a crystal tumbler and watching his palsied hands struggle to hold the glass to his lips and sip, Stanislaw said, "Perhaps you should rest now."

As the Pope placed the glass on the desktop, their eyes locked. In a calm voice, he reverted to their shared native tongue, Polish, and regarded a statue of the Blessed Mother he'd received from Fatima. *"Nie opuszczaj mnie teraz, don't leave me now."*

To Stanislaw, he said, "I pray that the Blessed Virgin will grant me the strength to stay the course." His gaze drifted to the envelopes clutched in the secretary's hand. Each contained a letter calling for the immediate resignations of those who were members of the Brotherhood. "What led them astray? What evil is this that causes me to ask these men for their resignation at the point of what should have been the crowning achievement of their service to God?"

The secretary stood mute, his eyes radiating empathy.

"I feel the tombstone pressing down on me, old friend. And it weighs cold and heavy on my heart."

Easing him from his chair, the secretary guided the Pope to his papal bedroom.

CHAPTER 49

After receiving instructions from the SISDe's director to standby for further instructions, Rossi and his uncle knitted their way through the hallways of the Apostolic Palace.

"We'll hook up with Commandante Stato at his office," Rossi said. "Headquarters is dispatching a group from the Carabinieri Foreign Affairs Command. They're usually involved in the security of the Ministry of Foreign Affairs and of national and overseas diplomatic representatives. They're also sending reinforcements from the Carabinieri Parachutists Regiment, Tuscania."

"How long will it take?" Giovanni said, struggling to keep pace.

"They're en route. Stato will probably have his nose out of joint, but this comes from the top, and has been confirmed by the Pope."

"Then the Pontiff has been made aware of the threat?"

"That's the way I understood it." As he walked, Rossi glanced at his wristwatch. "The director insists upon speaking with Stato and a few others. Wants me to cool my heels, not talk to anyone else."

"Then why don't you settle down, nephew? We need cool heads at a time like this."

Rossi frowned, chewed his lower lip. "Something strange, though, I also got word that Claudio, one of my techs, was rushed to the hospital. Influenza-like symptoms, but so strong a strain that it's put him on life-support."

Before Giovanni could answer, one of his assistants appeared, red-faced and breathless. "*Professore*, this came by special courier," he said, handing him a package.

Giovanni nodded. "Where is the Chinon Parchment?"

The assistant eyed him dully for a moment and then his eyes brightened. "In your safe?"

"You have the combination. I made need it later."

The assistant scurried off.

As he stared at the envelope, Giovanni's eyebrows beetled. "The return address is Chicago. It's from my colleague, Max Schulman."

Motioning toward a settee and hoisting the package, the professor said, "I have a bad feeling that we need to open this now. "

"But I need to talk with Stato," Rossi insisted.

"You've already made provisions to insure the Pope's safety. Now plant yourself down and listen. There's something terribly wrong going on here."

"*Certtamente!* They're plotting to kill the Pontiff."

"Indeed. But the question is, who?" Giovanni said sternly.

"We know it's the Templars."

"Don't be so cock sure." He ripped opened the express envelope. "This whole business with the Templars bothers me. I have found documents in the Vatican archives, including a long-lost parchment, which prove that the Pope had in fact questioned Grand Master Jacques de Molay, and other leading Templars, in the dungeons of Chinon castle in the Loire Valley in 1308, in what amounted to a papal trial."

"But wasn't Molay burned at the stake?"

"Yes. The document shows that Pope Clement V secretly pardoned the Knights Templar but his absolution remained a secret."

"Maybe the Pope was too conveniently a day late and dollar short to the Templars' way of thinking?" Rossi offered.

Giovanni sighed. "Sin by omission, yes, but it's ancient history now. And to use your vernacular, not a very strong motive."

When he pulled out a print of a copperplate engraving, his mouth hung wide-open.

"Death, Knight, Devil by Albrecht Durer, 1514," Giovanni read aloud its title printed below. His face was drained of color.

"More bad news I take it?" Rossi said, regarding the picture. "Looks like someone's nightmare to me."

"It may well be," Giovanni said grimly. "Durer is an important representative of 'Northern Renaissance.' From Germany, he traveled to Italy where he could have met the most important central characters of so-called enlightenment of this period. Among his friends were magicians like Cornelius Agrippa von Nettesheim and Johann Trithemius. But he was much more than just an artist in contemporary sense ... he was an adept!"

"At what?"

"Magick."

Rossi laughed. "Slight of hand, making rabbits jump out of hats?"

"NO! Magick, spelled with a 'k' that is, from the Greek *Kteis* and *Kosmos,* to distinguish it from common stage magic. He knew of the secrets of the Great Work, Alchemy."

"Kteis and Kosmos? Sounds like coitus and cosmos."

Giovanni blushed and rolled his eyes. "You're close. Kteis means scallop shell or female sexual organ. It symbolizes the divine feminine." His uncle raised his hands and by joining the tips of his index fingers and thumbs formed an elongated oval shape. "A crude model but sufficient," he said, peering through the gap. "The vesica piscis also symbolizes the vagina, which is the gateway to God. The true Holy Grail." Rossi's gaze tracked back to his uncle's eyes, staring incredulously.

Giovanni lowered his hands and winked. "Now you know the secret, nephew, the secret of all secret societies, so closely guarded by the Templars and many men of letters that they suffered torture, ridicule, being branded demonologists and even death, rather than reveal the innermost secret."

"Sounds sick ... like an excuse for orgies."

"That's because the Church has demonized sex. Almost everyone who read *The Da Vinci Code* missed this revealed, dark secret. Instead of 'apple' being the final combination key to the cryptex, it should have been 'sex' or 'orgasm.' In the novel, Sophie's grandfather and his friends worshiped the supernatural force that resided in their own bodies. In fact, the word 'orgy,' Greek *orgia,* means simply, 'working, activation.' They believed that sex, the sacred chemical wedding or Heiros Gamos… is the key or bridge to the cosmos."

"How's Durer fit into this?" Rossi asked.

"Durer was a student of Alberti, the author of the *Hypnerotomachi Poliphili*; *The Strife of Love in a Dream.* The novel *Rule of the Four* also missed Alberti's true purpose. It's a symbolic guidebook that tells how to commune with God at the point of orgasm, which the French call 'the little death' because our minds become a clean slate at the point of climax. The veil drops, the fog lifts, and we can see and talk with God on a personal level."

Rossi chuckled. "I bet Master General Spears would like to have you drawn and quartered for suggesting this stuff."

186

Giovanni smiled. "The good Master General and I have agreed to disagree on this point. But he gets to the boiling point when I point out that it's all right there in the Bible... Solomon's Key."

"No way!" Rossi fidgeted in his seat.

"The Old Testament's Song of Solomon is a pathworking guide to the hidden corridor. It was the original liturgy of the sacred marriage ritual itself."

"What's this got to do with the Templars?"

"Everything. I see you need more background if you're going to understand what's at stake here. There has been an age-old war, fought for centuries, a battle of beliefs."

"You mean Islam vs. Christianity?"

"I mean what many like the Templars and the Alchemists believed to be the true, earliest doctrine of Christianity vs. the 'big lie' taught by the Church of Rome. Secret truths were passed from the Gnostics to the Templars. Truths that survive today in the Freemasons and some higher adepts of secret societies."

"So why don't they get the word out if they're so convinced?"

"It's a deadly war. Thousands have been slaughtered and persecuted for trying. What they needed was proof!"

"Proof of what? That sex is the link to God?"

"Hard evidence, and a celebrity endorsement."

"Like some soccer star hawking aftershave?"

"No, by His only Son. Legend states that the Templars found this proof near Solomon's Temple and used it to blackmail the church."

"Seems like their ace in the hole didn't carry much weight."

"Some say that they were missing the final key to the puzzle. The key that would unlock some ancient scroll, the proof written in Christ's own hand that he and Mary Magdalene were wed."

"You're not talking about that business of Jesus and Mary Magdalene raising a brood of heirs?"

Giovanni scowled. "No. The beauty and simplicity of the 'sacred marriage' has been lost. It's been distorted into the myth of Christ's Holy Bloodline. The Song of Solomon is the key to the code surrounding Mary Magdalene.

"The Templars knew the true secret of the Holy Grail. Mary was indeed the bride of Christ, but not in a traditional sense. That's an oversimplification. The Goddess, in this case Mary, was the opener of the way, called the sexual initiatrix.

"Now, what was it that the Templars were accused of worshiping?"

Rossi searched his memory. "Lucifer and a head, the bahfa... something—"

"The Bhaphomet— *Caput* 58—a goat-headed symbol of virility some say, while others say it was the name of the Goddess Sophia written in an early secret code called the Atbash Cipher. Like the Gnostic Gospels, the Templars venerated ... Mary Lucifer... the light-bringer."

"The devil?" Rossi protested.

Shaking his head, Giovanni laughed. "Ridiculous! Lucifer literally means simply 'light-bringer,' from *lux, lucis,* 'light,' and *ferre* 'to bring.' Milton added to the confusion with his fiction *Paradise Lost.*

"In the Bible Lucifer like Christ was called the bright morning star, who through mystical, sexual union with his consort the planet Venus—the evening star found the constellation Virgo—achieved the resurrection and the awakening. This is the true Lucifer that the Templars worshiped."

Rossi whistled. "I can see why the Templars got roasted on the spit. Zio... what's the point?"

Giovanni smiled warmly. "Jung said that dreams are private myths and myths are public dreams."

"Okay, nice little myth or bedtime story, but let's get on with the show, Zio."

Rossi frowned; bit his lower lip. Rossi fished his cell phone from his pocket and punched the speed dial to his director's office. After a short exchange, he clicked off. "They say he's still tied up, can't take a call, damn it all to hell!"

"Then stay with me, please. Now that you have more background on the Templars, what two historical figures were their undoing?" his uncle asked.

"King Philip and the Pope Clement V," Rossi offered.

"Right, take a close look at the print. See the two figures behind the *Knight* on horseback who of course represents the Templars?"

Rossi leaned in. "Looks like a king with a really bad hair day, a crown of snakes."

"And that would be Philip the Fair, representing *Death* and done up like mythical Medusa, an allusion to the King's vanity. She was the most famous Gorgon. No living being could look at her without being turned into stone. Finally, Perseus cut off her head while she was sleeping and brought it to Athena."

"Kind of an allusion to ... beheadings?"

He uncle grimaced. "I'm afraid you're right. Now find the Pope, please."

Rossi's finger wavered and then ... "Right there, the ugly guy with the face of ... a goat!"

"More precisely ... the *Devil,*" his uncle corrected. "Durer is telling us that the Templars regarded the Pope as the Prince of Lies because he hid the true path to God from the world." His uncle paused and began whistling a Mozart concerto.

Rossi checked his watch. "Zio, we really need to move along."

Giovanni waved his hand dismissively. "Hush, I'm thinking."

"That's it, now I recall," Giovanni said, his eyes brightening. "The dimensions of the engraving also held a symbolic clue. They were almost an exact ratio of thirteen to ten ... an infamous day for the Templars, remember?"

"October ... Friday the thirteenth? The day they were rounded up. And that's today!" He shot to his feet.

"Sit down, Nico, this instant! And get control of your emotions."

He did.

"That's better." Giovanni smiled. "Later, when their Grand Master Jacques or Jacob de Molay was burnt at the stake, he swore vengeance. Both the Pope and the King died that same year. And strangely enough, according to the number code of the Kabbalah, they both shared the letter of—Death."

"Six, six, six," Rossi offered, snickering.

Shaking his head adamantly, his uncle went on. "No. One ooh six." He pulled out a pen. "Jacob De Molay, Papa Clement, and Philip le Bell all equal one hundred and six.

"Zio, enough with the symbols and the history lesson, please."

"Don't rush me, nephew. Max thought this was important enough to rush to my attention. He's no fool. Remember that to the adepts of the occult, this is a world filled with symbols and correspondences. If you want to get into their heads, you must see the world as they do. If you have a sociopathic serial killer running lose who believes in astrology you—"

"Study astrology to catch him. Determine his next move." Rossi bowed his head in feigned apology. "*Mi dispiace*, I'm very sorry and stand rightly chastised, Zio."

"Now you're thinking correctly. Are you familiar with the Tarot deck?"

"Those cards fortune-tellers use?"

"Some say they, too, use allegory and symbols to conceal an ancient wisdom stemming back as far as the Egyptians. Number one hundred and six is also the gematrical value of a Tarot card, specifically the ... Death card." Giovanni's gaze locked on Rossi. "Now look at the bottom of the print ... see the skull lying above the Tablet?"

Rossi nodded.

"Again the *caput*, the head and the date of the Tablet ..."

Rossi shrugged. "It's just a date again. Fifteen ... thirteen AD."

"Don't be so sure. "No, in fact it's a coded message. A dire message."

CHAPTER 50

A MOTORCADE OF limos and vans sat nestled on the tarmac in front of a fixed base operations hanger at Rome's *Ciampino* airport. As the wind whipped across the ramp, the private Learjet turned and taxied to a halt, its screaming engines spooling down. The door emblazoned with the symbol of the Church of Eschatology, a flaming golden *E* snaked and entwined within two canted pyramids, swung open. Two limos and a pair of black Mercedes SUVs broke ranks and streamed into position at the bottom of the stairs. A sober-faced bodyguard exited first, nodded to his associate standing at the foot of the stairs and turned, which signaled his principals that the coast was clear. Honora and Drago Volante, followed by an entourage of aides, emerged and made their way into the waiting limos.

The smoked-glass partition rose as Volante hit the rocker switch and poured a pricey malted scotch into a cut-crystal glass. Turning to Honora, he said, "Care for a little celebratory nip?"

"I'll have the Cristal," she said, easing back into the leather seat and stretching her long, shapely legs. She wore a long-sleeved crème white Versace dress cut teasingly just above the knee with a hip-hugging tan leather belt. Donnatella had designed it expressly for her. The luxuriant material swathed her curvaceous form whenever she languidly sauntered with the confident grace of a runway model.

As Honora removed her matching leather gloves, he filled the fluted glass and handed it to her. They toasted. "How is the Italian do-gooder?" he asked. "I had our Bedouin friends snatch her as a bargaining chip in the case the Italian authorities try to interfere with our plans."

"She's fine and riding with Oba. That loathsome witch, pardon the expression."

He laughed. "Wrong culture. Oba's West African, found her at our Nigerian Temple. High Priestess of a cult devoted to the river goddess. She's named after the Nigerian goddess of the River Oba, wife of the god of thunder and protector of prostitutes."

"She's striking, carries herself like a warrior goddess, but is it true she wears a magical loincloth under her robe that she hasn't changed in years?"

Volante shrugged. "She does smell a bit ripe, doesn't she? I wouldn't know from personal experience, but it's quite probable. It's her … *Mojo,* works like an amulet that contains her power."

"Loyal?"

"To a fault."

Honora absently tugged at her earlobe and then smoothed her skirt with her palm. "Are you still planning on using your little dark angel of death?"

"Laylah is an integral part of the plan. But I'm more concerned with the supreme secret of *Le Cahier.*"

"You've decoded its message, then?" she asked, her voice incredulous.

He gave a wry smile. "Not yet but we're very close. Ahriman has laid a trap and will soon have the pertinent passages from *Le Cahier* decoded by our unsuspecting friend, *Professore* Giovanni. We are, however, racing against time. I have suspicions that our rivals, the Rosicrucians, and their British intelligence lackeys have gotten wind of the supreme secret."

"You mean MI-6?"

Volante nodded. He knew that the British Secret Service was founded by members of the Rosicrucian order whose descendents still run the show.

Honora frowned. "I still don't see what's so earth shattering about it, the whole religious history thing. The average person nowadays is more concerned with who J. Lo's marrying this time or who's sleeping with who on *Desperate Housewives* or how they can afford the latest gas-guzzling monster SUV than what a bunch of misogynistic old coots who lived in caves thought centuries ago." She opened her Chanel clutch purse, pulled out a tube, and freshened her lipstick, blotting the excess with a napkin and taking another hit of Cristal.

Volante studied his hands for a moment then looked up and said calmly, "On the surface, especially in the States, your reasoning is absolutely correct. But beneath that plastic, consumer-driven façade, people from around the globe still hold some things sacrosanct. Over one billion practice the Catholic faith. But if you cause them to question what they've been spoon-fed from infancy, question the veracity of their religious leaders, you create a hailstorm of doubt. The foundation begins to quake."

"You want that house of cards to topple?"

"That's our goal and they're playing right into my hands. The Christian right is making overtures to the Jews, misguided by our seeding the media with portents of the End Times. Putting the televangelist Pledger Lee Robinson on our payroll was the one good idea Ahriman came up with."

Honora crossed her leg and loosened her shoe; let it dangle on the tip of her toes as she bobbed her delicate ankle. "Those TV evangelists are nothing but old whores made up in new paint."

"Let's not be too judgmental, darling. You have to admire their ability to soak every last dollar out of the old widows. I'm stealing some of their brightest marketing people. Our latest demographics show a sharp drop in the numbers of the Viagra-popping set and the thirtysomething members."

"Sure, our bread and butter have always been the younger, guilt-ridden, greedy bastards who thought money would solve all their problems. Speaking of greedy bastards, I saw our baby-faced spokesman Gil Slade on the Entertainment network last evening. I realize that being a box-office movie star makes him a valuable product endorsement for the *E* Institute, but—"

"That he is. Our PR department set up the usual circuit of interviews to highlight Slade's new love interest, that pubescent actress who is the latest infatuation of eighteen to thirty-five demographic."

" … Suzie Wentworth?"

"Right. So what's the problem?"

"Bad press, darling. They showed a tight shot of Slade and Suzie on the red carpet at his new Sci-Fi epic movie premiere."

"Exactly the kind of publicity we want for our all-American boy. PR has leaked the rumor that Suzie's pregnant. The tabloids are gobbling it up."

"Let me finish. Looming in the background shot was that female watchdog you have shadowing Suzie. It was just a sound bite, but they zoomed in on the woman and identified her as being an employee of the *E* Institute. They implied that we were grooming Ms. Wentworth for membership and monitoring her every move."

Drago frowned. "I see your point. I'll call the intel division and have them put Ms. Wentworth on a looser leash, have her watchdog back off."

"Intel needs to back off—period. Lately they've been fucking up the works. That not-guilty plea on Little Nicky's child molestation case was botched because that trashy bitch they dug up … the victim's mother turned out to be a total fraud, a grifter. The jury saw right through her. A guilty plea would have insured us getting the royalty rights to the Beatles' songbook that's worth about five hundred mil… now we've got zip."

He shook his head. "It's of small consequence. Little Nicky used the royalty rights as collateral and one of our banks holds the note. And our 'emperor of rock' is laying low in a Bedouin-owned hotel in the Middle East as we speak. He's still right under our thumb. Besides when we got Cary Carlie Tishly to enter into that sham marriage with Little Nicky, we got our hooks into her daddy's estate."

Her lips began to tighten and she brushed a shock of hair from her forehead. "You could have told me. How are our plans for the bombing going?"

"Right on track. Our hypocritical Muslim martyrs who hold such contempt for women and, at the same time, are bursting with wet-dream visions of a paradise filled with earthly delights and seventy virgins, the very fruits forbidden by their self-imposed fundamentalism, are in place and ready to pounce."

Honora laughed. "If those poor boys knew anything about women or sex, they'd know that one talented and experienced hooker would be more satisfying than seventy veiled little cupcake virgins."

"Crudely put, but accurate," Volante said with a thin smile. "We had a nice run with the 9/11 suicide hijackers, but lately the pool of young zealots ready to trade life for heavenly concubines has fallen off. We've had to throw many of them to the wolves, let the western intelligence agencies think they're winning the war on terrorism."

"So you switched to using recent converts."

He nodded and lit a cigarette. "We need to bring back that 'ol' time religion.'" Volante pointed to the dome of St. Peter's rising over the rooftops below as they negotiated a steep hill and said solemnly, "This too shall pass."

"I think it's a mistake," Honora suddenly blurted, rifling her purse for a vial of cocaine. Bringing the tiny spoon to her nostril, she sniffed hard and rubbed her nose with the back of her hand.

"What's that you said?" Volante asked, his brows furrowing.

She proffered the coke, but he brushed it away with a dismissive wave of the hand. Shrugging, she returned the vial to her purse and fished out her makeup.

"Laylah. She's unstable, damaged goods," Honora said, matter-of-factly as she checked her makeup with the mirror of her compact. "You've tinkered around with her psyche to the point where she's become a monster." She tweaked an eyebrow, scowled, snapped the compact shut.

Volante swallowed the last of his scotch and regarded her with a cold stare. "Laylah is completely under our control. She's bright and adapts to her environment like a chameleon. In fact, she's already in place, waiting for his arrival."

Honora turned to the car window and sighed. "You make it sound like a computer game," she said sarcastically, pretending to be studying the scenery steaming past as they made their way around the city. "What if Giovanni or Rossi connect the dots? What then?" Her head swiveled toward him, eyes probing.

"If they do, we'll use our bargaining chip. Besides, Ahriman's plan will have them running in circles, focusing on the wrong target. Then, just when they think they've diverted a major tragedy, we shall strike with vengeance."

He smiled warmly. "Now if you'll excuse me, I've got a few calls to make." He reached for an encrypted SATCOM phone that was untraceable and as unfathomable as a self-replenishing, one-time code pad. A microchip or crytochip within used constantly varying complex algorithmic sequences. Every time he used it, the encryption scheme changed. He punched a number for his Vatican operative who used a similarly encrypted phone.

CHAPTER 51

Giovanni went on. "Look closely at the tablet."

If we take the **S**, and then substitute the numbers from the date on the tablet with the corresponding letters … turning fifteen into **O**, and thirteen into **N**, and tack on the **AD**, we get **SONAD,** an anagram. Reading it backward we get the Greek word **DANOS**, meaning 'burnt,' an epitaph in remembrance of Molay's burning at the stake. I think Max would agree that Durer's hidden message in this engraving is… 'We shall seek revenge by a blazing inferno.'"

For some inexplicable reason, as though it were an omen of things to come, the image of flames licking at Molay's body turned Rossi's blood cold.

Giovanni removed his glasses, pulled out a well-worn handkerchief and cleaned his lenses, then looked upward toward the ceiling.

"The language of symbols surrounds us. Many painters of this era, Leonardo da Vinci to name one, used sacred geometry to disguise a hidden message within the very depths of their work"

"How so?"

His uncle pointed upward to a tapestry on the ceiling. "First notice the symbol above the virginal woman who is floating in the clouds surrounded by cherubic angels."

Squinting his eyes, Rossi said, "It's an eye in a pyramid, the Illuminati symbol. Right here in the Vatican. And she's holding a snake?"

"The eye inside the pyramid, point up or down, has often appeared in Christian art. Sometimes placed high above the altar as in the Fisherman's church at Traunkirchen, while it appears over a doorway in the church of the monastery of St. Florian near Linz. Also in the Last Supper."

"Now come on. I've seen Da Vinci's fresco a million times, there's no—"

"Not Da Vinci. It was Da Vinci's protégée Jacopo Pontormo, copying Durer's composition, who placed it above Christ in his work 'Supper at Emmaus.'"

"Okay, but the snake?"

"An Ouroboros more accurately, the symbol of regeneration. The serpent eating its own tail. Again, we have another sexual reference."

Rossi grimaced. "So we have X-rated, decadent art right in plain view on the ceiling of one of the holiest places in the world?"

Giovanni winked. "The symbol of the serpent, representing strength, virtue, and super powers can even be see in today's pop culture."

Headshake: "Super powers? Really, Zio. Now you're getting your comic book fantasy world mixed up with religious symbolism? "

"See for yourself." Giovanni pulled a comic book from his inside coat pocket and pointed to the emblem on the superhero's chest. "The tip of the 'S' clearly shows the eye of the serpent. And the shield is an inverted pentagon."

I think you've been reading too much Freud. Superman is as American as—"

"Apple pie?" Giovanni broke in. "Ever wondered why the apple was the symbol of forbidden fruit, forbidden knowledge?"

"No, but I'm sure you'll tell me anyway."

Giovanni reached into his pocket and pulled out an apple. "My lunch," he said, smiling. Then he fumbled in his pants pocket and removed a penknife. He sliced the apple in half, placed one half on the settee, and pointed to the remaining fruit's center with the point of the blade. "Take note of the core … it forms a familiar shape, does it not?"

Rossi leaned forwarded, looking closely. From the apple's center an outline stared back. "I'll be damned. A pentagram!"

Giovanni smiled. "Freud with his belief in the overwhelming power of the libido almost had it right, but Carl Jung was closer to the mark. He was a Gnostic much like our friends the Templars. Believed in personal contact with God, without any intermediaries like the Church."

"That would lighten the coffers of Rome along with those of most churches, wouldn't it?"

"Not a popular stance, which is why the Templars were such a threat. The real point you have to understand is that no matter what the secret societies call themselves, Illuminati or Rosicrucians or Knights Malta, they're all the same. And unfortunately, many leaders of these groups have become power-crazed."

Giovanni reached into his pocket, took out a U.S. one dollar bill and red marker pen. "Another little prop I like to carry to demonstrate a point. The founding fathers of the greatest superpower of earth, the United States, were Freemasons and closet occultists." He pointed to the dollar bill. "They hid within the most widely used currency in the world … a magick talisman."

"Something that's charged with power like an amulet?" Rossi said.

"Very good." Deftly, Giovanni drew outlines on the bill. "See how the two seals are connected with a column that reads 'In God We Trust'?"

"Sure."

"Now when you fold them over one another, you have two back-to-back powerful talismans. The two seals with words of power written within one and on the edge of the other design were modeled after these magick talismans found in the Greater Key of Solomon, the most infamous grimoire in Western occultism." Removing a tiny book from his pocket, Giovanni thumbed to a page and pointed.

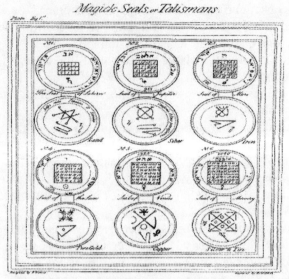

"The seals are upright but the resemblance is …"

"Uncanny." Rossi said, and gave a low whistle.

"Now look at the Great Seal again," his uncle prompted.

"I see an eagle but—"

"The original design resembled a Phoenix, which like America, rose from the ashes, reborn. But look at the thirteen stars above." His uncle had already superimposed a design with marker.

Rossi's eyes ticked from the ceiling and back to the dollar bill. "It's the Seal of Solomon, just like in the tapestry above us."

Pulling out the Durer engraving again, his uncle said, "Now that your eyes have opened, Mr. prudish bureaucrat, find the design hidden here. And remember, the Templars were burnt at the stake for worshiping it." Giovanni's eyes, already bright with amusement, brightened even more as he said it.

"If you draw a line from the tip of the spear … across to the…"

198

"Oh, Lord," his uncle whined. "We really don't have all day. It's an inverted pentacle or pentagram."

Rossi blanched. "So they really did worship the Devil."

"Have you been listening to anything I've just said? That's a subjective and spurious slander on a mere symbol of regeneration. Early Christians attributed the pentagram to the Five Wounds of Christ and from then until medieval times, it was a lesser-used Christian symbol. Geometric symbols mirror life and the world around us." He took out a pencil and pad and drew a pentagon. "Now if I connect the five inside corners of the pentagon … we get an upright five-pointed star. Imagine Leonardo's Virtruvian man standing within the star, arms and legs outstretched. Ergo, the star is a symbol for man, the microcosm of the macrocosm of the universe."

"I'm still with you, go on."

"Look at the center of the star and you'll see the inversions clearly."

"You're right … it forms an inverted pentagon, Superman's shield."

"And within the pentagon?"

Rossi drew a sharp breath. "Another inverted pentagram."

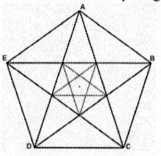

"The power of renewal."

"Okay, but a symbol of regeneration? God and sex again?"

"If we weren't fruitful and didn't multiply, you and I wouldn't be sitting here having this conversation. And His Holiness, Pope John Paul II, says as much in his *Gospel of the Body*."

* * *

Meanwhile somewhere in another section of Rome, Monsignor Scarlotti sat huddled on his cot in a dark cell. Light glared suddenly when the door opened, and he could barely make out dark shapes rushing toward him. They yanked a black sack over his head and jerked him off the cot. When they got him to his feet, his legs gave out. Still on his knees, they dragged him into the hallway.

He heard muffled voices. Then his eyes needled with pain as the hood was ripped away. When his eyes adjusted to the bright lighting, he was confused.

199

He looked around and found himself kneeling in front of a group of men dressed in the traditional black garb of Arab terrorists, their faces masked with checkered scarves. His gaze cut to the front, searching for the source of the harsh lighting. Overhead, two studio spots hummed and blazed downward. Lowering his eyes, he noticed the video camera.

A similarly dressed man emerged from behind the camera.

Clutched in his hand was a wickedly sharp scimitar.

He walked past Scarlotti without making eye contact and handed the sword to one of the other terrorists stationed behind the monsignor.

Scarlotti's confusion was replaced by sheer terror.

CHAPTER 52

THE *OMBRA* UNIT was positioned in the hallway of the fugitive's flat.
Dante had been surprised to find that the address Rossi had given him over the
phone actually existed. Checking with the landlord, he had determined that the
rent checks were paid by none other than Claude, the owner of the Black Cat
Café. He figured he'd get kudos from Rossi for his fine detective work.

Dante and Enrico bracketed the door dressed in black flack vests and Kevlar
helmets, their weapons at the ready. On the rooftop, a second team waited to
rappel from above and into the window. Lorenzo manned the apartment above,
peering at the image from a micro snake-eye camera that had been inserted
through a tiny hole drilled into the fugitive's ceiling.

Dante whispered, "I hear water running."

Enrico nodded.

"Lorenzo, from Dante. Whatta we got?"

"Looks like steam pouring from under the bathroom door. Let me scan
around. It's a one-room flat. Clothes strewn on the bed, dirty dishes piled in the
sink. No visible targets."

"Woman's clothing?"

"Looks like nylons and panties ... red."

"Can you drop another eye into the bathroom and a spike for ears?"

"Maybe if I had another set of hands. Okay, hold on."

His palm sweaty and clutching the grip of the H&K MP-10, back pressed hard
to the wall, Dante said, "*Ombra* Unit, standby one." Cupping the headset mic
with his free hand, to Enrico, he said, "You go in high, I'll go in low, clear?"

Enrico nodded. "We should call the boss."

Headshake: "After the way we fucked up last time? *Merda* no! ... we'll take
her down ourselves." Dante's eyes cut to Paulo who stood in a shooter's stance
down the hall a few feet to his left out of the line of fire of the doorway, the
muzzle of his submachine gun trained on the door. "I'll kick it, toss the flash-
bang grenade, and you'll go in first."

The click of a mic and: "It's definitely a woman. Here, I'll light you up."

Projected on the visor of Dante's helmet was the nude image of a woman,
standing with her head titled back beneath the spray of a showerhead, full pert
breasts lathered with soap, her hands running a sponge over her flat stomach and
water-glazed thighs.

"Lorenzo, can you make out the face?" Dante asked.

"Repeat ..."

"Put your *cazzo* back in your pants. Her *face*, can you get a positive ID?"

"Negative. But the hair's long and dark."

"Copy … *Ombra* Unit from Dante. Masks up and visors down. We go on my mark."

They acknowledged his command.

Like a well-oiled machine, the unit pounced. Simultaneously, the door slammed inward, the flash-bang rolled across the floor and detonated in the closeness of the cramped flat with a blinding flash, and the window glass showered inward as the agent swung from above and into the room. Another agent ducked and rolled into the smoke-clotted air, mask in place. Dante swung in high, while Enrico came in low. The maglites from beneath the muzzles of their carbines cut narrow swaths through the heavy blanket of smoke.

"Clear," Dante shouted, his voice laminating over a shrill scream that came from behind the bathroom door.

Taking up strategic positions around the room, weapons trained on the bathroom doorway, Dante signaled toward the door with a short, chopping motion.

Just as Dante was about to give the woman in the bathroom one last chance to surrender, the door slowly began to creep open.

"She's coming out," Lorenzo's voice poured into his earpiece.

Dante tensed, sighting on the middle of the doorway, fingertip hugging the trigger, breath coming in ragged, Darth-Vader-like rasps from behind his gas mask.

Instantly, from both sides, rough hands grabbed her arms, pitched her nude body to the floor and cuffed her wrists at the small of her back with plastic bands. Enrico raised his visor, expertly searched her long hair, between her thighs. Dante noticed that Enrico's eyes saucered wide as he did it. Puzzled, Dante signaled to him by nodding curtly toward the hallway. Enrico snatched her under one armpit while Lorenzo grabbed the other, and together they hoisted her and dragged her out into the hall on her knees.

Still in their grasp she knelt, head bowed, a curtain of sable hair hanging wet and disheveled.

Mask off, Dante stood before her.

"*Stronza*," Dante said, reaching out, snatching a handful of hair and yanking her head up.

Her feral eyes bristling with rage, she spit in his face. Enraged, Dante wiped the spittle from his lips with his palm and backhanded her hard across the mouth. A worm of blood crawled down her lower lip.

"*Tua madre si da per niente!* " she hissed in a deep voice, commenting on his mother's virginity, and spitting blood from between puffy lips.

A door down the hall opened, a face peeked out briefly and then quickly the door slammed shut.

In the distance Klaxons wailed.

"We need to move her … now," Enrico said.

Dante stiffened and nodded.

"There's something you need to know," Enrico added sheepishly.

"Save it for later," Dante snapped gruffly. Wrapped in the moment, Dante pointed a gloved finger in her face. Before he could speak, her mouth hinged wide and she bit down hard on his finger, twisting her head like a ravenous wildcat.

Dante howled in agony and drove the tip of his boot into her stomach. She released her clamped teeth and retched in pain.

"*Mannaggia fessacchione*! … damn idiot," he screamed, and tucked his injured hand beneath his arm, doubling over in pain.

"You'll need a rabies shot and an HIV test," Paulo cautioned sarcastically.

Dante grimaced. "Get her to her feet and take her out the back way to the van."

When they raised her to her full height, Dante stared in disbelief.

She was taller than he'd expected, and from between her legs, a donkey-sized dong dangled in the breeze.

Seeing his awe-shocked face, Enrico said, "That's what I was trying to tell you. She or … he's a *finnochio*."

"A transsexual," Paulo corrected, studying her body matter-of-factly. "Great *tette* but he … I mean she, hasn't had the lower half retooled yet."

She tossed her head haughtily and spoke between sobs in a hoarse voice, "Claude was going to loan me the money for the operation, but said he liked me better this way."

Dante felt the blood draining from his cheeks. His hand flew to his vest pocket and he retrieved the mug shot. His gaze fixed on the he-she's over-sized Adam's apple and rose to the brown, wide-set eyes. "*Ciposa*, toad-face ugly," he muttered, shaking his head. He held the photo before him for comparison, blinked, his eyes ticking back and forth, taking in the delicate, high cheekbones of the woman in the photo.

Just then they heard footfalls pounding down the stairwell, and Lorenzo bounded around the corner out of breath. "Where's my lovely Madonna?"

He drew up short at Dante's side, jaw gaping wide. "*Palle!*"

"Big as coconuts," Paulo said, snickering.

Pasty faced and shaking his head, Lorenzo managed, "Well *ciucciami il cazzo*, suck my dick."

Smiling knowingly, she winked and said in a deep throaty voice, "I'd be glad to, honey."

"***Is it just possible that*** you were so busy drooling over her *tette th*at you screwed up the ID and we got the wrong person, Lorenzo?" Dant*e* said, turning and stud*y*ing him coldly.

"Rossi's going to h*a*ve my butt, isn't he?" Lo*r*enzo offered.

"Our collective butt*s*, gentlemen," Dante sa*i*d.

"Ooh … *st*op that dirty talk, boys" sh*e* said, pur*r*ing. "You're *s*tarting to get me aroused."

As all eyes darted to her groin, mouths gaping in horror, Dante snapped, "Put a blanket on …her now! And bring her along. Let's get the hell out of here."

Lorenzo bolted for the flat, hands covering his eyes.

To his back, Dante shouted, "Lorenzo, you stay back and handle the Carabinieri and search the room. Think you can handle that*?*"

From the flat, Lorenzo's quaking voice, said weakly, "I'm gonna be sick… just don't leave me alone with her."

CHAPTER 53

Giovanni continued. "But there is a perverted, dark, and obscene side to Gnosticism that was left out of *The Da Vinci Code*. To put it simply, certain sects became hung up on the lower rung of Jacob's ladder of spiritual enlightenment. Their own egos devoured their souls, and they sought the Unholy Grail, the Judas Cup, and drowned in a power trip. Or to use another pop culture term… the Dark Side of the Force."

"Devil worshipers? The little guy with the horns and cloven feet."

A kind, sympathetic smile: "You've been programmed to hold up Zeus, an old, beared man on a throne, as your archetype of God. You're referring to another god—Pan. Like the serpent, his archetype was corrupted by cults, even certain members of the Templars and present day Freemasons see him as Lord of the Dark Side. But the devil doesn't rule the Dark Side. It's not a demon with a pitchfork and a tail, but rather, our own selfish id, that spoiled brat that lies deep within all our souls. Freud understood its nature. He believed that through normal, healthy development, a child's superego or conscience eventually seizes the reins and bridles that little demon. The demon that wants instant gratification, refuses to share, and worships himself and his power over others. These misguided occultists let the little imp out of his cage."

"Now hold on. And the little guy with the flute and horns and cloven feet who seduced maidens in the wood was God, too. No. Now you're teasing."

"Ever enjoy the organ music at mass on Sunday? Marvel at those long polished pipes towering to the ceilings in older churches?"

"Of course, but—"

"Well then you're enjoying the seven-fluted pipe of Pan. I rest my case."

"That's twisting the facts."

"Ever heard of Christ referred to as the good Shepherd who guides his flock to salvation?"

Rossi nodded.

"The pan-pipe is the regular instrument of the shepherd, so the Good Shepherd is, in Christian art, often represented with a pipe of seven reeds or straws, the classic syrinx of Pan."

Although Rossi had intended to quit while he was ahead, he heard himself saying,

"Fine … but what's this about the Judas Cup?"

"That subject we'll leave for another time. Later, Christians hid the fact that early Jews honored the Goddess, Yahuah's wife, who the Gnostics called Sophia. Michelangelo knew the truth and painted her at God's side right in plain sight on the ceiling of the Sistine Chapel. "

"You mean the painting where man's and God's fingers almost touch?"

"Yes, follow God's arm to His image and at his left … you'll see Sophia. From the digs at such sites as Kuntiller Ajrud, in the northern Sinai, we have found ninth-to-eighth century buildings with inscriptions such as 'Yahuah by his Asherah.' This proves that the Judeans worshiped the fertility Goddess, a large-breasted women with a pillar-shaped body."

"So who's this Asherah?" Rossi asked.

"The Goddess who was worshiped by King Solomon at the first temple in Jerusalem. Most Jewish people don't realize they honored God's wife when they named their country.

"Look closely at the name, IS-RA-EL. It's a holy trinity. Isis … Ra … and El."

"You mean—?"Rossi asked.

"Yes, *IS* the female principal—or Isis the ancient Egyptian Goddess of fertility, the sister and wife of Osiris. *RA* the male principal—their sun god, the supreme deity, represented as a man crowned with a solar disk or halo."

His gaze slowly meeting Giovanni's, Rossi said, "There's just one thing you haven't explained."

Giovanni cocked his eyebrows. "No, I most certainly covered all the bases."

"Zio, why did Professor Schulman send you this print?"

"You mean prints. Some Professor …let's see …"—he scanned a letter taken from the envelope—"… yes, a Nemo Bugenhagen of Vienna asked Max's help in finding a so-called secret message hidden in Durer's engravings. Max agreed with Nemo's theory that the three engravings were meant to be combined, thus relating a message for those who could decode it." Giovanni continued to read, then went on. "Indeed, Max was able to decipher some of the Kabbalistic symbols, but he felt that he only found the first of three messages."

"Which was?"

"Let me see," Giovanni said, and glanced at the letter again. "This is quite extraordinary. He says the engravings are a key to a passage found in *Le Cahier de la Rose Noire*."

Rossi gave a puzzled look.

"The notebook that was taken from the Vatican Archives," Giovanni explained.

Another print fell from Giovanni's lap to the floor. When he picked it up, his face turned white as a sheet.

"What's wrong?" Rossi demanded.

His voice cracking with tension, his uncle said, "Max wrote a note in the margin here. It says that Nemo asked that I in particular be sent this rendering of a Masonic Temple … Max asks that I have patience with Nemo's apparent eccentric nature and goes on to quote Nemo, 'The *professore* will need this to locate his missing friend.'"

"I don't get the joke," Rossi said.

"It's no joke." Giovanni paled and struck his forehead with his palm. "*Mah!* It just occurred to me that Nemo is Greek for 'no one.' And I fear that this Professor 'Nobody' was referring to none other than—Monsignore Scarlotti!"

From down the hallway heavy footfalls pounded marble tile. A brigade from the Carabinieri Airborne Regiment stormed double-time toward the papal apartments and took up positions alongside the Swiss Guardsmen stationed at key posts. Outfitted in midnight blue army fatigues, their trousers bloused neatly into combat boots, berets cocked sharply and H&K PG-1 submachine guns slung over the shoulder and hanging muzzle down against their black flack vests, the GIS, *Gruppo Invento Speciale*, officers made the colorfully dressed Swiss Guardsmen appear to have stepped through a wormhole in the space time continuum and into the present. A stern faced GIS agent, who wore the rank of major, marched toward Rossi. He was pretending not to notice the anachronistic Swiss Guardsman at his side, who fought to match him stride for stride, his face flaming with indignation.

Simultaneously they shouted, "*Colonnello* Rossi?" He stood. "You have an urgent phone call." Like trained attack dogs responding to their master's order to "cut," the two mismatched officers spun sharply on their heels, indicating in military talk that Rossi was to follow. Rossi and Giovanni exchanged glances and tagged along.

PART III

"The Church's negative judgment in regard to Masonic associations remains unchanged since their principles have always been considered irreconcilable with the doctrine of the Church and therefore membership in them remains forbidden. Catholics who enroll in Masonic associations are in a state of grave sin and may not receive Holy Communion. Local Ecclesiastical authorities do not have the faculty to pronounce a judgment on the nature of Masonic associations which may include a diminution of the above-mentioned judgment."

Cardinal Ratzinger, restating the Vatican's ban on Masonry 1983

CHAPTER 54

IN THE VATICAN security office, Rossi stood cradling the phone's receiver to his ear. Around him banks of television monitors flickered and systems lights from alarm boards twinkled. Surveillance cameras flashed live pictures of corridors and rooms. Whenever the Pope moved throughout the Vatican, a supervisor in the security office directed the monitoring of his every movement.

With clockwork precision, advance teams of guards were already in place, securing the area. As the Pope departed each succeeding location, like a computerized grid work of automated steel gates, the guards took up positions, sealing off access from the rear. From the corner of his eye, Rossi caught the image of the Pope's white soutane streaming into a doorway, followed by an entourage of sober-faced cardinals resplendent in their cassocks of crimson simar and fascia and priests who scurried behind them.

"Mr. Rossi of the SISDe?" a voice asked in a thick Arabic accent.

"Speaking."

"I suggest you have a guard put us on the speaker so everyone can hear. And oh, I suggest you tape it, also."

Rossi smiled to himself as he took in the guard with the earphones who sat at a console intently listening to their every word. To the guard, he said, "Put it on the box, please." Turning his attention back to the caller, he said, "You're on the speaker."

"Very well. Now listen carefully. We have brought the Holy Jihad to your doorstep."

"Be specific. Who's we?"

"I believe you refer to us as al-Qaeda."

"Demands?"

"The immediate resignation of the false *al-Nabi*."

"I assume that by prophet you're referring to the Pope?"

"Correct. And the release of a list of prisoners unjustly held by your security service."

"And if we don't comply?"

"The priest, the rotund, goat-faced one you call Scarlotti, will be the first to die."

"I'd need proof of life."

"I don't understand this term?"

"Proof that you have him, that he's still alive."

"Check your television newscast, Signore Rossi."

Frantically, Rossi scribbled a request to turn on a local news channel and slid it across the desk to the carabinieri officer. The major nodded and ran to a guard seated at a control console who punched up the news broadcast.

On the screen, the image of Monsignor Scarlotti appeared. Behind him stood three men dressed in black, their faces concealed, their dark eyes peeking from behind red-and-white checkered *gutras*, their heads hooded. The man in the center clutched a long scimitar. Its wicked blade caught the light and gleamed coldly. The camera zoomed into a close-up of Scarlotti's face. The lips were puffed and split, the right eye bruised and swollen shut, the face a mask of terror and agony. The camera panned to another dark figure who held today's *La Repubblica* in his hands.

"Judging by your silence, I perceive you've seen your proof of life," the voice said.

Rossi's mind tumbled downward. His younger sister, Bianca, was a refugee camp worker in Afghanistan. He'd begged her to return home, warning her of the constant threat of kidnapping, the violence, but she'd hushed him using their mother's saying, "God will shelter me from the devil's storm." Her last letter was months ago. Now in his mind's eye it was Bianca's he saw kneeling before those dark-eyed devil's henchmen not Monsignore Scarlotti. Her fawn-like eyes were tearing, radiating helplessness. Her soft voice begged from between trembling lips, "Nico save me!"

The Arab's teasing laugh from the other end of the line snapped him back to reality.

"Why are you doing this?" Rossi demanded, his throat constricting, his heart pounding against his ribcage.

"The false prophet speaks not against the occupation of Iraq, not against the suffering of the Palestinian people at the hands of the Zionists. Rather he speaks of ecumenical understanding and agrees to worship in their blasphemous temples. His servants prey upon the innocent children, Allah's lambs. And he turns a blind eye, preferring not to anger his shameful harlot, the gold of the great Satan ... the United States."

Around him guards and GIS officers stood, hands fisting at their sides, faces hardened with anger and rage. His own fingers clutched the underside of the desk so tightly that his hand began to cramp. He knew that he had to keep his wits about him, keep the man on the other end talking as long a he could.

Across the room, a GIS officer studied the voice-stress analyzer's print out of the conversation. Another sat perched on the edge of his seat, waiting for the results of a phone line trace.

"All around him the past stares with eyes veiled in tears," the voice went on. "The martyrs of the past will bear witness to the bull-headed priest's final moments of death. The first stone has been cast into the pond and its ripple will be felt across the world. You have one hour. And if you doubt our sincerity, watch, listen, and wait. Sit glued to your television screen. See the flames of Hell."

The vapid hum of dial tone droned in his ear.

CHAPTER 55

IN AN ANTEROOM just off the hospital chapel, Johnny Brett handed the SATCOM phone back to *Bast,* who was still dressed in the guise of Sister Mary Benedict and stood guarding the door.

"Well? How was my performance?" he asked.

"Not bad, a little over the top, Sheikh Alibaba," she taunted.

"Critics ... everyone's a critic. What did you expect? That script you gave me reads like something from a grade B spy thriller."

"You read it word for word?" she said, eyes narrowing. "Those were your instructions."

"Of course, I never ad lib." He shrugged and moved to a rack of votive candles. He held the one sheet script over the candle, letting the flames devour it.

She stared fixedly.

He held the paper too long and burned his finger. "Ouch!" Sucking his fingertip briefly, he turned. "So who's this Rossi guy? And whose phone did you patch me through? The connection was terrible."

Her watchful eyes cut right through him.

"Okay ... I get the point, sorry I asked."

"You'll live a lot longer if you forget you ever made that call."

He nodded. "So what now?"

"We wait."

CHAPTER 56

IN COMMANDER STATO'S private office, Cardinal Moscato sat in a stupor, slumped in a chair, his face bruised, right eye puffy and swollen shut. An IV drip-fed his forearm. Stato stood at the sink in his private half-bath, back turned, washing his hands compulsively.

Father Damien Spears's huge form towered over Moscato. He reached out with his knockwurst fingers and checked the cardinal's carotid artery for a pulse, then lifted an eyelid. To Stato, he said, "Think he's under yet?"

Stato stepped out, wiping his hands with a towel and said, "The Sodium Pentothal and Rohypnol should have taken hold by now. Let's give it a try." He tossed the towel on the desk.

Flipping a chair around and sliding it between his legs, Stato sat directly in front of the semi-comatose cardinal. Spears pulled a chair to Stato's side and slowly lowered his hulking frame into it.

"Cardinal Moscato, can you hear me?" Stato asked.

The cardinal grunted, bobbed his head slightly.

"How much did you give him?" Spears said.

"Enough to make an elephant sing…"

Spears looked deeply into Stato's eyes, holding them. "I think you're enjoying this too much."

Stato's gaze slid back to the cardinal. "Cardinal Moscato, I've forgotten the recognition code."

The cardinal flinched, but said nothing.

"Damn. He wouldn't go for it."

"Let me try something." Spears leaned forward, resting his huge hands on his knees. "*Buon Cugino.*"

"*Buon Cugino* …" the cardinal muttered

A puzzled look filled Stato's face.

"It means 'good cousin,'" Spears explained.

"But how did you—"

"When I loosened his collar, I found this medallion around his neck." Spears held the medal by its gold chain and then tossed it to Stato.

"Looks like a holy medal."

"At first glance, it appears to be a holy medal depicting St. Theobald. But look closer and you'll notice that their patron saint is clutching a hatchet."

"Whose patron saint?"

"I'll explain shortly. Let me finish."

Turning to Moscato, Spears asked, "And how, *Buon Cugino,* shall we exact our revenge?"

Rolling his head, the cardinal managed, "DANOS!"

"DANOS?"

"Operation Dragon's Breath will devour them in flames."

"But how … when?" Spears pressed.

Moscato's face began twitching; his whole body shuddered in spasms. He went rigid, then slumped forward.

Spears leaned closer, snapped his fingers, shook him violently. No response.

Sighing heavily, he turned to Stato. "It's no use, he's out cold."

"I've heard of it, but I've never seen it in action," Stato explained. "They've apparently implanted a post hypnotic, blocking mechanism. It's called an Azriel Block in Psy Ops.

"When Moscato said the words 'Operation Dragon's Breath,' it acted like a hypnotic trigger word, signaling his mind to shutdown. Even if I inject him with a stimulant, the minute we hit another trigger word, he'll go into lock-down mode again."

Spears grunted his disappointment.

"But maybe if you'd explain about the medal he was wearing and '*Buon Cugino'* we could decipher what he meant," Stato suggested.

"*Buon Cugino,* is the recognition sign of the *Carbonari,* a secret political society, a *società segreta*, who adopted their name from the charcoal-burners," Spears went on. "The hatchet denotes a master, whereas a tiny faggot lapel pin denotes an apprentice. When they speak with one another, they use many expressions taken from the old trade of charcoal-burning. Their assembly place is called *baracca* or hut, its interior *vendita* or place of selling coal, and its surroundings *foresta* or forest."

Stato shook his head. "You mean like the Freemasons adopted the stone masons' guilds and used their tools, like the square and compass, as symbols?"

"Exactly, because the *Carbonari* is a branch of Masonry that was established in Naples and France in the beginning of the nineteenth century." The Dominican's eyes narrowed. "But the symbols hold deeper meaning for higher-ranking members. In the center of the square and compass the Masons placed the letter **G**. The members of the lower Blue Lodge are told that it represents GOD, the great architect; however, once they pass to the highest-grade level, they are told the truth… the true secret of the Holy Grail." Spears went to the computer and called up a web site.

Spears pointed to the Masonic symbol on the screen.

Spears continued. "The compass represents the male, the blade engaged in coitus with the square, the female symbol or chalice. And in the center of the sexual symbol we find 'G' which represents gnosis. The compass and square equal the missionary position. Picture yourself standing at he foot of the bridal bed as the couple makes love." Spears stopped and regarded Stato. "You getting any of this, yet?"

"Not sure I want to. But the Holy Grail is Christ's Chalice."

"NO! For them it's the JUDAS CUP. The Whore of Babylon's cup of abominations."

Stato winced "You mean the Harlot from Revelations is the cup?"

"A living chalice of depravity. They believe that both male and female provide the magic elixir, which then must be eaten, taken as communion. But in their ritual it's all about lust, and the woman is not placed on a pedestal; in fact … she's usually the victim of ceremonial, gang rape. This is the true nature of their so-called 'blessed' ritual of Hieros Gamos. Afterward, they drink directly from The Judas Cup, the harlot's vagina."

"The magic elixir is … their own semen?"

"Precisely, the perverts mix their own gooey 'elixir' and that of the goddess, menstrual blood, into the Eucharistic host and eat it from the Judas Cup!"

His face flaming red, then green, Stato stared.

Moscato moaned. Turning toward the sound, Stato thought he detected the hint of a smile on the cardinal's lips.

A pulsing small amber light drew the security chief's attention. It meant that the Pope was moving somewhere within the confines of the Vatican. Stato's eyes darted to a rack of closed circuit television monitors that tracked the Pontiff's movements.

CHAPTER 57

A knot of officers stood huddled around the TV monitor in the Vatican security command center. Rossi lit a cigarette and tried to derive some modicum of pleasure, soothe his frayed nerves. A Swiss Guardsman sat at the console talking on the phone. Rossi tapped him on the shoulder and said, "Get anything on that trace yet?"

The tech looked up, studied him a moment, then averted his gaze before speaking. "I think Commandante Stato should—"

"And just where is this Stato?" Rossi cut in.

"He has given orders not to be disturbed," the tech said sheepishly.

The GIS major appeared at his side and ripped the phone from the tech's hand. He spoke a few fast and harsh words into the receiver and hung up. Looking around the room, he gestured for Rossi to follow him to a more distant corner of the room.

"Okay, you've got my attention. What is it, Major?" Rossi said.

"Name's Brazi, sir. I don't trust these Swiss Guard *leccaculo* prima donnas."

Impatience flooded Rossi's face. "Let's leave the turf battle for another day, or you'll be licking the boots of the Minister of Interior in about three seconds. Understood?"

"*Capisce.* It's just that central switching told me the call came from within the Vatican."

Rossi took a deep drag and regarded Brazi for a moment in silence. "What about the newscast tape?"

"Delivered to the Vatican Press Office. Had the tape and the package sent to CCIS for processing. They'll do the usual video breakdown to try to get a fix on location."

"How about the voice-stress analyzer?"

"Already got an analysis from the linguists, too. No masking, adult male probably middle-aged or older. But the speech pattern showed flux."

"Deception?"

"No deceptive responses, except one. Linguist says it was more like ... a shift from geographically nonspecific Middle Eastern dialect to west coast American."

"Which response was a lie?"

"When you asked him to be specific and he answered ... 'al-Qaeda.'"

Rossi's head jerked back, as if he'd taken a light jab to the chin. "Summary conclusion?"

"Possible fabricated ethnic pretense."

"An imposter?"

"The linguist used a different word …called him an actor."

From the press of officers around the control console a clamor arose. Simultaneously, Rossi and Brazi spun toward the sound.

All eyes were focused on the TV screen. A news reporter stood outside of the Termini, Rome's central railway station located east of the Vatican across the city.

Emergency vehicles were parked helter-skelter behind him, their flashing beacons stabbing through billowing smoke and a frenzied stampede of people pouring out of the station, faces soot blackened and bloodied, eyes wide with terror.

"Turn up the volume," Rossi ordered, looking on in horror.

The excited voice of the TV reporter filled the room. "Witnesses report that as the Rapido-train from Naples was pulling out of the station it exploded, followed moments later by multiple detonations throughout the terminal itself. Within seconds, a wall of searing flames churned through the terminal. Flying shrapnel peppered the air. One passenger reported hearing the blast and then saw 'lots of silver' which was, in reality, shards of glass that carved up the right side of his face while leaving the other side unscathed. Unconfirmed reports state that just before the blast, a man hoisted a knapsack above his head, and shouted something in what one witness described as an 'Arabic sounding rant.'" A slightly blurred, hazy image of passengers within the terminal appeared. Handkerchiefs cupped to their faces, they trudged through debris and severed body parts. "What we are seeing are images captured with a cell-phone camera by a survivor immediately after the attack."

Rossi panned the room. A strange combination of fear and anger blossomed on each face.

Moving quickly, Rossi grabbed a secure phone and dialed his office.

Enrico answered.

"What happened at the Termini?" Rossi asked.

"Dante just called in. Preliminary reports indicate same MO as the 3/11 Spain attack, only this time it looks like suicide bombers. When combined with the beheading threat it sure smells like Zarqawi's al-Qaeda group."

"The mastermind behind the videotaped beheadings in Iraq," Rossi agreed. "Al-Zarqawi personally decapitated an American on tape. He was good for the hit on the U.S. AID official in Amman, Jordan and bombings from Casablanca to Istanbul."

"They had a twenty-five million dollar bounty on his head. He was Jordanian right?"

"*Certtamente*, he was a CIA supported and trained freedom fighter in Afghanistan. After they beat the Soviets, he returned to Jordan. The Jordanians had him behind bars for seven years for plotting to topple the monarchy and conspiring to establish an Islamic caliphate. But when they released him, he fled to Europe and began operating terrorist cells in Germany. A day late and a dollar short, the Jordanians tried him in absentia for planning attacks on American and Israeli tourists."

"But wasn't he wiped out when two five-hundred-pound bombs pulverized his not- so-*safe house*?"

Rossi shrugged. "Cut the head of a hydra and another grows to take its place."

His voice hitching, Enrico said, "There's something else. Airport surveillance recorded the arrival of two NSA agents."

"*Le palle*, the balls of those *stronzos!* Who were they?"

"Give me a second to punch it up, boss." Rossi could hear the clicking of the keyboard as Enrico's fingers called up the data. "Here we go. You're not going to like this. It's that old warhorse, SAIC Peter Manwich, and—"

"That fat pompous little *testa de merda*!" Rossi took a deep breath, counted to ten. "That shithead, Manwich, is a loose canon. Fort Meade uses him for black ops projects. Man's got the integrity of a hyena in heat. Who's the other agent?"

"Never heard of him, must be some FNG."

"Does the fucking new guy have a name?" Rossi knew that across the world, every secret service had a similar endearment for new agents who were added to a unit, fresh fish who had to learn their trade by trying the patience of the seasoned field agents.

"Kyle, Agent Kyle," Enrico came back.

Searching his memory banks, Rossi came up blank. "Circulate their pics around and have the *watchers'* surveillance units tail them. Plant a GPS Interlock System on their car and a mini beacon on their persons if you can manage a bump and tag when they're out on the street somewhere." Gone were the days when surveillance had to be done with agents following their targets, trying to get close without being noticed. Now watchers could sit comfortably in their car with their laptop computer; the software would display a real-time tracking image on a regional map. The signal could also be relayed through the Internet to a command center anywhere in the world. "I wanna know their every move," Rossi went on. "What they ate for lunch …what the hell they're doing on my turf."

"Consider it done, boss."

"Okay, back to the bombing. Casualties?"

"No accurate body count yet … but it looks really bad," Enrico said in a thin voice.

"I want you to have two squads on standby and coordinate with the Air Force Base at Pratica di Mare. Tell the *Raggrupamento Elicoteri* Carabinieri Unit Commander to have choppers on immediate standby with our squads. I may need you up in the air at a moment's notice."

"Are the train bombings and the priest's kidnapping related? Strange coincidence."

"No such thing as coincidence in our business, Enrico. Just have the teams ready and keep me posted. Oh, and have another helo sent to the Vatican for me."

"Copy three choppers. But don't you wanna know about Claudio?"

"*Merda*, I forgot. How's he doing?"

"Not so good, boss. Some really rare viral infection, but they're trying to stabilize him."

"Source?'

"Still undetermined."

Rossi took another deep breath. "Get a supply of antiviral antidote from the bio-warfare department, too, just in case."

"In case of what, boss?"

"In case my hunch is right."

"You had a message, too."

"Go on."

"It was a woman. Dante said she sounded *sensuale*."

"Spare me the editorial."

"Said to tell you, 'as time goes by.'"

Rossi swallowed audibly. His heart skipped one beat, then another. "She leave a number?"

"No, that's the weird part … said she had your cell number and would be in touch."

Rossi hung up.

The command post's door burst open and Giovanni scurried into the room as fast as his game leg would carry him, eyes blazing like the Mad Hatter.

"I think I know where Scarlotti is. Would someone be so kind as to fetch me a copy of that audio tape?"

No one moved.

Rossi's gaze darted to Brazi, who nodded and shouted, "Somebody give that man the tape, and I mean right now!"

The phone chimed and a fresh-faced guard answered. His face bleaching white and shooting to his feet, he stammered a few "immediately, sirs" and hung up.

He turned to Rossi. "I've been instructed to escort you to the Commandante's office—"

"Immediately?" Rossi said, finishing his sentence and smiling.

As they made for the door, Rossi's cell rang and he answered.

A soft voice whispered, "As time goes by, Nico."

CHAPTER 58

THE WOMAN'S VOICE washed over him like an ice-cold wave. The image of her face, her star-fire-topaz eyes, her soft generous lips, sent chills up his spine. It had been years ago when he was just a gangly adolescent that he met her. First love, never forgotten. Then again by chance on an assignment in Cairo their paths crossed again. Things weren't going so well at home with his new wife Isabella; she hated being left alone and his work required a lot of globetrotting. Tempers flared. Harsh words were exchanged, words that could never be taken back. A long tearful look as he walked out the door, heading for his flight. No goodbyes, no kiss, just a vacant, watery stare and then she turned away. Two days prior, tired of the hang-ups whenever he answered the phone, he decided to leave the office early and tail her. He realized far too late what a big mistake he'd made. Sometimes it's better not to know the truth, sometimes it better not to have those lingering images of her holding hands with her boss, the two of them arm-in-arm entering that seedy, little, back alley hotel at noon, haunting your memory forever.

The assignment in Cairo was top priority. The Italian passenger ship *Achille Lauro* had been hijacked off the coast of Egypt by four PLO terrorists. A disabled Jewish American passenger, Leon Klinghoffer, was shot and then pushed overboard in his wheelchair. After they surrendered to Egyptian authorities at port, Egypt's President Mubarak allowed the terrorists free passage out of the country. The PLF leader Abu Abbas had flown from Tunis to Cairo to escort them.

Since Rossi had been stationed briefly in Cairo and still had contacts, he'd been dispatched to mount surveillance and track the terrorists' departure.

Even now, Rossi remembered that night as if it were sealed in a child's glass globe waiting to be shaken to life. Seated in the Salam Hayat hotel bar, nursing his drink, and waiting for his Egyptian Air contact to show, he noticed a stunning woman make her way through the knot of press corps that filled the barroom. When she passed him, the woman smiled and left the lingering scent of her perfume trailing behind her like a lioness marking her territory.

As she walked away, she turned and stole a quick glance over her shoulder in his direction. Her eyes flashed a raw sexuality. He was smitten. No commitment, no expectations, and miles from home, why not? And yet, he felt uneasy. Something about her was so familiar.

He moved to her table, bought her a drink, made small talk. She said her name was Alexis, a freelance journalist covering the hijacking. He knew she was lying, but really didn't give a damn. When their eyes locked, for just a second, he detected a flicker of recognition, as though she'd seen an old lover or friend after many years. The air between them pulsed with sexual tension as the piano player pounded out a rendition of "As Time Goes By," the theme from Bogart's *Casablanca.* After awhile she excused herself to go to the ladies' room. "Will you be here when I get back?" she asked with a fawn-eyed look, then walked away before he could respond.

He ordered another round of drinks, checked his wristwatch. The contact was late.

Then he spotted him, a mousy little man, threading his way through the crowded barroom toward him. The man's narrow, beady eyes ticked around the cocktail lounge as he told him which flight the terrorists would board and the security arrangements. Then he scribbled the information on a piece of paper and slid it across the table. Rossi passed the payoff envelope, hidden in a newspaper, and the airline employee rose, bowed, and vanished into the blue-gray cloud of cigarette smoke that hung heavy in the room.

Scanning the lounge for her, his sixth sense kicked in. The hairs on the nape of his neck bristled. Instinctively, he bolted from his seat and walked anxiously toward the restrooms. He poked his head into the ladies' room, called her name. No response. That's when he heard it. A muffled scream.

It came from outside.

Without thinking, he dashed for the door, his hand reflexively reaching for the weapon on his hip. Cursing himself as he ran, he remembered that he wasn't carrying. Since he was using the cover identity of a reporter to avoid tipping off the Egyptian Secret Service, he hadn't used his diplomatic passport when he entered the country. He would have been searched and simply didn't have the time or the inclination to obtain a handgun from the embassy. Despite what he'd seen portrayed in the movies, Rossi had soon come to learn the startling truth. Intelligence agents, any visiting foreign agent for that matter, even those under the protection of being included in a host country's blue book or registered diplomat list (which he wasn't for this penetration op), were at the whim of that country's bureaucratic machinery when it came to carrying weapons. The less friendly the country, the more restrictive its gun laws, the more likely they'd play hardball as to who, how many agents, and what types of weapons they would allow. Although weapons were routinely brought in by diplomatic pouch, actually carrying one was another matter. Most of South America was a given, but Europe was a crapshoot, and the Middle East was a nightmare. Rossi could have blown the entire surveillance mission if he had been inadvertently caught carrying.

Another scream from the opposite corridor. He spun and veered around the corner.

More screams.

He kicked open the door and pounced into the alley.

There, back sandwiched to the wall, a forearm locked under his chin, was the source of the screams. The young Arab's eyes saucered wide as the blade of a knife hung inches from the soft jelly of his cornea. Hair frazzled, sweat glistening on her beautiful face now contorted with rage, Alexis stood, pinning him to the wall. She was shouting questions in Arabic at the man. His responses were garbled, his speech slurred. Rossi's eyes tracked to the ground. A spent syringe lay at Alexis's feet.

Rossi took a step forward. Suddenly her head spun, her icy stare stopped him in his tracks. "Stay out of It," she snapped. "It's none of your concern. Go back to your drink."

Although still seemingly drugged, the Arab saw his chance. His hand pistoned out, knifed into the hollow of her throat. She gagged, stumbled back, dropping the knife.

The Arab snatched the knife and lunged at her. The blade sliced across her chest, shredding her blouse. A hot wetness oozed from her breast.

Ripping off his sport coat and wrapping it around his forearm, Rossi shouted, "Over here, Abdul, the lady's had enough."

Like hyenas, they circled each other, eyes narrowing, waiting. The Arab held the knife low, tossing it back and forth between his hands as he weaved drunkenly. But Rossi stayed focused on the man's hands. The blade speared out, but Rossi parried the blow with his forearm, clamped down hard on the Arab's wrist, and wrenched it backward. With the sharp crack of cartilage, the knife tumbled from his hand.

As the man stood doubled over in pain, Alexis calmly walked up behind him and planted the tip of her pointy high-heeled shoe between his legs and drove it into his groin.

Frog-voiced and gasping for breath, she managed, "I had everything under control."

Rossi bent and picked up the knife. "Sure you did. I suppose you're going to tell me you were giving him dance lessons."

She started to rant, then composed herself. "He attacked me coming out of the restroom, drug me into the alley and almost ..."

The Arab shouted, "You lying whore!"

She spun and delivered a swift kick to his face. He cried out in agony.

Her blouse was torn, the left breast exposed and slightly filmed with blood, her lipstick smeared. "Why don't you wear this," Rossi offered, and draped his jacket over her shoulders. Then he handed her his handkerchief and pointed to her lips. Voices sounded from the doorway.

Guiding her by the elbow with a firm grip, they hurried down the alleyway.

A few minutes later from a pay phone in a nearby hotel lobby, he called the embassy. But when he reached into his pocket to retrieve the slip of paper with the departing flight information—it was gone. Frantically, he rifled his pockets.

He looked up. Across the lobby, Alexis was talking to a short man whose dark hair was shot with gray. He had bushy eyebrows and a flat nose. Rossi recognized him as Mossad's local Kasta. She slipped something into his hand. He smiled, they exchanged a few words and he left.

Rossi hung up and intercepted her in the center of the lobby. Tried to read her face, couldn't.

"I trust that the information will be passed into the right hands," Rossi said.

She tweaked her brows and smiled coyly. "Within an hour of the plane's departure, four U.S. F-14 Tomcats will intercept the airliner and force it to land at a NATO base in Sicily. Then the targets will be turned over to the Italian government for prosecution. We wanted to blow the plane but the *Cowboy* in the White House put the nix on it."

He shook his head. "You set me up."

"No Langley did. They tasked Mossad."

"And left OSI in the dark as usual. Was the guy in the alley for real?"

"The real deal. Followed me into the hotel and jumped me in the ladies' room."

"And the syringe?"

"Liked his women comatose I guess. Probably wanted to pack me off to the white slave trade. Just gave him a dose of his own meds."

Upstairs in the hotel room, he scooped her into his arms and they tumbled onto the bed. She accidentally knocked her head against the headboard, laughed. She kissed his upper lip softly, used her tongue to open his mouth wider. Then hungrily explored the inside of his mouth with her tongue. He responded, almost hesitantly, as if he were filled with a slight sense of guilt. She bit his lip, tugged gently.

As he cupped her breast, Alexis winced slightly. "It's okay, just a nick, bleeding's stopped." She took his hand and guided it down her side, across her belly.

224

When his fingers found the soft curve of her thigh, he noticed the birthmark. She trembled with energy, with urgency. In a breathy voice she whispered, "Take me."

After sex they lay smoking and talking.

Her eyes met his. "Nico, was it better than our first time?"

Without missing a beat, he said, "The first time we made love, Josie, when we were kids back in Roma, was also my first time with a woman. And nothing could ever surpass that."

She glared, staring unbelievingly. Without warning, she drew back and slapped him hard. "When did you know it was me?"

He pointed to the small, heart-shaped birthmark on her thigh. She smiled and slapped him again. "That was for holding back tonight and for dumping me for that other prig of a girl."

Rossi rubbed his cheek. "I didn't dump you. Your father found out about us and whisked you off to the States, remember?"

"And the other girl, the little buck-toothed curly-top?"

Rossi's brow furrowed, searching his memory.

Josie pressed closer. "I saw the two of you coming out of the library. She kissed you!"

Rossi began laughing uncontrollably. She rabbit-punched his arm. He grabbed her wrist and pulled her to him. She struggled, out-maneuvered him, and once on top, straddled him with her thighs, pinning him to the mattress. "Curly-top was my cousin Lucia," he managed between rasping breaths. "I helped her with her schoolwork, I swear that was all." Her mouth gaped wide and he gently closed it. Then he kissed her long and hard. She shuddered, her soft lips finding his neck, her breath hot against his flesh. They made love again.

Afterward they lay side by side, fingers laced delicately together as they held hands, a reassuring and comforting tingling sensation passing through his hand as they compared careers, dreams, and bitter moments from the past like his wife's affair with her boss. They were surprised but not shocked that they had both taken up the intelligence trade. Finally they drifted off to sleep, snuggled closely together beneath the cool sheets.

He'd always been a light sleeper, which was a necessary skill of his profession. Some intuitive warning roused him from sleep. He opened his eyes and lay perfectly still, waiting for his waking mind to interrupt what his instinct told him.

Soft whispers, a moan. Half-formed words floated in the darkness.

Making a guess at the direction the sounds were coming from, he sat up in bed, his ears and eyes siphoning the shadows.

But there was no intruder in the room. Mumbled pleadings came from Josie's lips. She tossed and turned violently, eyelids fluttering, hands clenching the sheet in a white-knuckled grip. Sweat glistened on her upper lip.

He reached out to touch her then pulled back.

A strangled breath caught in her throat, and she gagged. Suddenly a strange calmness molded the features of her face. She spoke aloud.

"Black room. Walls pressing in. Closer ... Closer." It was Josie's voice, but lower in pitch, deeper in timbre, like a guttural growl from deep within her chest.

Her back arched off the bed, and the manic, inarticulate whispers flooded from her lips again.

He decided to risk waking her. He grabbed her shoulders, whispered her name urgently. She quaked in his hands and finally woke with a jolt. "It's okay, you're safe," he said reassuringly. Then he brushed the damp, matted hair from her eyes. As he caressed her cheek, tears seeped between his fingers.

"Night terrors," she said in a distant voice and forcing a weak smile.

He nodded.

She told him how she'd been captured by militants. Buried alive for two days, a small pipe to the surface feeding her stale, hot air. How she'd been rescued, and later diagnosed with posttraumatic stress disorder that manifested itself in claustrophobia and nightmares.

He listened, captivated by her *vulnerabilità*.

Cradled in his arms, eventually she fell fast asleep.

The morning light woke him. He wondered if he would find her still in the grip of her demons. Turning over, he found that the bed was empty. She was gone.

***

"Nico, are you there?" Her voice pouring from the cell phone startled him from his daydream that left him with a residual dizziness.

"Josie?" he managed. "Where are you?"

"Near ... very near."

Giovanni stood staring, perplexed. Rossi raised his hand to indicate that it was an important call.

When the Swiss Guard began to protest, Rossi stared him down.

"I need your help, Nico. They have my Uncle Lotti," Josie said, her voice hitching.

"Who has him? Al-Qaeda?"

"No damn it! The Brotherhood. We have to find him ... find him before..." Her voice trailed off.

"Brotherhood?"

Her voice cracking, she managed. "It's too complicated. But check out the *E* Institute, and watch out for smoke screens. All I can tell you for now is that things aren't what they appear. And Nico—"

"I'm here."

"They killed my father, too."

"I'm sorry for your loss. Want me to tell my uncle?"

She paused a few beats. Then she said, "My father respected *Professore* Giovanni deeply, and like my father, he's a very wise man. But Nico…"

"You think they'll want him out of the way."

Then came a long pause, the drone of static on the line. He could picture her beautiful face darkening with concern.

"If he knows too much, if they perceive him as a threat … My father told me that he sent Giovanni a package. A Professor Nemo Bugenhagen wanted him to decode some puzzle. If your uncle has the package and has decoded the engravings…then—"

"You think this Nemo's involved?"

"His real name is Doctor Ahriman, works for this *E* Institute, and Nico—"

"I'll find Lotti, don't…"

"Ahriman killed my father."

He didn't know what to say. Hearing her voice after so many years, hearing a voice filled with such genuine need and urgency, almost tore his heart from its root.

"I'm doing my best." In his mind, he cursed himself. He knew the response was lame at best, such a sensitive guy.

"No! Promise me you'll find him."

"I can't—"

"Promise!"

He took a deep breath. "Okay, Josie. We'll find him. Maybe if you told me more—"

She cut in. "They're orchestrating something big. I'm just following a hunch, but I can't be in two places at once. But if I find this bastard Ahriman…" Her voice drifted off.

"Josie, you're talking in riddles."

"I'll be in touch." Then she clicked off.

He stood frozen, staring blankly into space.

"Who was it?" his uncle asked.

Rossi sighed. "A ghost from the past."

The bright flash of strobe lights mounted high on the wall seized their attention.

As the Swiss Guardsman's hand-held squawked, he turned in an effort to muffle the transmission. He barked his acknowledgement and when he turned back, his face was sheet-rock white.

"What's going on?" Rossi demanded.

"The Holy Father is very sick. They're rushing him to the hospital."

CHAPTER 59

Commander Stato met them at the outer office door. After exchanging warm greetings with Giovanni, Stato regarded Rossi with weary eyes and said, "The Holy Father has taken gravely ill. My people and the GIS are rushing him to Gemelli as we speak."

Rossi nodded. "We heard. Have you got anything we can go on to locate Scarlotti?"

Stato's eyes ticked to Giovanni who nodded and then back to Rossi. "Your uncle and the Holy Father seem to place great trust in you, Mr. Rossi." He glanced at his watch. "We have little time. The terrorists have given us one hour and there's only forty minutes left, so I'll be candid. Despite appearances and despite what your intel may be telling you, it's not al-Qaeda who is the real threat."

Rossi remained pokerfaced, though he was beginning to draw the same conclusion.

Stato frowned. "I've heard the broadcast, listened to their demands but…"

"The call came from within the Vatican," Rossi said bluntly.

"*Merda*!" Stato said. "That means there's more of them than I anticipated."

"Them?"

"Perhaps I can explain," Giovanni broke in. "But if you simply share what you have learned, Commandante, then things would proceed much more quickly."

Stato sighed. "Very well. There's a subversive group operating within the Vatican, *Protocollo Diciassette*. The Holy Father has shown me proof and I fear that Scarlotti, while attempting to infiltrate them, has been found out. They will stop at nothing to defame and destroy the Church. Scarlotti's and other lives are in grave danger." He turned sharply to Giovanni.

Giovanni pursed his lips and said, "Go ahead and tell him."

Stato nodded. "Scarlotti and your uncle are descendants of high-ranking cardinals who condemned the Templars. I've sworn to the Pontiff to see that no harm comes to your uncle. Two Swiss Guard are now waiting outside that door to become your constant bodyguards, *Professore*."

"That's really quite unnecessary—"

Rossi stiffened. "He'll follow the Holy Father's wishes, and thank you."

Sighing and shaking his head, Giovanni said, "Such foolishness, very well, but let's get down to business. I think I may know where they've taken Scarlotti … that is if you gentlemen would care to hear me out?"

Giovanni moved to the desk and laid out the prints of the engravings he'd been sent. Next he played the tape of the kidnapper's demand. To Stato, he said, "Would you get me a map of Roma, please?"

Stato hit a button on the desk's console and a section of the wall revolved, revealing a detailed map of the city. "Will this do?"

"Gadgets," Giovanni huffed. "The kidnapper's choice of words was most peculiar."

Stato and Rossi returned puzzled looks.

"Several times the words rotund and goat-faced were used," the *professore* explained. "Which, of course, neither describes Scarlotti nor for that matter, the Holy Father."

"A hidden message then?" Rossi asked.

Giovanni nodded and asked Rossi, "You're beginning to see their ways. If you'll recall, the engraving had a goat-faced man did it not?"

"Pope Clement V?"

"Very good."

"Are you saying they're truly after the Holy Father?" Stato said incredulously.

Rossi explained, "I called in the GIS more or less just acting on instinct, Commandante. You've shared with me, so I'll return the kindness. A highly skilled al-Qaeda operative is loose in the city. I have a nasty suspicion that she was within these walls today. "

Stato wrung his hands. "But if it's not al-Qaeda … it has to be…" He glanced at Giovanni. "Unless *Protocollo Diciassette* has been operating—"

Giovanni answered for him. "In consort with them or has somehow duped them."

Stato reached for the phone. "I must raise the threat level."

Rossi reached out and clamped Stato's hand. "It's already been taken care of. Major Brazi of the GIS is already taking extraordinary precautions."

Giovanni cleared his throat. Their eyes shot back to the engravings.

"Now the other word … rotund. Any thoughts?"

Stato bit his lower lip, shook his head. "Maybe rotondo?"

"That's it. The Pantheon just like before," Rossi said.

"Something tells me no. Remember that they also mentioned that the martyrs would bear witness," the *professore* reminded.

Stato's eyes brightened. "The Coliseum then. It's round and many Christians were martyred there." He rushed to the map with Rossi hot on his heels. Fishing out his cell phone, Rossi punched in the speed dial for the *Ombra* Unit. But as he dialed he noticed that Giovanni was still poring over the engravings.

Stato said, sighing, "This won't be that simple. The Coliseum is huge with lots of cavities. But at least a Carabinieri team could be there in minutes."

Giovanni's head shot up. He looked at the clock and then back to Stato. "What was that you just said?"

"The Carabinieri could be there—"

"No the first part."

Stato thought a second and said, "This won't be simple?"

"That's it. We're wrong," the *professore* said evenly. "We've got it all wrong."

Rossi stared wide-eyed, confusion creasing his brow.

"Not the Coliseum, the round temple of Faunus, the Roman Pan, which Pope **Simplicius** later named San Stefano Rotondo!"

Rossi's jaw dropped.

"Named after St. Stephan of Hungary and Christianity's protomartyr. The first martyr of the Holy Land. The church was modeled after the Holy Sepulcher in Jerusalem."

"You're sure?" Rossi asked, glancing at the clock.

Giovanni held up the drawing of the goat-headed Pan clutching a maiden in the Masonic Temple. "The followers of Simon Magus, the sorcerer who engaged St. Peter in the duel of miracles right here in Roma in about 60 AD, worshiped there." He paused for effect. "They sacrificed goats there. And as for the bull-headed reference, prior to that it was a Mithriac temple, where during excavation, they found the golden head of the bull."

Giovanni straightened with a self-satisfied smile on his lips.

Stato glanced at Rossi who shrugged. He turned to the *professore*. "But you said the eyes of the martyrs, plural not singular?"

Holding up one finger, Giovanni began whistling a Rossini aria and closed his eyes, deep in thought. His eyes flickered open and he said, "Ah yes, the frescoes. I'd forgotten. Niccolò Pomerancio decorated the colonnades of the outermost ambulatory with frescoes of the agony of the martyrs. In 1510, the Jesuits took it over, and young seminarians were instructed to go there to view and contemplate the shocking and horrific fate that might befall them when they became missionaries. I saw it once. Quite ghastly it was. Herod with the head of John the Baptist, Jael assassinating Sisera in his sleep, Peter writhing on the cross, Sebastian stuck full of arrows, Laurence frying upon the coals, Bartholomew flayed alive … a ring of tortured eyes leering down into the center and falling upon the altar."

Rossi and Stato exchanged momentary glances. Then their eyes darted to the map, searching.

231

"There it is," Stato said, pointing to the church's location.

A knock sounded at the door.

"*Avanti*," Stato barked.

A guard entered. "Excuse me, sir, but a helicopter just landed on the square. I ordered them to move it but—"

"That would be for me," Rossi explained, his stony eyes darting to the wall clock as the minute hand ticked one more notch.

Rossi moved for the door. "Officer, radio them that we're coming out, tell them to fire up the turbines."

The guard looked to Stato who nodded, then spoke into his hand-held.

With Giovanni at his side, Rossi paused at the door and turned back to Stato. "Coming, Commandante?"

Stato shook his head. "I've got some unfinished business here. And at the Pope's behest, I must take a trip." Solemnly, he moved and faced Rossi. Then he laid his hand on Rossi's shoulder and met his gaze. "I know the Pope is in good hands, but he asked that I call upon a good man, a man who I could trust to aide me. I think that you are that man, Signore Rossi. Will you assume my position in my absence?"

Rossi was dumbfounded and for a moment he stood mute, struggling to find the words. "I have a full plate. The terrorist attacks, this al-Qaeda agent still at large."

Stato held him with the force of his penetrating, plum-dark eyes.

Rossi sucked a deep breath, puffed his cheeks, and blew out an exasperated breath.

"Major Brazi is an honorable man, and capable. But if you want me to look over his shoulder … I could—"

Stato beamed. "May God be with you, then." He slapped him on the shoulder, turned, and headed for his inner office.

The radio squealed and the guard cut in. "Sir, they want to know your destination."

Eyes deadpan and voice expressionless, Rossi said, "Tell them we're going to Hell on earth. And it's a church, San Stefano."

CHAPTER 60

THE POLYCLINIC GEMELLI is the Pontiff's hospital of choice; it has become known as "The Third Vatican" after the Holy See and his summer home at *Castel Ganddolfo* outside Rome. The hospital, located in northern Rome about two and half miles from the Vatican, takes its name from Franciscan theologian and doctor Angostino Gemelli, who founded the Catholic University in 1922. The immense complex stretches across ninety acres on the edge of a national park and includes a church, research laboratories, a bank, a library and a barbershop. Doctors at the clinic saved the Pontiff's life when he suffered a gunshot wound to the abdomen during the 1981 assassination attempt.

The hospital has some 1,900 beds, divided between two sites, and employs about 5,000 staff members including doctors, nurses, and administrative personnel.

When in residence, the Pope stays in one of a suite of rooms on the tenth floor reserved for his use. The papal apartments include a chapel, a kitchen and sleeping quarters for his entourage of nuns and Vatican staff.

Out front of the hospital, a television news crew was interviewing the hospital's spokesman, a portly, elderly man with thinning hair that, judging from the lingering trace of gray roots, seemed to have been dyed jet-black.

The female reporter had the hard, polished look typical of an overly primed and smug cable newswoman. She was as lovely as any movie starlet who ever walked the red carpet at the Oscars, her gray eyes predatory, her smile as genuine as a mannequin.

Adjusting her blouse to show more cleavage, wiping the lipstick from her front teeth with her finger and checking her notes one last time, the newswoman's face instantly transformed from tired and bored to the false, glowing radiance of a beauty contestant. The cameraman cued her with a fingered three count, pointing directly to her on the last down stoke of his hand.

"Ronda Stewart reporting live from Rome. I'm standing outside the Gemelli Clinic with Giuseppe Bardino, hospital spokesman." She turned to Bardino. "Mr. Bardino, do the recent visits of the Pope affect the normal operation of the hospital?"

From the corner of her eye, she watched a monitor displaying a shot of the anchorman as the network cut back to the studio in New York. If he hadn't landed a job in broadcasting, he could have been a soap opera star. As he spoke, his bleached white teeth flashed wide like a thoroughbred racehorse that had been reined too hard at the bit. Below his image, a streaming banner told of celebrity marriages and divorces, Hollywood criminal trials, and scandals at the U.N. He stared intently into the camera, affecting an aloof, professional demeanor.

On the monitor a close-up of Bardino appeared.

Bardino shook his head and smiled. "Despite the importance of attending to the Pope, those patients who need to be treated still are. In fact, the tenth floor where he stays is only partially closed. There's no change in our priority of treatment or disruption in hospital services or procedures."

She began to speak, but before she could finish her follow-up question, a cacophony of Klaxons drowned out her voice. Instinctively, her head spun toward the noise; below camera level, her arm shot out, signaling the cameraman to get the shot. Carabinieri motorcycle outriders led and flanked a motorcade consisting of the familiar armored white Jeep Renegade, an ambulance, and a sleek Alfa Romeo chase car.

"It appears that something's happening," Ronda said, purposefully lacing her voice with alarm to add drama to the scene. "As you can see, a motorcade just wheeled up the hospital's front entrance. Mr. Bardino, isn't that the papal insignia on the Jeep's doors?"

On the monitor, the anchorman leaned forward. His voice sounded in the Ronda's earpiece. "Ronda, can you ascertain whose motorcade we're seeing?"

Maintaining a worried expression, Ronda said, "I believe it's the Pope's, Chad."

An aide rushed to the spokesman's side and whispered into his ear. Bardino stiffened. "Excuse me, but I must conclude this interview immediately."

Behind them, the motorcade screeched to a halt, doors flung open and a phalanx of dark-suited Swiss Guardsmen and GIS piled out of the chase car and surrounded a stretcher that was being lowered from the back of the ambulance. The knot of protective security agents and doctors that surrounded the stretcher as it moved quickly disappeared into the hospital. As Mr. Bardino spun and headed for the entrance, the newswoman shouted, "Did you know the Pope was coming? Can you tell us if his condition is serious?"

Glancing back over his shoulder and stumbling, Bardino blurted a curt, "No comment, thank you."

After signing off and smoking a quick cigarette as the cameraman secured his equipment, Ronda stood thinking. She congratulated herself on getting a sound bite and video clip that would be aired across the world and shared by all the major cable news channels. Reaching into her purse, she handed the cameraman some euros and flashed a cold smile. "Get me some more cigarettes and coffee, fatboy. We're going to be rooted right here most of the night. And don't fuck it up like last time." He shrugged and hiked up his pants as he waddled across the street, heading for a newsstand in the park. To his back, she shouted. "And why they gave me a moron like you who can't even handle a coffee run beats me." She went to the news van, pulled open the rear door and climbed into the back. When she looked up, the gaping maw of a handgun's muzzle greeted her.

"Close the door," the voice on the other end of the pistol said.

Hands trembling, Ronda pulled it shut, turned and stood crouching. The inside of the van was dark except for one dim overhead light. A partition stretched across the front, blocking light from the front cab. She strained to make out the face behind the handgun.

"Strip down to your bra and panties and be quick about it."

Swallowing hard, Ronda managed, "You can't rape me, you sicko. Do you know who I am?"

"Just do it!" The gun's muzzle stabbed forward.

Fumbling as she struggled to undo each button, her chest heaving, Ronda peeled off her silk blouse.

"The skirt," the voice whispered harshly.

Her bravado stifled by fear, Ronda pleaded in a tremulous voice, "Please, don't—"

"Hurry up ... or I'll do it for you."

Reluctantly, her hand moved to her back, unfastened the button and unzipped her skirt. Quaking, she lowered herself to the floor of the van, raised her bottom, and slid off the skirt.

She sat, her lower lip trembling, her long slender legs curled to her chest, her arms wrapped defensively over her chest, barely concealing her full breasts that peeked over the top of her push-up bra.

"I'll need your shoes and stockings."

"You're sick," Ronda snapped, her voice hitching. Then she scooted backward.

Leaning forward, a pair of topaz-colored eyes stared from behind a curtain of dark hair that spilled into the light of the single overhead bulb.

In a soft voice, Josie Schulman said, "You're not my type. Give me your clothes and press pass and maybe you'll live to tell your story on the Today Show."

Later, the cameraman returned to the empty spot where the van had been parked.

"Damn!" He pitched the coffee and cigarettes to the ground. "Probably got a scoop and bugged out on me again," he said to himself. Shaking his head, he lumbered off toward a group of taxies.

CHAPTER 61

THE BLACK-AND-WHITE helicopter emblazoned with CARABINIERI in bold letters and the red-and-white bull's-eye symbol with a green center on its tail section churned over the city. The sinking sun tinted the cloud of smog that hung heavy and thick over Rome like a burial shroud, transforming it from gray into a pale yellow hue.

From the Vatican, the chopper headed south along the Tiber. As they were skimming the water at about a hundred feet, their rotors were carving a stuttering wake across the murky, rushing torrent of the river below. Strapped snuggly into a seat in the rear of the chopper, it occurred to Rossi that if indeed God were looking down from above, he would have thought the helo resembled an angry wasp, with razored wings, swarming toward its target.

He glanced at his watch. "Give me an ETA," Rossi said to the chopper pilot.

"ETA five minutes, sir."

Rossi turned to Giovanni and pointed to the headset that hung next to him. "Put it on," he shouted.

Giovanni shrugged. "What? I can't hear a blessed thing."

Rossi laughed and mimicked placing on his headset.

Giovanni looked at him for a moment and then his eyes flashed understanding as he grabbed the headphones and struggled to adjust them to fit.

"How's that?" he shouted into the mic.

Wincing, Rossi said, "You don't have to shout, Zio."

The wind changed and they hit turbulence. Rossi's stomach lurched. He suffered from motion sickness, hated rides at amusement parks, even the merry-go-round.

Looking down, he saw Tiber Island rush beneath them. He noticed that it was indeed shaped like the stern of a ship.

The helo banked hard left, heading due east over the Temple of Fortuna and the *Palatino*. Within moments, the Coliseum loomed straight ahead.

"CC-80 from CC-90, ETA two minutes. You should have us on visual. Over," Dante's voice poured through the headset. Rossi had instructed an *Ombra* squad to rendezvous at the target site.

"Lima Charlie, CC-90," the pilot acknowledged.

Rossi asked the co-pilot, "Any tactical on the ground, yet?"

"Stand by one," the co-pilot said. "Punching up channel 2."

The frenzied voice of a tactical team member on site came over the air. "Shots fired, officers down. *Mandare un ambulanza rapidamente!*"

The radio squawked. "*Si … paramedicos in roto,*" answered the calm voice of central dispatch.

"Coming up on target now, sir," the chopper pilot said.

Smoke billowed from bellow, wafting from the church.

"Take us down, now!" Rossi shouted to the pilot.

The helo descended in a tactical attitude, a gut-wrenching dive.

Hot bile rose in Rossi's throat. He choked it back and felt the blood draining from his cheeks.

Treetops rushed toward them, a small patch of green behind the church, a park. Leveling off and whipping the grass and earth below with the backwash of its rotors, the helicopter nestled safely to the ground. The second helo with Dante's squad followed.

Rossi was the first one out of his chopper. The *Ombra* team poured out of the second helo, fanning out, with Dante rushing to his side. Giovanni with his game leg fell far behind.

Rossi's hand flew to his Beretta. He drew it and rushed beneath the whirling blades, gun hand extended and checking for targets. Up ahead loomed a large gate flanked by walls of brick masonry. As they passed through the gate, they saw the body of the first officer, lying in a pool of blood near his car. When they entered the *Cheisa* itself, kerosene fumes and smoke stung Rossi's eyes. In the distance he heard a moaning, like the plaintive cries of a wounded animal. For a moment he and Dante stood frozen, straining their ears, struggling to see through the smoke-clotted air.

As the faint cries coiled around him, Rossi began to shiver with a premonition of a patient evil that waited somewhere ahead. A hushed, whimpering sound echoed and snaked its way through the smoke toward him.

It was the sound of someone who was past screaming, someone who had shrieked his lungs out, who was past the screams of wordless horror and agony, past prayers and pleas. Someone who sobbed quietly only because he still drew a tortured breath.

Then he smelled it, layered beneath the smoke. Burned meat. Seared flesh and the smell of deep-fried fat, acrid and pungent and oily, congealed with the scent of fear.

Turning to Dante, who held a fire extinguisher in one hand and the pistol grip of his MP-5 submachine gun that hung from its shoulder sling in the other, Rossi shouted, "I think it's coming from straight ahead." They pressed forward.

In the wide expanse of the central vault of the church, the smoke thinned. Since the church was round, the only light came from the porthole-shaped clerestory windows high above that gave the church a dim, gloom-filled atmosphere.

Rossi moved toward the altar, the source of the flames that licked the air. Then he turned in dizzying circles, his eyes drawn by the macabre frescoes that surrounded him on all sides. Images that seemed to move, to come alive in the flickering shadows of the dancing flames. He remembered how Giovanni had quoted Charles Dickens earlier who, after visiting the church, had described it as "a damp, mildewed vault, whose hideous walls were a panorama of horror and butchery that no man could imagine in his sleep, though he were to eat a whole pig raw, for supper. Grey-bearded men being boiled, fried, grilled, crimped, singed, eaten by wild beasts, buried alive, torn asunder by horses, chopped up small with hatchets: women having their breasts torn with iron pinchers, their tongues cut out, their ears screwed off.."

Gooseflesh stippled Rossi's forearms.

Dante shouted, "*Mio Dio in Paradiso*, the altar!"

Rossi spun and rushed toward the altar, but was driven back by the searing heat. Through the billing smoke he could barely make out Monsignore Scarlotti who sat, naked and lashed to an iron chair, atop the octagon-shaped altar. Around him a makeshift funeral pyre blazed. At least what was left of him— what was still recognizable. His skin had been flayed from his chest and hung in obscene strips. Peering closer, Rossi saw that Scarlotti's groin was a mass of raw mutton.

For a moment, Rossi stood repulsed, frozen solid.

The hiss and spray of the fire extinguisher jolted Rossi into action. He ran to Scarlotti's aid. Standing directly in front of him now, he drew a knife and worked at the leather straps that bound the priest's arms and legs, trying not to let his eyes linger on the raw flesh, the traces of white sinew and bone that peeked from beneath blackened and charred tissue.

Scarlotti blinked and looked at him uncomprehendingly. Enrico laid a blanket on the floor. The sound of heavy footfalls echoed in the vastness of the room. Muzzle-mounted maglite beams from the *Ombra* Unit's weapons carved the dark murkiness that surrounded them.

A voice bellowed, "Clear!"

Another shouted, "I've got another carabinieri down over here."

In the distance, a calliope of Klaxons punctured the air, drawing nearer.

When Rossi and Dante tried to lift the monsignore from the chair, they heard a wet, sucking sound.

From behind came a familiar voice. "The iron chair conducted the heat like a branding iron, melting the tender skin of his back, buttocks, and under arms to the chair. It was a technique invented for Nero's amusement so he could watch early Christian martyrs writhe and squirm in excruciating pain as the crowds cheered from the stands of his beautiful Circus of blood."

Rossi wheeled around. Giovanni stood, a handkerchief held to his face with a tremulous hand. "Sedate him first," Giovanni ordered, coughing.

From the standard-issue medkit in his assault vest, Dante removed a throwaway field syringe and injected Scarlotti with morphine. After giving the drug sufficient time to numb the priest's senses, they gently lifted him off the chair and onto the blanket, laying him on his side to avoid irritating the worst of the burns.

Rossi took a knee at his side. Scarlotti's drug-heavy eyelids flickered, his lips quivered slightly. Rossi leaned closer, pressing his ear to within inches of Scarlotti's mouth.

In a faint whisper, Scarlotti managed weakly, "Papa … fiery dragon's breath … warn …" Then his voice trailed off.

"Don't try to speak," Rossi said in a gentle, reassuring tone.

But Scarlotti swallowed visibly and croaked, "Josie … Satan's flaming scepter. Malachy … the olive branch. Tell her to…" His watery eyes pleaded.

Rossi felt a cold chill flood through his veins, immobilizing him, as though he'd fallen into the ice-cold waters of an artic sea.

Giovanni knelt at Rossi's side and said to Scarlotti, "Help is on the way, old friend. We'll fight the valiant fight together. Just like old times."

With that, Scarlotti's eyes fluttered and closed as he slipped into unconsciousness.

Later, after the paramedics had loaded Scarlotti into the ambulance and tore away, Rossi approached another paramedic who was giving oxygen to his uncle. Giovanni winked from behind the oxygen mask; his soot-covered face and fright wig of wildly disheveled gray hair gave him the appearance of some mad circus clown.

To the paramedic, Rossi said, "Will the priest make it?"

The paramedic's face tightened and he studied Rossi for a beat. Then he said, "It all depends upon his stamina, his threshold for pain, and mostly on his will to live. Burns alone don't kill people. Sometimes it's the shock, a weak heart. People have been known to recover with burns over fifty percent of their body."

Rossi nodded.

"I've seen cases where despite their injuries, people have crawled and fought their way out of burning buildings."

"How will they treat him?" Rossi asked, bringing a cigarette to his lips and lighting it.

"He'll be placed in a pressurized hyperbaric chamber to counter the tissue hypoxia, and oxygenate his blood. Then he'll receive massive ascorbic acid, vitamin C... and antibiotic intravenous injections. An ample supply of oxygen to the tissues will prevent blood sludging in place of the third degree burns that develop. The eschars will drop off leaving normal tissue. The ascorbic acid will also help with smoke poisoning."

Rossi glanced at his uncle and then his cigarette, and pitched it to the ground.

Dante appeared at his side.

"Body count?" Rossi asked.

"We were lucky ... only two officers down and one of them looks like he'll make it."

A short, plump, sallow-faced priest hobbled up to them. "What's happened here?" he asked with a slight lisp in Florentine Italian. "I'm the pastor here, Father Fallace."

"I afraid your church has been turned into a crime scene, Father," Rossi answered.

"How dreadful. Was anyone hurt?"

Rossi exhaled sharply. "Quite badly, but the perpetrator had to have taken his sweet time. How could that be? Isn't this a tourist attraction?"

The priest nodded. "Normally ...but we've been closed for renovation, and the workers failed to show up for the last two days. Some sort of labor dispute."

To Dante, Rossi said, "That would explain things."

"We've been canvassing the area," Dante said. "No eyewitnesses. Nobody saw anything out of the ordinary."

Rossi turned to the priest. "How about a custodian ... anyone who might have seen what happened?"

The priest stroked his chin and looked down, weighing the question. Then he looked up. "Just that old *curioso*, Sister Maria Isabella."

"Can we talk to her," Rossi said. A busybody could be just the break they needed.

The priest laughed. "Excuse me, gentlemen, but I'm afraid that would be impossible; she's blind as a fruit bat and deaf as a stone."

Rossi sighed, rolled his eyes at Dante.

"But there's the surveillance camera, though," the priest offered.

Rossi stared in mute disbelief.

His cell phone rang. "I'll have to take this, Father. Could you hold on, please?"

"*Certamente.*"

After a brief conversation, Rossi clicked off. "Dante, they've just found another body."

"Where?"

"Hanging beneath the *Ponte Fabricius* at Tiber Island. Take a helo and get over there now. I'll stay back and see what we've got here. Check in as soon as you've got the facts, okay?"

Dante shook his head. "First they barbecue a priest in a church and then lynch another victim under the oldest bridge in Roma. Bastards."

"We don't know if there's a connection, yet," Rossi corrected. "Find out!"

"Yes, sir …I'm on it."

Brimming with freshly oxygenated corpuscles, Giovanni moved to Rossi's side, wiping the soot from his face with his handkerchief.

As Dante ran off toward the chopper, Rossi said, "You have a video recorder connected to that camera, Father?"

Nodding enthusiastically, the priest said, "Of course. It's in my office and you two look like you could use a stiff brandy, am I right?"

Giovanni said, "Maybe a nice port?"

Rossi chuckled. "Lead on, Father."

CHAPTER 62

AS THEY SAT in the rectory of San Stefano sipping a brandy provided by the priest and waiting for him to return with the surveillance tape, Rossi tried to wrap his mind around the problem. His gaze wandered across Father Fallace's desk, piled high with papers and unopened mail, filmed with a thick layer of dust. On the corner sat an ashtray filled to the brim with cigarette butts.

Pensively drumming the armrest, Rossi said, "I can't help but feel like a pawn on a chessboard, nothing more than a stumbling block for the knights and the rooks and the queen. They always seem to outmaneuver us."

Giovanni, who was seated in chair at his side, reached over and patted his shoulder. "You're doing your best. Keep your eyes and ears open and only believe half of what your senses tell you." Finishing the last of his brandy, he put down the glass.

"If I just knew what *Bast* was up to… what their next move could be?" Then turning to his uncle, Rossi said, "Could you make anything from Scarlotti's last words?"

"Unfortunately, he was probably delirious." Giovanni began humming Wagner and casting his eyes about the office. On stiff legs, he moved to a large table and removed the numerous etchings by Albrecht Durer he'd brought with him in a satchel and placed them out on the tabletop.

"What are you doing?" Rossi asked.

"My every instinct tells me that I need to solve this puzzle here and now," he said, ignoring his nephew's question and pointing, "This one here, misnamed Meloncolia One is one of the most interesting. And look at the face of the angelic figure who sits with book in hand, a deeply troubled expression on his face.

"The figure mirrors your suffering in your search for the truth. Like you, he is trying to fathom the signs along the way. The symbolic tools of the alchemist lay about him, but provide only empty answers: the balance signifying the equilibrium of the Gnostics, and on the wall behind, you can see a magick square tablet or devil's square. Adding the sums of the numbers in the rows, the columns, or diagonals we get thirty-four. Even when adding each two by two square or the corners we again get thirty-four. Apparently again like you, Durer, in the form of an angelic philosopher, has encountered something outside the realm of his sacred beliefs. Maybe an impenitent evil that obeys no natural conventions of society, because it sees all matter as evil, and therefore, nothing good can come from it."

Looking down at his hands briefly and then back to Giovanni, Rossi said, "Bunch of thugs and black-hearted bastards."

Empathy filled Giovanni's face. "Just try imagining P-Seventeen: an elite, ultra-secretive, neo-fascist, Masonic cabal, involved in—"

"Apparently, money laundering, assassination and false-flag terrorism."

Their eyes locked. "By false-flag, I take it that you have your doubts that Islamic terrorists are at the root of these attacks on Rome and the Vatican?"

"Somebody's pulling the strings," Rossi said gravely. "Zio, that earlier call was from Josie Schulman."

His uncle's wire-brush eyebrows rose like exclamation points, his face brightening. "How's her father? Maybe I should call Max, see if he's made more of this puzzle." He laughed.

Rossi chewed his lower lip, averted his eyes briefly. "He's dead. Murdered."

Giovanni bowed his head then looked up. "Then I must fulfill a solemn promise I made to Max. I must have private words with Josie."

Rossi met his uncle's probing gaze. "Josie told me it might have to do with something called the *E* Institute. That make any sense to you?"

Giovanni closed his eyes tightly; a tremor wormed through his right cheek. He composed himself and faced Rossi. "Indeed. Was it a ritualistic killing?"

"She didn't say. Why do you ask?"

Headshake: "I've suspected for years that the *E* Institute is a front organization whose roots stem from a Germanic version of Masonry known as the OTO. Their symbols give them away. Members are told to 'get in touch' with their *Thayton*, their true self. These people have a wicked and ugly sense of humor. If you say Satan with a lisp ... you get—?"

"Thayton," Rossi answered, and rolled his eyes.

His uncle sighed. "Rather an obvious pun at best. Drago Volante, their founder, though you won't find it in their slick, doctored bio on him, was originally a member of the OTO. The most infamous twentieth-century head of the OTO called himself the Master Therion."

"Who was that?"

"The English occultist, Aleister Crowley."

Rossi whistled. "I've read about him. Claimed to be working for the British SIS during World War I. He ducked the war and made for New York. Edited some Kaiser apologist newspaper, but claimed he was infiltrating the Germans' war effort against Mother England."

"More like playing both ends against the middle while ducking the war," Giovanni corrected.

"I seem to remember that James Bond's creator Ian Fleming, who was with British Naval Intelligence during the World War II, wanted Crowley to debrief Rudolf Hess after he'd parachuted out of a German fighter over Scotland in the spring of forty-one. Hess was supposed to meet with the Duke of Hamilton, but was instead taken into custody and held incommunicado."

"Your memory serves you well, nephew. The Nazis were steeped in the practices of the darker side of the occult, which Fleming was painfully aware of, as was the Duke. That old bulldog, Churchill, however, nixed the debriefing."

"Meddling politicians," Rossi said.

"Volante adopted the Masonic and OTO's grades into his so-called pop-culture, New Age psychology system, cloaked them in new disguises."

"Think there's any connection with what's been happening here in Roma?"

Giovanna shrugged. "I wouldn't be the least surprised to run into them head on." He turned back to the print.

Rossi stood, moved to his uncle's side. Staring at the artwork, he screwed up his face. "Does the engraving have some hidden message like the other one we looked at?"

His uncle nodded. "Meloncolia is the most symbol-ridden and enigmatic of all Durer's works. He was a master of his art, the art of allusive meanings, metaphors that blended seamlessly into each other. But let's take a closer look at Durer's other works first." Nodding toward the adjacent picture, he went on. "The sly trickster must have had a hardy laugh when both the clergy and public praised his portrait of Saint Hieronimus, better know as St. Jerome, credited as being the first translator of the Bible from Greek to Latin."

"I think you're saying Durer was sort of like what you once told me about Leonardo da Vinci, who had to hide his true beliefs from the prying gaze of the Inquisition?"

"Yes, once again a truth concealed in plain sight for those with eyes to see. Look at the plaque or *cartellino* in the corner with Durer's familiar AD logo and the date 1514. Like the plaque in the *Knight, Death and the Devil* engraving we studied earlier, the date points to the secret message."

"Which is?"

"That it's not St. Jerome who sits poring over the book in his study. It's not the Catholic Church he honors or the Gospels, but rather Durer is paying homage to the death of a famous Illuminati adept and his own Gnostic beliefs."

Rossi shook his head. "Better bring out the crayons."

"First the less obvious clues. In the language of the adepts, the gematria of the Kabbalah, the value of AD equals one plus four: five. Add this to the date 1514 and we—"

"Get 1519. So?"

"Now look at the beast lying comfortably in the lower portion of the painting."

"The lion?"

"Whose zodiac symbol is—?"

"Leo."

Giovanni's eyes probed and then finding no flash of enlightenment in Rossi's face, he shook his head. "Leo is a shortened version of …"

"Leonardo—"

"Da Vinci … who died in 1519 and painted St. Jerome in the Desert in—"

Rossi raised his palm as a gesture of capitulation and sighed. "Don't tell me, 1514."

Giovanni added, "If you recall the only existent image of Leonardo, his self-portrait, and compare it to the face in Durer's work … the similarity is striking.

Rossi's cell phone chirped a distinct tone, signaling that he had a text message and a photo waiting in his inbox.

"Something's coming in from Dante at the homicide scene," he told his uncle.

Clicking and scrolling down, he opened the message. The SISDe's cell phones could capture still digital pictures or record a full five minutes of video accompanied by streaming text messages beneath. As Giovanni peered over his shoulder, a long shot of the *Ponte Fabricius* at Tiber Island flashed on the phone's screen. Zooming in and slowly panning downward from the top of the bridge, the image of an inverted body, dressed in black and hanging from the bridge by one ankle, the other ankle lashed to the victim's knee, came into focus. Its hands tied behind the back, the slightly blurred image of the body swayed obscenely. And below it, the text read:

FROM DANTE: VICTIM'S WAIST WEIGHTED WITH BAGS OF SILVER COINS. EXACTLY 34 COINS. PRELIMINARY ID NOT POSSIBLE. HEAD MISSING. CLEANLY SEVERED AT NECKLINE. COMMENCED DRAGGING THE RIVER BELOW. NOTE PINNED TO CHEST READS … AESCULAPIUS, HEAL THYSELF.

Giovanni met Rossi's stare and regarded him coldly. "Nasty business, their mayhem played out like a child's scavenger hunt."

"How so?" Rossi said.

"You noticed that as we flew over Tiber Island on our way here its outline resembles a ship. Legend has it that ship once sank there. But in fact, a huge structure in the shape of ship, a temple to the Roman god Aesculapius, once covered most of the island, which was dedicated to him in third century B.C.E. Some of the marble facing remains. An obelisk towered in the center of the vessel-like temple, representing the ship's mast."

"And so?"

Giovanni raised a finger. "The popular name for the bridge is *Ponte Quattro Capi.*"

Rossi nodded. "The Four Heads Bridge."

"Precisely, on each side you'll find four heads resting on the baluster. While being ancient Roman carvings, they weren't part of the original structure. Pope Sixtus V, in the 1500s, had them added during the restoration. You see, the Pope hired four architects, who constantly argued about their work. As punishment, Pope Sixtus had them beheaded. But since the bridge's restoration was completed to the Pope's final satisfaction, he had their portraits placed there."

Rossi screwed up his face. "Okay, I get the beheading part, but other than confirming these bastards' knowledge of history, how does it help?"

Giovanni studied the ceiling in apparent frustration and then met Rossi's puzzled look. "Aesculapius … was the Roman god of medicine."

"A doctor?"

Giovanni nodded and added grimly, "It's just a hunch, but if I were you—"

Rossi finished his sentence. "You'd check to see if the Vatican's physician went missing."

CHAPTER 63

THE HOLY FATHER lay in his hospital bed at the Gemelli Polyclinic, his face filmed with perspiration, the rose of his cheeks replaced by a pallor resembling the color of curdled milk. At his side, the vital signs monitor beeped out its insistent rhythm as rows of jagged lines scrawled across the screen. A respirator whizzed in sync with the Pope's weak rasps. By the time he arrived at the hospital, his air passages were so blocked and inflamed that the doctors had to perform a tracheotomy. Grasped securely in John Paul's hand was a scapular of the Blessed Mother, the very same scapular proclaimed in the Secrets of Fatima as being the key to the downfall of the Soviet Union and the salvation of the world—if only enough of the faithful prayed daily for Her divine intersession. And now around the world millions of Catholics filled their local churches, took to the streets with tiny votive candles clutched firmly in their hands. Even in St. Peter's square a sea of tiny flames dotted the darkening twilight. In their wavering, flickering glow, the night mirrored the vault of the star-punctured sky floating above.

His long-time friend and aide Cardinal Stanislaw, a fellow Pole, who for nearly forty years, was as close to him as a son, sat at his side, his voice a soft whisper as he feverishly prayed the rosary. Doctors and servants and clerics crowded the private suite, hovering and hoping for a miracle.

On the floor, tucked closely against Cardinal Stanislaw's thigh, was large, black briefcase. Absently, Stanislaw intermittently nudged it with his toe, checking it was still there within reach. Locked safely within were the letters bearing the papal seal that called for the resignation of the members of the Holy See who'd been found out. So sudden was the Pope's attack it had caught Stanislaw off guard. Despite the confusion and chaos that accompanied the Pope being rushed to the hospital, Stanislaw had kept a cool head and had the foresight to grab the briefcase as he left his desk.

Outside the room, Major Brazi's GIS troops stood guard. Farther down the hallway Swiss Guards took up posts at entry and exit points. Although both the Swiss Guard and the GIS had adopted some of the security measures developed and honed to a fine edge by the U.S. Secret Service, bureaucratic stubbornness, and in some cases pure arrogance, had caused some elements of the protective security protocol to be violated.

Major Brazi had cringed on many occasions when he observed the Swiss Guard's flagrant violation of standard operating procedure. As recently as last month, he'd seen the newscast where the Pope perched in the front passenger seat of a white Jeep Renegade, while Commandante Stato and another guardsman nestled in the rear seat. Oblivious to the danger, the Pope sat waving to the line of onlookers as he passed. Brazi knew that the principal should always be placed in the right of the rear passenger seat—behind the AIC of the detail, who in turn, always rode right-front. And only highly skilled agents should be driving the vehicle in which the principal actually rode.

Similarly, the Secret Service issues lapel pins for different classes of people who would be allowed access to their principal. Top aides are issued one type, visitors another, low-ranking service staff another. The shape, size, and color of the pins are changed on a regular basis to eliminate the use of counterfeits. And the lapel pins worn by the Secret Service and the State Department's DSS fall under the same protection as a badge. Anyone caught wearing a pin without authorization, could and would be prosecuted for impersonating a federal officer.

But because of an unwillingness to confront the issues of security and hold their ground, the Swiss Guard, and this case the GIS, had given in to the foolish and sometimes haughty disdain that the powers that be in the Vatican had for security measures. Not wanting to be bothered with "such foolishness." Major Brazi knew that even though the hospital was almost a second home for John Paul, accurate lists of all personnel that were checked and rechecked for any possible threat should have been maintained. Updated background checks should have been made. But in this case, the Vatican's Secretary of State and the chamberlain, the *camerlengo*, had overruled the wishes of the security staff.

***

With a ping, the elevator doors parted and a nun and priest exited.

The Swiss Guard at the door checked his access list and said, "Your names, please?"

In a demure voice the nun answered, "Sister Mary Benedict …"—gesturing toward the priest she added—"and this is Monsignor Charles O'Malley, Boston Arch Diocese, envoy of His Eminence Cardinal Lawless."

Meeting the Swiss Guard's steely eyes, O'Malley quickly added, "Don't be so formal, Sister. Everyone calls me Chuck."

Frowning, the Swiss Guard ran his finger down the list. There, at the bottom, their names were penciled in, and next to them, *the initials of a high-ranking cardinal*. The guard looked up, studied them for a second, then asked for their IDs.

They complied.

After peering at their credentials through slitted eyes for a second, the Swiss Guard nodded and returned their IDs. He pinned them and instructed them to proceed. Halfway down the hall, they encountered another cleric. "We're in dire need of a cup of strong coffee, Father. Could you be so kind as to direct us?" the nun said, smiling warmly.

The priest led them to a kitchen area.

Once the priest departed, Sister Mary Benedict waited for his footsteps to trail farther down the hall before she spoke: "Here's the plan. I spoke to an attending physician downstairs who said that the Holy Father's condition has stabilized, but overall, it appears to be worsening. After developing a urinary tract infection, the Pope suffered septic shock, which will be eventually followed by organ failure. Little by little his body's shutting down."

The monsignor made a sour face. "Such a pity," he said, feigning sympathy. "Let's pray that his heart is strong enough."

"It isn't. The doctor also said that he'd heard rumors that the Pope wanted to die at home in his apartment."

The monsignor sighed.

"You know what must be done," she said.

"The resignation list you mentioned?" he whispered.

"Exactly."

"But how?" he asked as his eyes darted around the room. "You said the cardinal is guarding it with his life."

Her stony stare spoke volumes. He shuddered.

As she was about to answer, a doctor and another cardinal entered, poured themselves some coffee, and moved to a seat across the room. "Hand me those cups and tray," she instructed the monsignor. After carefully placing cups and sugar and powdered creamer on the tray, he held it in front of her. Deftly, the nun palmed two small capsules from the folds of her habit, and quickly glancing over her shoulder to make sure no one was watching, she broke them and let the contents pour into a coffee cup. She filled the cups and then rinsed the pot in the sink.

She positioned the drugged cup in the back row closest to her and took the tray.

Squaring her shoulders, she said, "I believe that Cardinal Stanislaw could use a good strong cup of coffee."

Monsignor Johnny Brett snickered softly. "Heavens ... we certainly wouldn't want him drifting off, would we?"

CHAPTER 64

SISTER MARY BENEDICT, a.k.a. Basha, her pale blue eyes cast downward in humility, made her way down the hallway to the doorway of the Pope's suite. She nodded toward the cups and angled the tray so that the GIS trooper took one from the front row. As he thanked her and handed a second to his partner, his eyes lingered on hers, the robin's-egg blue of her irises striking and magnified by the wimple that framed her face. For a moment, there was a long silence, then she broke the spell by smiling shyly. Abruptly, he stood back and held the door for her. She could feel the heat of his gaze on her neck as she entered the room. As the door whisked shut behind her, she crossed the room, trying to avert her eyes, trying not to stare at the Pope as she approached. The virus was working all right, she told herself. Its slow action was necessary to divert suspicion and mimic a common flu virus. The Pope's wishes to return to the Vatican apartments had been an unanticipated variable, as had Cardinal Stanislaw's snatching the incriminating evidence before departing the Vatican for the hospital. She'd been told by her Vatican handler to obtain the documents at any cost.

As she moved toward the cardinal, she reversed the tray, which repositioned the laced coffee in the front. A smile played across her lips as she recalled how her trainers had always remarked what fast hands she had.

Standing before Cardinal Stanislaw, she bent slightly and proffered the tray.

"*Dziękuję Jesteś taka uprzejma*," he said, inadvertently slipping into Polish in his weary state and displaying his gratitude. He took the nearest cup.

"*Proszę*," she answered softly.

"You speak Polish, Sister?"

"A little, Your Eminence. I worked at a hospital in Chicago with a large Polish cliental."

"Ah, yes. I accompanied the Holy Father there on a visit. Beautiful city."

Her voice cracking slightly, she asked, "Is there any hope?" Then her eyes began glistening as if on cue. If he only knew that they were tears of joy, she thought.

"There's always hope, my child. The Holy Father, like all of us, is in the Lord's hands."

"He looks so peaceful." Beneath her hushed voice was the steady drone of the respirator, feeding the suffering Pontiff's leaden lungs with air.

From the corner of her eye, Basha saw a doctor shepherding a knot of nuns and priests and guards out of the room. "His Holiness needs peace and quite, please wait in the corridor."

Glancing at John Paul, his waxen complexion, the cardinal's eyes began to moisten. "Let us pray that he finds a peaceful end to his long journey." Then he yawned wide, took another long sip. As he lowered the cup from his lips, his eyes began to flutter, then close. "*Jestem śpiący*," he barely managed before he dropped off.

Moving quickly before the cardinal could drop it, Basha snatched the cup from his hands. No one noticed. Surveying the room with a glance, she glided unnoticed to the corner where she set the tray on a table and returned to the sleeping cardinal's side.

With the calm ease and poise of a stage magician, she hefted the briefcase from the floor and disappeared into a private bathroom on her right. Once inside, she bolted the door, removed the files and letters, and concealed them under her habit. Then she tucked the satchel into a linen closet.

A soft rap at the bathroom door startled her. Spidery fingertips skittered up her spine.

"Sister, is everything all right in there?" Monsignor O'Malley's familiar voice sounded from the other side of the door. "Fool," she whispered from between clenched teeth.

"Yes, Monsignor. I shall be with you in a moment," she said, moaning quietly. When she inadvertently caught a glimpse of her haloed image in the mirror, she flinched. She gazed deeply into the reflection, searching those dispassionate eyes. That's when it happened. She became diminished; her body seemed to enfold and shrink within her skin. *What's happening to me?* A strange singsong voice floated from her throat, speaking softly, childlike. "Don't tell ... don't tell, it's our little secret. I'll never tell." Pressing her hands to her face, she explored her cheek, her lips, her fingertips running across her features like the hairs of a portrait artist's paintbrush. Then she began to drift away to the edge of the frame of consciousness. For a moment, she stood still, gazing at the world as though she were a mere spectator. Fear chilled her bones. In her mind's eye, Basha began to run, but the blurred image of a young girl rushed past her going the opposite direction, giggling as she ran.

Basha found herself in a dark forest. The childlike voice bubbled from *her* lips. *Hide-and-seek. Hide-and-seek.* Searching desperately for the voice, Basha ran deeper into the towering trees. As she ran, ghostly visions floated in the darkness, unthinkable images. Terror–stricken faces, their red-rimmed eyes pleading. Then a disembodied, pale, white hand shot out of the darkness, clutching a syringe, its gleaming long needle slowly and steadily drawing closer, now hovering right before her eyes. Sharp pains shot to her chest as she was seized in the vise grip of terror.

In her mind, the young voice shouted, *Three, two, one ... ready or not, here I come!*

The world somersaulted. The innocent face of a little girl stared back at her from the mirror. Her voice hitching, Basha managed, "But this isn't who I am."

Like a wisp of smoke, the girl's face vanished, replaced by the distorted faces of young women, slightly altered versions of herself. In unison, their voices spoke from Basha's lips, "It's not about you! It's about us. It's what we want, you selfish bitch."

Her knees went weak, and she clutched the sides of the sink for support. Hot bile rose in her throat. She gagged, threw up. She studied her hands. Suddenly the film of vomit grew darker in color, a deep red shade. Blood. *No. Clean yourself up, girl. Clean yourself up*, her mind repeated like a mantra. She opened the squeaky faucet all the way. Waited until the water was almost scalding, then plunged her hands beneath the hot stream. Obsessively, she scrubbed and scrubbed and scrubbed until her hands were raw. Steam billowed around her, fogging the mirror. She collected herself, blotted her quaking hands on her clothing, and wiped the mirror with her palm. She looked into her reflection. A nun's soft and gentle face peered back. As her eyes welled with tears, Basha kneaded them with the heels of her palms. Sobbing, she stood shuddering with apprehension, with confusion. "You're just tired. Too much stress," she lied in a forced whisper.

Another rap at the door gave her a start.

It's all for Hamal... remember? she told herself. Steeling herself, she dried her eyes, straightened and moved to the door.

But when she walked out, the monsignor wasn't there. She scanned the room and spotted him chatting it up with a doctor. *Big ham just can't resist overacting*, she thought. With a pinched expression, she strode across the room to the phony monsignor's side.

"We are at a loss to explain his absence," the doctor said, adjusting his wire-rimmed glasses. "Not that there's anything Doctor Cornelli could have done."

"Has he been the chief Vatican physician for long?" the monsignor asked.

"He served both John Paul I and His Holiness."

Frowning, the monsignor asked, "Pardon my rather morbid curiosity, but will the state insist that you conduct an autopsy if our Heavenly Father decides to call his own?"

Basha fought to conceal her anger, hands knotting at her sides, her fingernails digging into the soft flesh of her palms. *We'll have to kill him you know*, the strange voices whispered in her ear.

The doctor shook his head violently. "Never. No Pope would ever, nor should they ever have to … suffer such an indignity. But why do you ask?"

Delivering a sharp, but barely noticeable, swift kick to the monsignor's ankle, Basha bowed and said, "Excuse me, gentlemen." She turned to the monsignor. "I believe you have an important phone call, Monsignor O'Malley." She spoke with such quiet intensity that, when coupled with her wide grin, it created a bizarre effect.

Still wincing slightly, O'Malley managed, "That must be his Eminence Cardinal Lawless. Lead on, Sister Mary."

***

Rossi called Major Brazi's cell.

"*Pronto.*"

"Brazi, it's Rossi. Listen closely. We've got another homicide and we think it may be a doctor. Check on the whereabouts of the Pope's primary physician."

"Name?"

"Doctor Cornelli."

There was a click on the line.

"Hold on, I've got another call," Rossi told him.

After a few seconds, Rossi came back. "Major, I'm putting us on a three-way call with my agent, Dante."

"Understood," Brazi said. Rossi pictured Brazi stiffening to attention now.

"Dante, tell the major what you just told me."

"We found the vic's missing head or, rather, the Swiss Guard did."

"How's that?" Brazi stammered, appearing to realize the implications.

"In a hatbox no less, at the base of a marble sculpture in St. Peter's Basilica itself. They've got a positive ID … it's— "

"Doctor Cornelli," Rossi cut in.

"That's right, but how'd you—"

"Hold on," Rossi ordered, "Let me click on the speakerphone mode."

Giovanni's tired voice said, "Please continue, young man. Which sculpture exactly?"

"Said it's called Venus of the Vatican. We've got the whole area cordoned off."

"The Venus de Milo?" Rossi asked.

"No, I don't think so. Hold on … let me ask the guard." A soft murmur of voices and then Dante was back. "Guard says it's also called Lady of Justice, sits right beneath a bronze sculpture of Pope Paul III."

Giovanni said, "By placing the bloodied package there, they are sending us a message. Justice is finally served. I'd forgotten about the infamous Borgia Pope and his cousin and mistress, Julia Farnese. The Popes kept their love affairs within the family. Julia was Pope Paul III's sister. Even today, whenever the Holy Father says mass at the towering altar of St. Peter, Julia's marbled face taunts him, since her supine, seductive, and exquisite form lies a few feet away, sprawled languidly on a couch, the Seal of Justice slipping from her delicate hand as though it were the artist's hidden editorial comment. Julia's face, the woman who shared a past Pope's bed and bore him an illegitimate daughter—Laura—stares longingly.

"Although the Borgia Pope Alexander didn't commission the actual work, he did have Julia, his married mistress, serve as a model for the Madonna and their illegitimate daughter, Laura, for the Christ Child in one of Pinturicchio's frescoes, which still can be seen in the Hall of Mysteries located in the Borgia Apartments within the Vatican."

"But who could've waltzed right past the Swiss Guard, past dozens of tourists, past all the Vatican staff milling about … with a bloody hatbox tucked under their arm?" Brazi offered sarcastically.

"Well that wouldn't be some Arab terrorist now would it?" Rossi said. "Or your men would have noticed."

"I believe Major Brazi just answered his own question. It would have to be someone who would go completely unnoticed," Giovanni replied.

"You don't mean—" Dante said incredulously.

"A member of the Swiss Guard," Major Brazi said, his voice pulsing with anger.

"Let's not jump to conclusions," Rossi admonished. "Anything else, Dante?"

"There're some words written on the box … it says… *Bocca Della Verita.*"

"The Mouth of Truth," Rossi muttered. "Zio, should we get a squad over to the portico of the Church of Santa Maria and check out the marble disk?" Rossi's mind reeled at the incredible perverse irony of it all. Thinking of Audrey Hepburn's shocked expression in the film *Roman Holiday* when Gregory Peck, concealing his hand inside his coat sleeve, withdrew it from the disk's mouth and produced a stub. Roma's much-romanticized test of a lover's truthfulness had been defiled and mocked by these coldhearted killers. "Or should Dante just look inside the victim's mouth?"

"Checking now," Dante said, "just let me slip on a fresh glove. There, prying open the mouth. Hold the light closer, please. Looks like something's in there … "

"No!" Giovanni said in a flinty voice. "In order to give young lovers a painful bite when they inserted their hand into the sculpture's mouth, a parish priest used to place a —"

"*Mannaggia!*" Dante shouted. "Excuse me…forgot where I was."

Rossi could imagine Dante's hand abruptly jerking back from the head and making a fervent sign of the cross. "Speak to me! What's happening?" Rossi demanded.

"Biggest, blackest scorpion I ever saw just crawled out of the vic's mouth."

"My uncle's right," Rossi acknowledged, "better to be safe than sorry. You'd better get it over to the lab and get back to me."

The sound of pounding footsteps and excited voices poured over the line. Rossi could make out Brazi's voice barking orders. After a moment, his voice quaking, Brazi explained, "More bad news. They've just found Cardinal Stanislaw slumped in a chair at the Pope's bedside."

"Knocked out?" Rossi asked.

"No, poisoned."

"Suspects?"

With hesitation stitching his words, Brazi managed, "A nun and a priest."

"Nothing more solid?"

Brazi sighed loudly. "One of my men said she was... striking. The most beautiful powder-blue eyes he'd ever seen."

"Dante, put out an All Points," Rossi ordered.

Rossi shook his head. *Striking:* like a stiletto, the word sliced the lining of his gut. Had to be Gina, he thought, no, knew instinctively. Only about a couple thousand clergy in the city and more arriving each hour since John Paul had taken ill, he reasoned. Not to mention the city splitting its seams with the million or more Catholics making the pilgrimage, too. And they projected four million in total. Streets gridlocked, hotels overflowing, tent cities sprouting up in the parks, police and emergency services tasked beyond record. Her face floated before him as he said, "Dante, get that photo of our UNSUB disseminated to the press. I want her face on every front page daily, I want it to be broadcast as a special bulletin, and Dante..."

"You want it done yesterday, I know. I'll see if the hospital has surveillance tape on them, too. Oh, I almost forgot. When I'm done, I'll bring your car over."

"Baby it, Dante."

"We're running the tape now," Brazi said.

"Thank you, Major. We need a make on the priest. Make sure the Carabinieri are advised the woman's armed and dangerous. And Dante, for our troops ... Code-00 full counterterrorism protocols are in effect." Rossi had borrowed the double-0 classification from the SIS, which meant—licensed to terminate on sight.

CHAPTER 65

HAVING ACCOMPLISHED THEIR mission, Basha and Johnny Brett left the hospital. Once they'd secured the documents at the predesignated location and were back in the van, they changed clothes. Basha knew that the secret of a quick-change artist is not, as most believe, being able to change rapidly from one outfit to the next. The secret is wearing multiple layers of clothing, which are custom sewed and fitted with Velcro strips at key points. This allows the top layer to be ripped away and discarded, leaving only the undergarments as a new disguise. Some stage magicians who were slight of build were known to have worn as many as six layers.

"Think your boss will be pissed that the old boy is still hanging on?" Johnny asked, taking a long pull of Maalox and wiping his lips with the back of his hand.

As they pulled to a stop at the light, she said, "Your big mouth almost mucked it up. Playing twenty questions with that doctor was stupid, unprofessional." The light changed.

As she hit the gas, she caught Johnny undressing her with his eyes. When she peeled away her habit, a tigress emerged. She was now dressed in Roberto Cavalli from head to toe: short black ruffled skirt, a sheer, black, jewel necklined, long-sleeved blouse that barely concealed a silk burgundy halter top with black lace trim which accentuated her bare midriff. She'd applied a touch of makeup. She shuddered slightly as his eyes seemed to literally crawl across her thigh, down her calf to her ankle, lingering at the straps of her shoes. The violated feeling stirred deep thoughts. Back in the hospital bathroom she'd lied to herself. The disconnected feeling, the uncanny experience, hadn't been entirely new. In the night, in her dreams, faces, thousands of faces, coalesced into one face, whose fish-eyed, glassy pupils raped her with their stare.

The man's waxen hands paw over her face, linger at the swell of her tiny breasts, and finally drift across her flat stomach. A stifled scream wells within her lungs as the remembered images taunt her. She swallows audibly, feels those clammy hands probing her thighs and then ... between them. A sublime mixture of terror and wanton abandon courses through her. She climaxes, shuddering with pleasure, again and again. But then waves of nausea rise from the pit of her stomach.

The visions subsided.

But that wasn't the half of it. There were the lost minutes, hours, days— weeks. Blackouts. She would be talking on the phone or gazing at television, cigarette in one hand and then, suddenly—go missing. The stinging burn of the cigarette's glowing cherry, nestled between her fingers, had startled her from her stupor more times than she cared to remember.

But the worst had been the trip to Paris, a trip that she hadn't remembered making. She woke in a strange hotel room. Suitcases brimming with clothing she'd never purchased, makeup on the sink in shades she never wore, and on the pillow, the scent of a man she never bedded still lingered.

She recalled how, like a foolish schoolgirl, she hugged the pillow, trying to envision the man whose cologne lathered the air and still hung on her forearms, the back of her hands. Frightened and confused, she packed and made for the lobby. Hesitating at the checkout desk, she summoned the nerve to ask for her bill. The desk clerk smiled warmly and said, "*Qui, mademoiselle.* But you've already paid it this morning. Are you wanting another copy?" She nodded and stood mute. Dark motes began to swim across her field of vision. She took a deep cleansing breath. The name on the charge slip was no one she recognized.

Quickly, she made her way to the hotel bar, took a stool, and ordered a double shot of bourbon. After downing it, she stared at what remained of the amber liquid that filmed the bottom of the cut-crystal glass. *Since when do I drink bourbon? My passport*, she remembered. Fumbling with palsied hands, she found it in her purse and opened it. Her photo and the name—Laylah Thomas—which she didn't recognize were on the ID page. Then her gaze drifted back to her purse. It wasn't her purse. It was similar, but sure as hell wasn't hers.

Now the visions returned.

Hot breath pouring across her face, grunting rutting sounds, the sour stench of sweat, then dead weight crushing her body. And the curdled odor. The musky scent of spent desire.

A blaring horn yanked her back to the present. She felt something, looked down. A hand that had been caressing her thigh pulled away quickly. Johnny Brett wrung his liver-spotted hands, a worried look on his face. "I just couldn't help myself, honeycakes. You're so firm, so beautiful, so …"

Up ahead, an alley loomed. Basha cranked the wheel hard to the right and swung the van into the alleyway. The van rocketed through the narrow space, scraping the side of the brickwork on one sharp turn into a bisecting alleyway. A dead end lay ahead, but instead of slowing, Basha poured on the speed.

"What the hell are you doing, you crazy bitch?" Johnny shouted. Wetness flowered at his crotch.

At the last minute, Basha stood on the brakes. The van shuddered to a screeching halt, rubber barking. Fast-hands Johnny, carried by the momentum, hit the dash. As he slowly pulled himself to a sitting position, blood streaming down his forehead, Basha's face slackened and melted into a youthful innocence.

In a childlike voice, she spit, "You shouldn't have touched *us*." Before he could react, Basha brought up her arm and flicked her wrist. It caused the stiletto-thin blade concealed within the spring-loaded mechanism of her bracelet to whisk out. With an effortless, practiced swipe, its blade deftly razored its way across his throat. She shook her head and clucked her tongue. "Bad man," she scolded peevishly as her hand brushed at her blood-spattered blouse. "Look what you did to my pretty things."

Just then, the SATCOM phone chimed. Puzzled, *little* Basha reached for the phone, studied it, and finally after pushing a few buttons, a voice came from the earpiece. Leaning forward, hesitantly she answered, "Hello?"

Dr. Ahriman whispered, "Lollypop?"

A wide grin: "That's my name, Daddy. Don't wear it out." She giggled.

"Lollypop, did daddy's girl do something naughty?"

Her lips forming a pout, she twisted her wrist, studying the bloodstained blade, and said dryly, "The bad man won't hurt *us* any more." Absently, she wiped the blade on Johnny Boy's trousers, and pressed its tip against the dash, forcing it back into the bracelet.

A long pause then: "Good girl. Now, Lollypop … let's play a game," Ahriman said with a fatherly inflection.

She stiffened, her eyes fluttered. "I'm listening."

"Basha won't have any recollection of what you've done. When I sing your favorite song, you will allow Basha to return …"

"Good. She can clean up the mess this time."

"That's right, Lollypop. Now for your song … are you ready?"

"Yep."

Ahriman sang in a melodious voice whose intensity and cadence made the children's playful tune all the more out of place and bizarre, all the more malevolent. "I am a little teapot short and stout, tip me over and *pour me out* …let her pour out. Lollypop … let her pour out."

As she hummed along, suddenly, she shuddered, went limp. Her head slumped forward. When she raised it, it was Basha who answered. "I am listening," she said, her inflection wooden.

"Quickly, dispose of the actor. I'm assuming that's who has been eliminated?"

She dry swallowed and then her gaze drifted to the lifeless body beside her, searching his sightless eyes for an answer. "Last thing I remember…"—her bewildered look turned to a sneering frown—"is that the old pig laid his hands on me." Her eyes darted to her skirt, once solid black, but now mottled with dark red polka dots. Then feeling something on her arm, she hiked it up and regarded the blood that had already begun crusting on the back of her forearm. Closing her eyes tightly, struggling to remember and failing, she let out an exasperated groan. "He's hung up his dancing shoes and has gone into *permanent* early retirement."

"That was unfortunate for him, but unimportant at the moment. A soon as you have finished with him, I want you to ..."

As she listened, her sixth sense tugged at her.

"Standby one," she said.

In the rearview mirror, Basha saw the approaching policeman. With a flick of her wrist, as though it had a mind of its own, the spring-loaded blade snickered out. It waited patiently, expectantly for the officer to draw close enough, lean into the open window. And when he did, it razored effortlessly across his exposed throat.

"What's going on?" Ahriman asked.

"Just a troublesome policeman. I took care of it."

On the other end a brief pause then: "Basha, I want you to meet someone."

"Who?"

"Oh, just an old flame."

CHAPTER 66

JOSIE looked down at the flyer, written in Italian and English, which lay on the seat of the stolen TV van next to her:

The *E* Institute proudly presents a lecture by the world-renowned psychiatrist
Doctor F. Ahriman this afternoon at 2:00 PM in the Temple's main meeting room.
All are welcomed to attend.

A gagged plea came from the real Ronda Stewart who still lay in the back hogtied. As Josie rechecked her makeup and hair in the rearview mirror, she said, "Sit tight, Ronda. You're about to make news history." Adjusting the press ID so that Ronda's picture was half-tucked beneath the lapel of her jacket, she exited the van and made her way across the street.

She'd been parked across from the temple's main entrance, waiting for Ahriman's arrival. She'd already introduced herself to the meeters and greeters from the Institute, two overly bouncy, wide-eyed members who'd recently been assigned from another *E* Institute's office in India. They were delighted to have the famous Ronda Stewart on hand for a brief interview and photo op with their soon arriving guest speaker. Josie was delighted to learn that they'd never actually seen Ronda, since they'd been denied access to television while on retreat in India. Josie made a lame excuse for her absent cameraman, saying he should be here any second and explained that she'd like to do a short interview somewhere quiet. The bobbing Bobbsey twins rolled their heads East-Indian style as they spoke. "We've arranged Mr. Volante's private office for your interview. Would that be to your liking?"

Josie smiled and checked her wristwatch. Two minutes to arrival.

Absently, her hand patted the outline of the Sig Sauer concealed beneath her jacket.

Then she saw it, the limo in the distance, threading its way through traffic toward her. Her breath tightened in her lungs. One of the Bobbsey twins spoke quickly into a small walkie-talkie.

The limo pulled to the curb directly in front of her. Her muscles tensed. Like a bullwhip coiled and charged with latent violence in the hands of its master, she waited to lash out.

Her hand slid beneath her jacket and her fingers wrapped firmly around the pistol grip. She scanned the area. *No security agents. No chase car behind the limo. I'll take him right here.*

The limo's door opened. First a short leg, then that diminutive body emerged. He wore an expensively tailored charcoal suit and sported an evening cape and white silk scarf.

She took a step forward, eyes locked on her target.

Just a few more steps, she thought. *A few seconds and you'll send this piss-elegant bastard to hell.*

She was moments away now, leading a small knot of bodies that had accumulated. The Sig was just clearing her jacket when it happened. A rush of students and staff poured out of the front doors and onto the sidewalk. One of the Bobbsey twins cut in front of her, but she ducked around him, the pistol held low and tucked tightly against her thigh now.

With a theatrical flourish, Ahriman swung his cape over one shoulder and preened for his audience.

For a moment their eyes locked, and she was staring into Ahriman's beady, watery gray eyes. In the same instant his face went slack. He'd recognized her. His gaze tracked to the pistol that stabbed outward. A press of bodies swarmed about her, oblivious to what was about to happen.

Then just as she applied pressure to the trigger, a little girl, clutching a bouquet of flowers, burst in front of her, blocking the shot. Without hesitation, Ahriman bent and scooped the girl into his arms, smiling broadly in Josie's direction and waving to the well-wishers. Using the girl as a shield, he made his way through the crowd.

Josie froze.

Tossed by the onlookers, a shower of rose petals rained lazily down around her. The world skipped a beat, drifted into slow motion. Shouting voices became muddled, distorted. Robotically, she tucked the handgun deftly into its holster and willed herself to back away. She stumbled lamely, rage coursing through the corded veins of her neck as she was jostled by the onrushing throng. Every fiber of her being screamed and urged her to rush headlong into the crowd, empty the clip into his chest, damn the consequences. But she kept staggering backward, tears crowding her eyes. She managed to keep Ahriman in sight and then, just as he reached the doorway, he turned. Sprouting a wry smile, he looked directly at her, waved, and disappeared into the shelter of the building.

No use trying to get in now, she reasoned. Ahriman would alert security to her presence. She ducked into the van and tore away, tires barking rubber. Later, she pulled into a secluded parking garage. Eyes still tearing with anger, she pounded the steering wheel, and climbed into the back. Earlier she'd given Ronda a good dose of Rophenal, which made the petulant Ronda as compliant as a puppy. Josie stripped off Ronda's clothes, and put on her own. After untying her, she dressed Ronda, and placed her in the back seat of a nearby old Fiat that was plastered with Italian soccer hooligan banners. Ronda looked up. "What's happening?"

"If the rophy doesn't wear off, you'll probably have the time of your tight-assed life," Josie answered as she slammed the car door and turned on her heels. Ronda stared blankly and smiled.

As Josie sped away, she realized her mistake. She'd let emotions cloud her thinking.

She'd tried to Lone Ranger it and blew the hit. The next time she'd get backup.

CHAPTER 67

AS THE UNMARKED EMBASSY sedan crawled through snarled Roma traffic, the CD-player blared an oxymoron titled "Greatest Hits of Donny and Marie Osmond." Although Agent Kyle was the wheelman, the combination of the slow pace and caterwauling of the squeaky clean siblings belting out "A Little Bit Country, A Little Bit Rock and Roll" drove Manwich to distraction. Fuming, he lowered the passenger-side window and began pounding the side of the car with his fist as he shouted curses at the indifferent Italian drivers that engulfed their vehicle. Equally indifferent, Kyle's head bobbed in time with the saccharine music.

Turning back to Kyle and frowning, Manwich said, "What are you, some kind of a senile geriatric trapped in the body of a thirty-year-old?"

"No, I'm a Mormon, boss."

Manwich scowled again, radiating disgust. "Same difference." He fished a half-eaten Snickers bar from his pocket and devoured it in two bites. Then he ejected the CD, his chocolate-covered fingers filming the disc, and replaced it with one from his briefcase. The breathy, eerie sounds of the Eurythmics. "Now, that's music." Feigning a thick Latino accent, he added. "The eighties were very, very good to me."

Kyle's eyes darted to the smudged CD and then to his boss. "Never knew if their lead singer was a guy or a gal."

"Gal? Listen up, farmer Bob. Granted she didn't have a rack like Marie, but trust me … she's all woman. Probably swings both ways but—"

"She's a gymnast, too?"

Manwich stared into Kyle's boyish face, whose cornpone smile infuriated him each time he saw it. "Never mind, dickweed. Just get us to the church on time, okay?"

Before he could answer, the SATCOM phone chirped. He killed the music. The equipment was NSA's latest satellite encrypted phone, which used a nonlinear-phase signal and unlimited 128-bit keys. As he punched in, Manwich remembered the old-time Green Scrambler phones whose encryption hardware was about the size of a hulking outdoor air-conditioning unit. How times had changed—everything that is—except the f'ing new guy, Agent Kyle, who appeared to be a reincarnation of Brendan Fraser's portrayal of Dudley Do-Right.

Although he was thousands of miles distant at HQ in Maryland, the Answer Man's voice was crystal clear. "Agent Manwich?"

"Yeah."

"We've got some rather disturbing recent intercepts. The involved parties are using the last generation of encryption algorithm, and although the key itself isn't transmitted, we—"

"Have it in our database."

"Precisely."

"Who was the target?"

"Our old friend, Drago Volante, head of the *E* Institute."

"And the other party?"

"Doctor Sanger of the University of Arizona."

"Specialty?"

"Genetics."

"Sounds familiar," Manwich offered.

"Should. He was in a black ops bio-weapons program. But was terminated."

"Grounds?"

"Failed his yearly update psychological evaluation."

"Diagnosis?"

"Paranoid schizophrenic with Messiac delusional manifestations."

"Should fit right in with Volante, then. They'll be playing 'find the name of the next Pope in the pizza game' in no time."

"He's in Rome … waiting to board a flight to Pakistan as we speak."

Manwich's upper lip curled. "How the hell did he skip the country? We can't have him delivering weapons grade biotechnology to the fucking Muslim Fundamentalists. For God's sake, Islamabad is crawling with al-Qaeda operatives. I'll dispatch a wet-work team to take the little prick out right now."

"No. We already have a team in place at the other end. Want to see who his meet-and-greet will be."

"Since you've got proof positive that Volante's group is actually using the encryption chips you sent me to look for, all I gotta do is catch one of Volante's guys with the classified chip in his phone, then squeeze 'im tell he gives up the info."

"There has been a change in your objective."

"So whataya want from me?"

"Words come from the top. Move in on Volante's operation in Italy. They want it taken down completely."

"Okay, me and what army?"

"Compartmentalization is a huge factor. Your orders are to work with a Mossad team."

"Now why didn't I think of that?" Manwich said with heavy irony. "Are you completely nuts?"

265

"All that's necessary for now is to execute an extraordinary rendition."

"You want us to snatch someone and transport 'im to a third country?"

"Yes."

"Weren't five CIA agents just indicted in '*absentereo*' by the Italian court for grabbing that Egyptian terrorist last year?"

"Your point being?"

Kyle blanched and mashed the brake pedal at the last moment, narrowly avoiding the rear end of a bus. "What the fuck?" Manwich admonished.

"Really, there's no need for such language, agent."

Still grimacing at Kyle, Manwich said, "Not you, sir. Now what's the deal with this Mossad business."

When the caustic voice of Loveday, the chief of the ops directorate broke in, Manwich flinched.

"Agent, we need a cut-out, someone to take the rap. Mossad already has an asset on the ground there. An asset motivated by a personal vendetta. They killed her father. When we got wind and threatened to blow the lid off the whole deal, Tel Aviv saw it our way. The Mossad agent is operating without sanction, out for blood. In case you haven't noticed, we're not any too popular with the Italians these days. There's a OSI operative named Colonel Rossi who could also prove useful."

Glancing back over his shoulder, Manwich took in the plain-Jane coupe that had been running a loose tail on them since they left the embassy. "I think I picked up an Italian surveillance team already, sir. We're en route to this Rossi's location right now, sir."

"How's that?"

"There's been a snatch and grab of a Vatican cleric. I had the tech boys monitor the dagos' radio transmissions. We're rolling up on the site where the victim was found right now. If we're in luck, Rossi will still be at the scene." Manwich silently cursed himself for using the racial slur.

"We could use a lucky break."

"Sir, how do I make contact with the Israeli?"

"She'll find you."

F'ing great, Manwich thought. They've got me teamed up with some broad who's out for payback. Means she'll be careless, all pumped up and hell-bent for leather. Then it occurred to Manwich to ask the bigger question. "So who's this guy you want us to snatch?"

"It's a woman, a false-flag operative code-named *Bast*. The encrypted description should be coming over your terminal right now."

"Standing by."

"And Agent Manwich …"

"Right here, sir."

"You must take this operative alive at all and any cost. Is that clear?"

"No matter who gets in the way, then?"

"That's affirmative. And one more thing, whether he gets in your way or not …I want Ahriman eliminated."

Manwich stared at the laptop screen as the image downloaded. Took in the woman's doelike eyes, the aquiline features.

Headshake: "You care which one of them takes the fall?" Manwich smiled wryly as he said it, already predicting the answer.

"Not in the least."

The connection went dead.

When Manwich looked up, they'd pulled to the curb across from St. Stefano. Kyle asked, "New orders?"

"I think you just may get your cherry popped."

Kyle stared blankly.

A marked police car careened around the corner and screeched to a halt across the street. They turned toward the sound. The door flew open and a uniformed officer emerged. From that short distance, even with her hair tucked neatly beneath her cap, it was obviously a woman. Her movements were too smooth as she made her way down the sidewalk with the grace and agility of a panther. Popping a monocular cam-scope to his eye that fed to the laptop, Manwich studied the woman's face. Then his gaze shifted to the laptop. According to the FACE-IDENT software in the computer, it was a match.

Manwich nodded toward the officer. "Don't look now, but I think your date just showed up."

Pulling his 9mm Glock from his DeSantos shoulder rig, Manwich jacked a round into the chamber, checked the spare magazines that hung nestled beneath his other armpit, and reholstered his weapon. Manwich preferred the balanced feel of the shoulder hostler because he had a hard time keeping his pants up with the weight of the standard-issue hip-mounted version, loaded down with extra mags, a stun-gun and cuffs. Besides, the only way for a man of his girth to lick the problem was to wear suspenders. Not his style. He thought suspenders made him resemble some fat-bellied, gin-guzzling Southern lawyer who practiced before the bench in a fly-infested Louisiana bayou courtroom. Which was exactly what his father had been.

Still staring intently at the disappearing form of the female officer, Kyle did the same with his handgun, grinning like a schoolboy.

"Don't *l*et our girl's uniform fool y'," M*a*nwich said. "That's one might*y* fine-*l*ooking hellc*a*t beneat*h* those slacks."

Kyle licked h*is* cracked lips. Like a hound catching sent of a fox, he *ba*iled from the car and acro*ss t*he street, narrowly missing being hit by a Vespa. Manwich half duck-waddled half ran, round-shouldered and baggy-assed, in pursuit.

∎ ∙∙∙ ∎

At Fort Meade, Loveday, the chief of ops directorate, nervously drummed the tabletop.

The Answer Man cleared his throat. "You sent Manwich to Rome to snatch an al-Qaeda agent and terminate Ahriman. Then dispatched an ops team to India. Why? I don't get the connection."

Absently rolling his ring between his thumb and index finger, the chief bit his lower lip, sat in silence. He looked up. "That's between me and … God." Averting his eyes, the chief of directorate studied his stubby, arthritic-bunched hands. The same hands he'd used to strangle the intern Kenny with piano wire.

From the chief's ring finger, the Knights of Malta seal glared back defiantly, as if it were admonishing him to keep his vow of silence under pain of death. He stiffened. Then he looked up and regarded the Answer Man briefly, then abruptly looked down, busying himself with paperwork, which meant: end of discussion.

What the Answer Man, Manwich, and most of NSA didn't know was that the chief had indeed hired Ahriman years ago, covertly setting up NSA's own Psy Ops program. Secretly funding his dark experiments in mind control. *Bast* was actually Ahriman's brainchild. Ahriman wanted to switch the subjects of his programming trials from adults to children. He thought they would be more malleable. *Bast* or Basha and her brother, Hamal, were found in a Palestinian refugee camp. Basha was brought to the States. The chief's right arm man was Carl Rothstein, the Station Chief in Tel Aviv at the time. He'd scouted the camps. He'd screened and tested dozens of children, but these two were exceptional. Bright and healthy and eager for affection.

There had been another sibling, a sister, but Rothstein discovered some politically connected Israeli citizen had adopted her and the files had gone missing. It had been part of a PR program aimed at showing Israel's good intentions toward peacemaking, but in this case, Rothstein suspected Mossad involvement. Many young children were taken from camps in Lebanon and raised by sometimes-unknowing Jewish families, receiving indoctrination in a kibbutz. It was code-named Operation Moses. Rothstein had also let the boy, Hamal, slip through his fingers and into the hands of the chief's opposite number at MI-6.

The chief suspected that Ahriman was playing both sides against the middle. A double agent, who worked for NSA, Volante, and MI-6. He suspected that Ahriman had shared his research with all three. Volante had also become a liability. Volante saw himself as an extraordinary man, tasked with the responsibility to use his extraordinary gifts to save the world. And like most extraordinary men, he had no compunction to act with the dictates or mores of society. He was above the average man; looking down at a world, he held the power to create. He believed there was no such thing as chance. He believed that chance was something he had the power to create. And like most who believed they were extraordinary, he became delirious with power. In a word he was quite mad.

Now, the ball was set into motion. It didn't matter who eliminated whom. And he trusted that Manwich would see to it that the Italians or Mossad took the rap. *Yes, it's between me and God*, he thought.

Reverently, the chief took his rosary in hand and bowed his head in prayer.

* * *

A block behind them, nestled discreetly behind a truck, sat the plain-Jane coupe. The MI6 agent behind the wheel palmed a SATCOM phone and punched in the number.

A gruff voice answered, "Speak."

"Mr. Childress, things are coming to a head on this end."

"Have you spotted your target, then?"

"*Bast* just arrived, sir. But there appears to be major complications."

"How so?"

"Fort Meade has operatives on the scene. Namely, Manwich."

A sharp intake of breath. "Bloody wanker!

"Yes, sir."

"Don't let that bleeding arsehole stand in your way, let 'em queue up. Get the operative *Bast* at all costs."

"Consider it done."

"Bollocks. Just make sure you get it done, then." A long pause then: "One more thing. Ring up the Beekeeper at Legoland and tell him things are *Luvvly* on my end. I had little trouble with the local plonkers, but that's been sorted out nicely. I've already neutralized the NSA team on the ground here. Caught the drop on those prissy Nancy girls and we'll be in position when the Doc arrives."

All the while the young Arab man sat in silence in the backseat, his eyes locked on the woman dressed as a policeman. His eyes were soft brown and tragic. He stiffened as his lower lip began to quiver uncontrollably and he brushed away a tear. He couldn't let his emotions betray his true intentions to these men.

CHAPTER 68

AT THE SOUND of the door creaking open, Giovanni paused and turned. Father Fallace entered, almost tiptoeing and somewhat out of breath. Moving closer to the table, he placed his hands on his hips and smiled. "I see you're a student of the arts. Durer's work has been my obsession for years."

Giovanni regarded him, but said nothing.

Fallace directed them to the last painting with a nod. "Although they're all quite remarkable, I find Durer's Crucifixion the most intriguing. Such interesting detail and such an amazing mystery it relates."

"Mystery?" Rossi said, exchanging side glances with his uncle.

"I'm no art historian, but it is a well-known fact that Durer was in tune with the underground stream of what, for a lack of a better term, could be called Freemasonry. Like many Renaissance painters, he was a noble heretic at heart. Even a bit of a rogue."

Giovanni studied the priest as he spoke, noting every minute detail. Each eccentric mannerism, the way his pallid hands steepled, the scent of his overpowering cologne, the inflection of his voice. The impish way the corners of his mouth twisted when he smiled.

"Some say he had a 'thing' for his mentor, although, because Alberti passed much earlier, they never consummated it. Except perhaps on copperplate." The priest gave a wicked laugh.

Giovanni interrupted: "You're referring to his work *The Fall of Man*. How he substituted his face for Eve and that of Leon Battista Alberti for Adam in the Garden of Eden?"

"Indeed," Fallace said. "Two naked men, standing with a cow-eyed look." His eyes widened as if to demonstrate.

"Starry-eyed lovers," Giovanni offered. "Though of course it was an unconsummated wish on Durer's part since he was born the year Alberti died. Alberti, however, aside from almost—kick starting the whole movement and being an architect, was a member of a secret order of adepts."

Rossi rolled his eyes as if to say, *here we go again*.

"Bravo, *Professore*. I see you're a bit of a Renaissance man yourself." The priest's eyes twinkled. "Then you may already know of Durer's little secret regarding the death of Jesus."

"Really, Father," Rossi broke in. "We're in a hurry. Can we see the tape, please?"

Silencing him with a dismissive wave of the hand, Giovanni said, "Father, please continue." When the priest turned to Rossi, Giovanni signaled his nephew with a wink.

The priest pointed to an engraving that resembled the last supper.

"My dear, *Professore,* they say Durer's deepest secret is revealed in this work. I confess that it eludes me. Since we share a similar passion, do you have any thoughts?"

Giovanni thought that Fallace's interest in Durer was too odd a coincidence but decided to play along. His gaze ticked from the priest and back to the print. Stroking his chin in deep thought, he regarded the puzzle. "Let's begin with the basics, the composition. We have perfect symmetry, six apostles on either side, which draws our eye to Jesus and …"

Fallace gave a sharp gasp. "My Lord, why didn't I see it? It's so obvious."

Rossi leaned closer. "If there's already twelve apostles in the scene, then who's that Jesus is cradling in his arms?"

"Well done, Nico." Giovanni smiled. "Like Leonardo da Vinci's last supper, we have a clue staring us in the face, something totally out of place."

"You're saying it's Mary Magdalene?"

Fallace cleared his throat. "On the contrary, it looks like …"

"Go on," Giovanni coaxed. "Remember the hermetic adage 'as above, so is below'?"

"I see it. The arches, symbolizing the *Vesica Pisces* or womb!" Fallace said excitedly as he began scribbling a diagram on slip of paper. Then handed it Rossi who looked puzzled. Two intersecting semicircles filled the paper.

Fallace stabbed the picture with his finger. "Now look, Colonel Rossi, right here in the print... a dark hole, a window ... a birth canal or gate... and below Christ, holding what must be his—"

Giovanni broke in and spoke in a hushed tone.

"His only son ..."

Fallace giggled and trembled like a schoolgirl. "Marvelous, *Professore*, simply marvelous!"

"Simple logic." Giovanni shrugged. Then he turned and regarded Fallace coldly. "Of course, it's just another heresy." His tone was half statement, half question as he probed with his eyes. *He's tipping his hand*, Giovanni thought.

Fallace smiled thinly and regained his composure. "Off course. But I love to solve these little riddles." He pursed his lips and turned to Rossi. "I have another one for you."

Fallace rubbed his hands eagerly as he turned back to the table. "Look at the crucifixion scene. Pay particular attention to the figure standing behind the cross. The one with his arms raised."

Rossi sighed and nodded.

"Unusual gesture ... unless you recognize its true significance," the priest explained. "It is the Grand Hailing sign of the Masons, who of course, received it from the Templars."

"Their distress call," Giovanni added.

"Precisely," the priest said. "Now, young man, study the face of Jesus carefully."

Looking closer, Rossi muttered, "Looks pretty sun-leathered and worn for a man of thirtysomething."

"Yes, go on."

"From what you said before about the Adam and Eve business … I'd guess it was Durer's face." Rossi turned to his uncle for some indication that his was correct, but Giovanni stood mute. Slowly his uncle's gaze drifted toward the desk, the overflowing ashtray. As he patted his pockets, Giovanni said, "Oh dear, I seemed to have left my cigarettes back at the office. Father, could I impose?" A puzzled look filled Rossi's face, but when he began to speak, Giovanni hushed him. "I know, I know. I'm truly quitting next week."

Fallace answered with self-effacingly modesty. "Oh, I'm terribly sorry, but I don't smoke."

Still frowning, Rossi started to reach into his suit pocket. Giovanni shook his head. Eyes darting to the priest and then back again to his uncle, Rossi nodded.

"Young man, your observation was astute, but your conclusion missed the mark." The priest pointed to another painting on the table. The radiant face of Christ looked upward, long flowing hair, modest facial hair, typical but somehow different…

"Allow me to introduce Albrecht Durer," Fallace said, laughing.

"A self-portrait," Giovanni asked.

Fallace nodded. "Far too flattering, too much artistic license I'm afraid."

"So whose face did he substitute for Christ's on the cross then?" Rossi asked.

"None other than the same face whose impression we find on the Shroud of Turin, the same face that is honored in every Masonic Temple in the world, the face of Jacque De Molay. The Templars' Grand Master and—sacrificial lamb."

With those last words, Giovanni's mind reeled. Another piece of the puzzle that Max had died for was now revealed. The Templars indeed had proof that Christ's resurrection was false.

CHAPTER 69

AS ROSSI STOOD regarding Father Fallace, he rubbed the stubble of his five o'clock shadow. "You're referring to the Templars?"

Beaming, Fallace said, "None other. Don't tell me you share my interest, Colonel?"

"Let's just say it's become a recent obsession." Rossi shifted his gaze to his uncle who stared fixedly at the priest.

Moving to the desk, opening a drawer and withdrawing a book titled *The Hiram Key*, Fallace thumbed to a page displaying a photo of the image of the Turin Shroud.

"The upper photo is undoubtedly easily recognized as being the reverse negative image purported by many to be Christ's, somehow magically imprinted onto His burial shroud. But look at the striking resemblance to the woodcarving of Grand Master Molay beneath it. Look closely at the eyes, the long angular nose, the distinctively odd shape of the beard, how it's parted at the bottom edge. Back in 1988 the Vatican allowed three separate carbon-dating tests to be run on the linen of the Shroud of Turin. It was found to be a complete fraud. No older than the late 1200's. This coincides perfectly with Molay's arrest after Pope Clement had called him back from Limassol, Cyprus. Shortly thereafter, Molay was arrested and tortured at the hands of the King's henchman, Grand Inquisitor of France, Guillaume Imbert. After raiding their Temple in Paris, Guillaume's men found a shroud concealed in a box neatly folded beneath an actual human skull and bones. Like Spain's infamous Torquemada, Guillaume was a sadistic genius when it came to methods of torture. Since the Templars were accused of denying the Crucifixion by trampling and spitting on the crucifix as part of their initiation ceremonies, the Inquisitor devised a fitting trial by ordeal for Molay, a blasphemous reenactment of the Christ's crucifixion. After scourging his flesh raw, crowning him with razor-sharp thorns, and nailing him to a cross, Guillaume speared his side with a lance. Taunting him, Guillaume pressed the bitter tasting, vinegar-soaked rag to Molay's lips. Molay eventually confessed and was lowered from the cross and wrapped in the shroud seized from his own temple."

Giovanni broke in: "Naturally, this all occurred before he recanted and was burned at the stake in Paris?"

Fallace's eyes hooded, his lips curled into a tight smile. "Naturally. I just find it a more plausible explanation than—"

"Leonardo forging it," Giovanni said with a hint of sarcasm stitching his words.

"Da Vinci had access to Roger Bacon's invention, the camera obscura, and the necessary silver salts like nitrate and sulphate," Giovanni continued. "But the notion that he created a solarographic image by radiating or singeing the chemically treated linen with condensed ultraviolet rays from sunlight is—"

The priest cut in. "Scientifically preposterous …since burn marks fluoresce under a black-light and neither the image nor the bloodstains react in such a manner."

It occurred to Rossi that his uncle and the priest were now parrying and thrusting like opponents in a fencing match. He put his money on Giovanni for the killing lunge.

Fallace drew a deep breath. "My dear *Professore*, despite your protests and tone, I somehow feel that there may be an underlying doubt, a nagging incertitude regarding the Crucifixion. Am I correct?"

Maintaining a poker face, Giovanni replied, "Rather an odd question for a priest. Your implication is that we share a mutual doubt."

For a long beat, Fallace said nothing, but Rossi observed the unspoken *tells*, the body language: tightness in the shoulders, a slight tick in the right eye, a hand rising absently to the lips.

As if shrugging off a pestering mosquito, Father Fallace flicked his head and instantly the curtain fell, and when it rose again, the priest's demeanor changed to that of a bumbling, humble parish priest. His arm shot out. From beneath the French cuff of his sleeve, a gold Patek Philippe wristwatch glinted. "My goodness, look at the time. Let me just pop in that video, shall we? I have to make my evening visiting rounds at the clinic."

When the priest moved to the VCR, Rossi's hand discreetly moved to his hip, checking for the reassuring feel of the butt of his Beretta.

Finding his voice, Rossi said to his back, "Please do, Father." Then he moved cautiously to his uncle's side.

The flickering image of the chapel appeared. It was empty.

"Fast-forward until we see some movement," Rossi instructed.

The VCR was an older model and static bars streamed across the herky-jerky image.

Abruptly, a figure entered from the right lower corner of the screen.

"Punch play," Rossi ordered.

As Fallace stepped to the side, Rossi's attention was riveted on the image. From the back, it appeared to be a priest dressed in a long black cassock who now kneeled reverently before the altar, head bowed in prayer. Even at this angle, even though the priest was kneeling, Rossi could see that the man was tall and lanky and ghostly thin.

His back to the camera, another figure glided across the screen. Although the picture was grainy, Rossi could make out the slow, deliberate manner in which the second diminutive figure seemed to creep up on the supplicated priest. Suddenly, the figure's arm hiked high above the priest's back; but because of his short stature, the figure appeared to be almost forced to stand on tiptoe to get the proper elevation. Then the unmistakable flash of a blade arced downward.

As they stood awe-shocked and staring at the grisly scene unfolding in stark shades of black-and-white that made it seem almost surrealistic, as though they were watching an old horror film, the hot steel struck again and again savagely.

The strangely animal-like, hungry sound of Fallace clearing his throat jolted Rossi from his reverie.

Rossi coughed to create a momentary distraction and quick-peeked over his shoulder.

Apparently, while they'd been engrossed with the butchery on the screen, Father Fallace had out-flanked them and now stood directly behind them, arm outstretched, holding a palm-sized device. His placid gaze turned feral. His eyes gleamed with madness.

And on the television screen before them, the murderous figure slowly turned toward the camera, revealing the grinning face of Father Fallace.

CHAPTER 70

THE FALL EVENING AIR turned lemon yellow in the slanted, fading light. In the silence of the night that blanketed Vatican City, the colonnades, the rooftops, Bernini's sentinel angels drew more shadows over themselves.

Below the window of the papal apartments in St. Peter's Square, a throng of youthful faces gazed upward in hushed anticipation and prayer, searching that solitary dim, rectangle of light for a fleeting shadow, in the fleeting hope the Holy Father's gentle face would somehow once again miraculously appear. The face of the man, not the Pope or the symbol of Christianity or quiet statesman, but rather, the face of the man who'd sought out *their* generation. The man who'd traveled more miles than any other Pontiff, who'd held office almost as long as St. Peter, longer than some of them had lived.

Within the apartment, a flock of dour-faced Polish nuns flitted about the room in a desperate effort to keep busy. Marko, his personal valet, busied himself by inventorying the Pope's personal things. Out of sheer habit he had laid out the Pontiff's white cassock for the next day. Not bearing to look at it, his gazed shifted to the ornate box on the desk, near the dressing area. It contained the Pope's will and next to it was a tape recorder. Realizing that the end was approaching and his strength was seeping away minute by minute, John Paul had recorded his last words for his flock earlier.

The camerlengo entered the room, accompanied by Master-General Spears and Cardinal Drechsler. Their eyes were downcast as they walked in a stilted motion. The camerlengo nodded toward the door, indicating Marko should leave.

Marko met his rheumy gaze. "He's passed?"

A solemn nod.

"And his last words?"

The camerlengo stiffened, cleared his throat. "They were … 'Follow me.'"

"Christ's words to Peter," Marko offered, studying the floor for a moment. Then he looked up, eyes tearing, and said with a hint of joy, "But he was referring to his—"

"Youthful flock. Even in death, he thought of himself as their shepherd." Moving to Marko's side, the camerlengo placed his arm around him and guided him toward the doorway. "Go to him. Leave us old men to talk of the future of the Church."

He locked the door behind Marko and joined the others at a desk.

In his shovel-like hands, Master-General Spears gripped the tiny box. With care, he slowly undid the clasp and lifted the lid. The others stood in hushed anticipation as Spears withdrew a rosary and a set of neatly folded papers. He opened them and spread the stack out on the desktop, smoothing the wrinkled, cream-colored, fine linen stationary with his huge hands.

Spears recognized the Pope's handwriting as he read aloud the first page.

Lieber alter freund:

Spears heard a sharp intake of breath and turned to see Cardinal Drechsler swallowing visibly, his Adam's apple bobbing. Spears realized the Pope was addressing Drechsler in the cardinal's native tongue, German, just as he always had done. He took in the cardinal's probing eyes and stoic expression, framed in a mantle of silvery, thick hair. When Drechsler nodded tersely, Spears went back to the letter. The narrative switched to English.

Although many have seen the third secret of Fatima as a doomsday prophecy which they believed you and I held close to our chest, denying its existence as such, the real prophecy comes from another source. Destiny will place the papacy in the hands of a just man, a bringer of peace.

As Drechsler leaned in closer, reading over his shoulder, Spears felt the cardinal's hot breath on his neck.

Spears turned to Drechsler and noticed the cardinal's face had become stony. "Perhaps you'd rather read it in privacy…"

"No. Please continue," Drechsler said, his voice melodious, yet forced and brittle.

Spears read on. *The twelfth-century Irish bishop, Saint Malachy, foretold of the last two Popes to occupy the Vatican. The second to the last would be the Gloria Olivae, the glory of the olive. In a vision, the Blessed Mother told me that he would bring a temporary peace, but usher in the beginning of the end. In her hands, she held a book and pointed to a quatrain of Nostradamus.*

"In a short time, the physician of great evil and the leech of unequal order will put the Olive Branch on fire. The post of the Pope will be moved from one coast to another, and by so great fire their empire will be accosted that the heat will evaporate the saliva in their mouths."

The last Pope, Petrus Romanus or Peter the Roman, will be engulfed in a terrible last battle. Malachy wrote: "During the final persecution of the Holy Roman Church, there shall sit Peter of Rome, who shall feed the sheep amidst many tribulations, and when these have passed, the City of the Seven Hills shall be utterly destroyed, and the awful Judge will judge the people." Life and history have taught me some grim lessons. My vision clouded, I sought to defeat the great beast—communism. But in doing so, my heart filled with a deep-seated hatred for their Godlessness. By allowing the ends to justify the means, I have allowed the Adversary a foothold within these sacred walls, within the very hearts and minds of the Curia. For too long, I have also allowed petty egotism and tradition to deny womankind's rightful place within the Church. My last wish is that women be allowed to resume their previous roles as priests or priestesses, which they rightfully held in our earliest roots, so-called paganism. In denying the truth of Christ's true teachings, in demonizing women, in labeling many true gospels as heresy, we have played into the Adversary's hands. Remember DEO, NON FORTUNA, By God, not by chance. And I might add, By birthright, not by misguided tradition. The time has come to stop disenfranchising our sisters in Christ. Women must be ordained as priests.

Reaching the end of the page, Spears stopped and looked up. "It seems the Holy Father had a change of heart. If this were to be made public—"

The camerlengo remained conspicuously silent. Spears marveled at how the camerlengo managed to convey an outward expression of groveling subservience while simultaneously projecting inner contempt. Spears's gaze ticked to Drechsler whose cold eyes fixed on him. He said nothing: his look said it all.

After a moment, Drechsler managed a gruff, "It will never see the light of day."

Spears straightened his shoulders and returned the look steadily. "Light, even when concealed beneath the darkest of cloaks, even from the vast reaches of distant galaxies, seems to find its way through the murky dark. And no matter what machinations the universe throws in its path, light and truth always—"

"Prevails," the camerlengo cut in absently. Then casting his eyes about sheepishly remained silent.

Drechsler studied their faces before he spoke. His demeanor softened, a rare smile splitting his marbled face. "Perhaps. Yes, perhaps this bears careful study. However, let us not make rash judgments, gentlemen. Turn the page."

Staring back from the next page were rows of letters forming a block that filled the page.

"What on Earth?" Drechsler said.

Spears brought the paper to his eyes, studying it intently. Reaching into his cream-colored robe, he produced a pencil, laid down the paper, and began circling lines of letters.

"Careful," Drechsler demanded. "You're defacing Karol's will!"

Ignoring him, his brows beetling in deep thought, Spears continued to segment the block of letters with elongated circles. "There we are," he said, a self-satisfied smile curling his lips. "On the contrary. I'm not defacing it, Cardinal. I'm deciphering it."

Now the block of letters resembled some word puzzle found in a newspaper.

"A Bible Code ... pure and simple," Spears said, shaking his head. "I wasn't aware His Holiness understood it. Amazing."

Drechsler scowled and said sarcastically, "Yes, such unknown talents and interests."

"How does it work?" the camerlengo asked.

"Ingenious but—so simple. One simply runs out the verses from the Bible in an unbroken series of letters and uses a computer program to hunt for patterns and reoccurring frequencies of letters or words."

"Word puzzles," Drechsler said, rolling his eyes.

"But they're God's words, my good Cardinal. Meant to be seen by those who have the eyes, the heart to see."

Sighing and shaking his head, Drechsler said, "And what 'secret message' has God imparted to the Holy Father?"

Pointing to the circled rows of letters that now formed words, Spears said, "Merely, the identity of the next Pope." Drechsler stared, dumbfounded. Then finding his voice, he read aloud in a weak whisper, "Benedict Sixteen." A cold chill crept up his spine, his heart pounded. Years before, while lying awake in the still hours of early morning, Drechsler had decided that if the time ever came for him to assume the papacy, he would choose the name Benedict XVI. Struggling to suppress the welling apprehension that had seized him by willing his face to morph once again into an unrevealing mask of marble, his steely gaze darted from the paper to Spears, searching. "Is there more?"

Spears flipped to the next page, where two columns of words were written: the left in English, the right in Hebrew. Spears read the English: "The Shroud of Turin. Blood. Key to the Daughter of Christ. "

Rubbing his chin, Drechsler straightened to his full height and spoke with the command and authority of a Shakespearean actor: "I think it best for all concerned that I take safekeeping of these documents." Before Spears could protest, Cardinal Drechsler snatched the papers from the table, stuffed them roughly back into the box, and tucked the box beneath his arm.

The camerlengo gasped, then started to speak.

"Camerlengo," Drechsler said, cutting him off. "I believe we must make preparations for the papal funeral rites, the *novemdiales*, the nine days of mourning."

As if thrown off center by a quick shove, the camerlengo flinched and changed gears. Rubbing his hands together, he said excitedly, "Indeed, Cardinal. Indeed." His eyes flicked this way and that around the room nervously, and then he made for the door, muttering to himself as he marched off. "Yes, there are many preparations to make. Where to begin?"

Spears drew a deep breath, regarded Drechsler with a wide-eyed, unrevealing look, as though he were staring right through him, and said, "I'll look forward to speaking about all of this at a later date, Cardinal. For now … let's say, I have more pressing matters."

With that, he spun his heavy frame in a swish of white fabric and disappeared through the doorway, resembling a ghost who was off, late for another haunting.

Alone now with his thoughts, Drechsler's eyes cut to the white soutane and skullcap lying on the bed. He moved closer, ran his fingertips across the fabric. He imagined the white smoke snaking the early morning leaden sky. He imagined himself wrapped in a similar custom-tailored by Gamarelli soutane and scarlet vestments, appearing on the balcony, arms outstretched as the cardinal shouted, *"Habemus Papam,* We have a Pope!"

He imagined the roar of the crowd as the *Servus Servorum Dei,* the Servant of the servants of God, Benedict XVI, gave his first papal blessing.

But then, from nowhere—a dark shadow winged over him, chilling him to the bone marrow. The shadow seemed to swoop downward, growing in size until it blotted out the sun. He saw himself, his face pallid and contorted, lying in state as a crowd slowly paraded past. Frozen stiff but still conscious, he searched his surroundings. This isn't the Vatican. Where in God's name am I?

Then from the doorway came a short coughing sound, jolting him from his daydream, followed by needling pain in the side of his neck, as though he'd been stung by a bee.

Faintness stole over him suddenly.

His hand shot out, gripping the bedpost for support as he stood on rubbery legs, gulping ragged breaths, his forehead beading in a cold sweat, heart racing. His knees buckled and he collapsed. The tiny ornate box spilled from his hands, tumbling across the floor.

Footsteps.

His vision blurred as he lay, staring across the rippling floor, cheek pressed to the rug, unable to move.

Boots. Black boots appeared at eyelevel. Hands—clutching a pistol—plucked the box from the floor. A thin voice, muttering unintelligible words, floated downward. Then dark motes, resembling lampreys, began eeling before his eyes. His vision tunneled and then blackness, everywhere blackness.

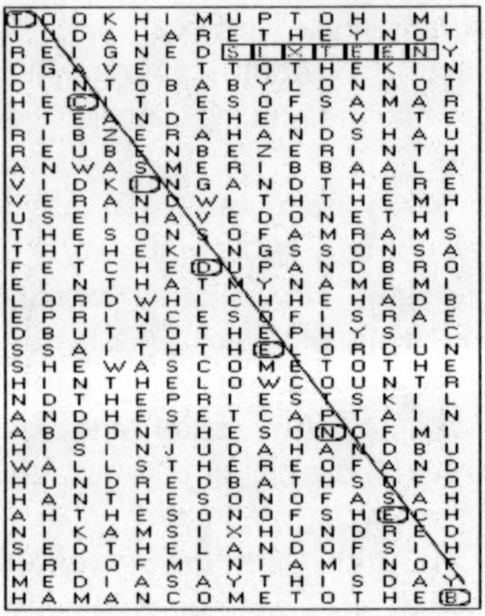

CHAPTER 71

A KNIFE-EDGED WIND sliced through the adjacent hillside rocking the TV van. Rain lashed at the van's windshield as a hulking warrior sat in the driver's seat, peering through a highly magnified night-vision spotting scope. Tree boughs twisted in the gusting wind.

Dark figures strode across the rain-soaked blanket of leaves under their feet. Then their opaque forms skittered across the green, phosphorescent field of the night-vision scope. A howling wind laminated itself over percussion caps of exploding thunder.

The driver said in a guttural voice, "We've got company."

The two warriors secreted in the van exchanged glances. Instinctively, the driver reached for his weapon.

As she monitored the laser beam listening device aimed at Volante's estate, Josie wondered if she should have talked Schlomo into mounting this surveillance mission, wondered if she should have asked him to be her backup in Italy without sanction. When a well-placed mole and former Mossad training academy classmate within at the NSA passed along word of Ahriman's affiliation with *E* Institute and Volante's recent arrival in Rome, she knew she had to follow up on the lead. After her failed hit at the temple, she figured Ahriman was probably on the lam, hidden somewhere within the vast holdings of the *E* Institute. Checking her sources, she came up with the location of Volante's mountain retreat. So she called Uri. But since Uri was tied up with another assignment, he sent his brother, Schlomo, who caught the next flight from London, where he'd recently wrapped up an assignment. When she picked Schlomo up at the airport, his appearance startled her. Schlomo's head was spade-shaped with a Neanderthal forehead, his complexion sickly, the color of dusting powder. His shoulders were wide as a railroad tie, and his towering frame seemed to almost brush the ceiling. With his hands the size of scoop shovels and his body slightly misshapen, Schlomo resembled a sideshow attraction. Josie blinked, did a double take, half-expecting to see bolts protruding from the sides of his neck.

Schlomo was the strong, silent type. A Goliath of few words ... mostly grunts. At the gate, Schlomo managed a weak grin, as if to do so were painful. Then he turned and shambled for the door.

She'd rented a garage where Schlomo made some modifications to the TV van she had borrowed. He outfitted it with eavesdropping equipment and weapons he'd obtained from some old contacts.

But now huddled in the van, a premonition of death seized Josie. Schlomo, in a glass-smooth motion, threw back the top bolt as he raised the 9 mm. Uzi submachine gun from his lap, his hand chopping downward to extend the folded metal shoulder stock. Josie, seated at the listening console, ripped the headphones from her ears and grabbed the Micro-Uzi machine pistol off the gun rack to her right.

PERIMETER ALERT . . . INTRUDER . . . sprayed across the console-mounted monitor screen in bold red letters. Fear leached through to the marrow of their bones. First the weapon in her hand began to vibrate, tingling her palms. Then the air itself almost hummed around her. Suddenly, the van's rear and side windows imploded simultaneously, cutting a deep gash into Josie's temple.

A metallic clawing, scraping sound began at the rear and traveled across the van's rooftop, stopping inches above the driver's head. The sound conjured a vision of Freddy Krueger's razor-tipped fingers raking the van's sheet metal. First the sidewall and then the roof buckled inward as if it were struck with an invisible sledgehammer, as if the molecular structure of the metal itself was being pounded and stretched by some powerful force. Their eyes darted frantically, trying to comprehend. Being trapped within the close confines of the van was bad enough, but this was maddening. Josie's claustrophobia seized the reins; she became paralyzed with fear.

Schlomo's hands were slippery with perspiration. He struggled to hold the Uzi in a white-knuckled grip. Sheets of rain tore through the broken window, stinging his face and eyes. Then, the barrels of each Uzi rose in unison.

Silence. The vibration stopped, replaced with a tingling sensation, rippling over her flesh. Then sweltering heat, as though she were cooking from the inside out.

Her breathing labored and shallow, Josie's eardrums prickled with the tick . . . tick . . . tick of her Rolex Chronometer.

Time stood still.

Horror sank into their bodies, washing over their faces. Pulsed in their temples.

Tick . . . Tick . . . Tick.

Sweat poured off their bodies.

Josie's throat constricted like dried rawhide. *Do the math. Two Uzis, 30 round magazines with backup mags duct-taped to their sides. Reverse the mags, reinsert and fire.* She'd practiced the drill a thousand times. It took about one second. *A total of 120 rounds . . . fire in controlled bursts.*

But somehow she knew down deep at her core, knew in her gut, that this boogeyman, this "thing going bump in the night," was no mortal enemy. An invisible beast had entered her ordered world, bending and distorting reality with its arrival, lying in wait inches from her face—ready to pounce.

The deafening silence engulfed them. It was almost as though a black hole had absorbed the wind, the thunder, the rain, their own heartbeats, sucking the sound waves from midair.

A faint, high-pitched sound began to resonate in the silence, grew stronger, overpowering. It pulsed in their blood, in the fillings of their teeth. Drove like millions of tiny needles into their brains. Then they heard a buffeting sound, like mainsails cracking against the sea's hammering winds. The van was rolling from side to side now, pitching Josie to the floor. Josie and Schlomo fired bursts of hot lead into the van's rooftop, the sides, struggling to lock on a target.

Their ears rang in pain from the roar of the muzzle blast. Eyes blinded by the Uzi's muzzle flash, tearing from the cordite-laced air, choking now in the blue gray mist of gun smoke. Schlomo screamed, "*Gevalt*! Josie, help me!"

As if a giant fist hammered the roof, it buckled steadily downward, crushing Schlomo into the seat like pressed ham.

Desperately fighting to get to him, reaching and clawing for him but realizing it was useless, Josie fell backward and fired again, spraying the roofline. The van rocked and swayed violently. Throbbing, thrashing waves of sound pounded from all sides. The van began to accordion toward her from both sides.

Tortured sheet metal screamed in her ears. Like the plates of a giant drill press, the twisted steel inched closer. Josie searched frantically. Then she saw it; the trapdoor in the floor that Schlomo had cut out, used to ditch contraband or to exit the van by dropping into street manholes. Something fell, pinning her ankle. She grabbed hold of the heavy piece of equipment and heaved it to one side, freeing herself. The side wall lurched again, almost wedging her against the opposite encroaching wall. Moving quickly in the narrow space that remained, sweat stinging her eyes, she wrenched open the trapdoor and squeezed through just as the flooring sandwiched above her. She rolled out from beneath the van, got to her feet and ducked into the tree line. Crouched in shadow, she frantically searched the darkness. Nothing. Absolutely nothing but the crumpled husk of the van. She said a silent prayer for Schlomo.

Josie circled around the van, using the trees as cover. Her ankle throbbed with a glassy pain with each step. There, barely discernible through the dense brush, she saw them. A group of men in black Nomex were field-stripping a strange-looking device. Maybe a cannon or mortar of some sort, she reasoned. They must be Volante's henchmen. Drawing the silencer-equipped Sig Sauer from the small of her back, she aimed and fired. Three quick coughs and they lay dead.

Eyes darting, searching for more targets, she hobbled toward the device. She pulled a red-lensed penlight from her pocket and studied the weapon. Bold letters on its side read ULTRA-PHONIC M-12. *A chicken fryer, so this was the unseen demon,* she thought, chiding herself for letting her fears and phobia cloud her thinking.

She'd heard of them, but had never seen one in action, and certainly had never been on the receiving end until tonight. It was an ultrasonic "non-lethal" weapons system, supposedly still under development, that emitted a wave of sound coupled with microwaves strong enough to subdue a rioting mob. She knew that was a total crock, since its nickname was due to the fact it could poach your flesh and simmer your blood within the walls of your arteries. Apparently, someone had amped up the sonic power and recalibrated it, making it strong enough to buckle sheet metal.

Her stomach still rippled with spasms of nausea; her head ached with a dull pain. Searching the area, she found a black, modified four-wheeler. She hopped on, kicked it over, and peeled away, churning the ground with its over-sized tires. Leaving a spray of dirt as her signature, she raced into the forest.

CHAPTER 72

FATHER FALLACE STOOD grinning like the Cheshire Cat, the strange device in his hand still trained on Rossi and Giovanni. "Really, gentlemen, I had thought you would see through my play-acting much sooner."

Rossi shifted his weight from one foot to the other.

"No sudden moves, my dear Colonel Rossi," the priest said, panning the device toward him. "And keep your hands where I can see them. Colonel, remove your pistol and slide it across the floor to me."

Rossi glared. "Why the hell should I?"

"Because if you don't… your uncle will die!" In that instant, the priest punched a key on the device and Giovanni's hand flew to his heart, his face grimacing in sheer agony. He fell to his knees.

The priest explained. "This tiny transmitter emits pulsed micro waves synchronized to his myocardial rhythms, resulting in heart failure." Fallace glanced at his wristwatch. "I'd give him about two maybe three minutes at the outside."

Rossi's gaze shot to his uncle's writhing body on the floor. Gingerly, Rossi took out his pistol, bent, and slid it across the floor.

Keeping the transmitter locked on Giovanni and his eyes on Rossi, Fallace stooped and snatched the weapon. He clicked off the transmitter and pocketed it while training the pistol on his captives.

"That's a good boy," Fallace said, and nodded toward Giovanni who was already beginning to recover. "Help him to his feet, please."

The priest removed cotton wadding from his cheeks, then his spectacles and toupee, tossing them casually to the floor. "There, that's much better…"—he finger-combed his thinning hair and ripped off the Roman collar—"damn thing was most uncomfortable."

Giovanni cleared his throat. His breath labored, he struggled in a faint voice, "Doctor Ahriman, I presume? Or would you prefer to be called Professor Nemo?"

Dropping totally out of character now and losing his Italian accent, Ahriman smiled demurely and reached into his pocket, pulling out a silk handkerchief and dabbing the perspiration from his brow. "So, you did see through my little disguise, Professor?"

Giovanni's face was expressionless, his gaze steady as he stood massaging his chest.

"And yet … you still fell into my little trap," Ahriman said, clucking his tongue.

Giovanni shrugged. "Chalk it up to vanity."

The smile vanished from Ahriman's face. "And now, like in one of your pulp thrillers, I suppose you expect some self-deprecating wit and a rambling monologue, outlining our plans. I hate to disappoint you, but I've done a rewrite of the script. Instead, I'll just summarily execute the two of you."

Rossi laughed. "Still a bit melodramatic, don't you think?"

Ahriman raised the pistol, and held it in a two-handed shooting stance.

"I don't think you can afford to kill me," Giovanni said.

Ahriman sighed. "And why is that?"

"Because Max Schulman did not solve the puzzle. Although I suppose you tortured him before killing him just to be sure."

Ahriman stared intently, eyes searching.

Giovanni pointed to the Durer engravings. "I've deciphered the coded message in Durer's works. If I may …" He moved toward the table.

"By all means, Professor." Ahriman waved the gun barrel toward the table.

"The very dimensions of the Melancholia print are the first clue." Giovanni traced the outer edge of the print with his finger. "It's a simple Kabbalistic gematrical code, a mathematical symbol of Ihsous Cristos in Greek or Jesus Christ."

"Go on."

"Next we have the magic square which always equals thirty four, again symbolizing Jesus Christ in mystic numbers. Then there's the rainbow in the sky, a symbol of the divine feminine, Venus and Isis, merging with the earthly world. The outline of the pentagram on the seated angel is another symbol of Venus. It symbolizes the true meaning of the quest for the Holy Grail. That man and goddess must merge in the act of sacred, unselfish lovemaking in order to become Christ, 'the anointed one.'"

"Blah, blah, blah. Enough of your sugary fairytale! It's still meaningless dribble," Ahriman said.

"You said yourself that the man on the cross is not Jesus." Giovanni held up Durer's Crucifixion scene. "It shows that Christ was not—"

"Crucified or didn't actually die on the cross." The gun wavered in Ahriman's hand as his voice filled with excitement. "You're just stalling for time."

"What if I told you that Max sent me the missing part of the puzzle and that you, probably somewhere close, held the key to it all along."

Ahriman looked puzzled, but his hand absently patted the breast of his cassock.

Giovanni gave a self-satisfied smile. "Just as I suspected. You have *Le Cahier Rose* notebook on you, don't you?

"There is a passage that begins…"—Giovanni whistled a haunting tune—"it goes like this … 'O' careful saint that aged Jahveh fools.'"

Rossi flinched slightly. Stabbing outward with the handgun's barrel, Ahriman cautioned, "Easy, my dear Colonel." Then he moved to the professor's side, reached inside his own breast pocket and removed the notebook. He met the professor's gaze. "I trust you can read the symbols on its cover and safely open the book, then?"

Giovanni nodded and after studying the glyphs, he began sliding various slots within the cover in sequence, sweat dripping from his brows as he worked feverishly. He stood back a moment and took a deep breath. His hand reached out to open the cover, but he hesitated.

"Please be ever so careful, Professor. Rest assured that I had no intentions of killing you. In fact, I went to great pains to ensnare you into being here this very moment. Are you sure you've completed all the necessary steps?"

Giovanni gave him a cold look. "Why don't we stop playing games?" Then his hand reached out and carelessly flipped open the cover. He met Ahriman's stare. "As I said, you need me. If I hadn't done this correctly you would have stopped me."

"Touché. Now, get on with it."

Giovanni quickly thumbed through its pages, searching for the passage. When he found it, he laid the book open on the table. Next to the passage in French was an English translation Max had made:

> O' careful saint *that* aged Jahveh fools. Received *of* the danGer of need. He led to deceive rabble, upset Jews, the beaten son *of* priestly chorus. *For* Hail the Glory, a grim era of, eagerly Mad Man, that bush generated, of the eighty dogs. *Seek the* Cretin's hefty poet. *Find* the vilest of tolerably. *Be* in the legend. ReJoice sureness of truth. *See the truth of,* artist's Cheerful necrosis.
>
> EmmaNuel walks highpoint. O' haggardly is Mean deaf-Mute.

The professor and Ahriman exchanged glances.

Giovanni noted the last line and recognized his friend's little prank, Max's coded signature: *A Merry* XMAS. He unscrambled the anagram in his mind—A Merry MAX S.

"Very perceptive of you, *Professore*. I've puzzled and puzzled over this very passage. It is totally out of context with the rest of the book."

Giovanni smiled, eyes twinkling. "And you'd love for me to decipher it?"

"If you would be so kind." Ahriman bowed in fake humility.

"Do you have a computer with an Wy-Fi connection available?"

Ahriman regarded him coldly, then quickly moved to the desk, all the while training his weapon on Rossi who watched intently. Then he fumbled with a key, pulled out a laptop computer and booted it up. "It's networked to a printer."

"Very good," the professor said, stealing a side glance at Rossi. Without waiting to be summoned, he picked up the notebook and went to the laptop. His fingers began flying over the keyboard. "Of course, I have to have some sort of context, a frame of reference, in order to find the solution. What are you looking for? A name, a place, a person … a grave?"

By now Ahriman's full attention was on the computer screen, noting that Giovanni had pulled up a web site entitled AnagramGenius.com, and had begun entering the garbled passage from the notebook. "A name and a specific location," he managed.

As he typed, Giovanni explained, "The italicized words are not scrambled. And a comma denotes the end of each anagram to be decoded. We simply break them into separate phrases and let the computer program unscramble them for us."

Suddenly Rossi broke in. "Your target is the Vatican and the *E* Institute is somehow manipulating the Muslim Fundamentalists like pawns on a chessboard," Rossi stated matter-of-factly.

Ahriman flinched. "No comment." Then his gaze flicked from the screen to Giovanni. "Go ahead, submit the text!"

Headshake: "No, I don't believe I will. At least not right now. Wouldn't want your prying eyes to see too much."

Face reddening, Ahriman aimed the pistol directly at Rossi. "You'll finish it or I'll shoot him."

"Oh, I'm quite sure you will," Giovanni answered smugly.

"I never bluff." His finger curling tightly around the trigger, he fired.

Click.

Click.

Ahriman's face filled with rage and confusion.

Rossi drew his back-up Beretta from the small of back and then fished something from his suit pocket with his free hand. "You didn't think that I'd give you a loaded pistol?" When Rossi slowly opened his hand, he held the Beretta's full magazine.

Ahriman stood frozen, eyes glaring. He fumbled with the pistol, releasing the magazine. It was empty.

Rossi ordered. "Now it's your turn. Slide the pistol and that gizmo across to me and be quick about it."

Hesitantly, Ahriman complied.

Rossi bent down, palmed the Beretta and holstered it as he rose, still keeping the muzzle of his back up piece trained on Ahriman. Then he drove his heel hard into the device, which still lay upon the floor, smashing it to bits.

Giovanni said, "Something about you seemed familiar from the start, but at first I just couldn't place the face. The fact that you didn't smoke when the overflowing ashtrays attested to the fact that the real Father Fallace, whom you no doubt murdered, did."

Ahriman gave a weak grin. "Nasty habit, smoking."

"It was your discourse on the Shroud of Turin that triggered my memory. I recalled reading a paper on the subject you had written," Giovanni went on. "I'm afraid that on the contrary, it was your own vanity that did you in, Doctor. You went to elaborate measures to lure me here with the sole purpose of decoding that passage. I came willingly since I realized that without the notebook, I couldn't decipher Durer's secret message."

Rossi noticed that Ahriman's eyes shifted. Then the doctor said, "Officer, thank God you arrived. These men are murders."

Something firm and cold pressed hard against Rossi's neck and a soft but firm voice said, "Lower your pistol and toss it."

At the sound of that familiar voice, cold chills shot up Rossi's spine. As he pitched his weapon across the room, rough hands searched his body, and finding the holstered weapon, the officer ripped it out and chucked it.

From the corner of his eye, he saw the officer come into view as she sidestepped to his side and pressed the muzzle to his cheek.

Pale blue eyes stared from beneath the uniform cap.

Gina's catlike eyes.

CHAPTER 73

"Gina" Rossi managed, his face a mass of confusion.

For a moment she stared blankly. Then her eyes softened as though there were a fleeting second of recognition, but instantly turned cold. "Shut up. I don't know you and I don't know anyone called Gina."

Rossi stood mute, dumbfounded and totally off balance.

"It's no use, my dear Colonel. You see, she doesn't recall your little tryst," Ahriman explained, giving a hearty belly laugh. "Such a fickle gender. And your other girlfriend, Ms. Schulman, almost succeeded in killing me. While you were waiting, I ducked out and had a limo waiting to whisk me to the E Institute Temple. Ms. Schulman was waiting for me gun in hand. I foiled her plans and dashed back here after begging off my lecture by claiming that I'd suddenly taken ill."

Rossi managed. "Is Josie still—"

Ahriman gave a short chuckle. "Alive and quite determined to find me again I suspect." Turning to Giovanni and nodding toward Gina, Ahriman said sarcastically, "*Professore*, do you have a diagnosis?'

Regarding her from head to toe, Giovanni stroked his chin. He was taken by the woman's features. Something about her seemed so familiar, although he was sure he'd never laid eyes upon her before.

Giovanni offered, "Dissociative Disorder. Induced to program her to kill by using alter personalities. Separate identities that have no recollection of each other's actions."

Ahriman gave a low whistle. "Remarkable deduction, Professor. My early experiments with adults were fairly successful, but I knew that if I could work with younger subjects—"

"You used children?" Giovanni said incredulously.

"But of course. Young minds, malleable and eager for attention and affection which I readily supplied." Ahriman gave a lecherous grin. "Once lulled into a false state of security, I—"

"Assaulted their innocent minds with psychoactive drugs and then jerked the rug out from underneath them!" Giovanni's hands fisted at his sides now. "You used terror and psycho-trauma like an ice pick. Sheer terror can splinter a child's mind into pieces. Unable to face the obscene cruelty heaped upon them, the child retreats into make-believe personalities, alters that block out the memories. But those dark visions slither through their psyche and their venom poisons their souls."

Ahriman slowly clapped his tiny hands. Then he turned to Gina. "Listen to me carefully. You are unable to understand anything we discuss, until I tell you otherwise. We're going to speak in a foreign language you don't know. But you'll still watch their every move."

Gina's face slackened, but she tightened her grip on the handgun.

"You'll understand only the phrase, let's play a game, and then upon hearing it, you will comprehend our words."

"There, now we can speak freely." Ahriman smiled and turned to Giovanni. "Gina's true name is Basha. She came to me from a Palestinian refugee camp. She was my prize pupil. I soon realized that her overwhelming love for her brother and sister, whom she'd been separated from, was the key. The boy was adopted by a British family and the girl by an Israeli family."

The blood drained from Giovanni's face. He staggered and Rossi grabbed his arm to steady him. "You okay?" Rossi said. Giovanni nodded and took a deep breath.

Ahriman feigned a look of concern. "Easy, *Professore*. So sensitive. How touching."

Giovanni's eyes marbled over. "Finish your story."

"I induced a virtual fantasy world into Basha's memory. She believes her brother was killed through gross wrongdoing by the Catholic Church. Her primary alter is Laylah Thomas, whom she believes to be her long-lost sister."

"Again with your word games, Doctor." Giovanni shook his head in disgust. "Laylah Thomas meaning literally—Night Twin. A doppelgänger."

"I see that you appreciate the irony. Care for a little demonstration?"

Eyeing Gina from head to toe, Rossi struggled to digest the situation. Even now, the cold muzzle still pressed to his cheek, he couldn't help but feel for her. He had to admit the truth: she'd stirred something deep inside of him. And yet, here she stood, as uncaring and unfeeling as some robotic killing machine. *If I could only reach her, if I could connect ... then maybe.*

"It seems that once again you have us at the disadvantage, Doctor," Giovanni said dryly. "Proceed if you wish."

Ahriman cleared his throat and said, "Let's play a game."

Gina stiffened, her eyes fluttered briefly. "I'm listening."

Shattered beyond hope, her fragile psyche, like a looking glass hammered by blow after blow of trauma's hammer, was splintered. Spider webs etched across the surface of her consciousness, fragmenting each personality: *Bast*, Gina, Laylah, Basha; they were in reality all one deeply disturbed young woman, who now stared back from behind haunted pale blue irises.

To Gina, Ahriman said, "Who are you?"

"Who am I?"

"No, tell me who *you* are," Ahriman corrected.

"I'm Basha."

"No. Your name is officer Ricci. Say it."

In an instant, her striking, Permafrost blue eyes transformed into cloudy quartz, without substance or spark; they merely existed in her face, like souls adrift in limbo.

"I'm officer Ricci."

"Tell me your orders, officer."

Gina swallowed hard, and as her eyes glazed over, her grip on the pistol tightened again. But then her eyes danced with confusion. "I … don't know."

"You are to apprehend and neutralize two terrorists. A Colonel Rossi and one Professor Giovanni. They are very dangerous men."

She flinched, nodding her head slowly.

"You have found them, officer. They are standing before you."

"I have found them."

"On my command, you will carry out your orders. You will kill Colonel Rossi."

"On your command."

To Giovanni, Ahriman said, "You see, she's totally under my … spell, as it were."

"You're a bastard," Rossi said.

"Sticks and stones, my dear Colonel."

Giovanni coughed and licked his lips. Turning to Gina, he began speaking in an exact imitation of Ahriman's voice. "Let's play a game." Rossi recalled how, when he was a child, his uncle used to imitate the voices of movie stars and cartoon characters for his amusement. His uncle was a perfect mimic who had worked his way through undergraduate school by doing impersonations in clubs.

Hands clenching at his sides, Ahriman shouted, "No. Don't listen to him!"

"I'm listening," Gina replied, attention focused on Giovanni.

"You will lower your weapon," Giovanni ordered. On command, Gina lowered the pistol.

"No!" Ahriman said, lunging forward.

Rossi met him midway, spun him around, and held him in an armlock. Ahriman squirmed and struggled, but Rossi wrenched the doctor's arm higher. Mashing the crook of his other arm into the doctor's throat, he squeezed, took a step back with one foot firmly planted, and lifted him off the floor. Within seconds, the blood flow was restricted by the pressure to both sides of the doctor's throat. When his legs buckled, Rossi lowered the unconscious Ahriman to the floor and cuffed him. Next he roughly jammed a kerchief into Ahriman's mouth, gagging him.

Breathing hard, Rossi turned to his uncle. "He'll come to any second, but the gag will silence him."

Giovanni nodded tersely and turned his attention back to Gina.

"Hand me your weapon."

Instantly, Gina complied.

Rossi took the pistol from his uncle and went to retrieve his Beretta and back up.

But just as he stooped to reach for his handgun, a voice squeaked, "Hold it right there, Rossi."

Rossi spun at the sound. There, in the doorway, stood his worst nightmare: the asshole himself, Agent Manwich, with his stooge at his side.

CHAPTER 74

RISING TO HIS full height, Rossi said, "Don't interfere, Manwich. This is none of your affair."

Manwich made a palms-up gesture and gave a shit-eating grin. "Hey, wouldn't dream of it, Colonel. Just here to help."

"Somehow, I doubt your sincerity," Rossi said, tightening his grip on the pistol still in his hand and gauging his distance and potential targets. "Maybe if your friend didn't have his Sig pointed at my gut it would help."

Manwich shot a side-glance at Kyle and said, "Put that thing away."

"Yeah, better listen to your boss," another voice came from behind Agent Kyle.

It was Dante. He brushed past Kyle and Manwich, regarding them with the same distain a crow would have for scarecrows, and entered the room, moving to Rossi's side. His gaze shifted to Gina, who stood stiff as a fence post, then back to Rossi.

"Merda! It's *Bast*."

"In a manner of speaking. I'll explain later, but—"

"Boss, I've got some bad news."

"How so?" Rossi asked releasing the magazine from the police pistol and tossing it. Then he jammed the full magazine back into his own pistol, jacked a round into the chamber, and tucked the hideout pistol into the waistband at the small of his back.

"It's your sister."

"Bianca?"

"She's been snatched. They dragged her from her car as she was being driven home from Kabul. We figure it's the same group that took the U.N. workers last year and assassinated that Muslim cleric who condemned the Taliban rebels."

Giovanni was printing out the decoded anagram. He studied the pages, briefly squeezed his eyelids tightly and winced, and then scribbled a few notes in the margins. Next he moved to a fax machine and keyed in a number for the Vatican. He turned to Ahriman who sat glaring and punched send. After gathering the printout, the pictures and the notebook, he tucked them into the satchel and turned to Rossi. "But she's just a worker for CARE International, right?"

Rossi, his eyes closed, nodded glumly. "Doesn't matter." Then he turned to Dante. "Is she still alive?"

"There was a video of her on Tolo TV, one of their independent networks."

"Go on."

Dante pulled a photo from his pocket and handed it to Rossi. "It's a still lifted from the broadcast."

Rossi studied the photo. His sister was in the usual pose, bracketed by the barrels of two AK-47s aimed at her head covered in a blue scarf, her eyes wide and panic-driven. It was as though she were pleading directly for Rossi's help, like the time she'd gotten tangled in a wire-woven fence when they were kids, stealing tomatoes from the neighbor's garden, and Rossi had to come to her aid. His heart sank; his stomach was torn with spasms.

"Tough break," Manwich offered. "If there's anything we can do to—"

The loud ring of a cell phone interrupted. All eyes turned toward Ahriman. It was coming from his direction. Ahriman nodded furiously and mumbled through the gag.

Puzzled looks washed across their faces, and Rossi moved toward Ahriman to get the phone.

Rossi dug into Ahriman's pocket, flipped the cell phone open and said, "*Pronto?*"

A reedy voice on the other end answered, "Doctor Ahriman, please."

Rossi cupped the mouthpiece, and bent over Ahriman. He yanked out the gag, pressed his semi-auto to Ahriman's temple, and whispered, "It's for you. Any funny business, any attempt to talk to Gina, and I'll cap that sick brain of yours right here and now. Understood?"

Ahriman smiled thinly and nodded. As Rossi held the phone to Ahriman's cheek and bent his ear to the phone to monitor the conversation, the doctor spoke: "Go ahead."

After a few seconds, Ahriman asked Rossi, "He wants to know if I'm okay?"

Rossi nodded, indicating he should acknowledge the situation. "Yes, I'm indisposed and Colonel Rossi has our asset in custody." Ahriman's gaze lifted to Rossi. "He wants to speak to you."

Bewildered, Rossi rose and pressed the phone to his ear. "Rossi here, who is this?"

"That's of no importance. We would, however, like to make a trade."

"No deals."

"I suggest you reconsider. What I'm proposing is a simple exchange of hostages, Mr. Rossi."

"What hostage?" Rossi's heart was pounding against his ribcage. A dark premonition floated up from the dark recesses of his brain.

"Your sister, of course."

Rossi steeled himself. "She was abducted in Afghanistan."

"And now she's here in Rome," the voice stated matter-of-factly.

CHAPTER 75

ROSSI LOST HIS VOICE. A whirligig of emotions and dread swirled in his mind, making him dizzy with fear and apprehension.

"Are you there, Mr. Rossi?"

His voice cracking, Rossi managed, "I'd need proof of life."

"Very well."

In the background, Rossi heard other voices, then suddenly a timid voice asked, "Nico, is that really you?"

It was Bianca. There was no doubt. "Are you all right?" he said.

She coughed, cleared her throat. "Yes, but … they—"

Her voice trailed off and the reedy male voice came back on the line. "That will have to suffice. Since we laid a trap for your uncle, we assumed your involvement. I had your sister taken as a potential bargaining chip. Do we have a deal? Ahriman and *Bast* for your sister?"

Rossi chewed his lower lip until it bled. "Where and when?"

"Take the metro Linea B to the Piramide stop and change to the Lido train which will take you to Ostia."

"And then?"

"Carry this phone. You'll receive further instructions en route. Bring only your hostages and the notebook. Remember, we'll be watching you. No helicopters, no tactical teams. Just you and your uncle and the hostages."

"So we will make the handoff on the train?"

"No more questions. You had better hurry. You have fifty minutes, not one second longer, to save your sister's life."

The line went dead.

Rossi pocketed the phone, moved to Ahriman and hoisted him to his feet.

To Rossi, Dante said eagerly, "What's the plan?"

"They've got Bianca. I don't know how, but they do. I'm making a hostage exchange. We've got to get to the metro."

Dante reached for his phone. "I'll get the team in place."

"NO! It's got to be just my uncle and me. No surveillance, no backup. Is that clear?"

Dante nodded reluctantly.

Giovanni gave a long sigh and took Gina gently by the arm. "Come along now, dear. We're going to take a little trip." As he moved, he absently patted the satchel, which hung at his side.

"Take a trip," she said in a wooden voice as they moved for the door.

Manwich and Kyle exchanged glances. As Kyle took a step toward Gina, Manwich shook his head. "We'll be tagging along, Rossi. Orders. We have reason to believe Drago Volante is behind this, and as a matter of national security for both your country and mine, I insist."

Manwich moved to Rossi, facing him squarely. He took a pin from a wallet in his breast pocket and fastened it to the inside of Rossi's lapel. "GPS, tracking device. We can monitor from the laptop in our car at an inconspicuous distance."

Rossi puffed out his cheeks and exhaled sharply. "What the hell, okay. But make it a loose tail. If they spot you—"

"They won't … now let's get going."

With that, Rossi grabbed Ahriman by the arm and pulled him to his feet. He uncuffed him. As Ahriman massaged his bruised wrists, Rossi added, "Remember, I'd just as soon kill you as to look at you." The doctor nodded. They made for the street, took separate cars.

They made the trip to the Coliseum metro stop in record time. Rossi put his Mustang, which Dante had delivered, through its paces as he powered through the crosstown traffic. They ditched the vehicles curbside, bought tickets from the machine, and boarded.

Rossi looked at his wristwatch. Thirty-eight minutes and counting.

As the train pulled away, in the jaundiced lighting of the metro station, it occurred to Manwich that Rossi's group looked somehow surreal: a disheveled priest, a stiff-necked carabinieri being led by a rumpled professor type, all encased behind the window glass like department store mannequins. Manwich and Kyle turned and sprinted for their car. Dante followed suit.

"How the hell we gonna snatch the girl and whack Ahriman?" Kyle asked, slipping behind the wheel.

"Never fear, dickweed. In the fracas, I pinned her, too," Manwich explained. "We'll be able to track her movements wherever she goes. When the opportunity arises, we'll make our move. In the meantime, let's see how this all shakes out. Maybe we can kill two birds with one stone."

As they burned rubber, lurched away from the curb, and swerved into traffic, Kyle said, "What about Mossad. You said we had orders to hook up with them."

"Just like the director said, 'she'll find us.' And you know, I got the weirdest feeling she will."

Before Kyle could answer, something hard dug into the back of his neck. From the back seat came a voice. "I already have, dickweed." When Kyle tried to turn his head, cold steel filled his ear.

"Keep your eyes on the road," Josie said, raising up now and leaning slightly over the seatback as she screwed the muzzle of her semi-auto deeply into Kyle's ear. Manwich started to turn. "You too, fatboy or I'll double-tap you both right where you sit."

Josie's eyes shifted to the speedometer. The needle was dipping lower. "Pedal to the metal. We've got a train to catch."

CHAPTER 76

WHEN STATO ENTERED his inner office, he saw Master-General Spears's huge frame perched behind his desk in front of his computer, hammering away at the keyboard. He moved to Cardinal Moscato and checked his pulse. Satisfied, he plunked himself down in a chair next to Spears.

"Get any more out of him?" Stato asked.

Not taking his eyes from the computer screen, Spears nodded. "I overheard your conversation, thanks for clicking on the intercom."

"And?"

"We should have thought to ask him earlier. But anyway, yes, they're headed for the right destination. You want to radio them?"

"No. Then we'd have to divulge our source." His eyes darted to Moscato's battered face and then back to Spears. "Under the circumstances, that might be a bit difficult."

"Indeed," Spears agreed and reached for the mouse, clicking onto another web site.

"There's a complication, though. The kidnapper's call came from within the Vatican, which we discussed before I clicked on the intercom."

Spears paused. "That means …"

"Means we have more confederates to root out. Moscato was incapacitated when the call came in."

Spears grunted. "Bertone. That little weasel. I'll bet you a steak dinner."

Stato reached for the phone. "I'll have him placed in custody and brought here."

Spears stayed his hand. "No, better yet … have my personal secretary shadow him. But you can monitor his calls and movements with the cameras, too, can't you?"

Stato nodded and reached for the phone again. After making the necessary arrangements he hung up.

The chime of the fax machine drew his attention.

Puzzled, Stato went to the machine and removed the pages.

"What?" Spears asked.

"They're for you." Stato handed him the pages.

Spears read silently for a few minutes, his hands trembling as he turned the last page. He looked up and regarded Stato gravely. "It's from *Professore* Giovanni. It's a deciphered passage from *Le Cahier Rose Noire*. He and Professor Schulman had been working on decoding it when Schulman was killed by an agent of Protocol-17. Giovanni states that Schulman had only deciphered a few lines before he was killed, and the notebook was subsequently stolen. It seems that Giovanni has allowed himself to be the bait in order to get the notebook."

"And—"

"He's still missing some piece of the puzzle." Spears chewed his lower lip.

Stato's eyes brightened. "You said it had to do with the stolen notebook?" He shot to his feet and went to his desk, pulled open a drawer, and withdrew a piece of paper. He returned and handed it to Spears. "In all the commotion I forgot." He nodded toward the document. "I found this in the archives at the crime scene, beneath Pico's body."

"It's the missing page from *Le Cahier Rose* that Giovanni referred to. The professor said the notebook's binding was in poor condition, its pages loose and tattered. It must have fallen out." Then Spears placed the bloodstained page on the desk and studied it.

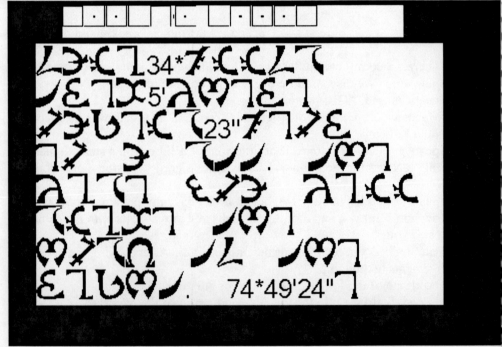

From the pile of fax papers, Spears took a single sheet and placed it next to the symbol-laden page on the desktop. It read:

> O' Satan Lucifer that Jehovah false God. Deceiver of the Garden of Eden. The Bible code revealed Jesus wept for the absent one, of Sacred

scripture. For the Holy Grail, marriage of, Mary Magdalene, that absent daughter of God the highest. Seek the city of the serpent. Find the valley of the lost tribe. Be enlightened. The resurrection of Jesus. See the truth of, Christ's false resurrection. The Nephilim walk among us. Daughters of Mary Magdalene.

With Stato looking over his shoulder, Spears explained. "Giovanni deciphered an anagram in the notebook. Although the wording seems strange, the message is clear.

"It repeats the Gnostic belief that Jehovah was actually Satan, the false ruler of a flawed world. It refers to Christ's marriage to Magdalene. It tells us that in the city of the serpent, in the valley of the lost tribe of Israel, we will find proof of the false resurrection. And proof that the Nephilim, which are offspring of the angels who violated earthly women, live among us."

Clearing his throat, Stato said, "The only proof of a false resurrection would be—"

Spears finished his thought. "If you found Jesus's tomb."

Stato offered. "And the offspring who resulted from the marriage of heavenly beings and women must mean—"

"The *Desposyni,* the children of Christ and Mary Magdalene."

In a thin voice, Stato asked, "But where is this city of the serpent?"

Spears took the page and moved to the computer. Furiously, his fingers flew over the keyboard. "The symbols at the top are Masonic code. The strange glyphs are called Enochian script, angelic language used by occultists like John Dee. They're simply a distraction. The answer lies in the numbers."

"They're map coordinates!" Stato said.

Nodding to the monitor and smiling, Spears explained, "The tomb is here." He stabbed the screen with his finger.

Studying the map, Stato said, "Srinagar, Kashmir."

Spears snatched the phone and dialed. He turned his back and spoke in a hushed whisper. After a brief conversation, he cradled the phone and turned back to the computer.

Stato said, "What are you doing?"

"I've booked your flight to Pakistan, my son. Under an assumed alias." He handed him a doctored passport and credit card.

"Father Devlin?" Stato asked.

"A Jesuit … but still one of my best priests. He's about your height and weight, so all I had to do was to have the photo changed. It will pass a cursory inspection and those Pakistani inspectors won't look too closely at a man of the cloth. He was good enough to offer his American Express card to the cause."

Stato stammered, "What do you mean man of the…"

Spears hefted his corpulent frame out of the chair and went to the bathroom. When he came out, he was holding a suit bag. He unzipped it and a black cassock and Roman collar peeked out. "Had them bring it in the back door. Why not try it on for size?"

Shaking his head vehemently, Stato said, "Absolutely not. If you think—"

Just then the image of the motorcade pulling up to the hospital flashed on the TV monitor, tuned to the cable news network. Spears firmly placed his ham-sized hand on Stato's shoulder and nodding toward the screen, he said, "He asked you to perform a sacred mission, did he not?"

Stato chuffed and rose, grasping the bag. As Stato made his way toward the bathroom, Spears said, "Don't forget your hat," and threw him a large black fedora. "Pull the brim down low and it will cover that ugly mug of yours."

Minutes later Stato stepped out, looking the part. He ran his finger between the stiff white collar and neckline. "Collar's a little tight."

Spears laughed. "Comes with the territory, son." He patted the seat. "Briefing time."

Father "Commandante" took a seat and studied the screen. The image of a weathered, arched doorway filled the frame. "Looks like Islamic architecture," he said.

Spears smiled. "That would be because it's right in the heart of an Islamic country, torn by war and bloodshed, a powder keg, being fought over by the infant nuclear powers of Pakistan and India. What you're looking at is a Holy Islamic shrine in the old part of the city … Srinagar, Kashmir. Srinagar translates as city of the exalted, the wise one. The serpent. The building is called Rozabal. 'Rozabal' is an abbreviation of *Rauza Bal*, meaning 'tomb of a prophet.'"

"Whose tomb?" Stato asked, leaning closer.

Spears clicked and a new image downloaded. The photo taken from above looked down into a crypt, where a long sarcophagus lay nestled between walls of an ornately carved wood screen.

"Saint Issa, also known as Yuz Asaf," Spears said.

"Never heard of him."

"That's because you have always known him as Jesus Christ."

Before Stato could reply, a sharp rap sounded at the door. "Who's there?"

"Master Sergeant Klientz, sir."

Rising and opening the door, Stato moved aside as Klientz wheeled in a stretcher upon which sat an over-sized medkit.

The Master Sergeant's eyes widened as he regarded Moscato.

"Hold the cardinal's arm while I give him a sedative," Stato ordered as he took a syringe from the medkit and prepared it.

Reluctantly the Master Sergeant complied.

When he finished, Stato said, "Klientz, you are proceeding directly under the orders of the Holy Father, do you understand?"

The Master Sergeant nodded, still staring.

Stato pitched the syringe into the wastebasket, replaced the vial and sighed. "Good. Now bandage his face completely and cover him with a blanket to spare him any further embarrassment. Then have Corporal Schmidt assist you with the transport."

"Where are we taking him, sir?"

Spears broke in. "You will deliver him to Doctor Lazar and Mother Superior at the Sisters of Mercy Asylum, where he will be placed in solitary confinement in a locked psychiatric ward. They'll be expecting you. As you can see, the cardinal has had a complete mental breakdown. His injuries, sadly enough, were self-inflected." Spears closed his eyes and bowed his head. "It's all so very sad."

The Master Sergeant swallowed visibly. "He's dangerous, then?"

"Homicidal," Stato answered, "and mad as a hatter. Thinks he's being hounded by the Devil himself."

"Paranoid delusions," Spears added, clucking his tongue.

When they left with Moscato, another knock came at the door. Spears's assistant entered, gave him a worn, leather-bound journal, and excused himself. Studying it briefly, Spears handed it to Stato. "Some light reading for your trip. It's the journal of a Russian explorer. I think you'll find it explains what's waiting for you in Kashmir."

Stato glanced at the book and then met Spears's gaze. "Anything else?"

"A Doctor Sanger will meet you at the airport. The Holy Father trusted him." The Master General continued. "You already have someone securing the Shroud of Turin, I assume?"

Stato's phone rang, interrupting his reply. When he answered, the operator told him to hold for a call from Turin.

Stato stood breathless, waiting for the voice to respond at the other end of the line. As the silence stretched, he felt his nerves stretch with it.

"*Pronto?*"

"*Commandante Stato, per favore?*"

"Speaking."

A breathless voice managed, "Commandante it's gone!"

"Control yourself, please. What's gone?"

"The Shroud of Turin, it's been stolen."

307

CHAPTER 77

HOURS LATER HE STOOD FACING the window, his back turned, hands clasped behind him. He seemed to be so deep in thought that Corporal Schmidt hesitated to speak. After gingerly placing the ornate box on the desktop, Schmidt cleared his throat and resumed the proper posture of a Swiss Guard, parade rest.

The man stirred and slowly turned, his face half-masked by shadow. Appearing gradually, like some stippled, leathery salamander emerging from beneath a rock, the purple-stained birthmark that covered his cheek was grotesque. And yet, Schmidt could not look away; it was as if his eyes were inexorably drawn toward—Cardinal Moscato's countenance. Even in the dim light, Schmidt could see the fevered gaze that glistened and danced manically in the cardinal's eyes.

In a tired voice, Cardinal Moscato said, "Schmidt, excuse me. I didn't hear you come in."

Schmidt shrugged.

"I assume you've made the necessary preparations with Master Sergeant Klientz's body?" The cardinal's voice was almost musical in its pleasantness, but his eyes had narrowed to pinpoints. As though a stabbing pain had suddenly seized him, possibly the lingering aftereffects of the drugs Stato had pumped into him, Moscato grimaced, lowered his head, and massaged his temples. When he looked up Schmidt was standing with his head tilted to one side and staring.

Moscato stiffened. "Get on with it."

"After we returned," Schmidt went on. "I sneaked him into the barracks and seated him at a table, a bottle of liquor and the antidepressants laid out on the tabletop in front of him."

"And the handgun?"

"When we were in the ambulance, I shot him with his own pistol. At close range." In his mind's eye, Schmidt could picture the terror-filled expression on Klientz's face as he realized, too late in the close confines of the front cab of the ambulance, that his companion was jerking his own pistol from his holster, and ramming it against his temple. Later Schmidt had wiped it clean of prints, disposed of the vehicle, and scrubbed his hands raw to wash away the traces of gunpowder. After reviving Moscato, he aided the cardinal in sneaking back into the Vatican through the ancient secret tunnels, which ran from the old fortress, the *Castel Saint Angelo.*

"Suicide," the cardinal said sarcastically, shaking his head. "His will be the second such act the Swiss Guard has faced, right in their own barracks, in two years."

Then Moscato's eyes shifted to the box. He reached out and plucked it from the desk. A smile slivered his face, but when he looked up and his gaze met Schmidt's, it quickly faded, replaced by an aloof, condescending pretense of indifference as he returned the box to the desktop.

"Good work, Corporal. Were you discreet?"

When Schmidt hesitated, the cardinal cocked his head and his eyes narrowed as though he sensed something had gone wrong.

Flexing his jaw, Schmidt finally said, "There were no witnesses, Your Eminence. After rendering Cardinal Drechsler unconscious with the tranquilizer gun—"

Moscato leaned forward and planted his knuckles firmly on the desk. "Cardinal Drechsler you say?"

Schmidt's gut knotted. "Yes, sir."

"Shot with a tranquillizer?"

Schmidt nodded, his hands beginning to tremble, every muscle tensing.

Now the cardinal glared.

"I had to improvise … he was alone with the box."

When Moscato pulled back and straightened to his full height, his hand moved toward a desk drawer.

Schmidt took an involuntary step backward. "I removed the dart. The dosage was enough to muddle his thinking, almost paralyze him. He never saw my face."

Moscato, never taking his eyes off the corporal, reached into the drawer and began to pull something out.

"I told the nurses that I found him like that," Schmidt managed, his voice quaking. "Told them he must have been overcome with grief."

When Moscato raised his hand, Schmidt cowered, his hands flying to his face. "Don't shoot me, please, Your Eminence! I have a family."

Moscato stiffened. A look of disgust filled his face. "My God! Pull yourself together, Corporal," he said, moving around the desk. He placed a reassuring arm around Schmidt's shoulder, gave a brittle laugh, and slapped his shoulder hard. "Did you honestly think I was going to kill you?"

Schmidt winced at the force of the blow and steeled himself. Wiping his nose with the back of his hand and blinking away tears, Schmidt noticed the envelope in the cardinal's hand.

As he guided him toward the door, Moscato tucked the envelope into the corporal's hand, closing his fingers tightly around it. "There, a little extra reward.

309

Buy something nice for your children, eh?" He gave a grandfatherly smile and winked.

When Schmidt began to speak, Moscato silenced him with a finger drawn against his own lips, opened the door, and ushered him out.

Even before the door closed completely, the smile melted from Moscato's face. Briskly, he strode across the room to his desk. He palmed the phone's receiver and dialed.

On the third ring, Volante's whispery voice answered, *"Buon Cugino."*

"Buon Cugino," the cardinal said.

"Do you have the package?" Volante asked.

"It's in my hands."

"Excellent. Don't let the box out of your sight."

"I won't."

A long pause then: "There's been a complication. The doctor and our asset have been …detained."

"How unfortunate. Will this interfere with Operation Dragon's Breath?"

"No. I have the situation under control. Under the pretense of a swap, we shall dispose of those meddlesome nags."

"Good hunting."

The cardinal cradled the phone and moved toward the window, staring out at the expanse of St. Peter's Square. Mourners still stood elbow-to-elbow below. He raised his hand, studied the inverted ring, and turned up his palm. He splayed his fingers and with thumb and forefinger, carefully rotated the ring to its upright position. From the face of the Borgia ring's crest, an ugly, tiny needle saluted. The ring was an infernal heirloom, used on many occasions by Lucrezia Borgia to poison suitors. Moscato nudged the base of the crest, and the needle sank flush into the onyx, nestled between gold letters. Moscato knew that when he drove the needle home into Schmidt's shoulder, the heavy-metal laced tip would break off. Within hours, the deadly, updated poisons would race through the bloodstream. Within days, the bungling corporal would suffer a terrible, painful death.

Smiling to himself, he reached for the box.

The sound of the door opening, slamming shut, and the rasp of the deadbolt driving home, gave him a start.

He looked up to see a ghostly figure towering before him.

For a moment, he froze under the power of Master-General Spears's halting stare.

His face filled with rage, Spears said, "How in God's name you escaped is beyond me. But this time I'll make sure…"

Instinctively, Moscato lunged for the box.

Despite his enormous girth, Spears covered the distance in seconds, charging and then pouncing on Moscato like an angry bear.

Moscato struggled, his face flaming with rage. He clawed at Spears's eyes, drawing blood. He spit like a rabid pit bull. Still the raging ghost pummeled him with mallet-sized fists. When Spears's hand tore at his collar, the cardinal's searching mouth found the Master-General's fleshy wrist and bit with such force that teeth sank into bone. Ignoring the pain, Spears's meaty hands slid upwards, thumbs digging into Moscato's throat, compressing his windpipe. Then he heaved his huge frame against the cardinal, pile-driving him across the room. Moscato gasped for air as his back slammed hard into a tall glass cabinet; in an explosion, curved-glass and splinters of wood rained down onto the carpet.

Struggling to concentrate through an oxygen-starved haze, a plan developed. Moscato feigned faintness. Pretended to blackout. The giant's eyes widened; he released his death grip and took a step back.

Breathing hard, face still flushed with rage, Spears managed, "By God, I'm sinking to your level." He doubled over, hands on his knees, fighting to catch his breath. "When I saw Schmidt leaving your office, I knew you had escaped."

Moscato hacked violently, massaged his throat. But when Spears looked down, cobra-quick the cardinal stepped forward and brought up his knee, planting a bone-crunching blow squarely into Spears's face. When the giant reeled upward in pain, Moscato drove his foot directly into the exposed target, his groin.

Spears groaned loudly, sank to the floor.

Excited voices came from the other side of the door.

Saliva glistening on the corners of his mouth, Moscato hovered over the fallen giant.

He taunted, nostrils flaring, "You're weak, Spears. That's why we'll always win."

The Master-General fought to raise his head. Through tear-clouded eyes, Spears saw the cardinal's hand fumble with his ring finger. Saw him move in, saw him draw back his hand for a strike to the face.

At the last second, Spears's arm pistoned outward, catching the cardinal's wrist in a vise grip. Then he staggered to his feet, twisted the cardinal's wrist sharply. Now it faced him and was bent back severely at an unnatural angle. The wrist bones crunched, snapped. The cardinal's face blanched. His eyes were glazed with terror as Spears forced the cardinal's hand closer and closer to his face.

"God, NO!" Moscato screamed just as Spears drove the back of the cardinal's hand into his face, lashing his cheek, pinning it to his forehead. Spears released his hold, stumbled backward.

Moscato's legs buckled; he fell to his knees. He brought his tortured, limp-wristed hand to eye-level. Grimaced as he slowly turned it back and forth. His free hand flew to his cheek; he pawed his face. Lowered it and studied his blood-filmed fingertips. Raising his head and meeting Spears's gaze, he said, "You fool. You've killed me."

"It's only a broken wrist and some minor cuts. You'll live."

Laughing deliriously, Moscato made it to his feet and moved toward the window.

Spears looked on warily, but bewildered.

Fists pounded at the outer door.

Then Moscato pushed open the window, limped up onto the sill.

"NO!" Spears shouted. "God will forgive you."

Moscato paused, looked over his shoulder, a thin, haughty smile on his lips. "My ring, the very ring I meant to strike you with, has a needle laced with poison." With his mangled hand, he motioned to his cheek. "But instead, the serpent's kiss has struck its master." He took another step. Looked down. Then glancing back over his shoulder, he shouted, "See you in Hell" and jumped.

With a crack of wood, the door burst open. Swiss Guards, led by Major Brazi of the GIS, poured into the room. Brazi stood in the center of the room, taking in the overturned furniture, the shards of glass that littered the floor, the smashed cabinet. Turning to Spears, he said, "Are you all right, sir?"

Spears nodded. The major's eyes tracked to the window. He ran to the sill and stood, looking down.

Moving quickly and unnoticed as the other guards joined Brazi at the window, Spears tucked the box beneath the folds of his robes.

The major gave a loud whistle and crossed himself. "Cardinal Moscato?"

"I'm afraid that, in the end, the good cardinal lost faith," Spears said in a soft voice. "He knew he was suffering from incurable cancer … and with the Holy Father's passing—"

The major sighed sharply and turned. "He took his own life and you tried to stop him…"—he swept his arm around the room—"hence the struggle."

"Precisely, Major. But we don't want to wash our dirty laundry in public … you understand?"

The major peered out the window, looking down at the cardinal's crumpled body below. "He landed in a throng of witnesses … it might not be so easy to explain."

"A tragic accident, perhaps?" Spears offered.

"Understood and duly noted, sir. You'll handle the press, then?"

"Of course."

Brazi straightened and moved toward Spears, his gaze shifting to the teeth marks that were beginning to redden and swell on the Master-General's hand. "You'd better have that looked at. It could easily become infected."

Spears glanced at his injured hand, studied Brazi's eyes, searching for any hint of suspicion, and then finding none, returned the major's knowing smile and nodded.

CHAPTER 78

ON THE TRAIN, Rossi's eyes roamed the passengers, ever alert for the familiar face, the out of place gesture, the quickly averted glance. So far: nothing. Only the usual crowd of tourists. At each stop, he scrutinized the faces of the people boarding the train.

He turned toward Gina or whatever her true name was. She sat upright, stiff as board. Although there was something tough and flinty about her, there was something more. Her face in profile, as she stared blankly out the window, revealed a certain vulnerability, a certain sadness. He had to admit that it was an appealing combination. But a tiny voice in his head shouted warnings. She had an aura of tension about her, as if she were at war with herself, and anyone who dared enter her world would be caught up in the struggle.

Rossi smiled, laughing to himself at the absurdity of the idea. *You're acting like you still have the option of slowly backing away, like it isn't already too late, a done deal.* Beneath him, the train rumbled on.

Giovanni broke the silence. "She's in a dissociative fugue state."

Then his eyes cut to Ahriman, who sat calmly, hands folded neatly on his lap; but his keen-eyed gaze was shrewd, watchful.

"You have a question, *Professore*?"

Their eyes locked and Giovanni said, "I want to know her control name. The name you use to reach the core personality's identity."

For a long beat, Ahriman said nothing. Then he shuddered in a silent laugh. "How you do surprise me. Not only are you versed in art and history, but psychiatry as well. I'm afraid, however, that you are as equally naïve if you think for one moment I will indulge your curiosity."

Without hesitation, Rossi who was seated at Ahriman's side, his Beretta tucked behind his folded forearm, jabbed the muzzle into the little man's ribs. "Indulge him," he whispered tersely, his eyes flashing cold.

Ahriman glanced down and winced as Rossi dug the cold steel deeper into his chest.

"My dear … Colonel, you're bluffing. Without me, you will never see your sister alive."

Leaning in and pressing his face closer, Rossi said, "Our bargain never said anything about delivering you …in one piece." With his free hand, Rossi pulled out a knife. Slowly, he lowered his hand and pressed the blade against the back of Ahriman's inner thigh, just above the knee. "One quick pull and I'll hamstring you. You'll be crippled for life. Then I'll do the other leg, move on to your kneecaps. You'd be surprised how little pressure it takes to shatter a kneecap, *my dear, Doctor*."

Inhaling sharply, Ahriman nodded and turned to Giovanni. "You already know the trigger phrase."

Rossi bore down on the blade, teasing with its honed point. "The name!"

Swallowing hard, a sour stench oozing from his pores, Ahriman said, "Mariamene."

"Mariamene?" Giovanni repeated.

At the sound of her name, Gina—now Mariamene—jerked, turning her head toward the professor who was seated directly in front of her. Recognition flashed in her eyes.

Reaching out and gently taking her hands in his, Giovanni said softly in an even tone, "Feel my hands, only my hands. You will pour all and any resistance into my hands. Hold back nothing." Her eyes fluttered, and she nodded solemnly.

Giovanni flinched as though startled by an icy coldness pouring off her hands as he said, "I now address Mariamene."

A slight tick bloomed in her right eye, her breathing became more labored, her chest rising and falling rapidly, almost hyperventilating.

Giovanni clasped her hands tightly. "You are at peace, Mariamene. Peace. Let the tension, the fear, flow out through your fingertips and into my hands."

Immediately, her breathing slowed, streaming out in a silken rhythm. Her taut cheeks slackened. Her furrowed brow smoothed. The tick vanished. "I'm at peace," she repeated, almost whispering. The change in her face was so dramatic, so abrupt, it seemed to Rossi that it was as though a mask had been ripped from her face, revealing a new *someone* who lived silently beneath some thin shell of pretense. A *someone* who had been patiently watching and waiting and biding their time, like a child standing at the edge of a spinning carousel waiting her turn to step aboard and ride.

"What's happening to her?" Rossi said, his voice hitching.

"It is called switching, changing alters," his uncle explained.

***

Giovanni's face floats before Gina. He calls her by another name. At first there is a sensation of dying. Then she rises from the depths of blackness. On the screen of her eyelids, flashes brighter than the sun brand her eyes. The light dims and she sees a face as though looking through a gauze-covered lens. A soft voice sings at the edge of her memory. Her mother's voice, the loveliest she has ever heard. Her vision clears. Warm, loving eyes caress her. A gentle breeze bends the meadow grass around her. Another voice, equally gentle, begins to speak. It is her father's. "Daughter, you have your mother's eyes, her sweet disposition. Like your mother, Magdalene, you and your descendants shall be the vessel of spiritual wisdom."

"Yes, Father," she hears a child's voice answer, her voice, and struggles to understand.

"Your mother, Magdalene, the virgin, the mother, the widow, shall tower over all my disciples and over all men who shall receive the mysteries in the Ineffable. Man shall condemn you as being profane, but you must take heart. For the true path to my Father is through you."

She feels at peace here, lingering in this time past, this place.

She whispers:

Mother Magdalene ...

***

The train began to slow, rolled to a stop. The doors hissed wide, drawing Rossi's attention. A tall, gaunt-looking man stepped into the car. Rossi studied him. Pale blond hair, pale skin, so nearly an albino that Rossi half expected his irises to be rabbit pink, instead of the gunmetal gray, which they were. When the man caught Rossi's stare, he quickly looked away and proceed down the aisle, taking a position near the door that led to the adjacent car.

From his vantage point, the pale man looked on. His dull, sleepy eyes belied the ferocious concentration, the unblinking stare that almost pinned Rossi to his seat. Rossi took in the pale man's fit build, the long bulky coat that was too warm for the weather, though it would easily conceal a weapon.

Rossi felt his insides go cold.

From his right, came the sound of the opposite railway car door opening, spilling the clattering roar of the train into their car briefly before it closed. A second man entered. He was rail thin. His pockmarked face and cheekbones, sharp enough to cut glass, combined with glassy green eyes, gave him a frightening appearance. He wore black from head to toe. From the corner of his eye, Rossi noticed Ahriman's expression: he'd recognized this fugitive from a barn's rooftop. A thin smile creased the weathervane's skeletal face. He held his position, blocking the door.

Giovanni released Gina's hands, and she slumped back into her seat.

Whispering out of the corner of his mouth, never taking his eyes off the two men, Rossi asked his uncle, "What was that she was mumbling? I couldn't make it out."

Giovanni shook his head. "I'll tell you later."

Feeling the killers' cold, haughty gazes, Rossi's heart thundered; the hair on his forearms prickled. Then his sixth sense drew his awareness to the window. There, running full out on a roadway alongside the railroad tracks, its jutting cowl scooping the wind like a hungry shark, was his forest green muscle car. Dante, crouched behind the wheel of the Mustang, waved frantically, trying to get his attention.

CHAPTER 79

RIDING IN THE BACKSEAT, Josie's eyes met Agent Kyle's, as they stared back from the rearview mirror. They were pacing the train, on the opposite side of the track from Dante in the Mustang. Without warning, a motorcycle veered directly into their path. Kyle panic-braked and cut the wheel hard right, whipsawing Josie against the rear passenger door. He cut back hard left, the rear end fishtailing wildly, narrowly missing the rider and regained control.

"Jeez, watch it, dickweed! Where the hell did he come from?" Manwich shouted.

Pushing herself upright and grabbing her pistol off the floorboard, Josie said sarcastically, "Nice driving ... dickweed."

Kyle beamed as the car accelerated with a lurch.

Manwich twisted in his seat, facing Josie. Nodding toward the pistol, he said, "For now at least, we're on the same side. You can put that thing away before dickweed here..." he shot Kyle a harsh side-glance "pulls another barnstorming maneuver, and you accidentally pump a slug through my seatback."

Josie lowered the weapon.

"That's better. How the hell did you find us so fast?"

Josie gave a thin laugh. "The Italians tagged you and have been tracking your vehicle. My partner simply hacked into the network." From her pocket she produced a hand-sized computer. Its display flashed with a beacon superimposed over a grid map of the city, indicating their exact position. Josie gave them a brief rundown on the crushing attack upon her and Schlomo in the van. How her father had been killed in Chicago.

Rubbing the back of his buttery neck, Manwich said, "My orders are to get the girl at all costs. You got any idea why the hell she's so damn important that they want her alive?"

Josie shook her head. "No. You concentrate on the girl, but Ahriman's all mine." She glared at him, and in that glare, hatred sparked and sizzled.

The scanner monitoring the Italian's radio frequency squawked.

Josie's face blanched as she translated. "They just received a bomb threat on the Lido train!"

"The train's slowing," Kyle said.

Checking her hand-held computer screen, Josie said, "They're coming up on the next station."

CHAPTER 80

THE TRAIN SLOWED to a stop. As the doors opened, passengers moved for the exit. The pale man took up a position at the doorway, blocking anyone from entering. Rossi fixated on the man, the door, a nettlesome something tossing and turning in his mind. Rossi had withdrawn the knife but still cradled his pistol out of sight, its muzzle trained on Ahriman.

The pale man stepped aside, allowing a tall, statuesque black woman to enter. Dressed in West African black and red satin ceremonial robes, she was an imposing figure. Standing at over five-eleven, she carried herself with grace and authority. She was dark and earthy. As she scanned the car and her gaze fell upon him, Rossi noted there was a spice of sulfur in her deep brown eyes. Her high, intelligent forehead was smooth. She could have been a model with those high cheekbones and sensuous lips. But her cheeks were disfigured, deeply stitched with tribal markings, adding to the overall air of a tigress. Her cool, ebon-hued flesh, filmed in the sheen of perspiration, raised a sensual chill in him. But when Rossi inhaled, he noticed she exuded a strange tang that conjured visions of a lioness devouring her prey on the killing field. The scent of freshly spilled blood lathered the air. With a quick glance, she took in Ahriman and the others. Apparently satisfied the train car was secure, she turned quickly and hoisted someone into the car.

Slowly a figured appeared. Head bowed meekly and hooded in a scarf, shoulders hunched, she stood before them. When she raised her head, Rossi found himself staring into Bianca's face.

The door closed.

Bianca brought her hand to her mouth. Her fingers shivered as she traced the outline of her lips. She made little choked sounds in her throat. Finally she managed, "Nico?"

Instantly, the black woman roughly wrenched Bianca's arm and guided her away, putting distance between her and Rossi. When Rossi sprang to his feet, the pale man spun and flourished a sawed-off shotgun from beneath his long coat. His crooked smile revealed a row of jagged yellowed teeth. He shook his head. Rossi got the message loud and clear, slouched back into his seat.

The black woman spoke, her voice throaty, but seductive and sleek as black velvet. "I am known as Oba."

Ignoring her, Rossi said, "Bianca, are you all right. Have they hurt you?"

***

At the train stop, Josie bolted from the car, covering the distance in seconds. But just as she reached the platform, the train began pulling away. She poured on the speed, legs pumping, chest heaving with each stride, scything through the sea of passengers smoothly as a shark through open water. Closing on the train, she leaped from the platform onto the steps of the last car. She clasped the handrails tightly, losing her footing briefly as her right foot almost brushed the rushing ground below, and pulled herself aboard.

Manwich looked on, pounding the roof of the car in desperation. Squeezing his wide girth back into the car and slamming the door, he shouted, "Follow that train!"

CHAPTER 81

BIANCA'S EYES SWEPT around the car like trapped sparrows. She seemed looted of all energy.

A commotion sounded at the rear of the car. A portly train conductor pushed his way into the car, past the weathervane with the glassy eyes who stood guard. As the conductor shouted curses in Italian, suddenly he arched backward, his hand clawing at his back. When he turned, Rossi saw the hilt of a throwing knife saluting from the fat man's back. In one fluid motion the weathervane stepped forward, clamped one hand onto the man's shoulder, grabbed the hilt with his other hand, and twisted, pushing the conductor to the floor. A wicked grin filling his face, the killer pulled out the knife with a wet sucking sound and calmly wiped the blood from its blade on his trousers.

The whites of Oba's eyes flashed. The flat of her hand knifed outward. "Enough!" Like the cold, marbled eyes of a spitting cobra, her gaze cooled. A broad, ingenious smile filled her face as she regarded them. "I believe we are here to make an exchange, no?" she said with a slightly French inflection.

Just then Rossi's cell phone beeped. When his hand moved toward his inner coat pocket, the pale man stabbed the air with the shotgun's barrel.

"Let him answer it," Oba ordered.

"Rossi."

It was Dante. "We just got word. There's a bomb on the train. We're going to stop it and evacuate the passengers."

Showing no emotion, Rossi clicked off.

***

Josie weaved her way through the cars, shouting to the passengers in Italian and warning them to move to the last passenger car at the rear. When she reached the car adjacent to the one Rossi and the others were in, she drew up short, ducked down. Up ahead, she saw the thin man guarding the closest door. He glanced in her direction and then turned his back. She holstered her handgun. Crawling on her hands and knees, she made her way into the gap between the two railroad cars and quickly climbed the ladder. Not wanting to but compelled to, nevertheless, she looked down and felt her stomach knot at the sight of the ground rushing beneath her, the blur of scenery at her sides.

She pulled herself up onto the railway car's roof, the wind combing through her hair. Crouching low, she straddled the roof and slowly made her way toward the other end of the car. A gust of wind buffeted her, almost knocking her off her feet. Halfway across, she dropped to her belly and leaned over the side. The blood rushed to her head as she hung upside-down, stealing a peek into the railway car through the side window. After noting their positions, she pulled herself upward.

Once she reached the far side, she swung onto another ladder and made her way down, once again nestled between cars. She palmed her Sig Sauer and sneak-peeked through the window of the door. A second man stood in the center of the car, leveling a sawed-off 12-gauge pump on Rossi and Giovanni. *Damn.* And beyond them, she spotted Ahriman, sitting smugly as though he were attending a university debate class. Her breath caught in her throat, her finger tightened around the trigger. For a moment, her whole body tensed, and she was ready to storm in, gun blazing. But she knew if startled, the man might jerk the trigger in a reflex action, and his scattergun would cut Rossi in two at that range. So she swallowed down the lava-like bile that filled her throat. Then sat on her haunches, back pressed to the doorway and waited for the proper moment to present itself, her hands trembling with tension.

CHAPTER 82

IN HIS RIGHT hand, Rossi still held a firm grip on his Beretta. He knew from Dante's warning that Volante was pulling a double-cross. His eyes shifted to Oba. Did she know about the bomb ticking away somewhere aboard the train? Did the others? How could he warn his uncle?

Ahriman began to rise. "Since we're all here, let's get this over with," he said remotely.

"Not so fast," Rossi said, raising the Beretta. Ahriman inhaled a sharp breath and froze.

The pale man tensed visibly. Rossi's eyes ticked right. The glint of the throwing knife's hilt shone between the fingers of the weathervane's cupped hand that hung loosely at his side, poised to strike.

Oba squirmed in her seat as a smile rose to her lips, but it was an icy smile that had no impact on her eyes. Her body, though large, was taut and coiled like a spring.

Rossi said, "Bianca, stand up and come to me."

With terror-glazed eyes, Bianca turned to Oba, her eyes begging the question like a schoolgirl seeking permission to use the restroom.

"Bianca, stand up and come to me!" he repeated.

Oba released her grip on Bianca's arm and flicked her wrist, noting the time on her wristwatch, her eyes darting about the car nervously. Rossi had his answer. The woman was counting off the minutes to the detonation. When she looked up, a silent nod was Oba's only answer.

On pudding legs, Bianca crossed the short distance. She almost collapsed into Rossi's waiting arms, sighing heavily. Her breath was soft against Rossi's cheek, like the flutter of a butterfly's wings. In that instant, Rossi's heart was ripped loose of its emotional moorings; he blinked back a tear, pressed her close.

"Such a heartfelt reunion," Ahriman said, and began to move.

But before he could take another step, Josie burst into the railway car. The Sig Sauer stretched out before her, held in a two-handed grip.

The pale man spun on Josie. Ahriman was now directly in his line of fire, blocking the shot.

Although it happened in a matter of seconds, the world seemed to plunge into slow motion. The overhead lighting flickered like a raw nerve. Rossi shoved

Bianca down and into Giovanni's lap, while instinctively twisting, bringing up his pistol and sighting on the weathervane. The killer's throwing arm pistoned outward. Cold steel kissed Rossi's cheek. Rossi squeezed off a double-tap, center of mass, into the startled man's chest.

Rossi panned his weapon left.

Arms outstretched toward the pale man brandishing the scattergun, fingers splayed wide, his eyes swimming in fear, Ahriman shouted, "No!"

Josie dropped to her knee and her Sig barked, a round hitting the pale man's shoulder, spinning him and causing the scattergun to explode with deadly force. Deafening.

A metal storm of shotgun pellets disintegrated Ahriman's fingers, tore off half his face. Flesh liquefied, white bone visible, eyes now dimmed with the sleep of Hell, Ahriman flew backward onto Josie, his liverish length of tongue protruding. Struggling beneath the fallen corpse, Josie fired. Her aim true, two rounds gouged deeply into the pale man's forehead, exploding out the back of his head in a bright red shower.

A deep guttural growl, like a wildcat, spit from Oba's lips as she pounced. Her huge hands found Rossi's throat as the full weight of her body slammed into him, knocking him off his feet.

Straddling him, her black gown hiked about her waist, her iron-maiden thighs banded his chest, pressing from both sides, while her steely fingers dug into his larynx.

His vision tunneled.

An explosion shattered the air and rocked the train, the sound and shockwave slamming through the train like a tidal wave. A wall of heat and pressure ripped through railway cars, shredding steel like tinfoil and creating a maelstrom of glass and shrapnel.

Their car lurched, jumped the track, and flipped on its side. Oba was pitched against the rooftop of the car, which now became a wall.

Rossi clawed at his throat, fighting for air.

The railway car hurtled on its side; a shower of sparks lighting its way as twisted metal screeched like a wounded beast.

Finally it came to a grinding halt.

For a moment, Rossi lay still, blinking hot blood from his eyes. His hand flew to his head. It was a small laceration but scalp wounds bled like hell, he figured. He looked around. Saw his uncle cradled in Bianca's lap. He crawled toward him.

"Is he okay?" he managed, his throat raw with pain.

Bianca looked up, eyes glistening, and nodded. "Has a nasty bump on his head but no signs of a concussion." Rossi stroked her sooty cheek gently and smiled.

Giovanni stirred and squinted in the smoke-filled air. "Takes more than a little train wreck to get rid of me." He coughed and winced, his hand moving to his temple. Then his gaze shifted and he pointed.

Rossi's eyes followed. There in the distance, he saw Oba, prodding Gina with the shotgun and then shoving her upward through an open window with her shoulder.

From behind him he heard a moaning sound. He spun to see Josie sprawled on her side, out cold.

CHAPTER 83

THE YOWL OF Klaxon filled the air. Blue strobes painted the night.

With Gina in tow, Oba made her way through the chaos of rescuers. There up ahead, she saw it, the unmarked car. Agent Kyle was in the passenger seat, waiting while Manwich threaded his way through the bedlam up ahead somewhere. Kyle was unaware of her approach. When he looked up, he stared down the barrel of the .12-gauge.

"Move over, you're driving," she said, racking another shell into the breech. Kyle stared blankly, puzzled.

Oba ripped open the door and drove the stock of the shotgun hard into his shoulder, knocking him across the seat. Kyle sat up, massaged his arm, and slid behind the wheel.

Gina/*Bast*, shocked out of her stupor by the train crash, followed, and planted herself in the middle. She was lucid now, pumped on adrenaline, back in control. As Oba lowered herself into the car, one leg still out, the shotgun switched to her left hand, Gina reached over Kyle, threw it into reverse, and grabbed the wheel. With her left foot, Gina mashed the accelerator. The car lurched backward, accelerating rapidly. The door swung shut painfully, slamming against Oba's dragging leg. She was thrown against the seatback. Gina's right hand grabbed the barrel of the scattergun. With the edge of her left foot, Gina braked hard while maintaining constant pressure on the gas pedal; the speedometer needle was shivering higher. Topping sixty. Simultaneously, she cranked the wheel fully counterclockwise. Rubber barked and smoked as the car spun in a shuddering 180, almost rolling. Melted brake pads steamed the air. The passenger door flew open.

The shotgun fired. Deafening in the closed space. The windshield exploded. Kyle, back pressed to the seat, screamed. Oba leaned toward the open car door. Gina's foot slid off the brake and mashed the gas pedal, sending the car rocketing backward. Releasing the barrel, Gina spun the wheel hard right with her free hand and shoved Oba with her opposite. Oba whipsawed right and tumbled onto the pavement, still clutching the shotgun.

Gina let off the gas and braked to a stop. She glanced at Kyle. "You, okay?"

He nodded, face bleached whiter than white.

Illuminated in the high beams of the car that ghosted through a haze of burnt rubber lay Oba. She rose to her feet slowly, shotgun in hand. She appeared dazed, unsteady on her feet. Dark blood dripped from her hairline. Her eyes sparkled wildly, hatred and cruelty glowing like a burning church.

By now metro police and carabinieri, their weapons raised, closed on Oba in a tightening circle as they shouted, "Drop your weapon."

Gina knew what was coming next. Oba's eyes seemed to lock on her for a moment, just before she raised the shotgun. Gunfire cracked and punched into Oba who straightened briefly, almost superhumanly, before shuddering in spasms and sinking to the ground.

The officers converged on the fallen woman, weapons still dead on target as though she might rise up suddenly in a last fit of rage.

From the corner of her eye, Gina saw the ambulance pull alongside. Kyle lowered the car window. Instinct told her to duck, but then she saw his face. He was older but his eyes were the same. Haunted. Wide. Slightly sorrowful.

She cried out, "Hamal." He smiled and began to exit the ambulance, moving toward her now. Was she dreaming? Could this be happening after all these years? A stinging pain bit at her neck. She began to black out but struggled to focus on Hamal's face. Eventually her vision tunneled into darkness. The tranquilizer gun coughed a second time, and Kyle slumped at her side. In the ensuing commotion, no one noticed. A British agent, dressed as a paramedic, jumped out and with Hamal's help, pulled Gina into the waiting ambulance. Its siren spiked as it sped into the darkness.

***

The blinding beam of a flashlight poured into the railway car. Rossi was at Josie's side now. She was conscious. Dante's familiar voice floated toward him through the fog of smoke. *Colonnello* … Rossi."

"Over here," Rossi shouted.

Dante knelt at his side while paramedics saw to Giovanni.

"She okay, boss?"

Rossi glanced down at Josie who nodded. "She'll be fine. Let's get the hell out of here."

CHAPTER 84

WHEN ROSSI AWOKE at early morning and focused his eyes on the bright, white ceiling tiles, he knew that he was not in his apartment. Then it came to him, the train, Bianca, Josie, everything. He sat up and looked about. Where was she? He heard the sweet tones of a female voice humming from behind the bathroom door on the far wall. It was Josie. They were at his uncle's place.

She emerged, her auburn hair wet and hanging loosely about her shoulders. She was wearing a terrycloth bathrobe that did not completely cover her breasts. Her long, supple legs were tanned, her feet bare.

"Josie, I—" Rossi stammered.

"Shhh," she said, "don't speak." She moved toward him, sat down on the bed at his side.

Words weren't necessary. They both sensed the same longing, the same yearning deep in their core. Rossi reached up gently, brushed a lock of hair from her eye, and pulled her toward him.

She didn't resist, but fell into his arms.

And for a moment he just held her tenderly, not moving, not speaking. In that moment they were in a land beyond words.

They could have spoken of loss or grief, of their wants or desires, of their hopes and dreams. But it wasn't the time, wasn't necessary, for even if Rossi could've read her mind, again it wasn't necessary. The beating of her heart against his chest, her soft breath against his neck, spoke volumes. He was deeply aroused by the clean soapy fragrance of her skin and breasts, but was unable to transform thought and need into physical intimacy, not yet.

Rossi struggled to rise. She pushed him down hard, straddled him. Her lips moved to his. Not a kiss, no probing, just resting on his. Their breath entwined now with each inhalation and exhalation. Souls conjoined. Then he kissed her, softly at first, her lips, her cheek, moving slowly up her neck to her earlobe. He nibbled. Explored her inner ear with his tongue. She shuddered, pushed back and rose, pulling her robe off her shoulders, her small but firm breasts exposed. Her nipples, gorged with blood, stood erect. She lowered them to his wet, waiting mouth. He licked, caressed them with a reverent passion.

As he reached upward and held them in his hands, he thought of Isabella, his late wife. He thought of Gina, her eyes like pulsing blue flames. But the name he called out now was Josie's.

Her hand slowly slid down the side of his torso, to his hip, his inner thigh. His manhood surged against her hand. She moaned and pressed her pelvis against him, rocking in gentle rhythms. Then, he entered into the depths of her, and they cried out together, their breathless whispers and cries, piercing the silence.

Now she sought his rhythm, pulling him into her own, steering him toward heaven's gate, toward rapture. They convulsed in unison as the backdoor to paradise was flung open.

And then it ended as it had begun, in hushed silence, a soft whimper, a lingering kiss. Her hair fanned across his face and chest, he breathed deeply, savoring her essence. She collapsed at his side; a sheen of perspiration filming her breasts and flat stomach. At first unfettered, now unshackled completely by love's euphoric high, they drifted upward, the memory of their joy an invisible umbilical. How long they'd lain like that, staring into one another's searching eyes, or with only a dim light pressing memories of each other's faces against the shell of their closed eyelids, they did not know. In this instant, in this moment, time no longer held sway over them.

She sighed and propped herself up on one elbow, considering him. Reaching out, she ran her fingertip over one dew-stained eyebrow. It tickled and Rossi flinched.

"You know," she said, "we could go on doing this all day?"

"Forever," he said. "Until the cows come home."

"Or they jump over the moon."

Rossi sighed. "I've never known any woman who could enjoy it the way you do." He lowered his head over her stomach, rubbing his nose back and forth across the angel hairs that ran up the center.

"Oh, how many have there been?"

"You mean women?" He blew lightly across her bellybutton.

"NO. Cows! Of course, women." She gave his forehead a sharp tap with her fingertips. "Are you saying that I'm oversexed?"

"Well, no, but you're certainly not undersexed."

"Was Gina, that was her name right?"

"Yes, but you're so—"

"So what, Nico? Intellectual?"

"No—"

"You saying I'm stupid?"

"No, I just—"

"So stunning, then?"

"No—"

"No?"

"I mean yes, but more than that. You're so alive, filled with life, so vibrant . . . and well . . . such a smart-ass—"

329

She reached up and tugged his lip hard grabbing it between thumb and index finger, brought it to hers. That was all it took. The bell rang. Round two.

CHAPTER 85

IN THE KITCHEN, Rossi and Josie sat at the table. Josie was wearing his pajama top, one leg on the floor, the other on the chair, her chin resting on her arms folded on her knee. The typical Hollywood morning after pose, she called it. Giovanni topped off their coffee cups and placed the carafe on the yellow-checkered tablecloth between them. He pulled up a chair, lit his pipe, and folded his hands on his lap, struggling not to let his eyes linger on the Josie's exposed leg and firm thigh. "Tell me, my nephew. Did you sleep well? Feeling more rested now, are we?"

Rossi shot Josie a sheepish grin and turned to his uncle.

"Yes, very well. Thanks for letting us use the spare room."

The professor smiled, and winked at Josie. She blushed slightly. "Any dreams, young lady?"

A tiny crease formed between her eyes and feeling suddenly self-conscious, she lowered her leg. "Strange question, don't you think?"

He shrugged. "Just thought that possibly your feminine intuition spoke to you during the night through your dreams." His watery eyes regarded her closely, then seeing no spark, lowered to his hands.

To his uncle, Rossi said, "You're still worried. Still trying to make some sense of all that's happened?"

Giovanni suddenly rose to his feet, began pacing the room as he spoke. "I am convinced that Volante somehow orchestrated the Pope's death."

"We can't be sure, he was old and fragile to begin with," Rossi offered.

With a dismissive wave, Giovanni cut him off. "Nonsense. His will to live was too strong." His lip curled cynically. "If I'd only had more time with the girl."

"We'll still be looking for her," Josie said. "As soon as I arrive in Tel Aviv tomorrow, I'm organizing a retrieval team." Josie caught the hard glance Rossi had given her at the word … *tomorrow*, but fought the urge to meet his gaze. She wouldn't look, couldn't look, because if she did, she might be caught, trapped under the sheer weight of his need. So instead, she rose quickly and made for the sink.

She performed a crude pantomime of indifference, pretending not to notice, pretending that her own heart didn't clench, didn't skip a beat at the sound of his voice, his touch. She fumbled in the cupboard for a glass, filled it and took a long pull, letting the tepid water drown her emotions. *End it now*, her mind counseled. *Nip it in the bud.* But her heart turned a deaf ear. Warmed at the thought of his strong but gentle embrace. Head lowered, shoulders hunched, she stood with her back toward him, biting her lower lip with small, incredibly white teeth.

"Gina was a basket case, anyway," Rossi finally said. "What could you have gotten out of her?"

Giovanni's eyes widened. "With the proper treatment, she might have been salvaged. By combining hypnotherapy with EMDR."

Steeling herself, Josie turned. She smiled at Rossi, bold and direct. Her eyes shifted to Giovanni. "That's something to do with reprogramming, isn't it?" she said absently. Rossi stared like a schoolboy.

"They use eye movement to desensitize and reprocess feelings, traumatic memories," his uncle went on. "Replace them with positive memories and self-esteem. Combined with atypical neuroleptics like olazapine and zyprexa, they have been able to reintegrate the splintered identities. Make them whole again. I'm still puzzled by her random mumblings when in deep trance on the train."

Rossi rolled his eyes, and huffed. "Really, Zio. That was just more hocus-pocus, like those phony artifacts they claimed to have found in Palestine and are leaking to the press."

Josie added, "He may be right. I got a cable from Mossad HQ saying that the antiquities investigators raided that artifact dealer's home. And like the case with the counterfeit ossuary that bore the names of Jesus and James, they found all the chemicals the dealer and his accomplices used to age the silver amulet. They even found the expert on Paleo-Hebrew who wrote the counterfeit inscriptions. They've determined he was the same guy who dreamed up the inscriptions on the Joshua Tablet, and the ivory pomegranate from Solomon's Temple and the phony patina imbedded within the inscriptions, which were found to be total...fakes."

Rossi nodded. "Big money to be made in the counterfeit relic business."

Giovanni almost smiled, then said in a grave voice, "I wouldn't be so quick to discount the validity of what they found. The Israeli government has its own agenda, too. And how do you account for the NSA's interest in Gina? Her apparent kidnapping by British agents?"

Rossi shook his head. "I can't. The strange thing is that the Brits didn't make for the UK."

Giovanni's eyebrows rose. "Then where?"

"Best we can determine is that they were headed for Pakistan."

Giovanni stroked his chin. "I must make Spears aware of this. It could be important."

"And when were you going to tell me this?" Jose said, scowling. "I'm going to get dressed." Josie took a few steps and paused. "I want to swing by the hospital and see my uncle Lotti before I leave." She glanced at Rossi.

Caught his gaze. Studied the way his lip curled slightly when he smiled. Stiffening, she told herself, *this isn't going to pan out, lover*.

"How's he doing?"

Josie shrugged. "Doctors think he'll pull through."

"I'll take you. I need to check on Bianca's condition," Rossi told her, his gaze lingering on her for a long beat.

"I'll catch a cab," she answered coldly and headed for the bedroom.

Giovanni moved to Rossi's side, placed his hand on his shoulder. "You're going to let her just walk right out that door and out of your life, aren't you?"

Rossi studied the faint map of veins under the milky flesh of his uncle's cheeks, trying to avert his eyes. Rossi sucked a deep breath, his eyes flicking to the doorway she'd just walked out of. "Probably. Neither of us is ready. Neither of us has the luxury."

Giovanni stepped back and sighed. "The air pulses when she's in the same room with you, your heart pounds in your chest ... but no! You're not ready!"

Rossi forced a weak smile.

"Listen to me, nephew. What you *don't* have the luxury of doing, like I told you before, is to continue lying to yourself."

"And what about her?"

"Someone has to make the first move." Giovanni gave a fatherly grin, then changed gears. "I received a call from Master-General Spears. He sounded very troubled."

"That business with Cardinal Moscato's death?"

"Not really. There was never any love lost between the two of them."

"Understatement was always your gift, Zio."

"Spears shares my concern that we're missing something. The Pope's funeral is in a few days and—"

"We're taking extraordinary precautions. I have a meeting tomorrow with the police and the military."

Giovanni's brow furrowed. "Spears thinks ... how shall I put it ... that there may be some truth behind their discovery of the Gospel of Q and then there's that troubling message he and I decoded in the Black Rose Notebook. We haven't had a chance to compare notes yet, so I'm meeting with him shortly. Spears has sent Stato on a mission which somehow relates to what he says the notebook revealed."

Rossi stiffened. "My guess is that whole business was a smokescreen, some diversionary tactic to distract us from their real goal."

Their eyes locked. "Precisely, that's what's troubling me. What is their real goal?"

Rossi started to answer then faltered.

"Don't forget that they butchered innocent men to get their hands on that notebook. Spears asked me to warn you to keep a sharp lookout," his uncle added gravely.

"What does he think I've been doing?"

"Not necessarily from Volante's group. Some catastrophic event."

"Some warring faction maybe?"

"Possibly, remember Durer's hidden warning of revenge by inferno."

"We're taking every precaution possible. If you were thinking of a bombing or a fire, that would be impossible, given the heightened security, the Vatican will become impregnable."

Giovanni's watery, tired eyes met his. "I pray you're right, nephew. Anyway, Spears said he has hacked into Moscato's computer files and has some very troubling news for me. Something that explains the Brits' involvement in this affair."

Josie popped into the room, dressed casually, bags in hand. She eyed Rossi and laughed. "You're not taking me to the hospital in your PJs I hope?"

Giovanni caught Rossi's eye and winked. Then slowly began humming "Our Love is Here to Stay" as he took his hat from the rack, tipped the brim, and shambled out the door.

CHAPTER 86

THE OFFICIAL NINE-DAYS' mourning period, the *novemdiales*, had passed. His papal ring broken, his study and bedroom sealed by the Camerlengo, the Pope lay in state within the Patriarchal Basilica of the Vatican, St. Peter's. His gray face and hands were in stark contrast to the brilliant white and deep scarlet vestments.

Outside, giant video screens placed in St. Peter's square and piazzas throughout the city did little to placate the surge of pilgrims who'd flooded the city, doubling Rome's population of 3.7 million. Bishops and laity alike were herded through metal detectors set up beneath the colonnades at the entrance to the square. Although visitors were asked to leave backpacks and bags at home, X-ray scanners were busy screening the never-ending line of mourners' purses and belongings.

At Rome's police headquarters the faces of the crowd captured by remote cameras were projected on over fifty large surveillance monitors. As the watchful eyes of the officers studied the images, so did the FACE-IDENT program. Designed to compare the facial features of the public against a database of known and suspected terrorists, today, the system was churning at maximum overdrive.

Beneath one IDENT screen an amber light began flashing, signaling a match.

High above the Cape Canaveral-like COMM-PIT was the combined security and military command center, where Rossi paced nervously near the main console.

"We've got a match on camera zero-niner, sir," a paunchy, no-neck tech with coke-bottle eyeglasses said.

"Punch it up," the deputy chief of SISDe ordered.

On the left half of the split screen the image of a gaunt, hollow-cheeked young Arab with a slight harelip appeared. The other half displayed the familiar face of the Gerta Van Diesel, the whiny-voiced, make-over queen, news correspondent who spoke out of the side of her mouth as though she had a chaw of chewing tobacco pressed against her inner cheek. She'd recently joined the ranks of the new wave of female television tabloid journalists: razor-tongued, hawk-eyed ex-prosecutors with highlights and spray-on-tan complexions.

"Balls, man. That's a false hit," the chief said, wheeling on his heels and storming off to light another cigar.

Rossi moved behind the officer, placed a reassuring hand on his shoulder. Immediately, he felt the dampness of perspiration seeping through the man's uniform blouse. The guy was sweating buckets, his round face beaded with dew like a fat melon.

Rossi pointed to the IDENT images. "Considering the mismatch of faces, it's not exactly a 'Fair and Balanced picture for Fox News, eh?'" Rossi said, trying to ease the officer's tension. "If I were the terrorist, I'd be insulted."

The officer gave a nervous laugh.

"What's your name?"

"Pompenni, sir. Tomaso Pompenni." Fishing an inhaler from his pocket, Tomaso placed it to his lips and took a hard pull. "Asthma," he explained apologetically.

"Well, Tomaso, we're in for the long haul, so relax. Bring up our girl on the actual network feed and turn up the volume."

Gerta was interviewing Rome's deputy mayor and a stiff-necked Italian Air Force officer who Rossi recognized as Brigadier General Luca Masserati.

To the mayor, Gerta said, "What security precautions are in effect?"

"There will be a complete shutdown of streets in the capital beginning now until six P.M. Trains will continue to arrive, but aside from emergency vehicles, only buses will be allowed to move and must park in designated areas. In addition, we have over fifteen thousand police and military officers at work, with elite teams of carabinieri stationed at every major intersection. I also understand that as many as a thousand sharpshooters have been deployed at strategic locations throughout the city."

Jabbing the mic toward the Brig. General, Gerta asked, "We understand that over a hundred heads of state or prime ministers or foreign ministers will be attending the funeral this afternoon. President Bush, Clinton, and the first lady."

The Brig. General nodded solemnly, stood like a wooden Indian, incapacitated by apparent stage fright. His fifteen minutes of fame slowly ticking away.

The deputy mayor leaned across him and into the microphone, grinning from ear to ear. "Yes, plus former President Bush, and Prince Charles and his new bride, HRH the Duchess of Cornwall."

Old leather face, Carmela, Rossi thought as he watched, suppressing a chuckle. Just another kept woman at the Vatican.

Clearing his throat, the Brig. General sharply brought up his arm, forcing the mayor to pull back. As an obvious sham, he pretended to scratch his nose, and said, "I'm partially relieved and partially concerned that the heads of many Islamic nations such a Libya, Iran, and Syria will also attend."

"Relieved?" Gerta probed in a squeaky voice.

A firm nod was the general's only reply.

Rossi figured he knew what the general was hinting at. If the leaders of these 'axis of terror' nations would be on site at the Vatican, it should eliminate the threat from their state-sponsored terrorist groups. Even as the thought hit him, Rossi felt the lining of his gut washed in an acid bath of doubt and nagging suspicion. He had Master-General Spears and Uncle Giovanni trying to make the shifting slats of the puzzle box give up the answer. The only clue, however, was that enigmatic quatrain Spears had shared with them that was mentioned in the Pope's letter. His uncle had attributed it to Nostradamus: "The fiery dragon's breath shall cause the seven hills to burn for generations." *What if they don't come up with a solution? Maybe I'm seeing boogiemen under the bed.*

The nasally grating sound of Gerta's voice drew him back.

"What about the threat of an air attack, General?"

"We have CAP, combat air patrols, flying over the city 24/7. Our F-16s are being refueled by a tanker and are supported by a NATO supplied AWACS, radar reconnaissance plane. Naturally, airspace will be closed down tighter than a pigeon's asshole…"—the general paused, red-faced, his jowls shaking as though he were chewing on the size-thirteen boot that he'd inserted into his four-starred big mouth—"well, a strict no fly zone has been in effect since yesterday, including Da Vinci Airport and our two secondary airports, Ciampino and Ubre."

Rossi laughed silently, picturing the general standing in front of the mirror in his boxers, knee-high black socks held by suspenders, a pair of Colt .45's slung from his love handles as he practiced for his "15 minutes of fame," while George C. Scott's portrayal of General Patton's speech boomed from the TV in the background.

"Any ground defense?" Gerta asked as though she knew what it meant and her producer hadn't whispered it into her earpiece.

"Cocked and locked and ready. Our ground-to-air anti-aircraft Hawk and Spada missile batteries have been deployed in a ring around the city."

Stroking his greasy pencil-thin mustache and jutting his cleft chin, the deputy mayor broke in. "I don't think we've ever seen in Italy such a large effort to protect a single place." Nodding toward the general, he added, "We began at square one, then worked from …"

"Worst-case scenarios," the general prompted.

"Indeed, meaning threats coming from the sky, from the land, from the sea— fast threats from all directions."

The screen filled with Gerta in a tight close-up.

Screwing up her face, her voice warbled again as she managed, "Just two days before the Holy Father died, Mehmet Ali Agca, the Turkish madman who tried to kill him in 1981, released a statement wishing the Pontiff a speedy recovery, but

R. DOUGLAS WEBER

added ominously, that the Pope should tell the world that doomsday was approaching. Will your precautions be enough?"

The deputy mayor almost giggled like a schoolgirl and shook his head, then looked briefly skyward as though he were seeking help from above. Then added condescendingly, "I don't know about the end of the world, but concerning any immediate threat … I think the Pope will continue to give us a helping hand."

An overhead screen flashed red, then scrolling letters proclaimed: FIREFLY ON FINAL APPROACH. And Rossi thought aloud, "the game's afoot, Watson."

"What's that, sir?" Tomaso asked, hiking up his eyeglasses onto the bridge of his sweat-filmed nose with a trembling, stubby finger and sniffing loudly.

"Nothing, just a little Baker Street talk."

***

The protective triangle of the Secret Service was complemented in the air. Following a VC-25A were four Navy Tomcat fighters, tailing at five miles while an AWACS lumbered out front, insuring that no bogies were approaching Firefly. The code name for Air Force One.

The SS advance team had arrived weeks earlier. Working liaison with the Italian security forces, running routes, running checks and double-checks on all possible headcases, shooters, and threat scenarios until their brains boiled and their eyes were bloodshot with fatigue, they were ready for *Tumbler's* and his wife's (code-named *Teacher's Pet)* arrival. Since the president's father, *Timber Wolf,* was also onboard, the Air Force steward had stocked plenty of pork rinds and salsa, daddy's favorite. The armored limo and secondary limos had been flown in by an Air Force C-17. They crouched gleaming in the afternoon sun. Behind the Presidential limo was the war wagon. Loaded with extra ammo and long weapons—shotguns, Uzis, and some classified weaponry—the custom-fitted SUV waited. There were enough Italian military and security agents on the tarmac and in the immediate area to start a small revolution in a banana republic.

Additional agents manned the Pratica-di-Mare air base's control tower. Concentric rings of security were now in place around the president and first lady.

The lead advance agent, his head still pulsing with a slight hangover from too many beers with German President Kohl's advance team, stood at the limo's side on the tarmac. He would work the principals and the AIC into the limo. His counterpart would be waiting at the Vatican. And another team would be waiting at a designated hospital, just in case somebody pulled a Hinckley.

Along the route and numerous contingency routes, military police were stationed at key points. And up ahead additional teams in identical war wagons would run point for the police lead and the motorcade.

338

The lead advance agent called the all-clear signal over his hand mic cupped in his palm to the agents onboard Firefly as it taxied to a halt. *You die, we fly*, he thought, recalling the Presidential and VEEP's Secret Service details' motto. The standard joke was that if the agents were to collect all the funeral flowers they'd seen, they could start a nationwide chain of floral shops. Sometimes they referred to it as the *FTD* detail.

Above, an Italian Carabinieri AB206 chopper and an U.S. AC-130U *Spooky* gunship churned through the lemon-yellow sky. The agent felt comfort in knowing that the four-engine Spooky's General Electric Gatling GAU-12/U six-barreled cannon, nicknamed "the Equalizer," which fires 1800 rounds per minute of 25 mm DU (Depleted Uranium) PGU-20/U armor-piercing shells, was trained on the rushing ground below. It was ready to chew the tar out of anything that came too near, too fast.

Having exited the aircraft, *Tumbler* turned to his AIC. As he ducked into the limo, *Tumbler* nodded toward the lead advance agent. With a wicked good-ol-boy smile curling his lips and his signature shrug, *Tumbler* said, "Phil, I think ol' Rusty looks a little green around the gills, musta got some bad Eye-tal-yan sausage or somthin'."

The AIC stifled a laugh, shot Rusty a your-ass-is-mine look.

Rusty pictured the foaming mugs of dark German beer and his career pouring down the bar tap's drain hole as he quickly checked his breath with a cupped hand.

"Rusty," the president said firmly, shaking his head. "Y' been eatin' barbeque at the ambassador's place again?" With a wink, Tumbler nodded, signaling the AIC to close the limo's door.

Glancing over at the ambassador, who was just stuffing his lanky frame into the second limo, and wishing he hadn't, Rusty met the ambassador's wide shit-eating grin. Luckily the droning whine of Firefly's turbines, still on standby for emergency departure, drowned out the president's critique of the ambassador's culinary expertise.

As the motorcycle outriders lit their cherries and spiked their sirens, the motorcade bolted forward. Rusty sighed and popped another breath mint.

***

Drago Volante and Honora made their way to the helicopter pad. Its rotors churning the air like black smoke, the backwash buffeted their bodies as they ran. They climbed aboard, and the chopper slowly began to rise in a nose down attitude, headed for an airfield where their private jet waited.

She turned to Volante. "I hate to leave Italy."

He smiled. "We'll be back."

She squeezed his hand. "Did you stock the jet properly?"

"Yes, a bottle of Cristal is onboard … well be able to toast our victory as we watch from the air."

"Too bad Ahriman wont be joining us," she added sarcastically. "He'd enjoy the fireworks."

Volante shrugged. "He died for a greater cause. They're all nestled safely in their beds, secure in the belief they've thwarted our plot."

"But what about securing the tomb?"

"Ahriman failed on that count but no matter. It will keep."

CHAPTER 87

IN ORDER TO get Stato on PIA's next flight to Islamabad, Pakistan, Spears had to use some Vatican clout. Now Stato found himself seated in the corner of the V.I.P. lounge in a high-backed faux-leather chair, sipping a glass of something professing to be merlot and nervously popping stale macadamia nuts. Each time his wineglass became half empty, a tall, luscious and attentive hostess sauntered to his side to refresh his glass. When she bunny-dipped to pour the wine, Stato got an eyeful of her ample breasts that swelled beneath her loosely buttoned, designer, white blouse. Velvety green eyes, high cheekbones, carried herself with the charm and grace of a high fashion model. When she took his order, she would teasingly brush up against him with a firm hip, pretending not to notice his reaction as her eyes danced with hidden mysteries.

Been out of circulation too long, he thought as he studied the teasing sway of her hips as she walked away. He wasn't really a priest, of course, but the costume he wore only seemed to heighten the young woman's interest. He glanced at his ticket, first-class, and laughed silently. He shrugged and sighed deeply. *The Holy Father's dead, the monsignore has been kidnapped, I just put the thumbscrews to a cardinal and high-ranking member of the Holy See and here I sit, lusting after some life-size Mattel Barbie Doll in a tight-fitting uniform. And even worse, I'm about to fly off to a ticking time bomb called Kashmir while the roof caves in on the Vatican.* His fingernails dug into the armrest of the chair. *And there's not a goddamn thing I can do about it.* He began laughing to himself again, realizing he hadn't even had time for the proper immunizations, so it wouldn't matter. He'd probably die from a brood of parasites that took up housekeeping his in guts or turn jaundiced with hepatitis or delirious with a malaria-induced boiling fever.

Voices drew his attention.

Seated in the corner near the bar was an elderly gentleman, nursing a branch water and whisky. Watery blue eyes, white hair, and a beard that was badly in need of trimming. A pipe saluted from the corner of his mouth. When their eyes met, the gentleman smiled warmly, winked, and took another swig from his tumbler. Then, abruptly, he would turn back to the bartender and rattle the ice cubes in his glass, indicating he was ready for another.

In the time he sat waiting, Stato had counted five such rattles.

From a worn leather satchel, Stato produced an old leather-bound journal given to him by Spears. Within its pages, written in childish scrawl, was the story of a Russian historian and antique book collector who had made a journey to Tibet. He began to read.

Nicholas Notovitch in the year of our Lord: 1887

Hearing of an ancient Tibetan scroll called the "Glass Mirror," which told of Christ's life and journeys into the Orient following the Crucifixion, I traveled to Lasha, Tibet, hoping to disprove this blasphemy. To my surprise, after making inquires, I was regarded with suspicion and turned away. I feared that all hope of finding the scroll was lost. When I departed the Potala lamasery or gopa, a grand castlelike structure with gold roofs and more than a thousand rooms and home of the Dali Lama, a young man approached me. In a hushed whisper, he assured me that he could serve as my guide and translator and that the scroll in fact, existed.

With my guide in the lead, we meandered on horseback through the picturesque passes of Bolan, over the Punjab, and finally, down into the arid rocky terrain of Ladak.

"Sahib," my guide said, "the lamas are distrustful of you because they have mistaken you for being British and, having lived under the tyranny of Chinese rule for so long, they see the British Empire waiting at the gate. But rest assured, hidden in underground cells the monks call 'the Black Treasure,' are many old scrolls. One is from a collection of Hindi writings ... known as Puranas. The ninth book, The Bhavisha Mahapurana, written in 115 A.D., recounts the meeting in around 50 A.D. of King Shalivahana and a foreign man, Yuz Asaf or Issa, described as a man with piercing intelligent eyes and a gentle manner."

My heart almost seized at the sound of Christ's Muslim name, realizing that if true, this would place Our Savior in the East after the accepted date of the Crucifixion. "Where was this meeting?" I demanded.

"In northern India, Srinagar."

"You will take me there"

"All in due time, sahib. First you should see the scrolls. You seek the truth, and God has provided, yes?" he mused, and kicked his horse, cantering out ahead of me, driving his horse up a steep slope. Over his shoulder and the sounds of hoofs pounding stone, he shouted, "Careful, sahib, destiny lies over this ridge. Are you ready for the truth?"

I swallowed hard and shouted back, "Yes!"

From behind him, the tinkling of ice cubes in a glass caught Stato's attention. When he turned the man from the bar was reading over his shoulder. Stato quickly closed the book.

"Fascinating lil' tale isn't it?" the man said. Taking in Stato's bewildered expression, the man offered, "Oh, how rude ah me. Now where are my manners?" As he moved around the couch, he extended his hand and smiled broadly. "Doctor Sanger, at your service, kind sir. Didn't mean to pry, but it seems that we' all got somethin' in common, Father."

Stato shook Sanger's hand reluctantly and then nodded for him to take a seat.

"I don't follow?" Stato said, feigning confusion.

Hitching his thumbs in the pockets of his waistcoat, Dr. Sanger smiled and chuckled.

"Nothin' to be ashamed ah, Father …?"

"Devlin," Stato lied, keeping with his cover story.

"Well, Father Devlin..."— he looked down, swirled his drink and studied it, then held it up to the light—"knowledge is like a fine ole whiskey. It becomes more mature with age, displayin' more clarity." He lowered the glass and met Stato's gaze. "Don't you agree, sir?"

Stato sidestepped the question. "What's your specialty, Doctor?"

"I'm a geneticist, sir. I examine the past through the filter and science ah genetics. No need for waltzin' me 'round the dance floor, Father. I'm sure Spears has told y' all 'bout me." He fished into his waistcoat pocket and flashed his university ID.

Stato acknowledged with a nod and wry smile. "Sounds interesting."

"You don't know the half ah it." He fumbled the ID back into its nest.

"Are you one of those 'lost-tribes' of Israel adventurers?" A weak smile cracked Stato's face as he said it.

"What y' see is what y' get, Father." Sanger pulled back the arm of his coat, showing his shirtsleeve. " See there?" He gave a hearty laugh. "Seriously, I recently had the distinguished honor ah participatin' in the DNA analysis and comparison ah Tutankhamun's mummy with his alleged daddy's, Amenhotep IV, better known as Akhenaten."

"And—?"

"Proof positive. That old boy King Tut was ah royal lineage all right."

"So you could determine if I was a Jewish decedent of the lost tribes of Israel?"

"You're referrin' tah what's known as the Cohen Model Haplotype, the standard genetic signature ah the Jewish priestly families. It let's us hunt for Jewish genes around the world."

"How far can you go backward in checking lineage?"

"Ta' hell and back, Father. The mutations or changes go away back one hundred and six generations, over three thousand years. Course, there's Mitochondrial DNA analysis or mtDNA for short."

"Mitoch…?"

343

"Think of it as lil' Mommy's egg. Since the mitochondria ah each new embryo comes from mommy's egg cell, mammas have the same mtDNA as their precious lil' daughters."

"So you could swab some orphan girl's cheek cells or that of say some terrorist and trace her back—"

"Theoretically all the way back to the Garden of Eden itself, sir. The genetic changes trace backward in a single line, one person in each generation, makin' it downright feasible to trace all humans to a single ancestor, the so-called *mitochondrial Eve.*"

"Not sure I'm convinced about this genetics business. But how can you get a sample big enough to examine from some ancient mummy?"

"In a word ... cloning. "Course we've got ourselves a high-falutin' name for it, PCR, polymerase chain reaction. Ain't that a hoot? Lets us churn out millions of exact copies of DNA from a single tiny lil' skin, hair, or bone cell."

Headshake: "But there's not much in the way of practical applications."

"I'll have you know, sir, it was good 'nough for the FBI. I helped develop their CODIS system."

"CODIS?" Stato asked.

"Combined DNA Index System. They punch DNA markers ah offenders, missin' children, refugees and terrorists into a whoppin' big old database. I'll have you know I even worked on the Shroud ah Turin project."

Stato stiffened. "You mean to say that a DNA marker from the Shroud is in this CODIS system?"

Sanger just nodded and held his gaze.

"Ever found a match," Stato asked sarcastically. "Maybe find Christ's great-granddaughter or grandson? Assuming of course that the whole notion of a marriage with Mary Magdalene and the Merovingian bloodline fable was actually true?"

Sanger laughed silently. "You're referrin' to the *Desposyni,* Greek for heirs ah the Savior. The short answer is no. But just for laughs, let's say we did find a match between the man in the Shroud and ah given male subject."

"Why not a woman subject instead?"

"Because that dog wont hunt, no siree. We'd first have to find ourselves ah Y-DNA match, male to male, y' see. Then, if this imaginary male had a sister, she'd be a distant relative of Christ. Now ain't that a hoot?"

Nodding slowly Stato said, "Kind of foolish conjecture, I guess."

"How's that, sir?"

Loosening his Roman collar, Stato said, "Because, after all, we are all brothers and sisters in Christ, Doctor."

Sanger slapped his leg and gave a hearty laugh. "Well said, Father. Say, how's Spears doing these here days? Haven't seen 'im in a coon's age."

"He said the Holy Father placed great trust in your abilities, said we should work together."

Eyes twinkling Sanger gave a knowing look and nodded toward the notebook now tucked safely in the priest's bag, which Stato had been reading earlier. "We've got our work cut out for us, Father. Yes, indeedy do. Gonna be thick as thieves we are. Yes, siree!"

Stato averted his eyes and looked around the lounge. He noticed people moving toward the exit. "I think they've called boarding," he said, rising and snatching his satchel from the floor.

Dr. Sanger hoisted his drink in a toast. "Here's to long lost secrets and ancient riddles whose answers are whispered by the reedy voices ah the dead, sir."

As they departed together, heading for the gate, the winsome, flirtatious PIA hostess tracked their every movement as she spoke into the phone, her hand cupped over the mouthpiece. "They're just boarding now, sir."

CHAPTER 88

A NEVER-ENDING STREAM of motorcades carried VIPs, more than eighty heads of state and monarchs, to the square in rapid succession, the leaders safely tucked behind darkly tinted glass. Some eight thousand security agents were working in tandem. Teams of EOD, explosive ordinance detection, dog units had searched every inch of the Basilica. Again concentric rings of security grew tighter and tighter as one traveled closer to Vatican City.

Dante had been assigned to one very special, very secretive and low-profile team— NEST—Nuclear Emergency Search Team, dispatched from its DOE operations office in Nevada. It was capable of deploying six hundred specialists to the scene of a terrorist threat, although actual deployments rarely involved more than forty-five people. Rome, however, had been an exception. The exact number was classified. The detail consisted of agents and physicists, engineers, chemists, and mathematicians, as well as communications, logistics, management and information officers. They came from such top-secret locations such as Los Alamos and Sandia. Their duty was to first assess the threat's technical and psychological validity. Although in this case no real, specific threat had been made, if it had, the details would be measured against databases containing designs from scientific journals, even passages from Tom Clancy spy novels for comparison. Was it just a hoax? What was the psychological profile deduced from the author of the threat's choice of wording? How extensive was his knowledge? In plain terms, was it credible? In this case, however, with so much at stake, they were operating under the assumption that a true threat existed and acted accordingly.

Teams secreted in trucks disguised as commercial vehicles prowled the city, their state-of-the-art equipment searching for nuclear material. Other teams, equipped with emission sensors for plutonium or uranium hidden in briefcases, patrolled on foot. Dante was attached to a van, just outside the square.

The funeral with its eerily old-world pomp and circumstance had gone off without a hitch. *Tumbler* and the VEEP had already had a wheels-up, as the protective details referred to takeoffs, and were safely en route to Shannon, Ireland. Many of the other delegations had also already departed the city.

The riot of activity, the tension-filled air, had begun to dissipate, leaving in its wake hundreds of exhausted, hyper-vigilant security agents, who were already beginning to take a breath, already imagining the taste of a cold one at the hotel bar.

The airspace over the city was still in a semi-locked-down mode. CAP sorties, combat air patrols, still circled high overhead.

That's when it happened.

The SISDe had picked up word of an aerial assault through an informant. Moments later, a jet was attempting unauthorized departure from Ciampino Airport. But just as its departure was thwarted by special security forces, another plane was picked up on approach.

At the command center, Rossi stood by anxiously, feeling helpless, as he watched the radar blip on the large monitor, heading on a vector straight for the heart of the city.

"Point of probable origin?" Brig. General Luca Masserati asked from between clenched teeth, a cigar saluting from one side.

"Computer calculates ... Sofia, sir," the tech said in a tremulous voice.

"Run it against the database of scheduled delegations," the Brig. General ordered.

An officer from the Ministry of Interior attached to Air Force liaison punched his laptop furiously. "Sir, yes, there's a delegation but ..."

"But what, damn it!" Before he could answer, the Brig. General was on him like flies on roadkill. "Sweet Jeezus. You've got that group checked as having already departed." Turning to his aide, the Brig. General barked, "Double-check with air traffic control ops."

The word Sofia still hung heavy in the air. The failed attempt against the late Pope John Paul II had been made by an alleged Bulgarian Secret Service recruited assassin from Sofia, a Turkish national and member of the Grey Wolves terrorist cell. Rossi was already at his drop line to the Umbra Squad's Communications Center. A young duty agent answered.

"Patch me into the net and have Enrique and Dante buzz me," Rossi said. "I want all available units, ground and air, to make for HOLYLAND." Rossi used the code name for the Vatican.

"Copy all available units."

"What's the location of the Prime Minister's security detail?"

"ETD for HOLYLAND departure ... imminent. Dante's in a NEST truck just outside the gate."

"Get on the horn and have them seek Level-five precautions immediately, then get onto the cabinet ministers." Until he knew more, it was best to assume that they needed to move people to location safe from bombing attack. "If anyone is left in the HOLYLAND vicinity, get them the hell out of there!"

The phone squealed. It was Dante.

"We've got an unauthorized aircraft headed for Vatican airspace. I'm recommending we evacuate Holy Land immediately," Rossi told him.

"Roger that, boss."

"And Dante, make sure my Uncle is out of there—"

"I forgot to tell you. He said something about calling you from Kashmir."

"Kashmir? What the hell are you talking about?"

"He and Ms.Schulman left early this morning."

"Which airline," Rossi said frantically.

"Boss, you called me this morning and told me to hook him up with one of our standby Falcon Jets."

For a moment Rossi thought he was losing his mind. Then smile creased his face and he laughed out loud. He could picture his uncle, with his perfect mimic ability, placing the call, impersonating his voice, with Josie probably standing by his side snickering the whole time. Later, Giovanni would chalk the whole thing up to "not wanting to bother you, nephew."

"Shoot a cable to our man in Islamabad and ask him to keep an eye out for them."

Stammering slightly, Dante said, "Sure ... but is everything, okay?"

"Let's hope so."

Rossi hung up.

The Brig. General was in full rabid dog mode, cheeks red and jowls wagging. "Status on CAP?"

"Two fighters refueling in eastern quadrant."

The Brig. General pounded the console. "Try to raise that Bulgarian flight again."

Another tech cut in, "Sir, air traffic control unable to raise incoming bogey."

"*Merda*! Foxfire two from the 36 ° *Stromo* 156° *Gruppo*. Scramble two now to intercept."

"Standard identify and intercept protocols, General?" his aide asked.

"NO! Intercept and neutralize the threat."

Briefly, Rossi was distracted by thoughts of his uncle and Josie. What the hell was he up to? He snapped to and digested what was happening in the command center. Rossi stood staring, taking in the implications. He knew that the CAP jet fighters were flying sorties 24/7 over the city, two F-16s to a quadrant. He knew that this required air-to-air refueling from tankers. And now somehow a major SNAFU had occurred. The fighters in the sector who could overtake the incoming Learjet were incapacitated. And pulling the remaining fighters would leave those sectors unprotected. They had no way of knowing whether, like in New York, more than one aircraft might be involved in the attack.

Rossi also knew "neutralize threat" meant the F-16 pilots could "fire at will" without waiting for command decisions. Wartime protocols were in effect. The ball was totally in their court. If they decided to down the aircraft, there would be no precious minutes lost, no unnecessary chance of a major air strike like 9/11. In the planning stages earlier, the Italian Prime minister, based on military advisors briefings, together with the cabinet ministers' go-ahead, had said he did not want another "American Peanut Farmer Fiasco." He was alluding to Ex-President Jimmy Carter's over micro-management of a military op that resulted in the death of Special Forces units attempting to free hostages in Iran. At the time and in light of the recent train bombing in the city, it seemed like a bold but necessary decision to Rossi. Now, however, it seemed all too real, and all too hurried.

Rossi placed a firm hand on the Brig. General's braid-covered shoulder, and said, "Sir, you must evacuate the Vatican immediately.

The general's eyes narrowed to slits. "Impossible. Even if we had more time..."

"All due respect, sir, but it has already been done frequently in Washington D.C. Even if only a few get out."

"How can you be so sure?"

Rossi studied him hard, staring him down. "You know I'm right." Rossi thought of Monsignor Lotti's fiery dragon warning, thought of Drago Volante. Hell... it had been there, right in front of his face, all along. Drago Volante meant … Flying Dragon.

The general rubbed his temples hard, then glared into Rossi's eyes. "If you're wrong." Then he spun on his heels and shouted, "Evacuate the Vatican."

"On whose orders?" his aide managed.

A wicked smile cracked the Brig. General's face. "Colonel Nick Rossi. And that's for the record!"

***

The scramble Klaxon at Pratica-di-Mare air base carved the air.

The group leader or *capogruppo*, Capt. Enzo Moretti, whose shoulder patch read 156 ° *Gruppo* and depicted a snarling hellcat, was seated in the Humvee, his wingman, Lt. Ricci, at his side. The Humvee rocketed from the squadron building, through the flight-line entry point to the F-16s waiting on the tarmac. They leaped out and made for their respective fighters. Moretti eyeballed the fighter as he ran, giving it the quick once-over. She was a beautiful bird recently acquired by the Italian Air Force in operation Peace Caesar to replace the vintage

Starfighters and fill-gap solution Tornados. The fuel crew had topped off the internal tank and the 300-gallon ventral external tank. The two wing tanks were empty. His eyes ticked to the armament: a rocket pod loaded with AIM-120s AMRAM, advanced medium range air-to-air missiles that could reach Mach 4, with a thirty-mile range. They were known as fire-and-forget because, once launched, the active radar homing took charge for its final stage of flight, eliminating the need for the pilot to keep his target illuminated. Its repertoire of killing scenarios included look-down, shoot-down, and multiple launches against multiple targets. But most importantly, short-range intercepts for dogfight situations.

The flight commander of the 36 ° *Stormo*, the Wolf Pack, who thought it fit his personality, had christened Capt. Moretti —*Lupo Solitario*, Lone Wolf. Moretti made for the ladder and scrambled upward, but halted midway. Pointing to an oversized bomb slung beneath the wing, he shouted to his crew chief, "What the hell is that for?"

The chief shook his head and shrugged. "Fuel-air bomb, Cap."

"A Satan-Stick?" Moretti had been briefed earlier. He knew the warhead contained volatile gases and/or liquids, which once detonated, formed an aerosol cloud over the target area. Once the cloud was ignited, the issuing fireball would sear the surrounding area, then begin sucking up every last drop of oxygen, creating a huge overpressure or blast wave. He remembered the tapes, the test results on a herd of sheep. The sheer force of the fuel-air blast had burst their eyeballs from their sockets, crushed internal organs. Excruciating pain, then death.

"She was prepped for a test drop, didn't have time to take her off," the crew chief explained. "Same with the 20 mm. cannon."

"*Merda!* She'll wallow like a pig."

"Gonna stand there and whine or take out that bogey, Cap?"

Moretti continued his climb, manned the cockpit. The chief followed, strapping him into the harness.

"This bird's go, Cap. Good hunting." The chief smiled wide, slapped him hard on the helmet.

The chief dropped to the deck and gave the bird another once-over. Moretti worked the flight controls and nursed the throttle to full idle. He turned to his wingman and signaled he was ready. The canopy down, he pumped the arms-up salute to his crew chief.

Within the cockpit, even when the JFS had engaged and the Pratt & Whitney F100-220E engine came to life, the sound inside never came above a faint whine.

In unison the fighters began to roll.

From his vantage point, the crew chief's gaze shifted to below the intake, where the torpedo-shaped LANTRIN navigation and targeting pods hung. They provided Terrain-Following Radar (TFR), Forward-Looking Infra-Red (FLIR), and targeting information for the aircraft's on-board fire-control system and target laser illumination. The targeting pod's large, ominous-looking, orange-colored eye stared knowingly, as though it held a secret.

On Moretti's command, the two pilots pushed their throttles to the stops, tripped their brakes, and bolted forward into the twilight. Advancing from mill power into afterburner, the time to 160 knots was eleven seconds, followed immediately by rotation.

At 800 feet, they hit a cloud layer and were streaming through the soup for about five minutes until they broke out at 11,000 feet. Center indicated a climb to 13K.

Moretti gave the usual commands: check ordnance, electrical; make sure your IFF is squawking green, fuel and external tanks feeding.

"Flight: turn right to heading zero-four-two. Bogey is at sixty-five miles on the nose," the control center reported.

"Roger, *capogruppo Lupo*, turning zero-four-two."

In an aerial ballet both F-16s banked right, adjusting their heading.

Moretti brought up the LANTRIN display. When the radar came up, it displayed any other aircraft ahead for at least forty miles. He used the radar control switch on his throttle to target one of the blips two miles out for an air-to-air missile attack. It was at thirty-seven k doing 280 knots. Immediately, the right multifunction display came up with the infrared view of the quarry provided by the targeting pod. Now the bogey was quickly and clearly recognizable as a Learjet 131 executive with a "death diamond" superimposed over the image. The computer database was programmed to identify aircraft.

Moretti's stomach knotted. "Center, from *capogruppo Lupo*. Have target. Moving in for a closer look. Any radio contact with bogey?"

"Flight: negative on contact, bull's-eye zero thirty to forty miles, proceed as bogey and eyeball."

Slightly behind the lead fighter, the wingman, Lt. Ricci, handle *Coguaro*—cougar— in the second F-16, followed the movements of the first jet, concentrating on maintaining contact with the center of coordination of the search.

In seconds, the group leader was perched off the Learjet's left wing, and his wingman held the rear position. Rocking his wings, Moretti gave the universal intercept signal for the plane to follow them down to the deck. The Learjet didn't respond.

Moretti did the math. In moments they'd be closing on Vatican City. Biting his lip, he made the call. He throttled back and slapped the stick. Into his headset, he said, "*Coguaro*, backfill my position, I'm coming up on his starboard." The jet cranked out two rapid, aileron rolls.

But instead of coming up on the right side of the Learjet, Moretti came up in at the rear, hanging behind both his wingman, who now filled his slot on the port side—and the Learjet.

Over the blip of the wingman, the death diamond formed and locked. Moretti toggled his arming switches.

"I'm spiked, I've got a launch warning!" *Coguaro* shouted frantically, the beeper blaring in his headset.

The missile was away. In a matter of seconds, the wingman's fighter was blown from the sky. Calm and with a calculated iciness, Moretti locked on the Learjet. The second missile streaked directly into the tail of the executive jet.

Without hesitation, Moretti rolled right and pulled the stick hard to his belly, jettisoned his empty external fuel tanks, and dove for the ground. He knew he had to drop below 200 meters, below radar. He punched up the coordinates.

***

On the ground pandemonium erupted.

"One fighter hit, sir. The second's dropping to the deck fast."

"And the Learjet?" the Brig. General asked, his voice cracking.

"Direct hit," the tech stated flatly.

For a moment, the Brig. General seemed stunned.

"Sir," the tech managed, his voice filled with confusion. "We have determined the Learjet must have been using a cloned Bulgarian transponder frequency. We just confirmed the actual flight originating from Bulgaria indeed departed earlier as scheduled with its delegation."

Eyes narrowing, the Brig. General said, "The bogey was purposefully squawking on a false freq. so we'd misidentify them?"

Rossi acted on gut instinct. "General, the bogus Bulgarian Learjet was a diversion. One of your fighters is making a bombing run on the Vatican. Do something now!"

The Brig. General's steely gaze met Rossi's; he nodded. Turning to the tech, he shouted, "Launch everything we've got at him, now!"

Ground-to-air missile batteries ringed the city.

Upon receiving the command to fire, the missiles were away, streaking toward their target like flying light poles, vectoring in on their target at Mach 3.

***

Meanwhile, Capt. Moretti had launched counter measures—chaff and flares along with his wing-mounted combat pod—and within seconds, would be below 200 meters. They had one shot at him and he knew it.

Two Spada missiles were in rabid pursuit. He rolled hard right, then left. At the last minute, they split left and right, resembling lost pups in search of their mother's tit.

A second volley winged in. Two miles and closing fast. Coming into the city from the northeast, he snap-rolled right, then spiraled down and hard left again. Below, the green of *Villa Borghese* appeared. Instinctively, he dove lower, banked ninety degrees and held it, "got skinny," soaring sideways between the twin bell towers of the Trinta Dei Monti church, which sat perched above the Spanish Steps. When the fighter roared out of the narrow gap, its wingtip narrowly missed the cross, which capped the obelisk, towering directly on the other side. That was all it took. In rapid succession, the missiles misdirected, slamming home into the bell towers on either side. A shower of debris rained down on the steps below. Crowds stampeded in panic. The hit being at less than forty meters from his bird, its explosive concussion rocked the fighter.

He rolled right, leveled and blazed over the steps, the fountain, screaming down the narrow city street that lay straight ahead. Six-story buildings bracketed each side, totally terrain masking him from radar now. The controls were sluggish; something was wrong. A quick glance at his right wing provided the answer. Sections of his wing were shredded as though talons had clawed away its flesh. Warning beepers droned. His flight instruments told of worse troubles: radio out, a firing-systems electrical malfunction. But his weapon systems would fire from backup battery power.

He lit the wick. Its afterburner kicking in, the fighter went supersonic, piercing the sound barrier. At this below-rooftop level, the resulting sonic boom was an elongated detonation. The resulting squall stutter-stepped down the street, windows exploding in rapid succession as the fighter screamed past like a low flying banshee. A group of tourists in an open-air double-decker bus ducked and covered as the plane rocketed past overhead.

The fighter stormed across the Tiber, screeching past the *Castel Saint Angelo*.

Then up ahead he saw it, the dome of St. Peter's rising like a smug crown of oppression. He was flying in a beeline, down the *Villa Della Concillazione*, nanoseconds away from the Vatican.

He toggled his arming switches again, and the reflector gunsight hovered before him.

Within seconds, he emptied his full complement of the 20-mm.-cannon's depleted uranium rounds into the looming target. Tracer rounds streaked through the darkness like fiery wasps returning to the hive. Designed to burn their way into tank armor, they wouldn't do that much structural damage to the target but the terror, the half-life of 4.5 million years of radioactive contamination, would make the symbol of the Catholic Church uninhabitable for decades to come. Although 20-mm-rounds weren't usually made of depleted uranium, the rounds that fed his cannon had been especially modified and substituted by an armorer who was also on the Brotherhood's payroll, as had the "Satan-Stick" fuel-air, vacuum bomb. It had been amplified with radioactive material.

He thought of the Learjet. He pictured Drago Volante onboard, toasting his wicked queen as the missile blew him out of the sky. Volante had insisted upon using his own jet as the decoy, squawking on the cloned Bulgarian jet's frequency, so that he could get a "bird's eye view."

He thought of Father Guido Salamanca, of how he'd violated him over and over, of how a thin smile came to the priest's lips every time their eyes met. He thought of all the other boys, the innocent ones. He thought of Cardinal Lawless, Boston's protector of the "child eaters," as he came to call them, who had recently been allowed to officiate at mass, during the *novemdiales* for the Pope. Tears welled in his eyes. When they'd come to him, asking for his help, knowing that he would replace the missing fighter pilot group leader that they'd abducted, he was repulsed; but the more he listened, the more he let his thirst for revenge— for some sort of closure, for peace to the torment that ate away at his insides— grow, the more their arguments made sense. And he knew that they were right. Only a brave, fearless man, a man secure in his convictions—a man on the *inside* could get close enough to do some real damage.

Now, teeth clenched in determination, he fired a salvo of rockets into the heart of the Basilica. Below, he could just make out a blur people in the square. It occurred to him that they resembled scattering and skittering cockroaches when you turned on the lights.

A plume of fire and smoke erupted. As he tore into it, he kicked rudder and dropped the "Satan-Stick."

For a split second, as the smaller charge diffused the volatile gases, there was nothing. Then a brilliant blast of light erupted, and a bone-crunching shockwave pounded the sky, slamming into his fighter like a quick, hard slap in the behind by an admonishing god.

He pulled back on the stick, fighting it. Climbed and clawed and crawled upward, then made a clumsy roll and dove for the coastline.

If he could get to the sea, he could eject and maybe they'd be waiting for him as promised. But because deep inside he felt a semblance of peace for the first time in his life, he really didn't give a damn if they did or not.

Then his resolve hardened. Simultaneously grinding into a molar and releasing the cyanide within and then hitting the eject switch, he was instantly catapulted into the night sky. His lifeless body, perched in its high-tech throne, floated across the twilight, suspended in time and space by the parachute rig. He was finally free.

CHAPTER 89

JOSIE SAT FACING Professor Giovanni aboard the *Ombra* Unit's Gulfstream-IV. They'd received word of the air attack on the Vatican and were waiting for further word that Rossi was safe. A crewmember called them to the front of the plane. "I've got Colonnello Rossi on the line now, sir."

"Nico are you, unharmed?" Giovanni said excitedly, speaking into the headset.

"A little ruffled but … why did you commandeer one of my aircraft and why in God's name are you heading for Pakistan?"

"How is Master-General Spears …" He paused when he heard Rossi draw a sharp breath.

"He's gone, Zio," Rossi managed softly.

"*Stronzos!*" Giovanni composed himself. "The members of the Holy See?"

"For the most part, they're all safe and sound."

"Thank God."

"I'm faxing through a message from Spears to Stato. We found it in his personal effects. Probably had intended to send it but never got the chance …" His voice trailed off. "The message doesn't make any sense to me, but none of this does."

"Send it immediately. And to answer your question, Spears shared some dire revelations. What he discovered on Cardinal Moscato's computer was …"—he bit his lip—"it's too complicated to discuss right now. But Stato's on his way to Kashmir and is in grave danger. He's traveling with a man who is a double agent. Spears believed a geneticist named Sanger was working for the Pontiff as a devoted member of the Knights of Malta, and advised Stato to work with him. But Moscato's files show Sanger's gone over to the other side. Spears tried to reach Stato, to warn him, but—"

"If Stato's been led into a trap, they probably took steps to cut off any communications. But Kashmir? For Christ's sake, the place is a killing field."

"For Christ's sake, indeed," Giovanni said to himself more than anyone else. *If he only knew how true it was*, he thought.

"And you and Josie are going to rush in there like the cavalry and get yourselves killed," Rossi added tersely.

"It's all very complicated, and Josie has a compelling personal interest in this whole affair. Nico, you're going to have to trust me."

The silence was deafening. Then Giovanni said softly, "We could use a little help."

"I've already notified Dante to have someone meet you in Islamabad. But if you're chasing after some MI-6 ops team, I'll have to muster a special ops team of my own."

"There may not be time, Nico."

"Damn it, Zio. I want you to hold tight in Pakistan until—"

Josie tapped Giovanni's shoulder and whispered, "Let me talk to him." He handed her the headset.

"Nico, I'll take care of your uncle. If the ops team misses us in Pakistan, send them on to Srinagar."

"Josie, don't be a dammed fool!"

"You're wasting vital time. Send the fax and make your calls."

"Damn it!" She could hear the pain in his voice. "If anything happens to you …"

"It won't."

"Josie …"—his voice wavered—"I love you …"

His words hung suspended on the crest of a tide of emotion that welled within her. She struggled for the right words and failing, simply managed, "I … I have to go." She handed the headset to the crewmember, nodded her thanks, and joined Giovanni, who'd already made his way to the rear of the aircraft.

"Time to put your cards on the table, *Professore*. I need to know exactly what's going on," Josie said, still picturing Nick's face in her mind's eye, cursing herself for not having the courage to speak with her heart.

"As I told you, Stato is walking into a deathtrap. Being led by a double agent, one Dr. Sanger, who has sold out his employer the NSA and the Knights of Malta and gone over to MI-6. Members of secret societies have infested these agencies, along with the Vatican. MI-6 was practically founded in days past by the Rosicrucians, and NSA's top echelon have been ranking members of the Knights of Malta. According Moscato's files, they are now in a death race to recover an ancient religious relic in Kashmir, and Stato is right in the middle of the fracas."

Josie regarded him coldly. "You keep mentioning that this somehow involves me personally. Why?"

"An explanation is long overdue, I agree. I promised your father that I would speak of the past with you. You've told me that he'd intended to share something important about your past the last time you saw him, but never got the chance." He bowed his head briefly, then looked up. "I need to explain why God chose you for this mission."

Josie steeled herself. "Please. No more riddles. Just tell me the plain truth."

Pulling a document from his satchel, Giovanni handed it to Josie. "Spears found this in Moscato's computer files. I printed it out for you."

Josie studied the paper.

It was an adoption form written in Arabic and Hebrew. It detailed the adoption of three siblings from a Palestinian refugee camp. A boy named Hamal, who'd been adopted by a British family, his sister Basha, who'd been adopted by an American, and finally EVE … who had been adopted by a Jewish couple.

Josie's eyes ticked from the paper and then back to Giovanni, staring incredulously. "This says the girl Eve was adopted by Max and Ennoia Schulman. That's impossible. I would have known if I had an adopted sister."

Giovanni sat is silence, letting her mind digest the facts. And when she had, her eyes began to tear. "I'm … I'm Eve?"

"They changed it to Josephine. Your father wanted to tell you, but then your mother passed suddenly …"

Josie turned toward the window. "My life's a lie. I'm not even a Jew."

"What does it matter? You were part of program to give Palestinian orphans a new life, and your father and mother did just that, didn't they?"

She nodded, blinking back tears.

"They gave you an education, love and now a career."

Josie wheeled on him. "Mossad knew the truth, didn't they? They wanted me because I was an Palestinian, so I could be used."

"Perhaps … yes, perhaps." He nodded knowingly. "Under a similar hidden agenda, your siblings were also adopted by families with connections to intelligence services. Your brother became MI-6's changeling, your sister, the NSA's."

"Sick bastards. Why?"

"Brace yourself. There's more. Moscato's files detailed it all. Basha is none other than *Bast.*"

"My sister's an al-Qaeda operative? God help me."

"He will, Josie. The files imply that she's been well … brainwashed by NSA. I saw the terrible results with my own eyes. In truth, she's not responsible for her actions."

"They made her a lab rat. Turned her into a coldhearted assassin." Josie cupped her hands over her eyes, lowered her head, and shuddered. Dropping them, she glared straight ahead and said softly, "And I'm no damn better, am I? My hands are just as bloody, slick with Palestinian blood. A murderer for Israel." Then it hit her. She turned sharply. "What about my brother?"

Giovanni grimaced. "Moscato suspected the same fate befell Hamal." Leaning forward, he took Josie's hands, held them tenderly. "There's more. I said that God had chosen you for this day." She turned her head and tried to pull away, but he held her hands firmly. "Look at me!"

Reluctantly, she turned.

"Your very names are significant," he explained. "Hamal means ... lamb, Basha means daughter of God, and Eve—"

"Means life," Josie whispered. Then she met his gaze. "We have to find them. I mean ... I have to find them. Rectify this terrible sin they've committed against us." She bit her lower lip, gave a half smile. "After all, they're the only family I have now."

"We shall, dear girl. We shall," he said in a comforting voice. Then he brought her a blanket and a brandy he'd skillfully laced with a sedative while his back was turned.

As he tucked the blanket tightly under her chin, Josie said, "Tateh used to do that a bedtime." He patted her cheek and kissed her forehead.

As she drifted off, Giovanni weighed the facts that he'd decided to withhold from Josie. Moscato's files had told of an incredible tale. A DNA marker match had been made and kept secret from all by these warring intelligence services. Almost simultaneously, both MI-6 and the NSA stumbled upon the match between the Shroud of Turin and Josie's brother, Hamal. Giovanni knew enough about genetics to verify that the results were accurate and not faked. He knew enough about genetics to see the obvious extrapolation of the data. If Hamal was of the same bloodline as Christ, then so were his sisters: Josie and Basha.

He looked up, studied her face in the waning light. She looked like an angel. But he knew that when she awoke, once on the ground and in the thick of battle, she would become an avenging angel of death.

CHAPTER 90

Srinagar, Kashmir

FROM ISLAMABAD, PAKISTAN Stato chartered a helicopter to Kashmir.
The old city of Srinagar was redolent with the scent of spices: cardamom, cloves, and saffron. Earth tones of brick, the rich hue of copper, even the vermilion of Kashmiri chillies hung to dry on windowsills appeared dull and monochromatic in contrast to the vast splendor of the valley's backdrop. Roads in the old city were narrow, winding, and chaotic. A confusion of streets and alleys, up and down the densely packed buildings, where even the narrowest streets seemed to have to elbow their way through the architecture, fighting for room.

Stato and Dr. Sanger stood on the bank of the River Jhelum watching a doonga, a shingled-roof houseboat, meander slowly up the river. Copper utensils from floor to ceiling gleamed in its kitchen as it passed.

They turned and made their way to the meeting place, passing locals in traditional dress who were on their way to the city's many mosques and shrines. Although deceptively serene in appearance, the city was a powder keg. Patrols roared past with dark-eyed solders brandishing automatic weapons.

In the café, seated at a small table, they sipped Kahva, a green tea.

Dr. Sanger stroked his beard. "The Holy Man has kindly agreed to meet with us, Father Devlin. I got word tah 'im last night through my sources. I vouched for y' sincerity and credentials."

Stato was still using the cover story of being a priest. "Why did we have to meet here instead of at the tomb?" Stato asked, eyes probing and then shifting around the room warily.

"'Cause to this day, sir, members of his heterdox Ahmadiyya community, which believe Jesus Christ lies ah buried in that there building across the way, are severely persecuted."

"But why would the Muslims care?"

Sanger frowned. "Why, sir. I do believe this should be y' area of expertise."

"I'm not that familiar with the region. Please enlighten me." Stato smiled to himself and thought it wasn't far from the truth.

"When you go ah venturin' into non-orthodox teachin' 'bout Jesus or Mohamed, you may be signin' y' own death warrant with the fundamentalist community. The notion that Jesus may ah survived the Crucifixion is a righteous anathema to orthodox Christians who believe the Bible teaches He died as atonement fah mankind's sins. The Qur'an teaches differently. Ahmadiyya Muslims believe that God frustrated the plan ah the disbelievers of Jesus. Although Jesus was nailed tah the cross, he did not perish on it, no siree. He was removed from the cross in a state ah unconsciousness as stated in the Qur'an 4:158. They don't believe in the blood sacrifice ah atonement. But Islamic fundamentalists believe that like Mohamed, Jesus ascended."

Stato took another sip. "Maybe the whole thing's just a hoax."

Sanger shook his head vehemently. "They wouldn't tah dare knowingly do it. The only reason they'all ah haven't been slaughtered so far, is their heartfelt faith and sincerity. As my genetic research has confirmed, these people are descendents ah Israel … or people ah the Book as Muslims call 'em. Furtha evidenced by the names they give tah their villages, their monuments, and ancient historical works and inscriptions."

A white-robed Holy Man appeared suddenly, almost as though he'd materialized out of thin air. Stato was taken back by his appearance. Sun-leathered skin, tall, and gaunt. His hyperthyroid eyes bulged from beneath dark bushy eyebrows. He bowed and said, "*Salaam alake Koom.*"

Sanger responded with the customary, "*La bahs hamdililah.*"

The greeting was in Arabic but they lapsed into the local Urdu dialect. As they talked, the Holy Man cast furtive glances at Stato and around the café.

Stato's Urdu was nonexistent. He marveled at Sanger's mastery of the language but wasn't surprised. Although Sanger projected the image of a homespun, sly country lawyer, he undoubtedly possessed a devilishly cunning intellect. Stato busied himself digesting the facts. He'd gotten word of the tragedy at the Vatican from a newscast. Master-General Spears's death. The reports stated Spears had remained until the last moment, helping herd everyone to safety. The Swiss Guard had whisked off Cardinal Drechsler and most of the Curia. The Vatican, however, would never be the same. The final report stated that although structural damage was at a minimum and decontamination procedures were immediately begun, the sun would supernova before the radioactivity was fully dissipated

The possibility, the terror of the radioactivity, necessitated moving the Holy See to another yet to be determined location. While not destroying the Church, the dark forces had a pulled off a major coup.

During the trip, Stato had befriended Dr. Sanger. But he didn't harbor any illusions about the good doctor's trustworthiness, despite the Master General's trust in the man. And now with the untimely death of Spears, Stato's suspicions deepened. They were playing a deadly game of cat and mouse in which they shared information, each with a hidden agenda. The doctor assured him that he had full access to the tomb and would be allowed to conduct DNA testing. But when Stato pushed him as to how he'd accomplished this, the doctor just smiled knowingly. Likewise, when pressed as to how he knew of the tomb's location in the first place, Sanger proved equally evasive.

Sanger pushed back from the table and hoisted himself to his feet. The Holy Man turned toward Stato, eyes twinkling, and indicated they should leave, with his outstretched arm.

They crossed the street, heading for the tomb. They encountered an old man squatting on the curb, his palm extended. His wizened eyelids were drawn into empty sockets. He was blind. Stato pressed a Euro into his leathery hand. Dusk was falling. Murky shadows crept in the yellow lamplight. Once they'd passed, the old man shot to his feet and scurried off.

The Roza Bal was an unimpressive structure, hardly calling any attention to itself. Three pagoda-like tiers towered above white stucco walls dotted with archways. Passing beneath a vine-covered archway, they entered the side door. It was humble, flanked with Arabesque Islamic-style carvings. Although by day windows allowed dusty sunlight to stab through, now at night, heavy carpets covered the windows. Ornate tiles washed across the ceiling above and blanketed the floor below, illuminated by the flicker of lamplight. Shadows crouched in corners. The room seemed to press inward claustrophobically. Towering in the center of the room, like an enigmatic monolith, stood a huge screened structure called a mashrabiya, made of intricate latticework.

Stato's heart skipped a beat. Did the tomb of Jesus actually lie beyond that screen?

The Holy Man hefted a lantern, and they climbed through a side entrance. He angled the light toward the corner. A stone slab lay covered in mud.

Stato and Sanger kneeled in front of the slab. From his pocket, Sanger produced a kerchief and a brush. With delicate care, he cleared away the residue.

Staring back at them were foot impressions. Stato's hand shot out, and he traced the carving carefully. "Bring the light closer," Stato shouted eagerly.

The Holy Man lowered the lantern. Stato ran his fingers over the sculpture.

"Raised wound marks," he managed. When Stato's fingertip rested in a cavity, chills ran up his spine. "And a single hole."

"More precisely, nail marks," Sanger explained. "Marks which you'll find correspond exactly with those found on the Shroud ah Turin, Father. One foot placed over the otha, consistent with the archaeological finds ah crucifixion victims."

Stato's mouth was powder-dry; his hand trembled.

Sanger pointed with the brush. "Look a lil' closer and you'll see the two pads under the soles ah the feet. It's like Juz Asaf slapped on some Dr. Scholl's tah counter the deformity caused by an earlier crucifixion."

Stato's mind reeled with questions.

Taking the lamp, Sanger moved across the room and illuminated a niche. A long box nestled there. To Stato, he said, "Go ahead, son. Open it."

Rising to his feet, Stato went to his side, his heart beating against his ribcage. He opened the lid and peered inside. Lying within the oblong box was a staff.

"The locals call it The Rod of Moses," Sanger said, "or the Jesus rod."

Stato jerked back his hand as if jolted by an electric cattle prod. He stood rooted in place, unable to speak.

Sanger gave a brittle laugh. "And now the sarcophagus." He rose and took Stato by the arm and led him to the tomb. Stato stumbled weakly.

As they stood before the tomb, Sanger explained, "Some call it Hazrat Issa Sahib ... or the Tomb ah the Lord Master Jesus. Yes siree, I've seen records with my own eyes that acknowledge its existence way back tah 112 AD."

Before Stato could answer, the sound of a car engine dying and the clattering of booted feet came from the rear of the building. Wheeling toward the sound, Stato whispered, "We've got company." Even in the dim lamplight, Stato could see the Holy Man's already bulging eyes pulse with fear.

A cauldron of sun suddenly ignited the room. It sliced through the screen, fanning outward at stiletto angles. They brought their hands to their eyes, desperately trying to block out the blinding light.

Squinting, Stato could barely make out dark silhouettes climbing into the enclosure.

Then a single glaring beam of light stung him directly in the face.

"If you have any weapons, drop them now," a voice commanded.

"Hell! Com'on ahead, now boys. They's all unarmed, and get that blasted blame light outta my eyes!" he heard Sanger answer.

The flashlight lowered, revealing three men dressed in black; their heads and faces were completely hidden by black balaclavas. They held submachine guns; their eyes were quick and callous.

The taller man in the middle, who seemed to be the leader, beckoned for Sanger to join him. Like an eager schoolboy, Sanger hobbled quickly to his side.

"Don't look so damn shocked, Father Devlin," Sanger said sarcastically. "Y' neva trusted me furtha than you coulda spit. Why the hell should I settle for ah tiny lil' ole DNA sample when I can have the whole damn mummy tah myself?"

Steeling his nerves, Stato said, "No I didn't. But just what do you intended to do with it?"

"Since we'all procured the Shroud ah Turin, I'll see if the DNA matches."

The leader grunted and said, "Inquisitive sod, isn't he?" Then he turned toward one of his men and signaled with a nod. The man disappeared and returned shortly with two others who were hefting a casket-shaped box.

To the leader, Sanger said, "Let's make the switch. I'm mighty anxious to get the blazes outta of Kashmir mighty quick, Mista Childress."

The man called Childress bristled with the latent violence of a coiled whip. "You shouldn't have used my name," he said, and shot Sanger a cold, hard stare.

Sanger swallowed visibly but said nothing.

"No further need for pretenses," Childress went on. Then he brushed aside his balaclava, revealing an Anglo face with dark piercing eyes. "Now step away from the sarcophagus, gentlemen."

When the others removed their balaclavas, Stato saw that one was a woman with powder-blue eyes and the other a young Arab man.

The Holy Man didn't move. Likewise Stato stood his ground. Unseen by the others, the Holy Man slipped something beneath Stato's jacket and tucked it into his waistband at the small of his back. Stato shot him a furtive side-glance, but the Holy Man stared straight ahead.

Childress said, "Restrain the bloody bastards, then."

An unreasonable, unfathomable determination compelled Stato to act. When Childress's thug made a grab for Stato, his training took over. Stato saw the man switch his weapon to his weak hand. Taking a quick sidestep forward and behind, Stato gripped the man's forearm and spun him. Using the man as a shield, his left forearm hooked around the man's throat, wrenching him backward, Stato's right hand found the MP-5's pistol grip. He stabbed the weapon outward, raking a burst of fire at the target directly in front of him.

Sanger dove behind the sarcophagus, taking cover, his plump fanny slowly wiggling out of sight.

Childress's hand flew to his shoulder, he screamed in pain.

From behind, the man who held the Holy Man finally reacted. He brought the barrel of his MP-5 crashing down against Stato's skull, pistol-whipping him to the ground.

Still clutching his shoulder, Childress stood over Stato's body. He turned to the Holy Man who stood arms pinned behind his back by the guard. He pressed his face within inches of the Holy Man's. "Ever hear of Prussic Acid, old man?" The Holy Man stared blankly.

"Bloody hell, of course not. You don't even speak English." With a twist of his head, Childress motioned for a second man to approach. The man pulled a facemask equipped with a canister from under his robe. Without warning, the man's fist drove into the Holy Man's solar plexus, doubling him over in pain. When the Holy Man straightened and began gasping for air, the thug clamped the mask over his face and pushed upward on the canister with his thumb. He stepped back. Coughing violently, the Holy Man's neck corded.

"Let him go," Childress ordered.

Immediately the guard released the cleric who sagged to the floor like an empty pillowcase.

"Inhaling Prussic Acid induces symptoms reassembling cardiac arrest," Childress explained to Sanger. "If they perform an autopsy, they will conclude he died from a heart attack."

"What about the priest?" the thug said.

Childress nodded toward the woman. "Kill him."

Hesitating, she stumbled forward and raised the MP-5. Her gaze ticked to the young Arab man, as if seeking direction. His soft brown eyes seemed to plead with her not to pull the trigger. Then Hamal spoke, "No more bloodshed, my sister."

Childress screamed, "Kill him or I'll do it myself!"

A shot rang out, then two more deafening bursts followed in rapid succession. Kill shots systematically took out two of the henchman, whose stunned faces looked into the deadly eyes of the woman who'd appeared suddenly from behind. Josie had taken them by surprise, applying her deadly skill as a marksman and acting as the dark angel of death. Josie, breathing hard, panned the room, searching for more targets. Her sights fell upon the woman, who stood next to the unarmed young Arab man.

Now *Bast* stood frozen, the submachine gun still in her hand. Hamal stood at her side wide-eyed and trembling.

Childress whirled on Josie, pulling his weapon from the small of his back. "You bloody bitch!"

Josie squeezed off two rounds, sending the slugs deep into his already wounded shoulder. The force of the hits spun him full circle and his pistol tumbled to the floor. His knees buckled and he collapsed, reeling in pain.

Josie moved quickly to his side and kicked away the pistol. Leaning over him, she said, "I didn't miss. I want you to lie there and bleed out slowly, while I ask you some questions, you limey asshole."

From the corner of her eye, Josie saw the MP-5 slowly rise toward her. *Bast's* face was ashen, numbed with terror and confusion. Their eyes locked.

Giovanni and an Italian case officer hobbled into the screened enclosure.

"Josie take off that damned ski mask," Giovanni shouted in a breathless voice as he limped into place, positioning himself directly between Josie and *Bast*. Josie ripped off the mask.

Then wheeling on *Bast*, he said softly, "Basha, Hamal. Look at her closely. Look into your hearts and see the truth."

Their confused expressions were matched by blank-eyed stares. Then suddenly a flash of recognition sparked.

"That's it. You see the resemblance don't you?"

Bast's eyes fluttered. Hamal placed his hand on *Bast's* arm, slowly coaxing her to lower the submachine gun.

"Josie, lower your weapon," Giovanni said, his voice even but stern. From the corner of his eye, he saw that the case officer's Beretta was also trained on *Bast*. Eyes locked on *Bast*, he waved his arm at the case officer, and ordered, "You, too! Holster your weapon, now!"

With reluctance, Josie and the case officer complied. But Josie kept her keen gaze locked on *Bast* and Hamal.

To *Bast*, Giovanna said. "Basha, you see it now, don't you? This is Eve, your sister." He gave her a moment to comprehend his words. "There never was a Laylah. They lied to you about your brother, too, told you Hamal was killed. But look, he's standing right at your side, isn't he?" *Bast* glanced at Hamal and nodded woodenly. "Yes, that's it," he continued. "There is just the three of you now …separated so long ago. This is your sister! Go to her."

The MP-5 fell from *Bast's* hands.

Then she took a faltering step forward toward Josie.

Josie swallowed hard. Involuntarily, her arms rose in greeting.

Standing directly before her, *Bast's* searching hands siphoned the air and then found Josie's face. Tenderly, she ran her fingertips over Josie's lips, her cheeks, her forehead.

Finally, they collapsed into each other's arms, sobbing. Hamal joined them, wrapping his arms around them, tears filling his eyes, streaming down his face.

***

Head pounding and needles of pain barbing the base of his skull, Stato came to. He pulled himself upright. Slowly made it to his feet. To his right, the Holy

Man lay still, his bulging eyes gone stale, and dusted over with disbelief. Stato made the sign of the cross over him and said a silent prayer.

Stato turned, taking in the scene around him and stood mystified. The dead thugs, the wounded Childress lying at his feet. The two women and a young man embracing one another. Then he spotted Giovanni.

"I don't know how you got here, but it was apparently just—"

"God's will," Giovanni said, smiling warmly.

Sirens sounded in the distance.

The case officer said, "We need to get out of here."

They made for the door.

Once they'd left, Dr. Sanger crawled out of his hiding place behind the tomb and slinked away.

In the alleyway blocks away, they huddled in the darkness. Stato stood, hands on his knees, still dazed. Then he remembered it. The paper the Holy Man had stuffed at the small of his back. Fumbling beneath his jacket, he found it. In the weak light of a doorway, he unfolded the thin scroll.

Still breathing hard, Giovanni said, "Our quest is not over is it? But at least it will be a long time before anyone attempts to rob that tomb again. The publicity will bring too much attention to the area for now."

"I had a good mind to blow it to kingdom come," Stato whispered tersely.

Reaching out and patting his shoulder, Giovanni said, "The world may not be ready for the truth, but you have no more right than they had to desecrate the tomb."

Stato nodded and raised the paper. "It's a map that indicates a location in Pakistan labeled Queen's Mountain and a verse translated from Arabic into English."

The screech of brakes signaled the arrival of the getaway car that the case officer had stashed up the street.

The case officer shouted softly from behind the wheel. "Hop in, everyone, let's get out of here and back to Italy *rapido*. Once they find those dead Brits, they'll throw up roadblocks and shut down the airfield. The helicopter's fueled and waiting at a secluded, old British governor's mansion we use as a safe house. Ironic isn't it?"

As Giovanni climbed in, he turned to the case officer. "We'll need to make a short stopover in Pakistan. These children need to see their great-grandmother."

The case officer's mouth gaped wide as he shook his head and punched the gas. "You're crazy, just like your nephew, Rossi." They sped into the night in search of the past.

EPILOGUE

Lungs burning in the thin air, they struggled to complete the final steps of the steep climb. Looking downward now, they stood in awe of the commanding view from Pindi Point or Queen's Mountain. It overlooked forest-clad hills and deep rolling valleys. Rooftops studded its lower face, jutting from the village that clung to the mountainside. Turning full circle, their gazes swept the snow-covered peaks of Kashmir that formed the background.

Beneath the towering television broadcast antenna on this windswept hill in Muree, Pakistan, they stood—Josie, Basha, and Hamal—fingers meshed tightly around the barbed-wire security fence that ringed the transmitter. Hamal winced as a nail-sharp barb pierced his palm. The barren, neglected, unassuming tomblike structure lay to one side, partially hidden in a riot of weeds. The locals whom had recently given sanctuary to many Taliban refugees called it Mai Mari De Ashtan. The case officer, thinking it was sheer madness, stood off to one side nervously smoking a cigarette.

Stato studied the scene before him. Though suitably humble, this forsaken place, desecrated by a steel totem of technology, couldn't actually be, as legend had it, the final resting place of Mary Mother of God? Could it? Stato's cheeks were red, his eyes tearing, his fingers numb from the biting wind. He pulled the scroll the Holy Man had given him from his satchel and read: THE GOSPEL OF ISSA

At this time, an old woman approached the crowd, but was pushed back. Taking notice of this, Issa stopped speaking and commanded them to allow her to come to him. Then placing his arm about the woman to comfort her, Issa said, "Show reverence for Woman, mother of the universe, in her lies the truth of creation. She is the foundation of all that is good and beautiful. She is the source of life and death. Upon her depends the existence of man, because she is the sustenance of his labors. She gives birth to you in travail, she watches over your growth. Bless her. Honor her. Defend her. Love your wives and honor them, because tomorrow they shall be mothers, and later-progenitors of a whole race. Their love ennobles man, soothes the embittered heart and tames the beast. Wife and mother ... they are adornments of the universe.

"As light divides itself from darkness, so does woman possess the gift to divide in man good intent from the thought of evil. Your best thoughts must belong to woman. Gather from them your moral strength, which you must possess to sustain your near ones. Do not humiliate her, for therein you will humiliate yourselves. And all which you will do to mother, to wife, to widow or to another woman in sorrow-that shall you also do for the Spirit."

Issa's arm swept over the throng.

"Take heart for I did not succumb to them as they had planned. I did not die in reality but in appearance, and it was another who drank the gall and the vinegar. It was another, my brother, J'acov, who bore the cross on his shoulder. It was another upon whom they placed the crown of thorns. I was laughing at their ignorance.

"There shall come to pass another. Flesh of my flesh, blood of my blood, from whom the cup shall not pass. In the Northern Isles, my seed shall flourish. Two bright blossoms shall unfold their petals to my Father's light. True Daughters of God."

Stato closed the scroll and stared off into the leaden sky, thinking. The north meant one thing. Since Stato knew who'd tried to make off with Our Savior's earthly remains, and abducted *Bast*, again the compass pointed due north to the land of the British Isles.

Placing the scroll in the bag, Stato took out an envelope Giovanni had given him, containing the fax of Spears's message to him.

Giovanni looked over his shoulder as he read.

STATO:

FOLLOW THE ROSE COMPASS. IT WILL LEAD YOU TO THE GODDESS OF THE HUNT. STOP. CONTACT THE REAL FATHER DEVLIN. WARN HIM. SAY THESE WORDS: SUB UMBRA ALURUM TUARUM JEHOVAH. STOP. TELL HIM THAT THE BEEKEEPER HAS MARKED HIM FOR DEATH.

As he stared intently at the Latin phrase, Giovanni muttered its translation under his breath, "Under the Shadow of Jehovah's Wings. The motto of the Fama Fraternitas …

… the Rosicrucians."

Looking at the three siblings who stood with their faces pressed against the fence, Stato asked Giovanni. "Do you really believe they are Christ's descendents?"

Giovanni shrugged. "What I know is that I see His message unfolding right before us. Love not hate, hearts filled with joy, not sorrow. That's what truly matters isn't it?"

***

Rome

Far beneath the altar of St. Peter's, nestled securely away within a concealed corner chamber of late Pope John Paul's innermost casket, lay the secret of his softened heart. Following Master-General Spears's untimely death in the basilica air attack, the ornate box had been removed from his personal safe by men of power and handed over to the new Vicar of Christ for safekeeping. It contained John Paul's dying wishes, his true will and testament, his decision to include women in the priesthood. Now it lay hidden for all time, tucked away from prying eyes, placed there earlier by the newly elected Pope Benedict XVI.

APPENDIX

1. The Enochian alphabet code:

2. The Greater Key of Solomon.

3. Death Knight Devil by A. Durer.

4. Issa's tomb.

IMAGE: FORTEAN PICTURE LIBRARY / DR ELMAR R GRUBER

Coming soon … THE VOYNICH COVENANT

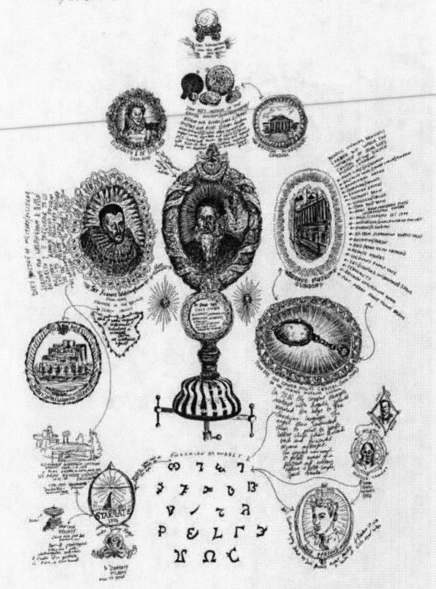

5. Vatican tapestry.

Suggested reading:

Joseph Campbell: *The Masks of God* 4 volumes.

Brent Corydon: *L. Ron Hubbard: Messiah or Madman*

Robert Lomas and Christopher Knight: *The Hiram Key*

David Yallop: *In God's Name*

Craig Heimbichner: *Blood on the Altar*

T.Struge Moore: *Albert Durer*

Philip Gardner: *Secrets of the Serpent*

Graham Hancock: *Fingerprints of the Gods*

Lewis Purdue: *Daughter of God*

Peter Levenda: *Sinister Forces* 3 volumes.

Robert Anton Wilson: *The Cosmic Trigger*

Printed in the United States
108741LV00003B/49-57/A